THE ENDING FIRE

ALSO BY SAARA EL-ARIFI

The Ending Fire Trilogy
The Final Strife
The Battle Drum

Faebound Trilogy
Faebound

SAARA EL-ARIFI

THE ENDING FIRE

HARPER
Voyager

Harper*Voyager*
An imprint of HarperCollins*Publishers* Ltd
1 London Bridge Street
London SE1 9GF

www.harpercollins.co.uk

HarperCollins*Publishers*
Macken House,
39/40 Mayor Street Upper,
Dublin 1
D01 C9W8
Ireland

First published by HarperCollins*Publishers* Ltd 2024
1

A catalogue record for this book is available from the British Library.

ISBN: 978-0-00-845050-2 (HB)
ISBN: 978-0-00-845051-9 (TPB)

Typeset in Minion by Palimpsest Book Production Ltd, Falkirk, Stirlingshire

Printed and bound in the UK using 100% Renewable Electricity by CPI Group (UK) Ltd

MIX
Paper | Supporting
responsible forestry
FSC
www.fsc.org   FSC™ C007454

For Jim, until the end.

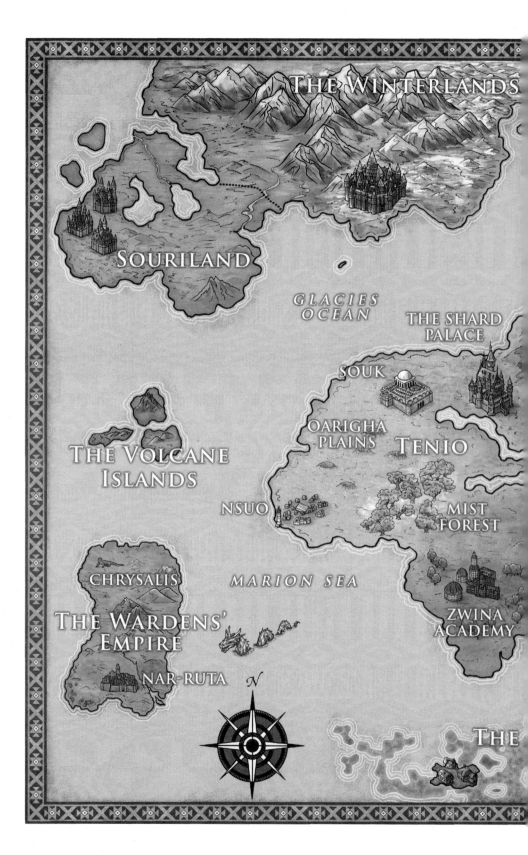

Recalling the events of *The Battle Drum* as told by Griot Sheth

The spoken word has been transcribed onto the page; the symbol of ✧ represents the beating of the griot's drum.

Back again, I see? You are drawn to my tales like the audience of a ripping. The blood and gore, the pain and torture.

And then the relief. That is what you come for.

When it all . . .

Stops.

✧ ✧ ✧

The end approaches, you must feel it cresting the horizon, creeping closer like the coming of night.

But before we venture towards the chaos and the plight, let us take a moment to linger in the colours of yesterday, and the yesterdays before that.

✧ ✧ ✧

Let's start with red, the heat of a burning ember, the shade of Sylah Alyana's blood.

A voyage taken to lands unknown
The Tannin taking a toll of souls
An abandoned port called Nsuo
Then bam! A cudgel knocks Sylah down
Wakes in a chattel cart, hands now bound.

I see you roll your eyes, knowing the Shariha's chains couldn't hold Sylah long. And it is true, our Stolen, our assassin, went on the run.

But then came the storm and acid rain, and the manacles of death tightened around Sylah instead.

And who comes to Sylah's rescue? Remember Jond, our fellow Stolen, a little disagreeable, a lot righteous? He was sent to Tenio as a penance, to be abandoned all alone. But together the old friends fled the Shariha's enslavement along with Niha, a healer, and made their way to Zwina.

Eyoh! Gone is the academy of wonders. Of eight blood colours and teachers. Floods have drowned it all.

But look skywards and you'll see the City of Rain where the councillors of the Academy have made a new home. And here we learnt the extent of their power.

The first charter is the law of growth. The power to grow what is given.

The second charter is the law of connection. The command of mind communication.

The third charter is the law of healing, putting back together what was once broken.

The fourth charter is the law of presence. Flighting from one place to another.

But once Sylah is healed, there is no aid to be had. Instead, we learn of the Zalaam, whose use of bone marrow has shifted the balance of the world. Earthquakes and acid rain! Floods and tsunamis!

Though, perhaps that is less shattering than the secrets at the centre of the Academy . . .

The fifth charter is the law of creation. To infuse life into the spiritless.

Disbanded and forgotten, the fifth charter was once led by the prophet of the Zalaam. Four hundred and twenty-one years ago he was executed, and his community exiled from Tenio. They set sail in eight ships, each segregated by blood colour.

Four boats settled on the Volcane Isles, and two the Tannin took as sacrifice to allow the final two entry to the land beyond. A land ripe for the plucking.

Red and blue.

Do you start to see it? The circle we have swum? Embers and Dusters are descendants of the Zalaam.

And the Tannin?

A monster formed by the Academy to hunt down the exiled. Whose nightly movements cause the tidewind that plagues us.

A monster that roams still.

So, while we linger by the blue shores of the Wardens' Empire, let's recall how our blue-blooded fared. Our disciple in the Keep, Anoor Elsari.

The Tidewind Relief Bill taken to the court
Anoor seeks allies to fortify her thoughts
Uka's life blood spilt over dinner
Gone is the mother, the warden, the sinner
Accused by her peers, Anoor seeks out the killer.

Focused on her salvation and not on the tidewind, Anoor stays in hiding while the wardens home in. Only her grandmother, Yona Elsari, seems to understand her, and takes over her efforts in making tidewind shelters.

With Anoor distracted, will Yona be the one to help the citizens of the empire?

Do you see my sly smile? You know something's a-brewing. And perhaps our Ghosting friend will know. To our very own hassa beetle we go.

A promise from a friend, a promise kept
Look after Anoor is what Sylah said
Hassa's time in the city is spent underground
But above she finds bodies with holes in their bones
Together with Kwame she investigates the unknown.

Bone marrow it was, taken from the hip bone and the back. A slow death, sucking them dry, worse than the rack. Does it remind you of anything I said a few moments ago, the Zalaam's power rooted in the magic of bone marrow?

But who was it, in charge of the shelters? Whose orders were followed? Who was Anoor's mentor?

So, we come to the final hue of the story, the yellow of sunlight. Our yellow-blooded member of the Zalaam, raised in God Kabut's eye.

Nayeli was the name she'd had all her life
Then claimed she was reborn as Kabut's Wife
Searching for the Child of Fire, the catalyst foretold
She ventured across the sea, across the colour threshold
And became warden, an empire controlled.

Nayeli, Wife, Yona. Three names she'd had until "grandmother" was uttered, and it was then that Anoor was discovered. Was she the one that the prophet foretold? The one whose Battle Drum will start the Ending Fire proposed?

Do you start to see the web of the story? The silver threads tying each piece to the other? But one is broken, ripped apart in the middle.

Kwame, a spectacle, a ripping, no longer with us.

It was as if the world felt the grief too, for leagues away the Shard Palace fell, and the Queen of Tenio was taken from the world.

The colours of yesterday have swirled to take shape.

Clear!
    Hassa's heart torn, like Kwame's organs. Now alone, she spends her time mastering bloodwerk.

Red!
    Sylah, whose fury inspired the Blood Forged, leaves the battle behind to return to her love.

Blue!

Anoor's been caught in the spider's game. The disciples, her new allies, aren't what they seem. The Sandstorm and the Zalaam are one and the same.

Yellow!

The Wife has found the Child of Fire. Now it's time to leave the empire.

Do you feel it? Cresting the horizon? The darkness drawing in, the shadows elongating.

The Ending Fire comes.

PROLOGUE

The tidewind came every night.

It billowed in from the Marion Sea between the clock strikes of nine and seven. A year ago, the hurricane ruptured the evening for only three or four strikes of the clock, but now its presence lingered, wreaking destruction like never before.

From Gorn's vantage point in the Wardens' Keep she watched the tempest roll in from the Farsai Desert. Her gaze followed its swirling path from the decrepit buildings in the Dredge in the distance, through the Duster Quarter and across the Tongue that bridged rich and poor—but the tidewind made no distinction between the classes of the Wardens' Empire. Whether your blood ran red, blue or clear, the tidewind wielded each gust like a serrated knife, tearing skin from muscle, muscle from bone.

Closer and closer the roiling storm came. It waged war against the architecture of the Ember Quarter and slipped its tendrils through the iron gates of the Keep. But still Gorn lingered by the open window. The promise of death stirred feelings in her chest that had long grown numb.

She shifted her weight, disturbing a stack of zines by her feet. The colourful pages spread across the floor. Anoor's room was just as she had left it. Where once jewellery and trinkets had littered her desk, now notes and half-finished sentences fluttered in the breeze. The pages were full of Anoor's dreams for the empire.

But her dreams had been waylaid, and so had Anoor.

Where did your grandmother take you?

The thought felt distant, like it had been whispered across a vast chasm where she had buried her pain. Her fear.

Gorn felt sand strike her cheeks and stick to the tears that flowed there. At first, the sand was a caress, the softest of touches from death, but then tears became blood.

She slammed her helmet closed with a clank. It hadn't been difficult to have Anoor's tidewind armour from the Aktibar trials altered to fit her. Just a bribe to the armoursmith and a few measurements. Gorn had paid a little extra to have the green metal reburnished to a dull bronze. She didn't want the wardens to trace the armour back to Anoor.

Not that she can be traced.

Gorn had tried for a time. She had hired an eru and ridden it all the way to the gates of Nar-Ruta, hoping to follow wherever Yona had taken her granddaughter. But when she reached the edge of the plantations she had hesitated. She watched the Dusters' welts glistening in the noonday sun as they hacked at the bark of a rubber tree. They fought against sand banks that ran deep into the groves, a testament to the increasing duration of the tidewind. Gorn realised then that finding Anoor was not the path destined for her. Perhaps if she still had Kwame by her side, they could have achieved it.

There was a sharp pain in her chest that felt faintly like grief, but she had hidden it so deep that it had become a dull ache.

Now I am alone and have other battles to wage.

The tidewind slammed into her side, bringing her out of her thoughts. A large piece of whitestone had caught her just below the ribs. Although it winded her, the armour did not suffer damage.

Anoor's room was not quite as lucky. Gorn watched through the reinforced glass visor as the zines were shredded to colourful confetti and Anoor's sheets ripped from the bed.

It should have hurt her to see her home destroyed so, but instead it fuelled Gorn's resolve for the war that was to come.

"I will leave them nothing of her," she growled into her helmet.

She pulled open the dressing-room doors and the chest of drawers, letting the tidewind take and take. Silks and taffeta were brought to life by the winds, dancing like ghosts made merry by firerum. Jewellery was plucked from stands by greedy gusts, adding beautiful sparkles to the frolicking procession. The pieces of clothing haunted the room with their empty-chested joy before being dragged out into the night. The gemstones were tugged along too, pulled towards the hearths of unsuspecting new owners.

And as the tidewind grew bloated with the remnants of the home she and Anoor had built, Gorn had only one thought before she left.

The wardens will come to know a mother's wrath.

PART ONE

❖

Recover

Patience has the ability to heal all things.

—Zalaam proverb

CHAPTER ONE

Hassa

KEEP TOWER DESTROYED BY TIDEWIND
Excavation efforts have begun in the eastern tower of the Keep
where the tidewind caused irreparable damage. Allegedly, it struck
the rooms of the former Disciple of Strength, Anoor Elsari, recently
accused of Uka Elsari's murder. No one is believed to be hurt, but
the tower will be uninhabitable for some time.

—The People's Gazette

Hassa lifted her gaze from the *Book of Blood* and into the eyes of a ghost.

It cannot be.

The apparition spoke. "Hassa?"

Drip. Drip. Drip.

Hassa's blood seeped down the pen nib and onto the floor. As each droplet hit the ground, the ghost of Sylah flinched.

"Hassa?" She said her name again. "Did you just bloodwerk?"

The table that Hassa had just pushed across the room with runes separated her from the phantom image of her friend. But Hassa didn't nod—she couldn't. Her body had frozen with disbelief.

Because it was not a ghost. Sylah was *really* here.

She looked like she'd weathered a storm. Her eyes were deeply sunken and her skin was sallow, ageing her beyond her twenty-one years. Though her hair had grown, her braids looked thin, the trinkets weighing them down, falling just past her ears. And if Hassa wasn't mistaken there were bald patches among the treasures, silvered and spherical like scars gifted by the moon.

Sylah took a step towards Hassa. A small frown growing between her brows.

"Are you all right?"

Was she all right? What a stupid question. Of course not. Kwame was dead. Anoor was missing, and the world seemed likely to implode at any minute.

And she could now bloodwerk.

Hassa carefully removed the quill from her wrist, then signed, *Yes, Sylah. I am all right. How are you?*

Sylah tried to smile, but her lips faltered in a grimace. "Yes, Hassa. I am all right."

They held each other's gaze, Hassa's a touch defiant, Sylah's a touch too knowing. Then they bridged the space between them until they grasped each other, holding onto the safety of their fierce friendship.

Hassa felt Sylah's tears on her shoulder, sparking a sudden terror within her. The embrace was too tight, her love too strong. Hassa pushed her away and stood back, trembling.

"Hassa, what is it?"

Hassa moved her arms, the sign for his name too painful to convey without pushing through the heavy weight of grief.

Kwame. Kwame is dead.

Sylah shook her head in disbelief, flinging tears left and right. "No."

Hassa nodded firmly and repeated the words, over and over and over again to match the even keening of Sylah's cries.

Then they were back in each other's arms, their bodies forming a mound of grief and loss. The only sound was the heaving of their breaths and the beating of their hearts in their throats.

They stood there for some time before Sylah rocked back on her heels and asked, "What happened? Tell me everything."

Hassa looked to her wrist and down to the space where a hand once was. The skin around the scar was a deep grey, dulled by the clear blood that ran through her veins. Like all Ghostings, Hassa'd had her hands and tongue removed as a babe—a penance to silence the indigenous people of the continent. But the Ghostings weren't silenced. They'd created their own language, and bided their time, because war was coming.

But what Hassa hadn't realised was that the battle had already begun.

"Hassa?" Sylah prompted her again.

She dragged her thoughts away from her ancestral scars and back up to the red-rimmed gaze of Sylah. Red like her blood. Red like an Ember.

Red like Kwame.

Her heart constricted as she was taken back to the scent of iron in the air. Kwame had died quickly—it took only twelve turns of the rack—and for that Hassa had been grateful. She had once seen a Duster make it to thirty turns before their limbs were finally torn from their bodies. She squeezed her eyelids, trying to shut out the image of Kwame's body. But it did nothing to stop the cheers of the crowd surging up from her memory. The Dredge-dwellers had rejoiced in watching an Ember murdered by the device used to kill only Dusters and Ghostings, those discarded to the edges of society. Hassa couldn't begrudge them their joy of vengeance.

But he hadn't been just an Ember to Hassa. He'd been her beloved.

Hassa stood and went to withdraw a bottle of firerum from her supplies. The Nest was all but empty now the Ghosting elders had left, but Hassa spent a lot of time in the underground cavern and had stocked it with the essentials. Firerum was the preferred vice of plantation workers. It numbed the wounds of the flesh and mind. Hassa knew they'd need it now.

She poured a tall glass for herself and Sylah.

There have been three deaths of note since you left, Hassa started. *First the Warden of Strength was murdered.*

"What? Uka Elsari was killed?"

Drink, Hassa commanded. *It will make it go easier.*

Sylah scowled and took a sip of the firerum. She grimaced. Hassa found it odd. Normally Sylah could finish a bottle without a twitch of a brow, and here she was balking at a mere taste. More had changed about Sylah than Hassa could know.

Warden Uka was killed in her home three mooncycles ago. Anoor was accused of her murder. As both her daughter and the person to have found her, it wasn't a difficult leap to make.

"Of course she didn't kill her."

Hassa looked up. Heat rose in Sylah's dark cheeks and the fierceness of her gaze was so scalding the edges of Sylah's silhouette blurred like a flame.

This is love, Hassa thought. Unquestioning, unwavering love. Because not for one second had Sylah entertained the thought that Anoor could have murdered her mother.

Hassa looked away. She had to, for she couldn't watch as she broke Sylah's heart.

No, it wasn't Anoor. It was an act of revenge—one of Anoor's Shadow Court, a new addition, killed her. Zuhari, she was called. But she inadvertently set up Anoor's demise, leading the wardens to think Anoor had done the crime. Anoor had no choice, she had to go into hiding.

The glass of firerum clinked as Sylah set it on the tiled floor with too much force. Her lips were a firm line. "Where is she?"

Hassa didn't want to answer the question. The last time they had gone to Anoor's hideout, she hadn't been there.

I don't know.

"What?" Sylah looked to the tunnels as if she were about to launch out into the tidewind to find Anoor.

Let me rejoin my tale, Sylah. Hassa chastised her with sharp movements.

Sylah waved a hand for Hassa to continue.

While Anoor was in hiding I discovered that people were going missing in the Dredge. Before Uka's death Anoor launched the tidewind relief bill, and one of the elements was offering succour and food to those who needed it. A shelter was built in the Dredge. But it became clear that those who entered didn't always come back out.

"What has this got to do with anything?"

Hassa bared her teeth. *It has to do with* everything, *Sylah.*

"Sorry," Sylah said, looking a little guilty. "I am impatient to understand what's happened to her."

I shared my findings with Anoor, and we decided to try and get someone inside to investigate. Hassa hesitated.

In that moment Sylah spoke.

"Wait, you said there were three deaths. The second must have been Kwame. Who was the third?"

When we took Anoor out of the Keep we brought her to Lio's. We thought your mother would protect her, given the fact that Anoor is Lio's blood daughter.

Sylah cocked her head and frowned. "Anoor was staying at my house?"

Hassa wanted to counter the comment and say that it wasn't *her* house any longer, that Sylah hadn't been here, hadn't known what they had all been through while she was away. But Hassa knew her next words would be a blow.

Lio agreed to go into the shelter to investigate. The first time she found nothing. The second time . . .

"Yes?"

She didn't make it.

"What do you mean, she didn't make it? She didn't make it out?" Sylah's voice was full of anger, but Hassa knew it wasn't directed at her.

She died, Sylah.

Tears were falling from Sylah's eyes again. Hassa watched them with a curious fascination. Sylah was frowning, her expression confused as if she were unaware that she was grieving, or rather, was in denial about it.

Sylah and Lio's relationship had always been complicated at best. Lio had been part of the Sandstorm rebellion—a group of Dusters who had stolen children from their cribs and raised them as weapons to one day infiltrate the empire. But then they had all died, killed by the Wardens' Army after they were discovered. Only Lio, Sylah and another of the Stolen, Jond, had survived.

I would rather have had no mother at all than Lio, Hassa thought.

Hassa's own mother, Dahlia, had been killed while pregnant with Hassa. Her father had been the son of an imir who hadn't wanted his line of succession sullied. Mixed couplings were illegal, so it wasn't difficult to have Dahlia killed.

But the assailants hadn't accounted for the Ghostings' tenacity for life. Once Dahlia had been left to die, Hassa had been cut from her womb and saved.

Hassa was still the only mixed-blood coupling she was aware of who had survived in plain sight of the wardens.

She drank from her cup of firerum, enjoying the burn down her throat. It numbed the old grief, just like she wanted it to. She pressed on with her telling.

Kwame and I found out not long after that the healers were draining people of bone marrow. He got caught during the investigation and paid the price. They ripped him, Sylah. Ripped him in half on the rack.

Sylah recoiled, her shoulders shifting backwards as if the words were hitting her like invisible runebullets.

Gorn and I, we went to see Anoor after Kwame was captured. And she was gone. We don't know where she is. Yona is missing too, along with the other disciples—

"The disciples are part of the Sandstorm." The words tore out of Sylah's throat.

Hassa had to reach for her firerum. She swallowed some before she signed, *Explain.*

"Jond told me. It's why I came back."

Sylah's expression splintered and Hassa saw something dark cross her features. Hassa wondered what Sylah had been through to make it back to the empire.

What happened?

Sylah began to answer, but no words came out. Tears rolled over Sylah's lips and into her open mouth. Suddenly her muscles went rigid.

"Did you say bone marrow?" Sylah whispered.

Yes, what do you know of it?

Sylah looked scared. Hassa didn't think she'd ever seen that expression on her friend's face.

"The Zalaam. The Zalaam are here already."

The tidewind had stopped howling by the time Sylah had finished her story. Hassa could see she was itching to go and search for Anoor.

Sea monsters and deathcraft. Queens and councils. You sound like a griot, Hassa signed.

"I know. I wouldn't believe myself if I hadn't lived through it." Sylah scrubbed her face with her hand, but the gesture couldn't smooth the lines of grief that now shadowed her expression.

Hassa had believed the Tannin was real, though many dismissed the sea creature as just another children's story. Hassa had seen too much to believe that monsters lived only in tales. Too often the truth was much worse.

But she could sense there was something Sylah wasn't telling her.

You say the Tannin will take a soul for every person who needs passage. And on the way there the elders sacrificed Embers. Who did you sacrifice to secure your homeward passage?

There it was again, the fracturing of Sylah's façade. But now Hassa understood what this expression was: guilt.

"No one," she said.

Neither of them acknowledged Sylah's lie.

"I had this." Sylah reached for a braid in her hair and held it up. In it was a small black sphere, no larger than a coin, covered in tiny runes. "It's an orb of creation, the fifth law."

You said there were only four laws: growth, connection, healing and presence.

Hassa was still reeling from learning that there was a type of rune that could *heal* people and another that enabled you to instantaneously travel from place to place.

"The council leaders disbanded the fifth law. The last fifth council member founded the Zalaam. He was their prophet, though his name has been written out of history. The orb of creation is what made the Tannin in the first place."

Sylah was looking at the sphere with a fevered expression.

"Though the fifth law takes its toll. Each act of creation takes a piece of your soul, and with every one, a part of your humanity is stripped away."

Irrevocably? Hassa asked, wondering how much Sylah had been practising with the runes.

Sylah shrugged. "I guess, it's why they say the prophet went mad."

And the bone marrow?

"Stronger than blood. It's what the Zalaam are using to fuel their army."

Army?

Sylah smiled and it was sickly. "An army of creations. The Ending Fire is coming."

The words rang in Hassa's mind, like the silence after the explosion she had experienced beneath the city.

So how do we stop them?

"The Blood Forged are reaching out across the world to try and band together a defence. But every country is suffering from the damage bloodwerk has done to the world."

What do you mean?

Sylah waved her hand upwards, towards the tempest of the tidewind above. A dismissive gesture that didn't match the seriousness of what followed.

"Bloodwerk, it's what causes the tidewind. It is altering the balance of the world, draining it of energy. By using bone marrow, the Zalaam are making it worse. Much worse." Sylah's voice turned lifeless, her gaze downcast. "If the Zalaam don't kill us, the weather eventually will. Either way they get what they want. Death to non-believers."

Hassa rocked back on her heels, shocked by Sylah's resignation.

Why did you come back, Sylah?

Sylah's eyes flashed, resurrecting them from their deadened state. "To warn Anoor about the Sandstorm—the disciples—remember?"

Hassa's mouth twisted with scorn. Anger pumped through her veins.

A war is coming, and you came back to help the woman you love. The woman who sent you away to bring back aid, if I remember correctly.

Sylah's gaze widened. Her eyes were still the red of Ember blood.

You come to me in my ancestors' home, a place born of fight and justice, to tell me you left the place where you could have helped the most to what, save a woman you once fucked?

Sylah did flinch this time. Hassa knew grief guided her anger. How dare Kwame leave her before the last battle? And here was Sylah, dejected and contrite, fighting not for life, but for love.

Hassa stood and found she was trembling again.

Get out. Go chase after her.

"Hassa—"

Get out. Hassa lurched forward as she signed.

Sylah's shoulders slumped and she nodded.

"I'm sorry," she whispered before retreating into the darkness of the tunnels.

Hassa wanted to call after her and apologise, to gesture that she hadn't really meant it, that she was scared and alone and afraid. And sad.

Oh, how she was sad.

But she didn't. Instead, she dragged her eyes back to the *Book of Blood* and the battle plans that had begun churning in her mind.

CHAPTER TWO

Anoor

Shine bright under Kabut's eye
Let his glow surround you
Succumb to faith and sacrifice
Let divine web bind you.

—Zalaam prayer chanted during the full moon

Anoor's knees knocked together as she edged onto the gangplank.

Three weeks of travelling and these were the hardest steps she'd taken yet.

The journey across the Wardens' Empire had revealed more sights and sounds than she'd ever seen in her twenty-one years confined to the Wardens' Keep.

But she'd been unable to appreciate them, for every time she blinked all she could see was the turning of the rack and the bloodied remains of her friend.

Click.

They had journeyed along the less travelled roads of the west coast, avoiding the larger cities of the empire. For a full two days the carriage had rattled through the vineyards of Jin-Eynab, where a small dirt track weaved between the fields. Every time they'd stopped, Anoor had devoured as many plump grapes as she could, leaving her fingers sticky and purple from their juice.

They rarely saw people; as the carriage had been packed with all their supplies, they had no need to stop. It was a shock when a group of eru riders had passed them on the outskirts of Jin-Sahalia on their final days of travel. The riders' noisy banter had felt harsh on Anoor's ears.

Now they had reached the end of their journey across the empire, to start another voyage across the sea. The gangplank swayed beneath her feet as she shuffled up the ramp to the boat.

"Don't dawdle, Anoor. We have many more days of travel ahead of us," Yona said from the ship's bow.

Click.

Anoor flinched from the image of Kwame's body on the membrane of her eyelids. The ramp moved beneath her and she sought stability from the metal railing. The coolness beneath her fingers soothed her rage and grief within.

Click.

Anoor breathed out slowly, willing the sound of the rack to abate from her mind.

Click.

"Stop, please just stop."

"Did you say something, Anoor?" Tanu came up beside her.

Anoor turned a tight smile to her friend and fellow disciple.

"No, nothing."

Tanu raised a dark eyebrow. "You're holding that railing pretty tight."

"Oh." Anoor's hands dropped to her sides. "I just haven't been on a boat before. I'd never even seen the ocean until now."

Anoor raised her gaze to the horizon. She had read so many descriptions of the sea, but nothing had prepared her for the expanse of it.

It stretched out further than she could have ever imagined. Like a tablecloth upon the land, it ran from shore to sky. And it moved like fabric too, with pleats and ruffles, lace and frills. Anoor imagined what it would be like to drape the waves over her body as she swam in the cool and unfathomable depths.

Somewhere out there is Sylah. The thought jarred her even more than the incessant clicking in her mind.

What would Sylah say if she saw me now?

Anoor started as Tanu answered—she hadn't even realised she'd spoken out loud.

"She'd say you were doing exactly what you set out to do: bringing down the empire and liberating those within. The Zalaam will help you lead an army to the Keep's gates."

Tanu squeezed Anoor's forearm. It was rare Tanu was this sincere, and it gave Anoor strength.

She walked the final steps up the gangplank onto the ship. The vessel was similar to the pictures she'd seen in textbooks, but larger, and entirely made of metal. The sail hung limply from the mast. She reached out to touch it, unfamiliar with the material. It scratched against her skin, the texture somewhere between straw and hessian.

Faro stepped into the sail's shadow and turned to her. "Joba-tree fibres. To withstand the tidewind." The former Disciple of Duty had been quiet for a lot of the journey north, only conversing with Qwa, their partner and former Disciple of Truth.

"That makes sense," Anoor replied.

There was the sound of clinking, and it was only when Faro turned that Anoor realised the noise wasn't resonating from within her mind.

Four people Anoor didn't recognise were loading the ship's hull with crates filled with vials. Through the slats in the crates, she could see the pale blue liquid in the glass. Each crate was packed tightly with ice.

"Do you think we have enough of the formula to win the war?" Anoor asked Faro. All three of them had been practising with the liquid every night, under Yona's regimented tutelage.

The runes that enabled godpower still astonished her. Last night she'd brought to life a spoon that could scoop her dinner onto her plate on its own.

Faro's brown eyes shuttered closed for a second before opening again, a little tight in the corners. "I'm sure the Zalaam have managed to produce more."

Anoor knew there was a lie there, somewhere. But she didn't press it. She was tired of secrets.

Ignorance felt safer.

Click.

She turned away from Faro to Qwa, who was overseeing the loading of the precious cargo from the shore. Qwa's forehead was peppered with sweat. He ran his hand over his brow, lifting the last hairs that remained on his head so they wouldn't stick.

Faro watched him with a small smile on their gaunt face. The braids they normally wore had loosened over the course of the journey and grown matted at the roots.

Footsteps rang out behind them as Yona marched across the metal decking of the boat.

"We're almost ready to depart," Yona said.

Tanu now stood by Yona's shoulder, her slight form the opposite in every way of Yona's looming presence.

"We are ready," Tanu said as if speaking for all the disciples.

Though Anoor wasn't sure she was.

I am the Child of Fire. The title felt like a collar around her neck. The closer they got to leaving the empire the tighter it felt.

"Anoor? Are you sure you're feeling well?" Tanu murmured to her.

Anoor nodded, trying to slow down her breathing.

Qwa joined the congregation on the boat. "That's the last crate loaded."

"Then we need to set sail immediately." Yona's voice had bite, though the muscle that twitched in her brow—so like Uka's—had smoothed now they were all on board.

The four sailors that Yona had hired stood to attention by the sails. Anoor was surprised that with the amount of money weighing down their pockets they could stand upright.

Yona had wanted not just the ship and the sailors but their silence. That hadn't come cheap.

Her grandmother turned to Tanu. "It's time for you to leave."

Anoor frowned. "What? Why is she leaving?"

Tanu jostled her shoulder with her own. "Don't worry, it won't be long until I see you again."

"But I don't understand—"

"There's no time for this," Yona interrupted.

Anoor stood firm and held her grandmother's gaze until Yona shook her head with a small smile.

"The blood of the endless flame is in you, I tell you. Tanu is going back to Nar-Ruta. She needs to sow the seeds of dissent and be Kabut's eye in the Keep."

"But you said it isn't safe, that's why we're leaving." Anoor refused to break eye contact with Yona.

"Anoor," Tanu said. "I need to go back. We need someone to cover our tracks, so they don't try and follow you."

"What are you going to say?"

Tanu grinned. "Don't worry, I've got it covered."

Anoor reached for Tanu and enfolded her in her arms. The bird-like girl felt more solid than Anoor expected.

Click.

"I don't want you to go," Anoor said into her hair.

"I know."

The smaller woman pushed her to arm's length. "You'll be fine. You're the *Child of Fire.*"

Tanu stepped away with a wink. "I'll see you on the battlefield."

Anoor jerked upright. *So easy was it to forget that war is coming.*

The thought seared across the walls of her mind, and though it was painful, it was a feeling she welcomed. It sparked the fire of her anger, the coals of which had never gone out. She clenched her fists so tight that her nails left crescent moons on the flesh of her palm. The mark of Kabut's eye.

Anoor's smile was grim and full of rage—the wrath of a god.

She wanted to oust the wardens more than anything. She wanted them to suffer, for Kwame, for the Ghostings, for everything they'd done in perpetuating the lie that the empire was alone.

But the empire wasn't alone.

There was land out there. People out there.

Click.

The boat moved away from the harbour, but Anoor wasn't looking back. She was looking out towards the sea.

Towards her army.

She didn't hear the sound of the rack again.

They had been travelling north for ten days when the sea began to grow rough. Lightning sparked across the horizon, shattering the twilight sky. Anoor stood at the railing of the ship, enjoying the onslaught of rain. The storm was exhilarating, the downpour refreshing. And as the boat dipped and dived, she could barely tell what fell from the sky and what surged up from the ocean. Sea water and rainwater collided, leaving her drenched from sole to head.

"Yona wants us to seek shelter in our cabin," Faro shouted from behind Anoor. They clutched onto the mainsail, the wind pulling at their clothes.

"I'll be fine!" Anoor shouted back. But as she said it, she felt her stomach lurch as the ship dropped twenty handspans off the cliff of a wave. Her feet lifted up and she found herself sprawled on the deck.

Faro crawled to her and together they made their way to the steps that led to their quarters. There they remained sequestered until the danger passed.

"Do you want to play shantra?" Anoor asked the swaying hammock above her.

"No."

Anoor prodded where Faro's ass would be with her toe.

"Get off." Faro's curt reply was as much as Anoor was going to get. But she wasn't giving up quite yet.

Each day away from the empire Anoor felt a small semblance of her old self come back. The pieces of her weren't the same: where they had once been as pliable as warm sand, they were now glass, fragile but sharp.

"Come on, please." She jabbed her fingers upwards where she estimated Faro's neck was.

"Stop that."

The boat jerked to the side, silencing them both.

"Where did you even get a shantra board from?" Faro sounded defeated. Anoor got out of her hammock to rummage in her pack.

"You know that ceramic tray Qwa dropped last week? I kept the pieces to make tokens. And look, I even used bloodwerk to magnetise them to the board, so the rocking won't affect the gameplay."

As Faro made to stand, the boat was thrown to the side once more.

"By the blood, what's happening out there?" Anoor stood up ready to leave their cabin, but Faro's hand darted out and clasped her wrist.

"We should stay here, it's safer."

"But the crew on deck, my grandmother."

"They'll be fine." Faro's grip tightened. Anoor looked down at her wrist where Faro held her so tightly, she felt a bruise blossoming.

"Get off me." Anoor's voice was glass too. Jagged and cutting.

Faro gave Anoor a thin smile before letting go. "Fine, but I don't want to be the one to explain to Yona why you didn't follow her orders."

Anoor hesitated by the door, her resolve weakening with every sway of the boat.

Faro added, "Besides, I'm pretty good at shantra, so maybe it is a good idea to leave now."

Anoor looked back. Faro's hollow cheeks were pulled upwards into a smile.

"One game," Anoor said. "And if the sea hasn't settled by then, I'm leaving this tin can."

Anoor crossed their small cabin and joined Faro on the ground. She lifted out the wooden plank she'd been using as a board and the ceramic tokens marked with bloodwerk.

Faro was looking curiously at the runes. Anoor wondered if her blue blood perturbed Faro but then they spoke. "These are cleverly made. Sometimes I wonder what the empire could have been if we'd given power to those with minds like yours."

"Minds like mine?"

Faro picked up a token and held it up to the runelight. "You understand that runes are a language, and with them you write poetry."

Poetry, Anoor thought. *I like that. But I wonder what poems I could write with the runes of creation.*

And how that beautiful violence could tear down the walls of the Keep.

A strike or so later, the sea had settled enough for Anoor to venture out of her cabin without worrying about Yona's wrath. It was still raining heavily, but the sea was no longer stirring like a boiling pot of soup.

Yona was standing on the bow of the boat. Her severe features were so still she looked like the figurehead of the ship, carved from metal like the deck beneath her.

"Grandmother?"

Yona didn't turn around. She wore her scars proudly; no wigs or long-sleeved gowns had left the empire with them. Instead, Yona wore translucent billowing fabrics that showed off her scars, like veining in granite, that ran the length of her body.

Her grandmother had always been striking but the marks made her more so. The scars were like beautiful filigree on her skin, and she wore them like armour.

Yona was still looking out towards the horizon as she replied, "One week, maybe more, and we'll be home."

"Home?" Anoor pressed. Her grandmother had told her so little about the Zalaam, and Anoor wanted to know so much.

"Yes, home," was all she said.

Anoor rubbed a hand across her eyes and looked around. The moonlight shone across the wet decking. It was then that Anoor realised they were alone on the deck.

"Where's Xan? Catt?" The two sailors had taken it in turns to play shantra with her in the evenings. Meda and Taloy were the other two hired hands, a couple that kept to themselves, but Anoor was still surprised Meda wasn't manning the sails.

"They fell into the sea. All four of them."

"What?" Anoor croaked, spittle lodged in her throat, and she coughed.

"They died during the storm."

Anoor felt like someone had punched her, but she didn't let the feeling hold her back. She lurched her chest over the railing and looked desperately into the ocean.

"We need to help them. Send down a rope!"

"Anoor, they're gone."

"They can't be."

"They are. Step back from there."

Tears were falling down Anoor's face and she brushed them away. She felt the glass within her cracking.

"Stop crying," Yona said. Though her words were harsh, her tone was soft.

Anoor tried to still the hiccuping of her sobs.

"Crying can be seen as weakness," Yona said.

Anoor jerked up her gaze to meet Yona's.

"I do not believe it to be," Yona clarified. "But there are others who see softness in tears and think that softness is an undesirable trait in a leader. Those are the people we must convince of your standing."

"Convince?" This was the first Anoor had heard of needing to convince anyone of anything. She was the Child of Fire.

Wasn't she?

"Do not let those doubts in, granddaughter." Yona had sensed Anoor's thoughts. "You are the Child of Fire as Kabut has willed it," she said fiercely, her teeth flashing.

Anoor tried to still the tears that flowed, but she had reached her capacity for grief. Her face crumpled once more.

Yona saw Anoor battling with herself and opened her arms. "Come here, child. Take comfort that their deaths were welcomed by Kabut."

Anoor let herself be held by Yona.

"Remember what I said that day your friend died?" Yona asked.

Anoor turned stiff as Yona's arms tightened around her.

Death has power. Let his sacrifice fuel you.

Anoor murmured the words through taut lips as Yona's embrace continued to tighten.

"Exactly. There is no space for grief in Kabut's eye. It is not the way. For grief denies the prosperity granted by Kabut."

Anoor was struggling to breathe as Yona's muscular arms tightened around her ribcage.

"Lead me in prayer now." Yona wasn't asking, she was demanding.

Anoor's mouth was pressed against the fabric on Yona's shoulder, muffling her voice. But she spoke the words her grandmother taught her. "Glorious one up above, you who knows no bounds or boundaries. You who spins the web of my future, take my pain, and bless me anew."

As Yona released her from the embrace, Anoor was once again able to take a deep breath, the sweet sea air filling her lungs.

And the truth was . . . she did feel better. Praying to Kabut had alleviated the pressure of loss that had built up in her mind. Because she hadn't lost anyone, not really, they were simply in Kabut's realm, waiting for her to join them.

She looked up at the moon and smiled.

I'll see you soon, Kwame.

Yona saw where Anoor's gaze travelled, and her lips drew up in turn. "Kabut blesses you, Child of Fire."

As Anoor turned back to her grandmother, something snagged on her eyeline. She frowned as she spotted a blue smear on the railing. She leant forward and touched it. The substance was tacky, and as Anoor brought it to her nose, she knew exactly what she'd smell—iron.

The smear was blood.

Yona came to stand next to her. She wiped the railing with her hand, removing the last bits of residue.

"One of the sailors must have injured themselves before going over."

Anoor nodded slowly, her eyes fixated on Yona's hand now holding the railing.

"I think I'll go back to the cabin," Anoor said quietly.

"Go, I'll see you at dinner."

Anoor retreated to her hammock, but sleep didn't come. She couldn't vanquish the image of Yona wiping the railing.

And the thin blue line of blood Anoor had seen encrusted under Yona's nails.

CHAPTER THREE

Jond

The Entwined Harbour has a long-standing relationship with Tenio. Queen Karanomo once brokered peace between the chief of the Wetlands and the captain of the Entwined Harbour. The outcome of which led to the chief acknowledging the moving domain of the Entwined Harbour's territory within the Ica Sea.

—Excerpt from *Politicking Across Borders,*
written by Rubo Oh-Kinsha

Jond's stomach lurched, and he fell onto his knees panting. He dry-heaved for a full two minutes.

The ground was soggy with rainwater, and he clung to the mud as if it could stabilise him.

"Bit dramatic, don't you think?" Kara said. Her scarf covered half of her face, but the scorn was clear in the crinkle of her violet eyes. They were the same colour as her blood, which was imprinted in runes on Jond's arm.

With his stomach still churning, he tried to focus on the runes. They had the same curves and dashes as the bloodwerk of the Wardens' Empire, but the strokes were different, unfamiliar to him. Like letters in a language he could read but not understand.

The councillor's way of writing the runes was different too. His own wrist was adorned with an inkwell, a cuff that held in place a stylus that pierced his vein, allowing him to write in blood. But the students of the Zwina Academy had learnt a different technique, a faster one: they carved runes into metal orbs that were then rolled over an open wound in the centre of their palm. The blood was then imprinted onto the object, and in Jond's case, onto his arm, to flight him to another continent. They called the practice "deathcraft".

"Is that the last time we're doing this?" The words spewed out of his mouth with another lurch of his stomach.

Kara snorted. "Do you see water?"

Jond groaned. The runes of the fourth charter—the law of presence—only enabled them to flight a few leagues at a time. They had been travelling bit by bit for what felt like forever and each time Jond was sick.

"We should reach the Ica Sea in the next flight. Come on."

Kara reached for Jond's wrist, her fingers soft, her nails sharp. She wiped away the old rune combination, now distorted from the rain. She cradled his arm against her chest, protecting it from the weather with the canopy of her hood.

The orb was flesh-warm as it rolled against his forearm. She deftly moved her hands, imprinting the runes onto his skin. The precision required to draw the right combination was a deterrent to those who would abuse the power—a power that drained energy from the world.

Just like the Zalaam were doing, Jond thought bitterly.

"Why are you grimacing?" Kara asked.

"I was thinking about the Zalaam and the power they strip from bone marrow. Will we ever be able to match it?"

"That's why we're going to the Entwined Harbour in the first place." She spoke slowly as if he were a child. "More allies means a greater chance of winning the war, isn't that what the Blood Forged are supposed to be doing?"

She had finished the combination and was working on her own forearm. Jond held his breath, knowing that at any second—

The world spun and suddenly Jond's feet were sinking into unfamiliar ground. No, *familiar* ground.

"Sand," he breathed. It wasn't blue like in the Wardens' Empire but instead a strange beige. The turquoise of the ocean beyond it was comforting, similar to the Marion Sea though the waves were much higher. A thick mist dwelled on the horizon and Jond squinted, trying to make out the mirage of shapes within it.

Kara appeared a second later and breathed a sigh of uncharacteristic relief. "Quickly, we need to move. The tide's coming in."

Jond turned, holding his hand to his stomach in an attempt to keep the bile down. "But where do we go?"

The island was small, a sand bank really, with no vegetation or civilisation in sight.

"There." Kara pointed to a rowboat a few paces away. It rocked in the waves.

She began to run towards it, her pack bouncing on her lower back as she went. Jond wasn't sure he was up for running. He was still feeling very delicate.

At least it isn't raining, he thought. Though it did make him wonder how the world's imbalance affected this part of the continent. He hoped the rains here weren't as awful as the acid storms on the coast of Tenio.

"Hurry up," Kara barked. The sea was up to her waist, but she was still a few handspans from the boat.

"I'm coming, I'm coming," Jond grumbled. But as he spoke, he felt a rush of water coming up to meet him. "What in the name of Anyme . . . ?"

In three breaths he was waist deep in the sea. In four it had reached his chin. Ahead of him Kara was swimming.

A vicious current pulled at his pack and clothes, threatening to drag him under.

"Kara—" Sea water filled his mouth. At first, he tried to fight it, his fists raised against the strength of the sea. But then his breath left him.

He opened his eyes as he let his body sink. Rays of sunlight slipped between the waves, illuminating the beauty of the Ica Sea.

Under the water there was a strange kind of silence, full of listening, as the creatures of the ocean welcomed him to their depths.

If I die here, I won't be alone. I'd never be alone again.

Jond barely registered the splash above him, too immersed was he in the concept of losing his sense of self to the sea.

But the oar, that he did feel. It banged against his skull, knocking some sense into him. The pain accompanied the memory of Rascal, the kitten he had rescued not so long ago. If he died, who would look after her?

Niha, of course. But Niha didn't know how to scratch Rascal's ears just the way she liked it.

Jond reached for the oar with the last of his strength and pulled himself to the surface.

The sun warmed his face as he broke through the waves. He gasped, drawing in a breath before reaching for the edge of the boat. He pulled himself up, his muscles straining with the effort until he fell, face forward, into the belly of the boat.

"Nice of you to join me." Kara's face scarf had fallen, the only indication of her discomfort. She looked more bored than worried that Jond had nearly died.

"Th . . . thank you," he stuttered out. He was *very* cold, but Kara seemed unfazed by the unexpected swim, her red hair already bouncing back into ringlets by her ears.

Jond sat up and looked back at the direction he thought he had come from. But the island wasn't there. He swung his gaze around, but it was nowhere to be seen.

"What . . . ?"

"Tide swallowed it," Kara said with a toothy smile. "The island only appears during low tide."

"How did you know it was low tide?"

"I didn't." She held up her chin, daring him to challenge her. It reminded him of Sylah and the thought twisted his gut. He looked away.

Jond cleared his throat. "Where shall I row us to?"

Kara had already reached for the oars. "I told the Blood Forged I could do this trip on my own. I never needed you, Jond, and never will."

Jond recognised the bravado in her tone. Always having to prove your worth was exhausting. He'd done it for most of his life.

He met her gaze until the tension in her shoulders released and she looked away. When she began to row her strokes were even and quick. Soon they were parting the waves towards the horizon where the shape of ships slowly came into view.

*   *   *

Jond had got used to having his understanding of the world shattered. And shattered again.

So, it was quite disappointing to see that the Entwined Harbour was exactly what the name suggested: a group of ships strapped together with twine.

Boats of different sizes were bound by their gangplanks and sails. The mass of vessels moved gently on the waves and Jond felt instant seasickness unfurl from the pit of his sour stomach.

Strips of multicoloured cloth hung from masts, and the pattern of them seemed too precise not to mean something—perhaps flags like the imir houses in the empire. The colours brought an innate cheerfulness to the view, and Jond found himself thinking that, despite the seasickness he was going to get, perhaps this trip might not be too awful after all.

With his curiosity sparked, Jond ran his gaze over the scale of the harbour, which grew bigger the closer they got.

Kara aimed for the largest ship on the periphery of the cluster, her sights set on a rope ladder that hung limply over the edge.

"How many ships are here?"

Kara tilted her head left and right. "Unsure. Maybe four hundred and fifty if you include the smaller fishing vessels. But that's less than half of the captain's fleet. Many ships are out foraging. So, the population of twiners fluctuates."

"Twiners? Captain?"

Kara made a frustrated sound. "Twiners are the nomadic people who live here. Their ancestry goes back many thousands of years. The captain is their leader, elected once every fifty years, but few captains' reigns last that long."

"Why? Are they a violent people?"

"Violent?" Kara laughed. "No, they're scholars at heart. And so, their political campaigns are often convoluted and intricate. Any captain who missteps is ousted, for even the smallest thing. One captain lost her seat because she tipped one of her servants. The opposition argued that it constituted an unauthorised expense."

"That sounds . . . exhausting."

"It is."

"Can they do deathcraft?"

Kara's shake of the head was sharp. "No, if anyone wants to study deathcraft they come to the Academy. Do you understand now why your land is so rare? Your knowledge so precious?"

She was talking about bloodwerk. The runes Jond had learnt in the empire were so different to the ones taught in the Academy. Bloodwerk was based on forces: to push and pull. Boring, really, compared to the power to flight from one place to another that Kara wielded.

A large wave crashed into the rowboat, knocking the oar out of Kara's hand. She retrieved it before Jond could help her. A few strokes later they reached the foot of the rope ladder.

"Go on up, I'll tie the boat down."

Jond nodded and did as he was bidden.

The ladder was slippery, full of brine and barnacles. He kept his gaze above and not below as he climbed.

He reached the top and let out a relieved breath, which turned into a cough as he looked around him.

Five soldiers levelled swords at his chest. They wore more pearls than cloth, the white beads illuminated against their dark skin. Most were freckled across their face and torso. Their curls were beaded so heavily that it pulled their hair straight.

Jond instinctively held up his hands.

"Jula bon bifra la hindra?" the woman closest to Jond said, her language smooth with rolling Rs and lilting vowels. She held the longest sword, just a few handspans from his heart, and Jond guessed she was the leader of the group.

"Huh?"

"Noba no yatu banglt?" This time her accent was gruffer and Jond wondered if she was speaking yet another language.

It was at that moment that Kara appeared beside him. All swords turned to her.

"Non-violent my puckered arsehole," he said to Kara through clenched teeth.

"Ity buto leckra, Kara," Kara said to the leader.

The swords dropped and they bowed low to Kara.

"What? How did you do that?" Jond marvelled.

"Tutu ity bu?" The leader jutted her head to Jond.

"He only speaks the common tongue," Kara said by way of explanation.

"Only one language?" The woman laughed. "What a primitive way of existing."

"Well, he is very primitive," Kara confirmed.

Now that Jond was no longer fearing for his life, he looked around. At this height Jond could see the expanse of the Entwined Harbour sprawling into the distance.

Children laughed and danced precariously along masts and balconies. They jingled as they ran, their clothing glittering with shells and pearls. None wore shoes, and when Jond looked back at the twiners in front of him he noticed that their feet were thick with calluses. The air was heavy with the smell of frying fish and something sweet, almost buttery. The aroma only added to his nausea.

"Come on. There'll be time to explore later," Kara said, pulling him by the arm.

The guards were leading the way across the deck. People stopped to stare at Kara and Jond who were so clearly outsiders.

Kara continued, "We will need to dress and wash before meeting the captain."

"She isn't the captain?" Jond tipped his head towards the woman with the longest sword.

"No, though you're right to point her out. Status among the ocean guard is indicated by the length of their blade."

Jond nodded.

Kara dipped out of view as she stumbled. Jond caught her, but she flung him off as soon as she stabilised.

"I'm all right. My leg just gave way." Her scarf had fallen again and Jond caught the exhaustion written into her features. The bloodletting had taken its toll on her.

Jond noticed her breath was coming out in quick, strained bursts as they were led down a wooden staircase in the centre of a lacquered boat. The stairs went deeper than Jond thought possible from the surface, and it reminded him of the *Baqarah*, the ship he had travelled to the continent on. Though that was all metal, and this was all wood, the corridor pressed in on him all the same.

The orange glow of light above them flickered and Jond looked up. He knew the light source wouldn't be generated by bloodwerk, as only the citizens in the empire knew those type of runes. He expected gas lamps, like in the City of Rain, but instead the light behind the glass was projected in strips . . . that moved.

"Lustre eels," Kara grunted. "They create light through their skin."

"The light we see is a chemical reaction as enzymes in their body collide and create energy," the leader of the ocean guard clarified.

"That's what I said . . ." Kara spoke through gritted teeth.

"No . . . you said . . ."

Jond drowned out their bickering; he was too mesmerised by the creatures swimming above him. It was hard to see the outline of their bodies against the brightness that emanated from them, but he could just make out the bulbous head and tapered tails of the eels as they swam past, one after another. The tube of glass ran through the centre of the ship, but Jond couldn't see where it ended.

"How do you feed them?" he asked, interrupting the guard's explanation of the differences in the definition between the words "create" and "reaction". Kara gave Jond a grateful look, but he was too distracted to appreciate it.

"The tube network is a circuit ending in a large tank in the front of each ship. The eels are free to pass through the tubing as they see fit."

"Why don't you just use gas lamps or torches? I imagine fire is much easier to control."

Everyone inhaled and one of the ocean guard's hands hovered by two green hoops by his waist.

Kara's nails dug into Jond's wrist as she hissed, "Do not speak that word again. It is banned in this country."

Jond frowned but didn't probe further. He changed the subject, trying to deflect from whatever issue he'd just caused.

"What is that hanging from your belt?" Jond pointed to the loops. The way the guard's hand had moved to them so quickly, Jond wondered if they were a weapon.

"Steelweed," the guard grunted. "Used to tie foreigners up." Then he smiled and Jond realised he was joking . . . maybe?

"It's a type of seaweed," Kara explained to him in that pedantic way of hers. "When it reaches maturity, it has the strength of steel.

The twiners use it for a lot of their rope and chains, as metal is hard to come by in the Ica Sea."

The procession stopped and Jond nearly bumped into the guard in front of him.

"We're here," the leader said.

The ship lolled to one side from the onslaught of a wave and Jond's mouth opened to retch. He contained it just in time.

"Do you have any ginger tea?" Jond asked the guard.

"Ginger tea?" she asked.

"For my stomach," Jond shrugged. "Seasickness."

The guards began to laugh, and it was Kara who stopped them.

"Bring him powdered gumo root in water." It was a command, not a question. It sliced through their laughter.

Kara opened the door to the cabin and stepped in. Jond followed, already pulling the pack from his shoulders with relief.

"No, no." She whirled on him. "This is my room. Yours is next door."

"Do you really think we should separate?" he said quietly, casting a glance towards the ocean guard.

Kara didn't reply, she just merely shut the door in his face.

The twiners in the hallway smirked, and Jond felt frustration spark a headache behind his eyes.

I wonder how many more times I'll come to regret accompanying Kara on this trip. He estimated the current number was north of fifty.

The ocean guard led him to the room next door and Jond entered, closing the door without a thank you.

His cabin was nothing like the metal tin he'd shared with Sylah on the *Baqarah*. It was warm and inviting, panelled in wood that smelt of sweet resin. And it was larger, with a bed big enough for two.

The light swelled in the room as two lustre eels swam past side by side in the glass pipe above. The next eel was solitary, projecting less light so that it invited the shadows to stretch from the corners.

Jond dropped his pack and it fell with a thump. It was made of the same water-resistant material of his coat, but if the contents were anything like his shirt, then it was unlikely they were still dry.

He unbuckled the bag and began to sort through it. Kara had insisted on packing for him. He'd thought it was because she knew the customs and dress of the twiners. But once he peeled away the damp layer of underwear and spare slacks, he found another bag encased in the first. He grunted as he pulled it out and uncovered the protected contents.

"She made me carry *books*?"

Jond's fingers ran along the spines with equal wonder and annoyance. He loved books dearly; ever since he'd learnt how to read, he'd consumed all the novels the Sandstorm had to offer, though that hadn't been much. The tomes had been stolen and intended for just one purpose—to train them for the Aktibar. But secretly Jond thought if he'd been given the choice, he would have loved to be a librarian. In another time and place, perhaps.

There was no other time and place. There was just now. Now and here.

But maybe once the war was over.

A dark thought lurked in the murky waters of his mind.

I won't survive the war.

He knew that for certain. No one expects the general that leads the troops into battle to survive. But he'd take a lot of the Zalaam down with him before he did.

There was a knock at the door. "Come in—"

But the guest had already entered. The woman was tall with sun-burnished skin that seemed to glow under the lustre light. Her eyes were citrusy, her jaw sharp. The hair on her head was cropped short with a single braid that fell by her ear, laden with blue shells. Her smile was full of curiosity and Jond felt his cheeks heat as she appraised him up and down.

"Can I help you?"

"Common tongue, eh, eh? But not so common looking . . ." She arched her back ever so slightly and it set the beads around her navel twinkling.

Jond's eyes rested on the smooth skin there a beat longer than was necessary. He realised what he was doing and looked away, but she only laughed. It sounded like waves swirling in shallow waters.

"I've brought you gumo root to settle your stomach."

Jond reached for the drink, grateful for something else to do with his hands. The woman made him nervous.

"I've also brought you some hot stones if you'd like to bathe."

She withdrew a bundle of cloth and unwrapped it, revealing three flat pebbles the size of Jond's fist.

He had spotted the bathtub in the corner, but the water in it was cold and he hadn't yet steeled himself to wash. "Thank you."

The woman nodded and went to drop two of the pebbles in the tub. The water hissed and bubbled as they sank.

"This one I'll leave for your wet clothes. You can wrap them over the stone for a minute and they'll be dry."

Jond nodded. He expected the woman to leave after that, but she didn't. He took a sip before saying over the rim of the mug, "I'm Jond, by the way."

"Nice to meet you, Jond By the Way."

"No . . . no . . . I meant . . ."

She laughed again, waves crashing on sand. "I know what you meant."

Another small silence.

"How do you heat up the stones without . . ." Kara had said not to mention "fire" and even without saying the word, only implying it, he saw the woman's eyes widen.

"A geyser," she said quickly. "We have an ocean-floor geyser that we lower the rocks into."

Jond nodded. Anyme damn it, he'd finished his drink.

"The bath won't stay hot for long . . ." Was she expecting him to bathe with her there?

Her gaze was playful, and Jond could feel the thrums of desire starting below his stomach.

Pretend to drink, pretend to drink.

"I'll leave you to it, eh, eh?"

Jond nearly sagged with relief as she moved to leave. He didn't want to ruin negotiations by sleeping with the first servant that was kind to him.

"I'm Shola, by the way," she said at the door.

"Nice to meet you, Shola By the Way." He allowed himself a little flirtation now she was safely on the other side of the doorframe.

He stepped forward hastily, closing the door. But Shola's foot darted out, stopping it. Her smile was sly as she leant into the gap in the doorway until their faces were a handspan apart.

Suddenly her mouth was pressed against his, warm and salty. Then she was gone, laughing her ocean sounds all the way down the corridor.

Jond shut the door with his lip between his teeth, tasting the remnants of her.

Between Kara's resentment and Shola's abrupt kiss, Jond felt ready to jump back into the sea.

He rubbed his hand over his face and said to the eel swimming above him, "Room in there for two?"

CHAPTER FOUR

Sylah

*WARDEN PURA: I've received several reports that Dusters have
been going missing after using the tidewind shelter in the Dredge.*
*WARDEN WERN: So? I think that's the least of our worries, Yona
is missing.*
*WARDEN AVEED: The tidewind shelter is no longer receiving
supplies without Yona's patronage, so that problem will resolve
itself. I agree with Wern, there are more pressing issues. Not only
is Yona missing, so too are all our disciples.*

—A section of minutes captured from the Upper Court

After seeing Hassa, Sylah spent the day drinking her bodyweight in firerum. It had been so easy to slip back into her old routine. Her feet had known to go to the one place guaranteed to numb her feelings: the Maroon.

As she stepped into her old haunt she felt as though she had crossed the threshold into the past.

A drummer sat in the corner. One of his hands moved lazily across the drumskin, rattling out an off-beat rhythm, the other held a glass of firerum. Two Dusters, who had clearly been there all night, crooned to the rafters, their duet trying—and failing—to keep pace with the drum.

"The sun rises, the sun sets, all we do is live and live," the taller of them sang.

"The moon swells, the moon wanes, all we do is lie and lie," the stouter replied.

Sylah stepped forward and joined them on the final line of the song.

"The sky spins, the sky twists, all we do is die and die."

The two Dusters laughed and clapped her on the back before weaving out towards the sunrise. From the welts on their arms and backs, it was likely they were going to the plantations.

Sylah jumped over a puddle of piss with a fond smile before settling at the bar. Nothing had changed here. The tables were still sticky, the aroma still sour.

And the firerum still strong.

The first glass slipped down less easily than it once had. She found her throat burnt for a few minutes afterwards—a feeling she'd never experienced before. Was this how Anoor felt when she'd tried firerum for the first time?

Anoor. Sylah winced as her name rang out like a chime in her mind. The reverberations of it lifted the hairs on her arms.

Where are you, my love?

Sylah closed her eyes. If Hassa had it right, then the disciples and Yona had taken Anoor somewhere. But where?

"Another," Sylah growled at the barkeep.

Neither the second nor the third drink did enough to assuage the feeling of helplessness. The edges of her mind still prickled from her argument with Hassa. But she couldn't muster up enough emotion to be angry back. Hassa was right.

I should have stayed with the Blood Forged.

The haze of firerum was welcoming but it still didn't do enough to blunt her feelings.

She lost all sense of time in the underground tavern. So, when she left the Maroon, she was surprised the tidewind had come and gone again.

The morning sun already brought with it a promise of sweltering heat. Blue sand rubbed between her toes and stuck to the sweat on her legs from the mounds of debris left from the tidewind.

"Theworldisfucked," Sylah slurred, swerving through the street.

A year on and nothing had changed. She was back in the city that had broken her, but without the woman who had pieced her back together.

Nar-Ruta without Anoor had returned Sylah back to the drab existence she had once lived. Anoor had brought colour and vibrancy . . . but most of all hope. Anoor had so desperately believed that she could change the empire for the better.

But as Sylah spun around on unstable legs, she saw nothing had changed. In fact, it had grown worse. More villas had collapsed from the tidewind's onslaught, and more Dredge-dwellers clustered in shadows trading joba seeds.

Sylah felt her mouth fill with saliva as she stepped towards those dealing the drug.

There was a bump against her legs and a cry. Sylah looked down into the face of a young Duster girl with two plaits, one running down each side of her head.

A girl with a crooked smile and two braids that hung by her ears—

Sylah faltered in her step, a vision of Petal striking her between the eyes.

"I'msorryPetalI'msosorry." Her words startled the young Duster who shrieked and dashed off.

It wasn't just grief that raked at her conscience but guilt too. First Sylah had failed to destroy the Tannin, her ploy with glass jars patterned with creation runes failing miserably. Seeing this, Petal knew that sacrifice was the only way to survive the passage through the Tannin's lair. So, Petal had jumped off the boat.

And Sylah, she had reached for her.

But to push her overboard or pull her back on the boat . . . Sylah didn't know. Or rather, Sylah didn't want to know.

She rubbed more fiercely at her eyes, trying desperately to vanquish the outline of Petal's face in her mind.

Her meandering steps led her out of the Dredge and into the Duster Quarter. The route she took was habitual. She didn't notice where she was until she reached the small joba tree sapling—neither Sylah nor Lio had ever cared for it—that stood in front of the wooden door of her old home.

"Sylah, is that you?" The voice was nasally and familiar. Sylah winced and didn't turn.

"Sylah? Lio told me you had gone east for work. Are you back now?" Rata, her mother's neighbour, was leaning precariously out of the top-floor window of her home. Her small eyes were scrunched tight, as if she couldn't quite believe what she was seeing.

Sylah had gone east, *very* east.

"Hello, Rata." Being face to face with her old front door had sobered her. "I am back."

"Lio hasn't been home for some time, I noticed her shutters aren't being lowered at night, just look at the mess on the stoop."

Sylah pushed open the door, displacing piles of sand that had gathered in the seams of the wood. Blue sand glittered down from the doorframe, adding to the dust that had wreaked havoc across the house.

"Eyoh, an upstairs window must be broken, look at this mess." Rata had been drawn closer by her nosiness, appearing behind Sylah's shoulder.

Sylah ignored her and stepped into her mother's old home. Rata tutted from the doorway.

"This will take a long time to clean. Tell Lio she needs to be more careful with her shutters."

"Lio won't be coming back here."

"Oh? Is she joining you east?"

"No, she is not joining me east."

Rata dithered, her long dress quivering around her legs. "Well, where is she then?"

Sylah let out a sharp breath before saying, "She's gone."

"Gone?"

"Dead." Sylah barked out the word louder than she had intended. She waited for the sharp pain of grief that the reminder of Lio's death ought to have brought but it didn't come. There was only so much pain she could hold.

Rata took a step back, her features slack. "What?"

Sylah turned her bloodshot eyes to Rata. "Lio's dead. Now will you get the fuck out of my house."

It was so much easier to be cruel than kind. She had known that a year ago, and right now, she wasn't sure why she had ever stopped speaking the thoughts that burnt up from her fiery core.

Rata closed the door on her way out, shifting more sand that hung in the rafters. It fell like tears upon Sylah's face.

Sylah surveyed the damage of the tidewind. It had ripped the kitchen apart, plucking at the cutlery and crockery that had been left out. Even the wooden fufu spoon that Lio had used to pound yams had been broken in the tidewind's path.

She bent to retrieve one of the splinters. It cut her finger, drawing blood, but she didn't mind. It was good to feel physical pain. At least it was something tangible. *Real.*

Sylah tipped her head to the side and wove the small piece of wood into a braid. A reminder of the mother that she had lost.

But she had never really been my mother, a mother loves, a mother nurtures.

And Lio had done none of those things.

She climbed the stairs to the second floor and moved to the bedroom. She lay on her old bed, hoping to bask in the smell of Anoor on the covers. But all traces of her had gone.

"Lio's gone. Kwame's gone. And now Anoor's gone too." Each name stoked the flames of her anger. With a surge of rage, she began to tear the sheets off the bed, shedding straw from the mattress. Then she turned to the cabinet and decimated anything the tidewind hadn't yet ripped apart.

The tears came slowly, like the beginnings of a storm. Then soon thunder struck, and Sylah's anger and grief merged into a heart-rending scream.

When her breath was spent, she fell into the mound of clothes and shredded bedding.

"Anoor, where did the disciples take you?"

The disciples had been part of the Sandstorm, and though Sylah didn't know their intentions, she knew they weren't good.

As Sylah pushed herself to her knees, her fingers brushed against something in the pile of clothes and bedding. Something smooth that wasn't cloth. With shaking fingers, she pulled out a packet of glittering red beads.

Joba seeds.

They must have been in the pockets of one of her old pantaloons.

Her heart began to race as she tipped them with shaking fingers into her palm.

The red skin of the drug glowed against her palm, and she wondered if this was her answer all along. Firerum could only do so much, but this . . . *this* could make her forget.

The seed felt familiar on her lips, like the kiss of a lover.

Like the kiss of Anoor.

She let the seed fall to the ground.

You are not the person you were a year ago, no matter how hard you pretend to be. The thought had Anoor's voice.

Sylah clenched her quivering hands into fists.

"I will find you, Anoor."

Sylah stood and made her way to the stairs, passing Lio's room on the way. Her mother's room was covered in sand. The only thing the tidewind had left untouched was a painting of the Sanctuary that hung above her bed.

The white farmhouse had been Sylah's home during her training under the Sandstorm. Lio had painted the picture the first year they had settled in Nar-Ruta, a reminder of the family they had lost there.

Sylah pulled her gaze away, tears already forming in her eyes. Old grief and new grief swirled like smoke in the hollowness of her chest.

She made her way down the stairs, then stopped. A thought had just struck her.

A Child of Fire whose blood will blaze,
Will cleanse the world in eight nights, eight days,
Eight bloods lend strength to lead the charge
And eradicate the infidel, only Gods emerge,
Ready we will be, when the Ending Fire comes,
When the Child of Fire brings the Battle Drum,
The Battle Drum,
The Battle Drum,
Ready we will be, for war will come.

The words sang out of her in a minor key, though stripped of emotion. She thought of all the Ember children stolen and raised by a group of Dusters. Had they known their cause wasn't the one they were fighting for? Had Azim?

Sylah raised a shaking hand to her hair where Loot's spider brooch lay. The symbol of the Zalaam. *The Sandstorm and the Zalaam are one and the same.*

But more importantly, Sylah now knew where they were taking Anoor.

There were no eru stables on this side of the Tongue, so Sylah had to cross the bridge into the Ember quarter. She was so consumed with her thoughts of finding Anoor that she hadn't noticed that the constant chugging of the trotro that carted food into the Ember market square had stopped.

As she neared the end of the bridge, she overheard an officer speaking to a group of Embers. "You'll have to cross the bridge and go to the Duster Quarter to get your wares today. The trotro's bloodwerk has been tampered with."

Sylah cast a glance at the tracks. Black ink had been painted across the ground, marring the bloodwerk runes. Sylah tilted her head trying to distinguish the shape the paint had been drawn in. It looked like writing.

"Truthsayer," she murmured under her breath once she'd parsed the word.

She checked again, just to make sure she wasn't misreading it. But as she frowned over its meaning someone came up beside her.

"The Truthsayer did this."

"Who?" Sylah asked.

The woman's eyes widened as if Sylah had asked what the sun was. Clearly more than the tidewind had changed around here.

"You been under a rock?"

"Not quite," Sylah replied. *Just on another continent entirely.*

"The Truthsayer's been the one causing havoc for the Embers. Ambushed a crate of Imir Gishla's food supply and redistributed it around the Dredge last week. Used the trotro during the night to move it all."

"In the night?" Sylah asked.

"Yes," the woman said impatiently. "Truthsayer only works at night. Every morning something's changed." With that the woman smiled, showing all her teeth.

Though Sylah was curious, she couldn't waste any more time on wondering who was sabotaging the Ember Quarter. Whoever they were, she was glad someone was fighting for the rights of those north of the Ruta River.

Sylah pushed through the crowd and picked up her pace. She had no plan beyond getting an eru and making her way to the coast. Lio's life savings jingled in her pockets. Her mother had always stashed her money under the third floorboard from the door, though Lio had never realised Sylah had known where her hoard was. More than once, Sylah had stolen from her to fund her drug habit.

Sylah found more slabs in there than the last time she had checked. They weighed down her trousers as she walked. It still wouldn't be enough to hire an eru, but her days as a Dredge-dweller had taught her the art of thievery. Or perhaps, less the art and more the stomach to do it.

The thought of travelling again made her footsteps leaden. It had taken her nearly a mooncycle to get to Nar-Ruta from the Tenio coast. She'd left the *Baqarah* moored to the east and begged for seats on cattle carriages going west. Although she still had the ambassador token from Anoor tied securely into one of her braids, she hadn't wanted to use it out of fear, just in case someone was looking for her.

The journey had been arduous. And to have arrived to find Anoor gone had stolen the last of Sylah's will to live. But she had to muster the last dregs of her fortitude to go on this final journey. To bring Anoor home.

The first stable she came across was on the bank of the Ruta River. She slipped through the barn doors and headed to the first pen. The eru in there was a ruby red and smaller than any eru Sylah had ridden before. It shrilled wildly and she wondered at the juvenile's temperament. But she didn't have time to wonder long. As Sylah began to saddle the eru she heard a cough behind her.

Sylah whirled around, annoyed that the drink had dulled her senses so much that she hadn't heard the newcomer's footsteps.

"Are you going to pay for that beast?" The stable hand couldn't have been older than fifteen. She could see from his brand he was a Duster.

"Wasn't planning on it," she replied.

"Okay." He shrugged. "But if you're going to steal an eru, I wouldn't go for her. She's just come back from a long journey from the northern coast. Probably only has a few leagues in her tonight. I've called her Berry."

Sylah scowled. "Well, which one should I steal then?"

"Probably Darg, he's the next pen along. Older too, less flighty."

Sylah nodded. "Thank you."

"No problem. I'm Tomi." He plucked at his short braids. "I've no love for my master. Plus, Berry here was gifted for free by the traveller, so we already have one more eru than we did yesterday." He patted Berry's nose fondly. The eru huffed into his hand.

Sylah snorted. "Tomi, why would anyone give up an eru for free?"

"Someone with more money than judgement. Only a fool would ride an eru so hard across the empire. Poor thing." He cooed at the eru. "Apparently, the traveller stopped only once."

"Sounds like they needed to get to the city fast. Speaking of, I too need to get *out* of the city fast."

Tomi gave her an apologetic smile. "Here, take the other woman's saddle. I won't get a whipping for that at least."

The boy had been kind, so Sylah swapped the saddle on Darg with the well-worn one he offered. Something slipped from one of the saddlebags and she bent to pick it up.

She felt the coldness of dread run down her back.

The paper was scrawled with runes repeated in a way that suggested someone had been practising. But they weren't bloodwerk runes. Sylah touched the orb in her hair. Her fingers running over the shapes that were replicated on the parchment in her hand.

"The law of creation . . ."

Someone from the Zalaam had ridden this eru.

"The traveller, what did they look like?"

The stable hand looked perturbed by Sylah's intensity, and he took a step back before answering. "She was small, short hair, curly on top." Tomi screwed up his face trying to remember. "Pointy nose?"

"Tanu." Sylah breathed her name into the musty air of the stable. It ignited her rage once more.

"I don't think I'll need an eru after all," she said.

"All right, well, I'll be here if you change your mind."

If there was anyone who could give her answers about Anoor, it was Tanu.

She started jogging towards the Keep with hope surging in her heart for the first time.

I'm coming, Anoor. We will be together again, you and I.

CHAPTER FIVE

Anoor

What is the Ending Fire? It is you, it is me.
What is the Ending Fire? It is the greatest sacrifice you'll ever see.
What is the Ending Fire? It is the purge that has to be.
What is the Ending Fire? It is when we will be free.

—Chant led by commune leader Teta

Three weeks after they had left the empire, they arrived at the Volcane Isles.

The sand was black, like the night sky had bled through the horizon. It also gave Anoor the same sense of awe as looking up at the stars. Like she was gazing at a vast world so different to her own.

And it made her feel just as small.

You are not small. You are wondrous, you are magnificent. Sylah spoke in her mind, filling her thoughts with a confidence she struggled to summon on her own. Growing up in the empire had hampered Anoor's boldness.

But this is not the empire.

A smile flickered across her lips. No longer did she need to carry her trauma's load—there was no space for it here on this new continent. She breathed in, feeling lighter than she had a moment ago.

She walked across the black beach towards the waiting procession. Nearly a full mooncycle on a boat had made her legs shaky, and the soil was much more compact than the shifting sand in the empire.

She tried to suppress the tremor in her legs, which was making it difficult to maintain a steady pace.

The beach itself was shallow, fading to a rocky cliff face where tufts of white bushes grew between boulders. Anoor wondered if the plants were the source of the pungent aroma. The air smelt like burnt rotten eggs, bitter and acrid.

"It's the sulphur," Faro said to Anoor's left. They had noticed her nose scrunching in distaste. "From the volcanoes and geysers."

"I don't know what either of those things are," Anoor said flatly.

"That big mountain over there on the furthest isle? That's a volcano, we have one in the north-west of the empire. All this soil, the rocks, are a result of the volcano erupting with lava many years ago."

"And the geysers?"

"Look over there. You see those sprays of water? They're not fountains. They're jets of steam from the earth's crust."

Anoor nodded in understanding, though she wasn't sure she really did understand. Even though she could see the volcano and the geyser they still seemed like abstract concepts from a dream.

And then she noticed a group of people standing on a flattened area of rocks that constituted a platform of sorts.

Anoor lifted her chin and pressed back her shoulders, locking eyes with anyone who dared meet hers. This new land had awakened her spirit.

Here I am born anew as the Child of Fire. Here I am free.

Free of the shackles of an empire that had long tried to dampen her abilities. Free from the constraints of a society that didn't celebrate differences, but instead vanquished them, *murdered* them.

There were eight people waiting on the shore. Anoor recognised them from Yona's schooling, though the colours they wore were enough to single them out as the eight commune leaders of the Zalaam. The fashion here was different, less rigid than the empire, with free-flowing skirts and trains that covered the ground around them.

The make-up they wore was simple, black kohl around the eyes and sharp black lines to accentuate their cheekbones.

But if you stripped away the clothes and the make-up, they could have looked like any group of people in the empire. The Zalaam did not look like gods, they were just like Anoor. It comforted her.

Yona reached the group first. She wore a translucent yellow dress the colour of honey, and on her head she wore a thin diadem of gold. It circled the scars on her scalp, ending in a single yellow gemstone on her forehead.

Each of the leaders held up their hands in a sign of respect—palms facing towards their faces, thumbs tucked into the centre, so eight fingers were held up in salute to the Wife. Anoor's own hand twitched with the repetitive memory of the movement. Yona had made Anoor practise each night before they went to bed.

Yona responded in kind, though her hands were by her waist, signifying that her interlocutors were of a status below her. She had taught Anoor to greet everyone with a lower rank, and to hold her hands by her chest.

Anoor did so now, signifying that the leaders were not quite as important as the Wife, but certainly of a higher status than everyone else around them.

With the formalities over, Yona extended her arms to the leader dressed in yellow. It had been a shock to learn of Yona's yellow blood—a shock to hear that there were in fact *eight* blood colours—but it gave Anoor strength to know her grandmother had hidden her blood colour just as Anoor had.

"I am sorry about Andu, he lived long. He lived proud. Our God will grant him paradise," Yona murmured to the woman in yellow. When her gaze met Anoor's she had tears in her eyes. A rare expression of emotion from her grandmother.

Yona had told Anoor that Andu had been the previous commune leader who had looked after Yona when she'd been young. It was strange to think of Yona as a child; it was almost as if her grandmother was too proud to have ever had a childhood. The carefreeness of youth seemed beneath Yona. And perhaps the innocence too.

"Anoor, this is Teta," Yona said. "She is the new leader of Yellow Commune. Of those with yellow blood like me."

"'New' may not be entirely correct. I have been commune leader these last fifteen years," Teta said as she turned to Anoor. Though her tone didn't have bite, Yona frowned as if it did.

Teta smiled at Anoor, her grin almost as wide as her jaw. As she dipped her head Anoor saw that her short hair had been shaved into a spider's web pattern.

"Welcome, Child of Fire." Though Teta's accent was strangely gruff, it also held echoes of Yona's guttural tone, a quirk Anoor had once thought was a result of Yona being raised outside of Nar-Ruta. Which she was—just even further outside than Anoor had realised.

"We have had a long journey. We need to rest, then we will convene in the open temple," Yona cut in before Anoor could respond.

"Yes, Wife. I have kept your quarters exactly as you left them. We can find suitable accommodation in the nearby huts for the Child of Fire—"

"Anoor will stay with me," Yona said as she began to walk away.

Anoor hesitated for a moment before following Yona. Faro and Qwa fell into step on either side of her and she wondered if Yona had asked them to.

Yellow flags hung from poles that lined the pathway and Anoor assumed that meant they had entered Yellow Commune. The rocky path wound upwards towards a settlement that sprawled across the uneven terrain. The huts were small, with circular openings in the centre that puffed out smoke and smells of frying fish. The buildings were made from a woven material. And as they got closer Anoor realised what it was.

"Are the houses made out of straw?" Anoor muttered in disbelief. "The tidewind, it'll destroy them all."

"There's no tidewind here," Qwa grumbled, his deep voice carrying further than perhaps he intended.

The roofs were laid with large palm fronds that had been braided into thick patterns that kept out rain and wind. They passed a man sitting on his stoop weaving some of the leaves.

Anoor stepped closer, watching his fingers deftly move. But as soon as he spotted her, he jumped up and pressed a salute to his chest before disappearing backwards into his home.

Yona guided Anoor back to the path by her elbow. "Indeed, Qwa, you are quite right. There is no tidewind here, though Kabut communes with us in different ways. When he is pleased, he shakes the ground beneath our feet, and so we must build our home from materials that make it easy to rebuild."

"The *ground* shakes?" Anoor asked, but Yona had already set off again at a brisk pace.

This new land was so unfamiliar to Anoor that the idea of the ground shaking was a concept she couldn't fully comprehend. She shuddered and continued on.

It was midday and the sun didn't burn like it did in the empire. Instead, the stares of the inhabitants did. They appeared in windows and doorways, on roofs and in trees, and held up their eight-fingered greeting in silence as they passed.

"This is eerie," Faro said. Anoor tended to agree.

They climbed shallow steps made of slate, eventually reaching a plateau in front of the summit of a small mountain. The path led towards the rocky surface, and Anoor realised that the crag housed a building within. She spotted windows set into the cliff face, the glass panelling looking out on the commune below. It took Anoor a moment to notice the door as it had been carved from the same grey as the mountain stone around it.

Yona stopped in front of it.

"This is the Foundry. It's where we are preparing the godbeasts for war. My homestead is inside. Faro, Qwa, follow Teta, she will house you nearby. Anoor, come with me."

Anoor shot Faro a helpless glance as they walked away, but Faro didn't look back at her. Though Anoor had got to know Faro a little more on the journey, in that moment she realised it wasn't a friendship. They weren't Tanu.

And they weren't Sylah.

Anoor swallowed the lump that formed in her throat. She wondered how Sylah fared as she had navigated the new land to the east. Whether she had missed her as much as Anoor did right now.

Her love for Sylah had become a dull ache that sometimes she reached for when she wanted to lessen the feelings of grief and loss. She reached for it now, not as a balm on a wound, but as a cloak of power. It lay against her skin full of the warmth of their memories and the security of their love.

And when Yona held out her hand Anoor felt not one flicker of trepidation. Even if Yona's hand was as lean and spindly as a spider.

*   *   *

The Foundry was even larger than Anoor had realised from the outside.

She gasped as she took in the breadth of the hall. It was the size of the Keep's courtyard, filled with rows upon rows of workbenches.

The ringing out of metal upon metal set the room chiming with a haunting melody. Anoor felt her heart begin to race as the workers closest to her stopped what they were doing. The scraping of metal against metal faded until the workshop was silent. Hundreds of eyes looked back at her. Her gaze skittered from one person to another. They all wore the same black apron. It looked as if it was thicker than cotton, the material stiff and protective. The youngest was perhaps eleven or twelve, the oldest nearing seventy. Each had the same curious expression on their face as they slowly brought up their fingers to their chest to greet her.

Anoor swallowed loudly. She felt the sound of it echo outwards into a sea of silence.

Was she meant to say something? Introduce herself maybe?

She opened her mouth to speak, but before she did Yona rescued her.

"Please, do not let us interrupt your work." Yona's voice rang out loud and clear, ending the painful silence. "It's more important than ever that you complete your godbeasts. War is coming. To begin we must end."

"To begin we must end," they repeated, a hollowness in their eyes that sent shivers down Anoor's back.

They returned to their work, the clanging sound of metalwork resuming.

Anoor, over the initial shock of so many eyes on her, stepped towards the nearest workbench eager to see the runes they were using.

"Anoor, this way," Yona said.

"Grandmother, may I see their work?"

"Later, first you must wash and rest."

It wasn't a request, and Anoor followed with gritted teeth. For a moment, Yona's tone reminded Anoor of her mother, but then she remembered: *No, my mother would have beaten me for asking a question in front of others. Yona has never laid a hand on me.*

Yona skirted around the periphery of the Foundry and down a corridor that led to a secluded area set deep into the mountain.

The first room looked like an office of some kind, with vials of potions and papers stacked five handspans high.

"This is my laboratory. It is in the centre of my chambers. To the right is the door to my room where a pallet will be brought up for you to sleep on. That room there is the privy. Bloodwerk is not readily known here, despite my attempts to send back my teachings." Yona scowled. "So, you'll have to pump your own water for the bath . . ." Yona sniffed. "Which I suggest you do now."

Anoor dipped her head and walked towards the bathroom.

"Leave your clothing outside the door, please. I'm sending someone to burn it."

Anoor looked down at her clothing and frowned. She had taken them from Sylah's room when she was staying at Lio's. The drawstring pantaloons and dark blue shirt may have had even more holes in them than when she left, but they had been *Sylah's*. That and her inkwell were all she had left of her former life. It pained her to part with the clothes.

But Yona had said to use her pain to fuel her own power. Perhaps this small sacrifice would please Kabut.

"I'll bring you a new dress to wear," Yona said from the door. "One more befitting your status."

The thought of a new wardrobe lessened the blow and Anoor proceeded to remove her clothing and leave it outside the washroom door.

The bathroom was much more rustic than she was used to in the Keep. The tub was copper, and green in the corners. The pump was rusted from disuse. She pressed down on it and warm chalky water began to pour into the bath. A few seconds later it stopped, and she had to pump it again.

"If I just added a few runes here . . ." she muttered to herself. It was a simple combination really, using the foundational rune *Ba* and then triggering it against pressure to move up and down.

The pump continued to fill the bath without her input. She smiled as she looked down at the runes in her blue blood. There was no better feeling than seeing her own bloodwerk.

"I never have to hide it again." And then she smiled and slipped into the bath.

CHAPTER SIX

Hassa

One cannot be both curious and dutiful. Curiosity breeds disobe-dience. Duty yields results.

—Ghosting proverb

Hassa moved through the tunnels beneath the city. The passages were as dark as her mood.

Her night had been a busy one. After Sylah left, Hassa had contacted a messenger through the Ghosting network and left them with a message for the Chrysalis detailing Sylah's news. Recounting it had been long and arduous and it only further incited Hassa's anger towards her friend.

She tripped over a loose rock and scowled as she stumbled.

This day continues to punish me.

At first Hassa had been elated to see Sylah, but then as the details of her purpose became clear, Hassa had grown frustrated. The war was bigger than saving Anoor.

If we forget the individual, we forget ourselves. The words struck her in the centre of the forehead, and she flinched.

She had resurrected her own words to haunt her. It had been less than a year since she first signed them to Sylah on the night Loot hunted Anoor.

What would Hassa have done if it was Kwame in Anoor's place?

Hassa felt some of her anger towards Sylah splinter away. She took a deep breath and when she let it out, she slumped forward, the tension easing in her chest.

She didn't agree with Sylah's choice, but perhaps she could understand it, just a little bit.

Hassa continued on down the tunnel. Though she had not slept, the oncoming of dawn had hastened her steps. It was time to report to Maiden Turin—though she was maiden no longer. No, Turin was now the Warden of Crime, having united Loot's old cohort of Gummers under her rule.

As Hassa began to climb the ladder up to the surface, she heard something in the distance. It sounded like someone pacing back and forth a few tunnels over.

She frowned. No one had attempted to use the tunnels since the gas explosion in the north of the Dredge. Except Sylah, who hadn't been around to know of Kwame's mistake.

Hassa heard the clockmaster call ninth strike above. She was going to be late if she didn't leave now.

Whoever it was, it didn't sound like they were exploring further than the ten paces they were repeating back and forth.

Hassa climbed the rest of the ladder and emerged into the Dredge.

She dragged her feet through the wreckage wrought by the tidewind. With her head lowered to navigate the debris and blue sand, she didn't spot the smoke at first, only smelt it.

"Fire, there's been a fire!" A Duster shouldered Hassa out of the way as they ran, picking up crowds as they went.

Hassa followed the surge of people towards the clouds of ash that billowed through the city. She was jostled to the edge of the masses who had come to a stop where the heat of burning wood singed her nostrils. But Hassa had been named after the hassa beetle, and she moved through crowds with the same ease as the insect.

What she found clogged the breath in her throat. And it wasn't just because of the smoke.

The tidewind shelter had been burnt to the ground.

Through a charred window frame Hassa watched as an internal beam collapsed and fell to the floor, billowing up charcoal and sparks. The whitestone structure still stood, but the bricks were blackened by soot.

This fire has been raging for some time, so little of what could burn is left, she thought.

Hassa looked to her right and saw a cluster of people with their heads bowed close together as they spoke. She slipped through the crowd towards them and listened in.

"But what did they look like?" a young Duster asked. They held a scarf against their mouth to guard against the smoke.

"I couldn't see, they were wearing armour of some kind. They just told us to take what we could carry from the supplies and leave before the tidewind struck."

"But where did you go?"

"They told us of a building that they had made secure in the south of the Dredge for those of us in the shelter without homes. Some refused to leave, but the Truthsayer made them."

"The Truthsayer?"

"That's what they called themselves."

The young Duster shook their head. "Why would they do this? Why would they burn down the one place that kept us safe."

It wasn't keeping you safe, Hassa wanted to shout. *It was killing your brethren, sucking them of their bone marrow.*

Whoever had burnt down the shelter had known about what was happening there. At least the Zalaam's supply was now cut off.

One less problem to deal with. Just the small issue of the oncoming battle left to come.

Hassa wheeled away from the wreckage of the shelter and made her way to Turin's. Hassa had some thoughts on how she could use the woman to her advantage.

"Where have you been?" Turin's lacquered nails felt like talons as she yanked Hassa through the door and into the living room. She wore a deep crimson dress that covered the curves of her chest and waist with ruffles, a style more modest than Hassa was used to seeing on Turin.

Hassa didn't bother replying. Turin only knew a smattering of the Ghosting language, and it wasn't enough to explain she'd been distracted by the fire.

Turin scowled at her blank expression and spun away, the frills of her dress twirling with her.

The old maiden house had been cleaned and rearranged as if to trick the eye into misremembering its former purpose. But the sickly smell of rose water didn't stop Hassa from recalling the hundreds of backsides that had laid upon the upholstery of the room.

The thick curtains had been drawn back for the first time, letting in the sunlight, and illuminating the new figures in the lounge. Hassa's eyes grazed across them as she went to join Ala, another Ghosting. Ala had remained working at Maiden Turin's despite Hassa offering them an escape more than once.

Hassa, good to see you. I wasn't sure you were coming. Ala had always painted her eyebrows a deep brown, a fashion that had started with Embers and seeped into the lower classes. Though it was rare to see a Ghosting with make-up, Turin had never banned her servants from the habit. She thought it made the nightworkers look more appealing to clients. But now Turin's clients dealt in contraband instead of sex.

What's going on here? Hassa asked.

I'm not sure, the newcomers arrived a strike or so ago. I'm sure Turin will tell us, Ala replied.

Hassa's eyes twitched, as she did not have as much faith in Turin's forthrightness. She turned the conversation to other matters.

There was a fire a few streets over, did you see? Hassa signed.

Yes, they are saying it was someone called the Truthsayer.

Do you know who they are?

No, Ala replied. Clearly uninterested in this new vigilante.

"Will you stop flapping over there. You've caused enough disruption, Hassa," Turin barked.

Hassa bowed her head, low enough to feign respect while allowing her still to survey the room.

Turin sat on an armchair, smoking a radish-leaf cigar. The red smoke curled around her like diaphanous fabric. She was flanked by two other maidens Hassa recognised as Sefar and Luta. On the sofa opposite was a notorious Gummer from Loot's old cohort known as the Purger due to her deadly skills with a knife. A few other Gummers were present, but certainly not the large number that Loot had once had in his employ.

There was only one person Hassa didn't recognise. He was tall and thin, with a faintly queasy expression on his long face. She looked to his wrist and saw what she suspected—no brand. This man was an Ember. She watched him with interest.

"So, as I was saying, I have decided to use my maiden house as the centre of my operations. With the recent mishap in the tunnels beneath the city I think it is safer for everyone if we stay above ground. It is time to bring the Warden of Crime's legacy into the light." Turin's smile was sly.

There were nods around the room, until the Purger spoke, her voice thin and raspy. "That's all well and good, but what legacy is there? All our joba-seed trade routes are compromised. We cannot operate them during the day due to the patrols, and we cannot operate them at night now the tidewind has grown worse." She shook her head with a bitter laugh. "We can't even keep the Dredge in check. Did you hear of this Truthsayer? They wouldn't have dared to burn a building if Loot were still here."

Turin's smile turned brittle. "Hassa, Ala, pour the coffee. I didn't hire you to gawk."

You didn't hire us at all, Hassa thought, but she did as she was bidden, Ala a step ahead of her. The coffee beans had already stewed and so it took them only a moment to pour it and pass it around. Hassa served the newcomer last, and when he picked up his mug, she noticed his hands were shaking.

Hassa recognised the pause to serve the coffee for what it was: a deliberate distraction from the thoughts of mutiny that had begun to swell in the room. It was almost enough for Hassa to foster a semblance of respect for the new warden. Almost.

When Turin looked up from sipping her coffee, her smile was bright once more.

"This *Truthsayer* gave me the idea for resuming our operations. Vahi here is an armoursmith." Turin nodded to the man Hassa hadn't known. "And he is going to make you all night armour to protect you from the tidewind."

There was a beat of silence before the room erupted into chaos.

"You can't expect us to go out in *that*?"

"Night armour? Like those lunatic messengers wear?"

"I can't die out there, I can't."

But Hassa didn't take her eyes off Vahi. He was frowning, his head shaking gently to and fro as if knocked by a breeze. His lips were murmuring something so faintly that Hassa went to fill up his mug despite it already being full. "Just the one job and you'll be free of her. One job, one job, and you'll be free."

So, Turin had something on him and was twisting the knife to get her way.

I need to find out what that secret is. Because an armoursmith is exactly what I need.

Turin cleared her throat, and the room grew silent. "Each of you will be fitted this afternoon. Vahi will procure and produce the armour by the end of the week. Disobedience is disbandment. And we have much to do, you and me. I've had it on good authority that three carriage-loads of joba seeds will be coming in at week's end."

"Three carriage-loads?" From the awe in the Purger's voice Hassa knew that was a lot.

Turin grinned; she knew she had them.

"And did I say that I pay double what Loot did? It's time we grew rich."

This promise changed the tide in the room, and soon nods and smiles joined their warden's. Except for Vahi who sat stoic, his lips murmuring the same words over and over.

"Soon you'll be free. Soon you'll be free."

For three days Hassa followed Vahi. Turin had set him up a forge in an abandoned villa a few doors down from the maiden house where the armoursmith could take measurements and work. Vahi spent most of his days confined to that one room. The amount of armour he was required to make vastly outweighed what Hassa thought one person could create in a week.

Turin had even requested the two Ghostings get a set. "Just in case they're needed on the road. I know that Hassa at least is capable of a lot more than just pouring coffee." Then Turin winked at Hassa, and she wondered how much the Warden of Crime suspected about the Ghostings' sleeping sickness ruse. Hassa had been at the heart of that operation for years, feigning deaths to the deadly disease in order to smuggle as many Ghostings out of the city as possible. Those who made it out alive travelled north to a secret settlement called the Chrysalis.

It was on the third night of watching Vahi that Hassa noticed something amiss. Usually he slept in the villa, the hammering of his anvil drumming deep into the night. She would linger in the tunnels beneath the forge listening to the *clank, clank, clank* until he took to his bed.

But tonight, there was no sound of the hammer or hiss from the forge. When Hassa crept out of the cellar and into his villa, she heard the front door close.

He's on the move.

She darted through the shadows of the forge and left through the front door. The tidewind was starting to stir, making just enough noise to dampen any sound from Hassa's pursuit, but not enough for the sand to draw blood.

Vahi kept his hood up and his face lowered as he shuffled through the street. But he still stood out in the Dredge. His coat was just a little too fine, his leather shoes too shiny. Few Dredge-dwellers could afford either item.

The Ember walked all the way through the Dredge to the edge of the plantation fields.

Hassa followed him through the forest. The fields smelt of pungent fresh rubber oozing from holes tapped in the bark. But there was another sharp aroma beneath the familiar smell of rubber that seemed out of place. It reminded Hassa of the infirmary, but she had no time to investigate because Vahi had picked up his pace.

He weaved through the rubber trees with purpose, and she felt a sense of trepidation. What was he doing out here so close to the tidewind?

A thought struck her.

Perhaps he is the Truthsayer.

The vigilante had made smaller moves since burning down the tidewind shelter. Imir Montera's newly ordered clothing had gone missing en route from the tailors and turned up in the Dredge, where it had been distributed too quickly to reclaim. The trotro had been fixed for one night, only to be used to carry the Keep's food supply from the Ember Quarter to the Duster Quarter, instead of the other way round. Many Dusters and Ghostings ate well that night.

If Vahi was the Truthsayer then he'd managed to carry out these revolts without Hassa knowing.

He walked so fast through the trees that Hassa started running to keep up. Then he stopped and spun. Hassa skidded to a halt, but it was too late. He had seen her.

"Why are you following me?" He didn't sound angry, merely curious.

Hassa hung her head and tried to look contrite. She shrugged her shoulders but still he waited for her answer.

"Speak, I can understand you."

If Hassa hadn't had years of practice in keeping her expression neutral, her jaw would have dropped open.

An Ember who could understand the Ghosting language? Unheard of—except for those Hassa had taught. Sylah had been her first pupil. Hassa had tried to keep her friend from her mind over the last few days, as she still stirred feelings of anger.

I wanted to see where you were going, Hassa signed.

Vahi's chin dropped to his chest. "Turin is having me followed? Isn't it enough that she keeps my daughter from me? I have done everything she asked. Everything."

So, Turin had Vahi's daughter hostage.

She didn't have me follow you.

"Then why, why are you here? Your name is Hassa, right?"

Hassa nodded, thinking. She needed to feign intelligence to manipulate the armoursmith to her task. But curiosity got the better of her.

Who taught you to understand the Ghosting language?

Vahi's frown softened into a smile. "My first love was a Ghosting."

Hassa was rarely surprised by anything anymore, and here this Ember had done it twice. For a Ghosting to have loved an Ember enough to teach him the Ghosting language was rare. Normally an Ember and Ghosting's love lasted as long as a bag full of money.

Except for Kwame. Hassa pushed thoughts of her former lover from her mind.

Vahi waited for Hassa's next question and though she had many, her plans were more pressing. She formulated the lie before she signed it. Hassa was good at lying, she'd had to do it enough times when spying for the elders. But there was something about Vahi that made her uncomfortable about mining his emotions in this way.

She steeled her nerve—he was an Ember after all—and signed quickly, *I know where your daughter is.*

Vahi's eyes widened with hope, leaving Hassa with a bitter taste in the back of her throat as she continued with her gambit. *I can free her. You know Turin will never let you leave. You are too valuable to her.*

Vahi's expression crumbled.

"I never wanted this. I didn't think nearly twenty years later she'd call on her favour. I'd made a name for myself as an armoursmith in Jin-Kutan. I didn't want to come back here . . . to where my beloved died—"

His voice broke and he looked away from Hassa. When he looked back his expression was resigned. "What do you want?"

Hassa pulled out a piece of paper from her pocket. The armoursmith took the page from her outstretched limbs. And though the breeze threatened to pluck it from his grasp he held it firm as he surveyed her scrawl.

"Is this what I think it is?"

Hassa cocked her head but didn't answer.

"You know it won't work with your blood?"

Make a mould for this design and I'll tell you where your daughter is.

Vahi looked deep into Hassa's eyes, searching for the sincerity there. He must have seen it because he nodded once.

"It won't take me long. Come back tomorrow just before the tidewind and it will be ready."

Tomorrow, then.

"Bring me word of my daughter."

I will.

One day to find out where Turin was keeping Vahi's daughter. If anyone could mine a secret, it was Hassa. She pulled in a deep breath, but the air had turned acrid, and she coughed.

The sharp aroma that had reminded her of the infirmary registered in her mind. Alcohol.

The smoke came next, billowing up on the rising tidewind. The fire moved quickly, from tree to tree, leaping from one alcohol-soaked bark to the next.

Someone was setting the plantations ablaze.

Vahi looked around, his brown eyes set alight with the reflection of the fire. "We need to leave now before we're trapped."

Hassa nodded, already moving.

Vahi let her lead as they ran through the plantations. They leapt over burning logs and ducked under falling branches. The wind was laced with sparks that struck Hassa's face as she made her way through the thinning trees until she reached the periphery of the Dredge.

Now safe, she turned on Vahi.

Did you set the plantations alight?

But she could tell by his ash-streaked expression that he was just as shocked by tonight's events as she was.

"No, it wasn't me. I went out there for a walk, to take in the view, it was where I used to meet Dah—"

The wind picked up, stealing the last of Vahi's words.

The tidewind was coming in fast, quickening the inferno of the blaze. They needed to seek shelter, but Hassa struggled to tear her gaze from the fire.

Vahi held up a forearm to his forehead, protecting himself from the sand and ash that swirled in the tidewind's breeze.

"We need to go inside, now."

Hassa nodded.

You go, I have ways to move within the city that are close to here. Then panic struck her as she remembered her original task. *You didn't lose the parchment with the schema on, did you?*

Vahi frowned for a moment, trying to parse Hassa's words, his Ghosting language rusty.

Instead of *schema* she signed *plans*. This he understood.

"I have it here." He patted his chest pocket, and she felt a sense of relief. "I will see you tomorrow with news of my daughter."

Hassa waved him goodbye and turned her gaze back to the plantations. She thought she had spotted someone moving among the fields furthest north.

Could this be the Truthsayer?

She squinted and leant forward, but a gust of wind took her unawares, causing her to stumble. The tidewind was getting too strong to withstand.

But still she lingered.

Seeing the plantation fields set ablaze was *beautiful*. Mesmerisingly beautiful. The most beautiful thing she had ever seen.

The fire grew in swirls of red and orange, consuming Nar-Ruta's greatest commodity with each surge of the tidewind. The gales lifted the blaze higher, twirling it into a tornado that wound a path of destruction through the trees.

Hassa realised she was laughing. Her throat raw from the smoke, her tears of mirth leaving soot-stained tracks down her face.

How the wardens will seethe. How the wardens will rage!

Eventually the tidewind grew too strong and Hassa was forced to duck below the nearest entrance to the tunnels. But the brightness of the fire was seared into her eyelids for some time.

It burnt with the vengeance of every Duster and Ghosting who had been killed by the whip of an overseer.

CHAPTER SEVEN

Jond

Mother sea harbours us,
Full of wrath and wonder
Mother sea harbours us,
Whether above or under.

—Initiation chant of the clerics of the Entwined Harbour

The gumo root had eased the worst of Jond's nausea and the bath the worst of his smell.

Knock. Knock. Knock.

Jond started, wondering if it was Shola returning for another kiss. He wrapped a towel around his waist before answering the door.

Instead, Kara stood there, leaning against the door with her arms crossed. She wore a face covering of purple silk that matched her dress, bringing out the violet of her irises. Her hair was bound tightly in an intricate knot on her head, the red hues shining like fire under the lustre light. She narrowed her heavily charcoaled eyes at Jond.

"You look nice," Jond said. It was an understatement, but he knew whatever he said she'd dismiss.

"You look wet."

"I just got out the bath."

"I can see that. Hurry up, the captain is waiting for us."

Kara's gaze was fixed determinedly on Jond's face, steadfastly refusing to venture south where the rivulets of water ran down his muscled torso.

Jond didn't let it bruise his pride. If she didn't care, then neither did he.

"I guess I better get changed then." He pulled the towel from his waist, revealing his nakedness.

Kara didn't even twitch. Was she even breathing?

She noticed him staring and quirked an eyebrow. "What . . . do you want a round of applause?"

Jond scowled and turned away. He dressed quickly.

Kara began to slow clap. "Congratulations, Jond, on your massive cock. Is that what you were waiting for?"

Jond felt his face flush.

"It is like a sea cucumber in girth . . ."

Jond ground his teeth as he pulled on his shoes.

" . . . and a cobra in length. Oh, how I will build a shrine for thee, sixteen floors high, though still smaller than your almighty dick."

"Shut up," Jond muttered as he pushed past her into the corridor. He stomped away with the brusqueness of fury. Twenty paces later he realised Kara wasn't following.

He looked back.

"Done with your tantrum?" She tilted her head to one side. "If so, follow me, you're going the wrong way. Oh, and bring the books I packed in your bag." She swivelled on her heel and marched off.

Jond wanted to throw something at her. Something big and heavy. Maybe the books. He knew he couldn't, the Blood Forged wouldn't forgive him for it. But he also knew that he wouldn't hurt Kara, not ever. And it was that thought that made him seethe all the more.

Kara led them out of the belly of the ship and into daylight. A member of the ocean guard greeted them there and escorted them across two more gangplanks.

"Is there anything I should know before I meet the captain?" Jond said under his breath.

"No."

"Any words I shouldn't say for example?"

"No, just that one."

"You are not being very helpful. If I make a mistake, it will reflect badly on negotiations, remember."

"You won't be making any negotiations. I just need you to sit still and look pretty."

"You think I look pretty?" Jond asked with a grin.

Kara's gaze turned stony, and she moved a pace away, ending the conversation.

The ocean guard led them to one of the largest boats in the city. It was nestled between four smaller vessels that were stationed with a platoon of ocean guards on each.

The soldiers idly sat watch, chatting and laughing between them. They were so different from the officers of the empire, though despite their joviality there was something hardened in their gaze. A look that Jond recognised as someone who had chosen a path of violence. He knew it because it was there in his eyes, too.

Jond wondered what they were guarding the captain from. The Ica Sea stretched on for leagues around them. He doubted they had much risk of invasion.

Then the thought came to him. *They're not protecting the people from intruders, they're policing the people from each other.*

He pulled the bag of books higher up his shoulder, as if they suddenly weighed more than they had a moment ago.

"This way," a guard said, indicating a staircase in the centre of the oakwood ship.

Jond trailed his hand along the polished nutmeg of the banister as he descended. He let out a soft "oh" as his feet sank into the velvet carpet at the bottom of the steps.

"Down this corridor to the left," the guard said. He pulled them along with an invisible tether and Jond found himself jogging lightly to catch up.

The lustre light illuminated the wooden panelled corridor and Jond found his eyes following the swimming of the eels above him until the glass tubes curved out into the opening of a grand hall. Here the lustre pipes twirled across the ceiling in intricate patterns.

The velvet carpet extended out to fill the wide expanse of the room. It was furnished sparsely with a set of driftwood chairs tucked into the corners of the hall.

It was then that the smell hit him. A soft odour of dust and paper, of ink and stories. He dropped his gaze from the ceiling to the walls, his breath catching.

The walls were filled with spines of books, lining every shelf like bricks. The air was dry, pulling the moisture from Jond's mouth. He noticed that heated stones were placed among the tomes, removing the humidity from the air. Lumps of coral bookended each row, keeping the books upright.

It was the most wonderous sight Jond had ever encountered. There were more books here than anyone could read in a lifetime, but Jond would have liked to try.

He stepped forward, his hand outstretched towards the nearest novel, titled *The Lost Seal Pup*.

"Do not touch," Kara hissed by his shoulder.

Jond shot Kara an irritated glance, annoyed that she had interrupted his exploration. "What use are books that you can't touch?"

There was a laugh behind him. A laugh he recognised, and he turned, taking in the room and its people in full.

Ocean guards stood by a throne of sea glass, tiled together in misty hues of blue and green. In the chair was the servant who had given Jond the sea-sickness cure.

Though she wore the same crocheted top and skirt she had before, upon the throne her clothes and jewellery appeared far finer than those around her. The sapphires braided into the weave of her dress sparkled brighter, and the pearls hanging from her waist beads appeared larger.

"Welcome." Shola's grin was full of mirth.

"But you were . . ." A servant? No, he couldn't say that. " . . . in my room . . ." he finished lamely.

"What?" The word was wrenched from Kara's taut lips.

"Yes, and now I'm here, Jond By the Way." She caressed his name with barely concealed pleasure.

Jond felt his skin flush with warmth. He could not deny the effect Shola's brazen behaviour had on him. Shola was unashamed of her desire, her gaze lingering on his as she slowly licked her lip.

Kara stiffened beside him.

"Captain Shola, thank you for taking audience with us." Kara's voice cut through the heat in the room like a shard of ice. "We bring you an offering." Shola dragged her eyes from Jond's to Kara's.

Jond didn't realise it was his cue to drop the books until Kara yanked them off his shoulder. She passed the bag to Shola's outstretched hands. The captain removed them, running her fingers over the titles.

"Some of the Academy's finest treasures. I thank you for this gift." Shola clicked her tongue and a young servant appeared. They collected the books with gloved hands.

Shola turned back to Kara and spoke in a language Jond did not know. "Ytumo jat, unoco bendo?"

Kara nodded in response.

"Teump la loa, isa?" Shola jutted her chin at Jond.

"Bendo, ula, Jond . . . le unoco la jat." Kara spoke the language as fluidly as Captain Shola.

"Eh, eh, I think we're being rude. Jond here is bored. Let's speak like commoners in the common tongue." Shola leant forward, the V of her top gaping open. Her grin was mischievous, and it brought out a bashfulness in Jond he rarely experienced. He found his gaze slipping down towards the curve of her breasts.

Kara cleared her throat and Shola gave her a knowing smile.

"You have journeyed far and must be weary," Shola said. "I have had my kitchens prepare a meal for us. Please sit."

Chairs and a table were brought out and placed in front of the throne. Jond and Kara sat down, and food followed shortly after: raw fish pickled in sea lemon and spices, bread baked with olives and sizzling prawns on hot stones, slathered in butter. Now his stomach had settled Jond could barely breathe for the food he shovelled in his mouth.

Shola watched him with glittering eyes. "Hungry?"

Jond paused and spoke with his mouth full, suddenly aware no one else was eating. "Is it poisoned?"

Kara kicked him beneath the table, but Shola just chuckled. "No, it is not. We don't poison allies."

Kara placed her fork down. "I'm glad you used that word, Shola. I wasn't sure you had remembered the deal we once made."

Shola's smile dropped to a flat line. "I remember, Kara, I remember. But do you, I wonder, remember the terms of the deal?"

Jond felt a strange tension build between his shoulder blades as the two women spoke of things he didn't understand.

"I protected you when the chief of the Winterlands detained your navy after stealing—"

"Reclaiming what was ours." Shola interrupted Kara without anger.

"They did not see it that way. Without my intervention you would still be in prison."

"Ever the peacekeeper . . . Kara." Shola said her name with the hint of a smirk. "But I suspect you don't bring us peace today. Instead, you come asking for war."

"You know the Zalaam are rising. You know the battle is inevitable."

"Perhaps."

"Do you not see the way the world changes? The palace—" Kara's throat bobbed and Jond saw the raw grief on her face for a brief moment before it hardened to anger. "We are already at war with the world."

Shola reached for some fish with her fingers. She chewed on the soft meat slowly. "The world does change. I see it. I feel it. You ask for our navy?"

"Yes."

"I will think on it."

"There is no time—"

"Do you remember the three days you spent in parle with the chief over my ships?"

Jond could hear Kara grinding her teeth.

Shola continued. "We lost twenty-seven people because the chief refused to send medical aid while you conferred."

Kara looked as if she might stand, so great was her rage. "I did everything I could—"

Shola held up her hand. She was smiling faintly and Jond wondered if that enraged Kara further. He hoped that it did: it was enjoyable to see Kara shrink beneath the power of the captain. "I know that, and I don't raise the facts of the past out of malice. Merely to remind you, time is important. Twenty-seven died, but twenty-seven hundred were saved. Though I am captain, I have my cohort of clerics that I must confer with. We cannot rush into a decision without weighing the stakes."

Jond's nostrils flared with annoyance. With every second that passed the Zalaam were destroying the world bit by bit. The imbalance caused by their bone marrow practice had already made Tenio all but inhabitable.

Time was not something they could barter with.

"There is nothing to weigh," Jond said. Frustration made his voice gruff. Kara tugged on his sleeve, but he pushed her away. "The question isn't how many will survive. No, the question is, will *any* of you survive?"

Shola's eyes rested on Jond with fondness, but he wasn't finished.

"You might not know what it's like out here, in the sea. But in Tenio the sky bleeds acid rain, and in the empire, a tidewind rips skin from bone."

There was a sharpness to Shola's eyes that wasn't there before. "You think we have not suffered? I think perhaps you will see. Very soon." She tilted her chin as she looked upwards towards the lustre light. The brightness of the eels above her lit the smoothness of her neck.

He followed her line of sight but had to avert his gaze. The creatures shone brighter than they had before. He blinked away black spots in his vision.

"The eels take shelter in the tunnel network. It is our only warning," Shola said.

"Warning for what?" Jond asked.

Shola's tone was grave as she said, "The storm to come."

Servants moved around them, clearing the table of food. An ocean guard asked Jond to stand as they proceeded to strap his chair to loops of steelweed tied to the ship's floor.

There was a fevered energy as people moved in and out of the throne room. Kara watched silently, her impatience wavering around her like hot air.

"I've been here when the storms have struck before," she said through gritted teeth. "During the monsoon season the ships are rarely still from the churning of the ocean."

But from the way Shola had spoken, these storms didn't seem normal, but Jond didn't want to contradict Kara. From the set of her jaw, she looked ready to chew him up.

When he didn't respond to her, she growled low in her throat and whirled away.

Jond looked for Shola, but the captain had slipped out of the room during the preparations for the storm. She returned a minute later with a family in tow.

"Hold onto the steelweed, there's plenty of room," she said to one of the children.

Shola saw Jond watching as she finished tying a baby's cot to the floor. The steelweed looked like it was more flexible than steel and could be tied in knots like a chain.

"The storm picks off those on the edge of the harbour. We lose at least three ships a storm," she said to Jond.

"How often do the storms come?"

Shola's face hardened. "Twice a day, sometimes more."

"Twice a day?" Kara said, clearly eavesdropping on their conversation. Her expression was troubled.

"These storms are nothing like what you have experienced before, Kara. They have all the qualities of the monsoons we are used to: lightning, wind, rain. But each force is wielded with one purpose—to destroy as many ships as possible. You had better strap yourselves in."

Shola turned away, returning to her throne where steelweed cuffs had been laid on the armrests.

Jond lowered himself into his chair and held on. Kara snorted softly before doing the same.

The silence was taut, ready to snap.

Kara began to tap the carpet with her foot.

"Will you stop that?" Jond said after the incessant noise drove him to speak.

Kara rolled her eyes and rested her chin in her hand, but thankfully stopped tapping her foot.

"This storm better hurry up. We've got to get the terms of the deal signed," Kara muttered, more to herself than anyone else. "The councillors are waiting for us."

"The Zalaam aren't," Jond said.

Jond looked at Kara and saw a flicker of fear in her eyes—no, less than a flicker, a half-shadow.

Kara opened her mouth to reply, but the ship beneath their feet spoke first. It growled and creaked as it was flung to the right, the whole harbour lurching in the clutches of the storm.

Jond looked to the books, but they were safe, held in place by a thin metal bar across every shelf. But the people were less secure. Some hadn't sat down in time and were flung hard against the walls or the furniture. They barely had seconds to right themselves before the storm attacked again.

No one made a sound. Not that Jond would have been able to hear it. The rain clattered above them like shards of stone. The thunder was a constant drone that rumbled in his chest.

A strike went past and still the storm didn't abate. Dried fish and water were passed from hand to hand, but Jond couldn't eat anything else. About three strikes in there was screaming from the corridor and a man appeared, wet from rain, his cheeks raw from the wind.

"Ohta Shola, dee ben, untoo. Dee ben! Dee ben!" he cried.

Shola had seemed to be napping since the start of the storm, but now her eyes snapped open. "Where is your vessel?" She responded in the common tongue.

"Outer zone seven." Jond could see the man's tears merging with the rainwater.

"You did not evacuate like we decreed? We identified that outer zone seven was unstable three days ago. Did you not receive the missive?"

"We did," the man wept. "But we thought it was overcautious. My daughter, she's still on the boat. I thought it would be safe."

"We are not safe. We are never safe even when the mother sea grants us her waters to sail," Shola replied sharply.

The man dropped to his knees. "Dee ben, Ohta Shola. Dee ben."

"I will not risk further death in rescue because you did not follow orders." Jond could see how the words pained Shola.

The man sobbed by her feet, immovable as the ship rocked.

"I'll rescue her," Kara said.

Shola lifted her chin, her gaze unreadable. The father began to babble his thanks, but Kara was watching Shola intently. Something seemed to pass between the women, a transfer of power, or maybe an acknowledgement of respect. Shola nodded once. Kara seemed to take this as silent permission as she turned to the man.

"Describe where your daughter is, as precisely as you can, and I will bring her back."

She removed the strap that held her orb steady around her palm, ready to imprint herself with runes.

The man gave her the directions to his home. Kara nodded tiredly and then with quiet precision, she imprinted herself with runes. A moment later she had flighted to the man's home.

A minute went past, and then another. And another . . . and another. Until nearly a strike had come and gone.

The storm was easing, the rain pattering less like boulders and more like pebbles. Jond removed himself from the steelweed straps and began to pace, his boots worrying into the velvet carpet.

What if she got the directions wrong and flighted into the sea? What if she drowned? What if—

There was a wet cough and Jond turned to find Kara holding the hand of a girl of five or six years old. They were both drenched, Kara's silk face covering plastered to her nose and mouth. She wrenched it away and took a deep breath in.

The girl ran to her father just before another gust of wind struck the ship. Kara stumbled, her eyelids fluttering. To anyone else it looked like she was simply unsteady on her feet from the storm, but Jond could see she was about to faint.

He jumped up and helped her to the floor. "You're all right. I've got you."

"Shut up," she mumbled, though without hostility.

"Yeah, yeah, I know. You don't need help," Jond laughed as he rested her back against his chest.

With the father and daughter reunited, and the storm coming to an end, the others in the hall began to resume normal duties.

Shola shot Jond a curious look from the throne, but she was distracted by a report from one of the ocean guards. Jond could faintly hear the guard list the toll the storm had taken on the harbour, but his worry was concentrated on Kara.

He looked down at her as she rested on his chest. Her breathing was laboured. "Here, drink this."

He offered her what he had left from the last water ration. She drank it gratefully. Some of it dribbled onto her chin and he held back the urge to wipe it away. He didn't want to lose any fingers.

"Why did you do it?" he asked.

"It'll help negotiations," she said.

Jond made a small sound in his throat, and she looked up at him. She seemed to weigh her words carefully before speaking. "I know what it's like to lose a child. And if I could save someone from that pain, why wouldn't I?"

"You had a child?" The question was out of Jond's mouth before he could stop it.

Kara's gaze went distant. He recognised the etchings of an old grief in her face.

"Th-they died in the womb. The pain . . . my husband, he could not take it . . . so I lost both of them."

Jond felt a flash of fury at the man who had abandoned Kara in need. Though he had shrouded what he could of his anger, Kara had seen it.

"It was a diplomatic partnership, Jond." Exhaustion had pulled down all of Kara's defences, and she looked at him now with an openness he had never seen before.

His hand instinctively cupped her freckled cheek. He brushed his thumb over the shadows of sorrow that gathered under her eyes.

To his surprise she didn't protest. Instead, he felt her leaning into him, a low hum emanating from her chest.

A flicker of a smile quirked at Jond's lips. The pain from her expression had gone; instead her features had softened, her eyelids shuttering closed. She looked more vulnerable than Jond had ever seen, and he tightened his arms around her.

Soon her breathing elongated into sleep.

"Is she all right?" Shola appeared, looking down on them both.

"I think she exerted herself, rest will help."

"Shall I have the guards help her to her room?" As Shola spoke two ocean guards appeared by her side.

Jond shook his head. "No, is it all right if I stay with her here for a little while?"

Shola cocked her head, her expression a little too knowing. "If that is what you would like, Jond By the Way."

"Just a few strikes, then I'll wake her," Jond said.

Shola spoke quietly to guards, before she turned back to Jond. "You won't be disturbed. But remember, no touching the books."

Jond nodded. He had no intention of disturbing Kara from his chest.

Soon he and Kara were alone.

Just a few strikes, he repeated to himself.

But there was something satisfying in providing Kara with safety and comfort. And so Jond held her there all night.

CHAPTER EIGHT

Anoor

I have tested every colour of bone marrow but there appears to be no significant difference in strength between the colours. The potency seems arbitrary, with no correlation between blood groups. The average volume, pale hue and viscosity of bone marrow is consistent across all blood colours too.

—Notes made by Nayeli Ilrase during
her first year as master crafter

Anoor soaked in the copper bathtub until her skin grew wrinkled and the water cold. It had been some weeks since she'd bathed. Though the washroom wasn't as opulent as the one in the Wardens' Keep, with all her oils and soaps, it was still soothing.

She tipped her head beneath the cooling water and brought her hands to her scalp. She washed the grime and sweat from her hair, feeling more refreshed than she had for a while.

For a moment her fingers weren't her own, but Sylah's. The memory of her unfurled like the softness of steam on water. Anoor let her mind drift back to the time when they had shared a bath.

Sylah's hands had been gentle as she had washed Anoor's curls, her legs lying on either side of Anoor as she leant against her. Anoor felt her heart constrict with the sharpness of missing her, and her eyes turned hot and wet.

"Anoor?" Yona appeared in the washroom's entrance. She held

swathes of fabric in her hand. "Oh good, you haven't drowned. Come on out, it's time to go."

"What's that?" Anoor pointed to the material Yona held.

"Your new dress."

Curiosity quickly drew Anoor out of the bath. Once she was dry, she inspected the garment Yona had left.

The dress was made of a pale heavy fabric with embroidered flowers and leaves patterned into the hem. Anoor was dubious about the style, it was less colourful than the dresses she usually wore, and the material seemed stiff and box-like.

She ran her fingers over the stitching and was surprised how coarse and bumpy it felt. Almost as if something had been sewed into the embellishments. But when she inspected it closer, she couldn't see anything out of place and dismissed the unusual lumps in the stitching as a feature of the unknown fabric.

"What is this made out of?" Anoor asked as she shrugged the dress on. It instantly weighed down her shoulders, causing them to droop.

"Buba flower." Yona was only half listening from the study room beyond. Anoor peered around the doorframe of the bathroom and saw that Yona was writing out a letter. Anoor strode over but could only catch the first line of the message: *To all the Blood Forged.*

The words meant nothing to Anoor, so she pressed on. "What's buba flower?"

"It's like the cotton in the empire, only thicker," Yona replied.

Anoor nodded and looked around. "Do you have a mirror?"

Yona didn't respond; instead her eyes scanned the paper in front of her.

"Grandmother? Mirror?"

Yona's eyes slid lazily to Anoor's. "No, I do not have a mirror."

She turned her attention back to the desk as she sealed the letter. Then Yona strode to the door of her chambers where a messenger was waiting.

"Deliver this to Jano Reduo," Yona said to the servant.

While Yona was busy, Anoor looked around the room for something to see her reflection in.

The wardrobe in the bedroom was made from metal and with a

bit of polish Anoor could see some of the features of the dress as it draped over her body. "Oh, *no*."

The dress looked awful. The sleeves created a cube-like shape around her arms without a ruffle or bow in sight. The patterned flowers, though colourful, were too delicate to see, so the beige fabric blended in with her skin. At a distance she must look like a naked rectangle. The collar was asymmetrical, cutting across her chest sideways to reveal another strip of drab fabric underneath.

Anoor loved fashion. And whatever *this* was, it was not fashion.

She marched over to Yona. "Grandmother, I can't wear this—"

Yona sighed, cutting her off. "Anoor, what you're wearing is a simple pattern made by one of our stitchers in the Green Commune. I did not have the means to send your sizing ahead of time, so I apologise that it does not meet the standards of tailoring you are used to."

Anoor's mouth shut slowly. Yona had taught her that each town on the Volcane Isles specialised in a different export, like those in the empire. The Green Commune must have dedicated their time to learning the craft of stitching.

They need more schooling. The thought was a mean one and she felt shame flush her cheeks.

"I'm sorry, Grandmother, I didn't mean to seem ungrateful."

Yona's gaze was stern. "It is not about being ungrateful. I care little for the stitcher who made this. What I care about is how you are perceived. Though we trade in other fabrics on the mainland, I thought it best you wore something grown from the soil of the land, as you were not born here. Everything you are seen to do, wear, eat, say, will be monitored. I warned you before that people will question whether you are the Child of Fire. And we must cast away all doubts."

Anoor smoothed the front of the dress, appreciating it in a new light. Though the material still felt heavy, she imagined it as chainmail. Protection against those who wished her ill.

There was a sound at the door, and a young man entered holding a mug of steaming liquid. He handed it to Yona, who nodded her thanks.

Anoor watched the servant leave before turning back to Yona. "What's that?" she asked.

"Bitter leaf tea."

Anoor scrunched up her face. "Does it taste bitter?"

Yona set the tea down before pulling out a pouch of red powder and stirring it in. "Not anymore. I like to add some barknut powder to sweeten it. Would you like some?"

Anoor nodded and took the mug from Yona's outstretched hand. She took a small sip and smiled. It tasted like honeyed almonds, with a slight citrusy note that cut through the sweetness of the barknut powder Yona had added. "It's delicious."

Yona smiled. "Come along. Let's drink and walk. I'd like to show you the rest of the Foundry."

Anoor felt a surge of elation as she followed Yona. The chiming of anvils striking metal sounded beautiful as they made their way through the main workshop. But instead of heading right, which would have led them outside, they moved left, deeper into the Foundry.

Workers looked up as they passed, but Anoor didn't have time to pause by their benches as Yona tugged her along. She wanted to linger by their sides to watch them carve runes into the metal. The godpower Yona had taught her over the weeks had astonished her more than anything else she had learnt in the last year.

She recognised the foundational runes of godpower drawn onto metal as she passed: to diffuse life, to infuse life, to mimic life and to take life.

Her hands tightened around the mug of bitter leaf tea as her fingers itched to practise herself.

At the end of the corridor was a wide set of doors made of the same stone as the walls. In the centre of the doors, where the door-knobs would be, were engraved two spiders, painted black. But they weren't what caught Anoor's attention.

On either side of the doors was a strip of glass panelling. As she got nearer, she realised they were greenhouses filled with foliage.

Anoor peered in, her breath fogging the glass. Behind her reflection were hundreds of hairy red spiders each the size of her hand. So not a greenhouse, but an enclosure.

Who keeps spiders as pets? she thought.

She would have stepped back from the glass cage of her own accord, but before she could a hand pulled her roughly to the side.

"Stay back from the habitat. No unauthorised personnel beyond this line." The guard motioned to a chalk circle that surrounded the two doors and the habitat.

"Excuse me?" Coming from Yona, the question sounded like a threat.

Another guard tugged on the first one's sleeve. "Prowa, I think that's the Wife, look at her scars."

Prowa shrugged them off. "Everyone has scars on their head nowadays. I only answer to one person. And I haven't been told to let you through."

There was the sound of running footsteps behind them. A man appeared, his pale skin wan as he saluted Yona.

"Wife, you may not remember me, but once you showed me kindness. And that path led me to my title as master crafter."

Yona looked to the man, her eyes widening a little. "Chah. The same name as my former husband. May he live in eternal paradise. I remember you."

Chah's expression didn't change, but a muscle worked in his jaw and his eyes became glossy. "I hope you will be pleased with the development of the Foundry in your absence."

"That will remain to be seen. And so far, I have not been granted access to the storage facility."

Chah turned a neutral expression to the guards. "Did you refuse entry to the Wife and Child of Fire?"

Prowa looked like he'd just swallowed a piece of sour mango. "Are you sure it's them?" he whispered to Chah.

Yona laughed. "Are you questioning our God?"

Prowa was shaking now. "I laid hands on the Child of Fire? I will go and purge my sins in the endless flame. Forgive me, Wife, Child of Fire." The guard scuttled off, his long braids bouncing on his back.

"Excuse me while I enquire about a replacement for Prowa," Chah said. "Wife, Child, do you require any further assistance?"

Yona waved him away. "No, go, find a new guard, and also, make sure everyone knows who I am. I know I left before most of these new crafters were even born, but your memory has not faded. So, pass it on to the others."

The slight reprimand warmed Chah's skin.

"Come on, Anoor, this way." Yona marched forward but Anoor stood firm.

"Why does Chah need to employ a new guard?" Anoor asked the question, though she suspected she knew the answer.

"Because Prowa is about to throw himself into the endless flame."

Anoor tried to hide her gasp, but Yona had heard it and shot her a bemused glance. "Remember that this life is temporary. Purging himself of his sins is a way to earn Kabut's forgiveness. When the Ending Fire comes, he will be welcomed into Kabut's realm."

Anoor nodded, trying to take comfort in Yona's words. It was hard to have trust in something she was unable to see.

If godpower exists, so must Kabut. Her reasoning was a little weak and Yona must have seen the confliction on her face.

"Drink the tea, it will soothe you," Yona said as she pushed open the doors.

Anoor wanted to retort back, but the tea's fragrance filled her mouth with saliva, and she leant in to drink more. When she looked back up, she almost choked.

The doors had opened out into a warehouse lit by hundreds of gas lamps that ran around the periphery of the room. They dazzled Anoor's eyes, leaving her with black spots in her vision.

Wait. Those aren't black spots . . .

Spiders the size of small villas went on for as far as Anoor could see. No, not spiders, *godbeasts*, made of metal and scoured with runes. The metal on their backs had been moulded to include a recess where the Zalaam could ride the creatures into battle. Anoor could see the slot where the vial of blue formula would go, to awaken the creatures. Their bodies were heavily armoured, their legs were double-bladed swords.

They were killing machines.

"By the blood," Anoor breathed out.

"These are the quellers, I perfected their schema when I was Foundry Master." Yona's voice echoed as she walked between the metal beasts. "They are our main offensive against the empire's army."

Anoor nodded, the mug in her hand shaking. She took a sip. The trembling in her hands stopped and she smiled. "The wardens won't survive this."

Yona's eyes glinted. "Let us hope not."

"I altered the rune placement on the quellers' backs," a voice called out. Chah had come to rejoin them. "It gives them added protection. I hope you approve of the changes, Wife," he said, bowing his head as he ducked under the nearest queller to point out the change.

A small frown of disapproval knotted on Yona's forehead, but as she joined Chah and saw the changes she murmured, "That was well done, well done indeed."

Anoor drifted away from them as they began to discuss quotas and efficiency. The drink in her hand steadied her as she moved between the quellers. There must have been at least a hundred of them, more maybe, but she wasn't counting.

She could see the final line of the godbeasts a few handspans away, and as she reached them, she realised that the quellers were on a platform above a wider expanse below.

She looked down and gasped.

There weren't hundreds, there were *thousands* of godbeasts. All different sizes and shapes. But there was one in the middle that had squeezed the air right out of her lungs.

"It's beautiful, isn't it?" Yona said, joining her on the edge. "We call it the clawmaw. It wasn't finished when I was here last, but the schema was all my doing."

The clawmaw stood on two legs. Each leg as thick as a joba tree. The arms by its sides ended in talons. The seat for the rider was nestled in its wide torso. It was gargantuan.

It was exquisite.

"The cone-shaped creations below are hollowers. They're mimicked from a mole that is native to the mountainside and will be helpful in building tunnels. And the smaller godbeasts are called sentinels. We used the anatomy of wolves to map out their schema. They're our main defensive line."

Anoor's heart hammered in her chest, but there was something else there, though it took her a second to identify it: joy. Joy that the empire would suffer, joy that the wardens would meet their death soon enough. It thrummed through her veins and filled her senses.

And when Yona said, "Do you want to see a queller in action?", Anoor's answering grin was more than enough.

* * *

They walked to the east side of the warehouse towards what Yona called the "testing strip". They passed a steel door that looked more reinforced than the others and Anoor asked, "What's behind there?"

"That's the laboratory where we create the formula. Do not try to go in there."

Anoor wanted to ask further but they had arrived at their destination.

The testing strip was a long room set into the stone of the mountain. A queller was at the end. The retractable ladder fused into its side was down.

Yona flicked her wrist and a person appeared in thick leather armour. They began to scale the ladder to the sentinel's heart.

Anoor had decided the Child of Fire was bold and confident—things the old Anoor had never been. So, she asked, "Can I be the one to ride it?"

Yona frowned, her lips parting to say no. Anoor interrupted her before she gave the word breath. "Would not Kabut be pleased to see his Child using godpower?"

Chah bowed his head at the invocation of the God's name. The movement drew Yona's eyes to his, and Anoor could tell her grandmother was weighing up her answer.

"Fine. But I will guide you."

Anoor gulped down the dregs of the tea and passed the mug to Yona before climbing the ladder. The dress twisted in her legs, but she managed it, if a little less gracefully than she'd hoped.

The metal was cool through the thick fabric as she sat down. The seat was a little snug between her hips, but it gave her security. From this height she could look down on the top of Yona's head and appreciate the beauty of her scars—the perfect spider's web, preserved in silvered skin.

Yona climbed the ladder halfway and reached over to hand Anoor a vial of liquid. Instead of being pale blue like the ones shipped over on their boat, this one was lilac.

"Is this a different formula? Why is it purple?" Anoor asked.

"It does the same thing," Yona said. She continued before Anoor could ask further. "You'll need to add a drop of your own blood to the vial before pressing it into the catchment."

"Oh, like when I was using Gorn's blood, in order to control the power, I must include a bit of myself."

"Exactly. Though you will have little control once the vial is in. As you can tell from the shape, we have mimicked the quellers to the movement of spiders. In this case the deadliest spiders we have on the Isles—the Red Quells. It is in their nature to destroy the territory of the prey they hunt."

"The spiders in the habitats at the front?"

Yona nodded. "Half of this vial will give the godbeast a strike of life, maybe more, so I recommend you use just a little. You remember the rune you must draw on your own body to tether the creation to you?"

"Yes," Anoor said. To take life was the most important of the godpower runes as it was what gave the creations their power. By drawing the rune on her body, the godbeast could take the strength it needed to live.

"I will observe in the next room. That window is reinforced glass. And Anoor, be careful," Yona replied.

Anoor waited for Chah and Yona to exit the testing strip. The observation window was at the end of the room with floor-to-ceiling glass. Their faces were mere specks from her height.

Giddy flutters swirled in her stomach as she used her stylus to pierce her vein. She opened the vial and watched as a bead of her blood swirled into the lilac substance.

Yona had said to use less than half the vial, but Anoor tipped the whole thing into the slot. Lilac liquid ran through the grooves made in the metal like an irrigation system that fed the etchings of runes.

The godbeast came to life.

Anoor screamed with exhilaration as the queller moved across the testing strip, gaining speed as it went. She had expected the jerking motion of riding an eru, but the scuttling of the creature's eight legs kept her steady.

The ground shook as its enormous legs struck the flagstones. The observation window at the end of the room rattled in its frame.

Anoor heard crashing and the grinding of moving stone. Then the glass windows gave way and shattered.

So much for reinforced glass, Anoor thought.

The queller was close to the end of the testing strip, and Anoor could see Chah scrambling to get out of the way of Anoor's path. Yona stood with her back against the wall, ever proud in the face of death.

The queller launched through the window's opening, causing destruction in the observation room before moving through the doors to the Foundry's main floor.

Anoor felt the first threads of panic. There were *people* in there and the spider's legs had proved that it could destroy anything in its path.

She racked her brain for the rune to diffuse the life of the creation. Terror had filled her mind, scattering her thoughts.

The ground was still shaking, the workbenches rattling, and she realised what was happening.

An earthquake.

Screams broke out as the sentinel's legs sliced through the bodies of those who couldn't get out of the way fast enough.

"Move!" she screamed.

Yellow blood splattered against the floor. The queller didn't stop.

The doors of the Foundry had been opened and the godbeast lunged through them, intent on more destruction in the town beyond.

As they lurched down the steps, Anoor was shocked by the damage already done by the earthquake. Her heart twisted as she took in the flattened huts, the walls and roofs turned to simply leaves and straw once more.

People searched through the remains of their homes for their belongings. Children were crying and screaming. But all the adults had the same blank expression born from years of suffering under the world's elements. Anoor recognised the look, as she'd seen it in the citizens of the empire whose survival under the tidewind had been a constant battle.

People looked up as Anoor flew past, the queller gaining speed as it went downhill.

The shore in the distance churned angrily in the earthquake's wake, and Anoor hoped the black sand would slow the beast's charge. But still it ploughed on, lurching towards the shallows. Sea spray struck Anoor's face, giving her clarity.

I will not let this beast drown me.

The rune for *diffuse* came to her and she drew it hastily onto the godbeast's side.

The spider went still as the life dispelled from within it.

Adrenaline spent, Anoor slipped from its back and fell to the ground.

CHAPTER NINE

Hassa

In Nar-Ruta alone, 285 mixed couplings have been prosecuted in the last twelve mooncycles. I petition the court to bring in stricter penalties for this crime. Of course, the Nowerks should continue to get the rack, but I suggest we look at firmer laws surrounding those who aid and abet people hiding pregnancies because of mixed-blood relations.

—Imir Raheeb of Jin-Kutan, year 402

Hassa had searched all of the rooms in the maiden house in case Vahi's daughter was hiding there but found no trace of her. It didn't help that she had no idea how old the child was, what she looked like, or whether she presented as a Ghosting or an Ember.

Hassa took her search to Turin's office, hoping to find clues at the very least. But her sleuthing came up short. There was nothing in the reams of paperwork on Turin's desk that indicated any sort of hideaway where the child could be.

The next evening came quicker than she had anticipated. While cleaning dishes with Ala in the kitchen of Turin's house, she turned to the other Ghosting and asked, *Ala, do you know of any safe houses Turin might be using at the moment?*

Ala paused, thinking. Her limbs flicked suds as she signed, *No, I don't think so, I think the warden would have asked me to clean them if so.*

Warden. Ala's allegiance to Turin was so deeply embedded it roiled Hassa's stomach.

Almost as a reflex she signed, *Are you certain with your decision to stay in the city, Ala? I can help guide you to the Chrysalis up north.*

Ala let a rare scowl show on her face. *I have no wish to leave my home and join the Ghosting settlement. To me, this is freedom.*

She waved her wrist around the kitchen. *Food and fresh water are provided. A roof is given. Though I must do unsavoury things, Turin has promised I will never have to work another day as a nightworker. That is freedom enough.*

Hassa shook her head. This was a battle she would not win any time soon. She knew many people like Ala who had remained in Nar-Ruta when emancipation had been offered.

Hassa went back to her more pressing issue.

No safe houses then?

No.

It was not the answer Hassa was hoping for. She was meeting Vahi tonight and he would not hand over what she had asked of him if she could not provide the truth he sought.

And if he didn't give her what she needed then her whole plan would fall apart.

And if her plan fell apart, she would have nothing. Nothing except her thoughts and the hollowness Kwame had left in her heart.

A plate slipped from Hassa's limbs and crashed onto the ground, shattering into many pieces. She watched the shards scatter, like the fragments of her thoughts sliced by the memory of her former lover.

Hassa, are you hurt? Ala signed before immediately starting to clean up the mess.

I'm fine. I'm sorry.

"What was that noise?" The clatter had drawn Turin's attention to them.

She swept into the room and surveyed the mess.

"Ala, you're going to have to clean that up on your own, because Hassa, I need you to take these papers to Vahi. It's more measurements for the last pieces of armour I need."

Turin looped a messenger bag over Hassa's head without warning. The pages inside the bag were light as they bumped against Hassa's hip.

Fate is leading me to Vahi's door sooner than I would have liked, Hassa thought.

"Do your legs not work? Go."

Hassa felt a slow hiss escape between her teeth.

Turin's eyes widened in shock before she let out a brash cackle. "You do make me laugh." Though her eyes twinkled, it wasn't with mirth but menace.

As Turin turned to leave the kitchen, she laced her fingers through the dirty wastewater before streaking it across her clothes. "Oh, and Hassa, when you return, I think this dress might need cleaning and pressing."

That was Hassa's evening gone.

She was used to being treated like less than a person. She was a Ghosting, the dregs of society. But the farce of servitude was getting harder and harder to maintain.

That was foolish, Ala stated as she crouched on the ground. She signed with a brush strapped to her limb, shedding fine pieces of porcelain.

Hassa didn't reply. Instead, she bared her teeth at Ala before marching from the room.

Hassa hesitated on the doorstep of Vahi's forge. Helplessness seeped into the edges of her mind like the shadows of the coming night.

I can always find another armoursmith to make the contraption.

It was true: Vahi's involvement in Turin's growing guild had been serendipitous. Hassa hadn't expected to be presented with the opportunity to have the schema made so soon.

But time was running out, and if what Sylah said was true, then war was coming sooner than they all realised.

The door opened before she could change her mind.

"Hassa, you're here, come in quickly, quickly." Vahi's wide brow was slick with sweat as he guided her through to the living quarters of the forge. The heat of the fire stifled the room and the air smelt like hot metal and coal.

Hassa dropped the messenger bag on the ground by Vahi's feet.

I have brought you more measurements from Turin, Hassa signed.

"Never mind that, what news do you bring of my daughter?" He pulled up a chair from the corner of the room and ushered her into it. He himself perched on the edge of his bed.

When Hassa hesitated, he sprang up and strode across the room. "Of course, of course, you'll want to see the mould first."

He knelt and withdrew a hessian sack that he handled with both hands. "It didn't take me all that long. I made it from whitestone, as it can sustain the temperatures of molten iron. You'll need pins for the hinges and a leather strap for the cuff, but here's a prototype I made with those elements added."

Vahi handed Hassa a metal contraption.

"May I?" he asked. She nodded, giving him permission to strap it to her wrist.

The metal was cool as it slipped over the scars at the end of her limb. He tightened the leather straps securing it in place before swivelling the stylus on hinges until it hovered above her vein.

"Your composition was ingenious, really. Without a hand in the way, a pivot rotating hinge sits flush at the base of your wrist, so it doesn't need to be specifically made for each user." Vahi smiled and flourished with one hand. "A Ghosting inkwell."

Not just any inkwell, an inkwell capable of mass production.

This could sway the tide of the war, she thought.

"You can position it above the vein, wherever that sits. Then lock it into place by pushing down on this pin. Though I'm really not sure what you need this for."

Hassa wasn't listening. Her left wrist had moved across to meet the end of the stylus. With a gentle nudge she pushed the sharpened end into her vein. Her blood seeped to the tip ready to be drawn into runes.

The pain felt like victory.

Vahi's hands twitched with anticipation, and he clasped them together in front of his stomach.

"Now I have given you what you required, tell me all there is to know of my daughter."

Hassa couldn't meet his eyes. She turned her attention to the inkwell and slowly began to remove the strap. Vahi saw her struggling and offered his help.

"Sorry, I should have made a loop in the end of it so you could release it yourself. It'll only take me a stitch or two."

He withdrew a needle and thread from his pocket and took the inkwell from Hassa's wrist. He cradled it so gently that Hassa found tears burning in her eyes at his kindness. She touched his shoulder, drawing his attention to her signing.

I don't know where your daughter is. Her throat felt raw as if the words had been torn from her throat. *I'm sorry, I never did.*

Vahi looked away, his shoulders drooping before he returned to stitching the strap. When he finished, he removed Turin's notes from the messenger bag before placing the inkwell and the mould in there.

"Take it. Whatever pageantry you need it for obviously meant enough for you to lie so well. I have no use for it."

Vahi's benevolence stretched further than was comfortable. Hassa hesitated at the edges of the room, unsure whether to go.

The armoursmith let out a long, haggard sigh before pulling out a bottle of firerum from under his bed.

"If you're not going to leave, then the least you could do is join me for a drink. It has been a long time since I spoke to a Ghosting. I'm finding my vocabulary a little rusty."

When she didn't move, he poured a shot of firerum into a chipped mug and handed it to her before taking a swig from the bottle.

Hassa sipped then put down the mug and signed, *How long is it since you last saw your daughter?*

Vahi's laugh was as harsh as the firerum. "I have never met her."

That startled Hassa. She'd assumed that Turin had kidnapped Vahi's daughter from his home.

"I see you know even less than I realised." Vahi shook his head sadly, but his words held no contempt for her ruse.

Despite deserving it, she thought.

"No, the story woven between Turin and I is long and complicated."

Maybe it was the firerum, or maybe it was the lingering joy of owning an inkwell, but Hassa found herself interested in an Ember's life for the first time.

Tell me.

"My lover, the Ghosting I told you about, she was one of Turin's nightworkers. My father thought I ought to be bedded when I turned twenty, and so he sent me there with strict instructions." The lines in Vahi's face softened as his mind travelled back through the years.

"That night, I couldn't . . . fortify myself . . . and in my failure I wept. My love was kind to me. She spent that first night teaching me the basics of her wonderful language. I met with her every day for a year—in the plantation fields where you found me a few days ago."

His smile faltered. "But my father was a man of means. Little did I know that his money had paid for Turin's eyes and ears."

This didn't surprise Hassa: being a maiden was a difficult business. Often it was wealthy Ember patrons who sustained the delicate ecosystem of wealth and influence that kept them running.

"When I found out she was pregnant, we planned to leave the city. I had been training in smith work for many years, despite my father's disdain for the career I had chosen. I found a forge in Jin-Kutan that would take me on. But—" The bags under his eyes grew deep and vast, gathering shadows of anguish and grief. He coughed, trying to hide the quiver of his throat, but Hassa had seen it, could feel the pain. "When I arrived at the meeting point, she was dead."

A thought struck Hassa between her brows like a lightning bolt.

"That was nineteen years ago. I left the city and vowed never to return. Until Turin sent a message to me in Jin-Kutan claiming that the baby had been saved, and that if I did these jobs for her, she would tell me where my daughter was."

Is your father an imir?

"How did you know that?"

The name, tell me the name of your lover. Hassa's wrists shook as she signed.

"I called her Dahli, but her full name was Dahlia. It was back when Turin had renamed all her nightworkers to have the names of flowers."

I know where your daughter is. Tears rolled down Hassa's cheeks, but she couldn't stop them.

Vahi shook his head. "It's all right, Hassa, I've made my peace with the fact Turin was probably lying. I'll do this job for her then leave on the morrow."

I know where your daughter is.

Vahi noticed the tears on Hassa's cheeks. "Hassa?"

It's me.

CHAPTER TEN

Jond

The Entwined Harbour has no currency other than books. Knowledge is what it values highest. At last count it was estimated that the country had over 5.5 million books aboard its ships.

—Extract from *A Nation at Sea* by Saleem Oh-Torak

It took three days for Captain Shola to reach a decision on whether to join the Blood Forged. Three days and six more storms. Jond was in one of the smaller libraries when the last one hit. The tomes had become his solace during his time in the Entwined Harbour.

"Jond By the Way, you do not fear the storm?" Shola entered the room, her eyes lifted to the horde of eels lighting up the tubes above him.

Jond hadn't even noticed the warning from the creatures overhead, his eyes had been so firmly glued to the text in his hands. *Beneath the Coral* was a story about a woman who lived alone on an island. Her peace was absolute until a sailor's ship was waylaid by a storm. Jond had just reached the part where the two characters had declared their love for each other.

Their lips pressed together with the surging force of the tide. The sun at their back was warm, but the fire between them was hotter still. He lowered her onto the sand, drew his hands around her waist and let his desire part her legs.

Jond closed the book with a snap, drawing a hiss from one of the nearby ocean guards. He placed the tome back on the shelf more carefully, ensuring that the book was secure behind the lip of metal that prevented it falling during the thrashing of waves. Then he removed the reading gloves he had been given. He'd had to undergo three strikes of training before being allowed to touch a book in the library. It was only due to Shola's intervention that he was even granted permission.

Foreigners were not usually given access to the twiners' riches. Even then, Jond was limited to only this small library in the corner of the captain's ship where the ocean guard could watch him. He didn't mind. He wasn't a fast reader and the stories here were enough to keep him sustained while he waited for Shola to reach a decision.

"I didn't see the eels' warning," Jond replied.

"Eh, eh, too involved in the words. What were you reading about?"

Jond whirled his gaze around the room, pausing on the green sea-moss earrings that hung from Shola's waist.

"The properties of sea moss," he lied smoothly.

Though he had a penchant for all books, he'd found himself drawn to the lustful romances in the far corner of the library. It eased some of the loneliness that had seeped into his mind during the last few days. Since the night Kara had fallen asleep in his arms, she had avoided him like he was a disease she didn't want to catch.

"Sea moss?" Shola's nose crinkled upwards, and it was clear that she didn't believe him. "Perhaps I missed that section in *Beneath the Coral*. It must have been after they lay together in the rock pools."

Jond laughed softly, abashed that he'd been caught in his lie. "I didn't think you would have read the fiction books in here. I assumed that twiners only read factual and historical research—things you can learn from."

"Are you saying you did not learn anything from *Beneath the Coral*?" Shola's smile was inviting, alluring even. But Jond looked away from the glistening of her lips.

It wasn't that he didn't find Shola attractive, oh, he did, but their flirtation felt depthless, like a sprinkling of dust without the sediment of connection beneath the soil.

Shola's grin faltered when Jond didn't immediately respond. It was then that the storm hit, throwing them both to the side.

"Come, bind here," Shola shouted over the cacophony of thunder. The captain had crossed the library to crouch by a metal railing. It looked recently screwed onto the wall, just for this purpose. She withdrew a ream of steelweed from her pocket and began to bind her waist to the rail.

Jond, pushed forward by the lurching of the ship, joined her quickly. He tied himself to the other side of the metal banister with the steelweed Shola offered.

For a while they sat listening to the winds howl outside. Jond's stomach roiled with the lolling of the boat.

"Do you know what books are the most valuable in my country?" Shola asked in the lull of the storm's rage. The brightness of the lustre light cast her features in a warm glow as she spoke.

Jond wasn't sure he could answer without being sick, so he shook his head.

"The stories that make us feel: the fables and the romances, the adventures, and the thrillers. Knowledge is not just about facts. Like muscles aren't just what make you strong."

She gave his arms an appraising look before continuing. "You know how to fight, not because of the muscles in your arms, but the training you have gone through. Stories are like that—they teach us how to feel, to love, to care. Stories nourish the mind and feed the heart."

Again, Jond nodded. What she said made a strange kind of sense to him. He thought about how *Beneath the Coral* had softened his feelings of isolation.

"Stories nourish the mind and feed the heart in ways that other knowledge can't," he repeated hoarsely. He thought Shola might not have heard him but when he looked up, she was watching him curiously.

"If it wasn't for the sea sickness, I'd say you were born a twiner," she chuckled. "Suck on the end of your steelweed. The sea salt in the plant's leaves should help until we can get you some gumo root."

Jond slipped the end of the steelweed twine into his mouth. The burst of saltiness was at first repulsive, but after a few swallows he found his stomach settling a little. The plant had a strange texture.

He expected it to be smooth like metal, but instead the leaves were finely serrated and he knew if he wasn't careful, he'd cut his tongue.

With his sickness temporarily at bay, Jond's mind was brought back to his purpose on the Entwined Harbour.

"Have you reached a decision about the Blood Forged?" he asked.

Shola nodded. "I came here looking for Kara."

Jond's upper lip curled. "If you are looking for Kara then you should know, wherever I am, she's the furthest away from that point she can possibly be. The woman can't stand to be around me." It was true that Jond had barely seen her since that small moment of vulnerability after the first storm.

Shola laughed, drowning out the sound of thunder. "Indeed, she does look like she's eaten a festered clam every time she's near you." Then she cocked her head. "Though you know some of the community think parasites make clams taste sweeter."

Jond coughed, hiding the retch that had started in his throat. "What?"

"All I'm saying is her face may say one thing, but her tastebuds quite another."

He shook his head, unsure what Shola was getting at. "But whether you enjoy it or not, parasites will still make you shit."

Shola barked out a laugh. "I like you, Jond By the Way, I think you might like it here if you stayed."

"I like you too, Shola, and I think I would like it if I stayed here too." He entertained the thought for a moment until another peal of thunder rattled his teeth. The smile he gave Shola was tinged with sadness.

"What is your decision? Will you join the Blood Forged, Captain?"

The light in the library subsided, the storm was abating, the eels' behaviour becoming less frenzied.

Shola removed the restraints and pulled herself wearily to her feet. The beads and pearls on her clothing chimed.

"Captain no longer, Jond By the Way . . . captain no longer."

Jond's brows knotted in confusion. "What?"

Shola waved his question away "Come with me. Hopefully one of the ocean guards has found Kara."

Jond rushed to undo the steelweed holding him in place and had to run to keep pace with Shola.

Is it my destiny in life to run after powerful women? Though the thought was born from bitterness, the notion wasn't entirely unappealing.

He snorted and shifted his gaze away from Shola's swaying hips.

As Jond and Shola entered the captain's throne room, Kara made a beeline for Jond. Her hair was damp and Jond wondered if she'd been helping the ocean guard search for survivors.

"Why are you with Shola?" she hissed.

Though Kara wasn't talking to Shola, it was Shola who responded. "Where have you been, Kara? Eating clams?"

Jond snorted. Kara's eyes swung from Jond to Shola, knowing but not understanding the hidden meaning in the woman's words.

"Shola," Kara's ire turned to her, "would you like to explain why there is someone else sitting on your throne?"

Jond looked past Kara to see what she meant. Indeed, the face that stared back at him was a hostile knot of frown lines.

"Captain Rani." Shola thumped her fist against her chest in salute. "I brought forth our guests."

"Foreigners," Captain Rani corrected.

Shola nodded and turned to Kara. "I am no longer captain. I was ousted this morning by the opposition."

"What? Why?"

"Does it matter?" Rani interrupted Jond's questions. "We are ready to share our verdict." Rani turned his blunted chin to Kara. "Unlike my predecessor, I hold no obligation to you or your people. The queendom of Tenio has long held too much sway over twiners' lives, the Zwina Academy even more so—"

"The Zwina Academy is neutral territory, it abides by no law, no politics—" Kara was interrupted before she could recite anything further.

"You come before me to tell me that the Zwina Academy is apolitical? You of all people?" Rani laughed, the sound grating and raspy.

"No, we will not join you in this war," he continued. "This is a war of deathcraft, a war of the Academy's own making. And so, you will suffer the consequences."

Jond felt his rage form into words.

"You will *all* suffer the consequences, not just us," Jond shouted. Every set of eyes turned to him, but Captain Rani was already standing, having dismissed them. At a stiff shake of Rani's wrist, a group of ocean guards surrounded Kara and Jond.

"You think a few guards will stop us?" Jond braced himself, about to charge through the foray of daggers and swords.

"Don't be a fool, Jond." Kara's voice was weary. She turned to Shola, who had moved away from the group of guards. "You know this is a mistake."

Shola shrugged. "I voted to join the Blood Forged, but I have no power anymore. The clerics have been working for some time to remove me from the throne. And there is one thing our people respect more than the sea—democracy."

Jond's mouth twisted. "I don't give a shit—"

Kara held up her hand and Jond quietened.

"Thank you for your time here, I wish you well. Come, Jond, we must pack our things and leave. The council must hear of our failure."

Shola pushed through the guards and held onto Kara's shoulders. She was smaller than Kara by a handspan or more, but it looked like she held the other woman up with the strength of her gaze.

"It is not your failure, Kara, it is the failure of our people," Shola said softly as if she knew her words bordered on treason. "May the ocean mist bless your journey, may the mother sea guide your current." Shola turned to Jond, her hand reaching down to a satchel by her waist.

She pressed a book into Jond's hands and said: "You have a home here among us should you ever wish to return, Jond By the Way." She closed her eyes and leant forward. Though she didn't kiss him, he felt her breath on his lips.

"And remember," she said, "stories nourish the mind and feed the heart."

Jond looked down at the book in his hands. It was the romance he'd been reading earlier, *Beneath the Coral*.

He turned to Shola to say thank you, but the woman had disappeared down the corridors of the ship, leaving a faint echo of her tinkling laughter.

* * *

Kara paced her room.

"Will you stop that? You're making me dizzy," Jond muttered. It had been a few strikes since his last dose of gumo root, and something told him that he was unlikely to get another. The hospitality from the twiners was at an end: guards were stationed outside Kara's door waiting for them to leave.

Kara paused in her march long enough to remark, "I'm thinking."

"Can't you do this thinking from the City of Rain? We need to go back and tell the council what happened here."

He was also keen to check in on the progress of students studying bloodwerk. *Soldiers, not students*, he had to remind himself. Everyone had their part to play in this war.

Kara's mouth moved as she spoke quietly to herself. Her words sounded like coordinates, but Jond couldn't be sure. A few seconds later she nodded sharply.

"I'm ready. Bare your arm."

Jond offered up his forearm to her with a weary sigh. "Here we go again . . . is there a way to make this feel less like my stomach's about to explode—"

The world shuddered around him, the panelled wall of the chambers disappearing in a blink. Jond fell to the ground and coughed.

"I guess not . . ." He wiped spittle from his lips and stood. Kara appeared beside him a moment later.

Spices scented the breeze, and the sun was warm on his neck. There was not one cloud in the sky. Jond looked around him. They were standing at a crossroads of winding streets that weaved between empty stalls and vacant shops. He only knew that they were meant to be shops because he'd been here before. But it had not been like this.

The last time he had visited the Souk, music and chatter had permeated the streets and the smell of honeyed dates hung in the air. The stalls had once been draped in swathes of patterned cloth that had hung across doorways and awnings. But now only copper glinted on their roofs.

"This isn't the City of Rain," Jond said through gritted teeth.

"How astute." Kara set off towards the market stalls.

Jond followed, his brow furrowed. The Souk was eerily quiet. It was like they were wandering through the skeleton of a body without the muscle and flesh that gave it life.

"Where is everyone?" Jond asked. Kara's eyes were troubled.

She reached out to touch the dust covering the beams of a stall. The wood crumbled beneath her touch, the copper awning clattering on top of her. Jond reached to save her, but it was too late, she was crushed.

"Kara, Kara." Jond's muscles strained as he pulled at the large metal sheeting. "Skies above, say something."

"All right. Hello."

Jond whirled around. Kara was standing behind him with a sardonic grin. Runes patterned her arm from her quick flight. Jond let out a shaky breath.

"Don't touch the stalls. I think the acid rain must have turned into acid fog. I fear we won't find the supplies for the journey here."

"What journey? Where are we going, Kara? I thought we were going back."

Kara looked up at him. "I can't, Jond. Not without good news. I can't return without a navy." Her voice broke at the end, the only indication of any emotion.

Jond knew what failure felt like. He'd failed Sylah, he'd failed the Sandstorm. He'd failed everyone he'd ever loved. "I understand."

She gave him a grateful smile, though it was brief.

"So, where are we going?" Jond asked.

"The Winterlands. I think I can convince the chief to offer us his longships. He doesn't have as many vessels as the Entwined Harbour, but it might just be enough."

"I'm guessing we'll need more clothing than this?" Jond plucked at the waterproof material of his coat.

"I was hoping to trade for something here. But we'll have to go back to the City of Rain." The slump in her shoulders was enough to spur Jond on.

"Why don't we look here first? If people were in such a rush to leave, it might be that they left some things. Why don't we look around first before we give up?"

Kara's lips lifted and Jond was glad to see her grin again without the sarcasm he was used to. Whenever she turned a genuine smile his way, it always felt as though they shared a secret. Like the curve of her lips were for his eyes alone.

"Why are you staring at me?" she asked, her brows knitted together, the smile slipping away.

Jond started, he hadn't realised he was. "Sorry, I . . . eh . . . Shall we start searching?"

Kara's eyes narrowed but she said, "All right, but stay close to me. Any sign of fog or acid rain, we leave."

"Sure."

They picked their way gingerly through the stalls, concentrating on those that looked like the owners had traded in fur or clothing. But if any merchandise had been left behind it had already turned to dust. Jond was quickly losing hope in their mission.

"Wait, I think I've found something." Kara lifted the copper lid of a crate. Jond jogged over and peered in.

Swathes of fleece and velvets frothed up from the lip of the container. Jond tugged on one of the collars, unravelling the piece of clothing against his chest. Layers of petticoats fell to his ankles in hues of soft pink.

"Kara, these are dresses."

"But look, they're thick, some are even lined with leather. These are perfect. Oh, there are gloves too." She held the lace gloves up to Jond with a wide smile. "A few dresses and a couple of pair of gloves and there you have it."

Jond had never been a fan of dresses—too difficult to fight in. He tilted his head back with a heavy sigh. But it was this or freeze to death in the Winterlands.

"Fine. Let's get changed."

The Winterlands were exactly what the name suggested: a land of perpetual winter. Everything was white, the sky, the ground, the rain.

Snow, it was called.

It looked beautiful, like glitter falling from the sky. But as the snowfall increased it robbed them of their sight, so Jond could barely see two handspans in front of him. Not that there was anything to see. Jond was yet to spot a building, or a tree, or anything beyond *snow*.

To make it worse, he could barely walk. The three dresses he was wearing were laden with frills and embroidery, making it difficult for him to move his legs. The gloves were even worse. They didn't fit, ending where his thumb met his palm, but he was glad of them, nonetheless.

"We don't make for the most impressive ambassadors," Jond muttered as he waded through snow. Kara huffed out a cloud of fog.

Despite wearing four gowns and a headdress she'd found—that Jond was pretty sure was actually a wedding veil—Kara still looked regal as she picked her way through the ice.

"We can change when we get there. Be thankful for the dresses, they're saving your life right now."

Jond believed it. Despite the mound of material weighing him down, he could still feel the chill in the depth of his bones. He'd understood the concept of snow before now, but the reality was something much worse than he'd imagined.

He paused for a moment, his teeth beginning to chatter.

"I was raised in a bloody desert, this is unnatural," he grumbled.

"Keep moving, you can't stop. It could be your death."

Jond growled and trudged on. The blizzard was growing worse with every step.

"If my coordinates were right, and they're always right, it can't be much further, keep going." Kara shouted beside him. But as the wind swirled around them, he could only hear every other word she said.

Jond stumbled, his hands taking the impact as he fell. "Kara!" He couldn't see her. Snow was up and snow was down. Something warm spread against his hand and he savoured it. But when he looked at his palm, he saw that something had cut through the layers of gloves, and he was bleeding. He watched the red blood mar the perfect snow. His ears filled with the pounding of his heartbeat.

"Get up, come on, you can't stop." Kara was there, tugging on the collar of his dress.

"I got cut."

"I don't care, come *on*."

But Jond didn't move. He could just make out the jagged shape of a slate tile sticking out of the snow. He frowned and reached for it.

"I need you to listen to me. Drop that rock and keep moving."

"I think it's a roof tile." His lips were frozen together. He tried again. "A roof tile."

Kara didn't understand or didn't care to.

Jond started to dig. It wasn't until he had uncovered the third tile that Kara understood. "No . . . it can't be," she said.

Jond laughed, a desperate, high-pitched sound. He stood, stamping his feet on the ground.

"They're underneath us," he said.

Kara's eyes filled with tears that instantly froze on her cheeks. There was a crack, and a shifting under their feet.

And then they were falling.

CHAPTER ELEVEN

Sylah

DISCIPLE'S NARROW ESCAPE FROM MOTHER-MURDERER
Reports from the Keep confirm that the Disciple of Knowledge,
Tanu Alkhabbir, has returned from the clutches of the convicted
murderer Anoor Elsari. She is the only disciple thought to have
survived the ordeal.

—The People's Gazette

Tanu walked with light footsteps through the Ember Quarter. It was eighth strike in the evening, the first time the disciple had left the Keep in four days.

Sylah watched the woman from her vantage point at the top of the water tower. Her progress in capturing Tanu had been slow. She'd tried to infiltrate the Keep twice, but they'd upgraded the security protocol since Anoor's escape. The only people going in and out with ease were the last few Ghostings left in Nar-Ruta.

Sylah could have asked Hassa. But she hadn't seen her friend since she'd thrown her out of the Nest.

Sylah ran a hand over her braids with a sigh. She understood why Hassa had been angry with her. Coming back to the empire to save Anoor was turning her back on the Blood Forged and her pledge to help save the world from the Zalaam.

But without Anoor there was no world.

The delay in catching Tanu had stretched the distance between her and Anoor. But today was the day.

The day Sylah would get her answers.

She jumped down from the tower to follow Tanu. The bag on her back hung heavy against her shoulder blades, made weighty by the rope and weapons in there. As the tidewind began to stir, Sylah rejoiced at its early appearance.

It would be the perfect cover for the sound of Tanu's screaming.

Sylah had heard the tale of Tanu's miraculous survival recounted in the taverns. Tanu had claimed that Anoor had drugged all the disciples and murdered Yona before setting sail into the tidewind. Tanu also claimed she had only escaped by feigning sleep before diving into the sea's depths. She had swum all the way back to the empire's shores. All the others were presumed dead in the tidewind's heart.

A ludicrous tale, more melodramatic than one of Anoor's zines, Sylah thought when she heard it. She quickened her pace as Tanu got closer to the Tongue. If she crossed into the Duster Quarter Sylah's plan would be shot.

Just before the entrance to the bridge, Tanu turned. "Maiden's tits, she's small but fast." Sylah was running to keep up as she made her way down a narrow street.

Tanu stopped outside a building—the sign hanging over the door said, "Sphinx Tavern". That moment of hesitation was her downfall.

Because it was in that moment Sylah sprang.

Tanu instantly bucked against Sylah's arms, jabbing her elbows sharply into her ribs. She made to scream but Sylah took the opportunity to stuff a rag in the smaller woman's open mouth.

Though she continued to struggle, Sylah had two handspans on Tanu and enough rage to give her the strength of a desert lion. Sylah pinned both her arms behind her back and tied them with the rope she had brought. The villas lining the streets already had their tidewind shutters down, so Tanu's throaty screams did nothing to help her.

Sylah kicked the back of Tanu's knees and she buckled to the ground. Then she bent down until her eyeline was on a par with Tanu's.

"Hello, fellow Stolen," Sylah said. "We have a lot to talk about."

Tanu growled in her throat but Sylah simply laughed. She pulled the disciple roughly to her feet and led her back up the road towards the Ruta riverbank until she reached the eru stable.

"Tomi? I'm here, you can go home now," Sylah called out as she guided Tanu's struggling form into the empty pen.

The stable hand appeared, his face troubled. "Is that who I think it is?"

"No," Sylah replied.

"But—"

"Go home, Tomi."

The stable hand hesitated for a breath. Sylah shot him a look of pure fury, and he all but ran from the stable, his pockets jingling as he went.

She had found a use for Lio's life savings after all.

Sylah turned her attentions to Tanu who had started moving slowly towards the pen door. "Oh no, you're not escaping that easily." Sylah bound the woman's feet before removing the gag.

Tanu spat in her face. "The wardens will hear of this, and you'll be whipped until you bleed to death."

Sylah wiped the spittle from her face before slipping her hand around Tanu's neck. "Don't worry. The wardens won't hear of this."

Tanu's eyes widened. "I know you. You were Anoor Elsari's maid-servant," she said with gasping breaths.

Sylah knew her laugh was manic. "Oh, I am so much more than that."

Tanu frowned.

"You have no idea, do you?" Sylah said, aghast. She rocked back on her heels, releasing her grip from Tanu's neck.

The tidewind slammed into the side of the barn door, making Tanu jump.

"Stolen, sharpened, the hidden key,
We'll destroy the empire and set you free,
Churned up from the shadows to tear it apart,
A dancer's grace, a killer's instinct, an Ember's blood,
A Duster's heart."

The chant drifted out from Sylah's memories and into the space between her and Tanu.

"You're one of us?" Tanu whispered.

"Yes. From another cohort. Did they tell you that there was more than one sanctuary?"

Tanu shook her head, and for the first time dread seeped into her features. "What do you want from me?"

"Where is Anoor?"

"Dead, at sea."

Sylah flinched, her greatest fear given voice. But she refuted it, her head shaking back and forth.

"No. Try again," Sylah said.

"She might be alive, but the boat was heading into the tidewind, I saved myself—"

"No!" Sylah slammed her fist against the wall of the stable. The eru in the pen along shrilled in fear. Sylah didn't want to hear any more about Anoor dying.

Anoor is not dead. Sylah's hand throbbed from where she'd struck the wall. The pain focused her rage.

"I don't know anything else," Tanu insisted.

Tanu's lies agitated the already swirling waters of her emotions and Sylah took three deep breaths to slow her heartbeat. Then she honed her mind in a technique known as battle wrath. The mental state crystallised anger into action and was often paired with combat training like Nuba formations.

Tanu's own breathing turned shallow. Perhaps she recognised the stillness that had come over Sylah and sensed the danger.

Sylah reached for her bag and pulled out a knife. She laid it across her lap. "Tell me again. Where is Anoor?"

Tanu pursed her lips until they turned pale brown, the blood leeching away.

"She sailed into the tidewind."

Sylah leapt across the pen and pressed the knife against Tanu's throat. The disciple looked defiant as Sylah ran the blade against the hollow of her neck. A fine line of red welled there.

"Kabut take my sacrifice," Tanu rasped.

The name struck a chord in Sylah. "You worship the Zalaam's God."

Tanu closed her eyes waiting for Sylah's knife to end her life, a smile on her face.

Sylah made a sound of disgust and pushed Tanu away with the hilt of the dagger. "I won't give you a quick death."

Tanu opened her eyes slowly and watched Sylah through slits. "Nor will I tell you anything," Tanu said.

"You already have. You've confirmed my suspicions that the Zalaam and the Sandstorm are now one and the same."

A muscle twitched in Tanu's jaw.

Sylah continued, "Though I don't know what part Yona played, I know that if Anoor is with the other disciples then she is on her way to the Volcane Isles."

Tanu's eyes widened. "There is no land beyond the sea."

Sylah shook her head sadly. "You do not need to keep up the ruse with me. I have just returned from the mainland."

Tanu's expression turned guarded. "No one has been to the mainland in hundreds of years."

"True. I was among the first to do so."

They both fell silent, Tanu considering Sylah's words, Sylah considering when to kill her.

She may not betray the Zalaam easily. I should slit her throat now and be done with it. The thought of killing Tanu satisfied Sylah's bloodlust. But she knew it wouldn't bring her any closer to finding Anoor. Somehow, she needed to get Tanu to talk.

The silence was punctuated by the battering of the tidewind against the barn's shutters.

"What will you do with me now?" Tanu asked.

"I'm deciding whether to kill you." Sylah twisted the blade left and right, cutting through the air.

Tanu's eyes widened, her jaw trembling.

Anoor would not want me to murder her. The thought was sudden and intrusive. Anoor was not here *because* of Tanu.

"You won't be able to break me," Tanu said through shaking lips.

It sounded like a challenge and Sylah's smile spread slowly across her face. "Perhaps a few days of starvation will loosen your tongue."

She had paid for Tomi's silence. It would be a simple thing to leave her bound in this pen.

Tanu's eyes glittered and she bucked as Sylah gagged her. Her defiance delighted Sylah.

Am I enjoying this? Her hands faltered.

She had never been one to take pleasure in other people's pain. But something had snapped within her. Since Petal's sacrifice to the Tannin—and her own involvement in it—she had struggled to be comfortable within her skin.

And now I'm taking joy from the pain of others. Her hands began to shake, but she finished the final knot before stepping away.

Sylah fled the pen, sickened by her own actions.

She needed to wait out the tidewind in the barn, as far away as she could get from where she'd left Tanu. She crept into the enclosure where the red juvenile eru slept.

"Hello, Berry," Sylah said softly. "Do you remember me?"

The eru lazily opened its eye before settling back down to sleep.

"You sleep, I'm just going to sit here for a while. I didn't feel like being alone."

Berry's tail flicked out to where Sylah sat. But it didn't strike her; instead her tail curled around Sylah.

Sylah smiled and leant into the eru's cool scales.

She tried to sleep but her thoughts were dark and troublesome. She worried about herself, about the tidewind and the Zalaam. But most of all she worried about Anoor.

When the tidewind abated, Sylah slipped out of Berry's pen and out of the barn. She had decided that a shower would help clear her mind before she continued investigating.

As she left the barn and crossed the Tongue to head to Lio's she thought she saw something in the distance. The sky was speckled with flecks of white like ash lifted on the breeze.

Had there been another fire?

Sylah watched as one of the white pieces fell on the ground in front of her.

No, not ash, but paper.

Someone had covered the Duster Quarter with sheets of parchment. Sylah picked one up and felt her stomach roil as she read: *There is a world beyond the empire. The wardens have been lying. The ground we walk was once the Ghostings', their penance brought about to silence them. All blood colours can bloodwerk, and everyone will need to bleed— for war is coming. Meet me where the plantations no longer bloom when the tidewind ends. I am building an army—Truthsayer*

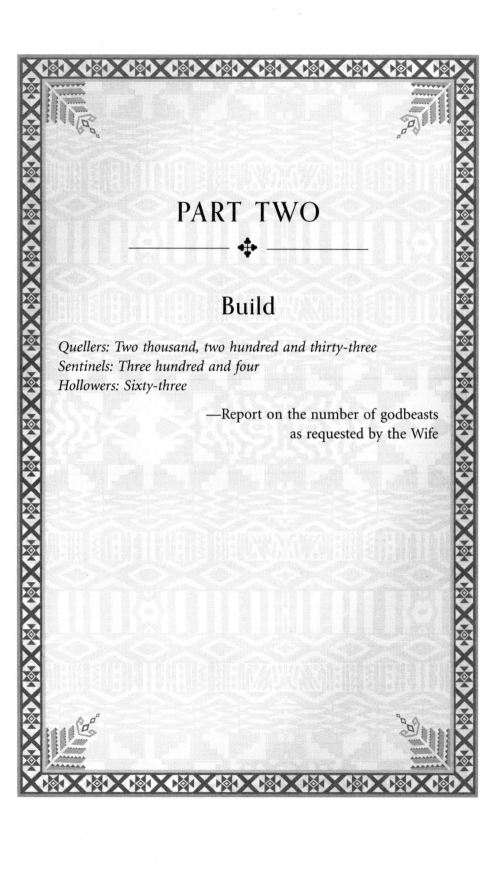

PART TWO

✣

Build

Quellers: Two thousand, two hundred and thirty-three
Sentinels: Three hundred and four
Hollowers: Sixty-three

—Report on the number of godbeasts
as requested by the Wife

The waxing fable of Queen Karanomo as told by Zenebe

As with all waxing fables, the storyteller adds their own knowledge to the story, which is shown here through italics.

O what there was, O what there wasn't.

Born to Queen Togla, Karanomo was an only child. Raised in the confines of the Shard Palace with little to do except explore its vast corridors and lush gardens. *School was a tutor brought into the palace. Playtime was hiding from Queen Togla's advisors.*

But it wasn't a terrible time, only lonely.

O what there was, O what there wasn't.

When Princess Karanomo was thirteen there was a terrible accident in the Shard Palace. Queen Togla, known for her lavish parties, had been hosting delegates from Bushica when she tripped and fell from a balcony. *The Royal Flighter had been sent away on an errand to the Academy and was not there to bring in a healer.*

Tolga died that day. And Karanomo became Queen.

O what there was, O what there wasn't.

Thirteen, grief-stricken and a Queen. Karanomo did not let her age dissuade her. Instead, she used her time to learn all she could of her country. *First, she spent three terms at the Academy learning all she could of flighting. But that wouldn't be her last time among scholars.* Then she spent two years with her Sea Lords and three years with her Earth Lords.

But an heir is required to further the throne, and so at twenty,

Karanomo put in place her first contract with Emperor Alperlo of Bushica.

O what there was, O what there wasn't.

But a child was not forthcoming. Grief once more plagued the Shard Palace. Their marriage was annulled and Karanomo sought no further partners.

But it wasn't a terrible time, only lonely.

O what there was, O what there wasn't.

Before the Zalaam waged war on the world, Tenio lived in prosperity and peace. But all things are fragile, the Shard Palace has shown us that.

Gone is the Queen and her court. Gone is the world we once knew.

But we remember the peace our Queen brought to the world. And the love we have for her still.

CHAPTER TWELVE

Anoor

Choice is a greater boon than a wish.

—Ghosting proverb

Anoor woke in an unfamiliar place. The panelling above her seemed different today, the paint duller than she remembered. *I'll ask Gorn to help me redecorate*, she thought.

"Anoor? Are you awake?" The voice drew her back to the present. She turned her eyes to Faro's.

"I thought I was back there, in the Keep," Anoor said.

Qwa's face appeared next to Faro's. "I think she must have hurt her head."

"No, I'm fine. I think." Anoor pushed herself to her elbows. She was lying on a pallet in Yona's rooms.

Everything came back to her in a rush of panic. "The queller . . . oh, by the blood, the people it killed. *I* killed. How many were there?"

Faro and Qwa exchanged a look.

Qwa spoke first, his voice gruff. "I'm not sure. The earthquake caused some casualties too."

Anoor felt tears wet her cheeks. "I was such a fool. I couldn't remember the diffuse rune. Remember how many times Yona made us learn it those first few weeks? Over and over?" Anoor's voice careened into a wail.

Faro laid a stiff hand on her shoulder. "Yona—the Wife," Faro corrected themselves, "told us she would be here soon. She is over-seeing the repairs to the Foundry, but she said you might benefit from bitter leaf tea when you wake."

Faro picked up a mug from the bedstead and handed over a steaming tea.

"She taught me how to make it for you, with extra barknut powder to make it sweet," Faro said softly.

Anoor sniffed and took the mug from Faro. Her lips shook as she took a sip, trying to stop the sob that was caught in her throat.

The tea instantly soothed her. Once she was certain her words wouldn't come out as a cry she said to Faro, "Thank you."

Footsteps echoed down the corridor outside. The door slammed as someone closed it behind them with a lot of force. Not someone. *Yona.*

With a look, the Wife sent Faro and Qwa scattering. Anoor sat up in bed and prepared herself for her grandmother's wrath.

Yona took a seat on the edge of her own bed on the far side of the room. She smelt faintly of smoke.

"I'm so sorry, everything just went out of my head. I should have used the *diffuse* rune sooner," Anoor muttered. "So much loss . . ." Her eyes grew hot again.

Yona stood and came to stand by Anoor's pallet.

"Yes, there was loss today, and I too am sorry for it."

Tears splashed onto Anoor's cheeks. Yona gently eased the mug in Anoor's hands to her lips.

"Drink, it will make you feel better."

The tea lapped at Anoor's lips from where Yona tilted the cup. She swallowed two gulps before murmuring, "All the families destroyed, all the children who have lost their parents."

Yona made a small sound in her throat and Anoor glanced up. Her grandmother looked at her in bewilderment.

"You mourn for the *people*?" Yona asked.

"Yes . . ."

Yona brought a hand to her forehead and closed her eyes. When she opened them again her gaze was edged with annoyance.

"Each person who died today, died in service to Kabut. Their sacrifice, though unintentional, was still a sacrifice. Let it fuel you, not hinder you. Death is power, do you not feel more powerful?"

Anoor swirled the tea in her hand as she thought about it. Did she feel any different? She took another sip. The liquid filled her with a pleasant warmth. Though her nerves felt frayed she didn't physically feel too bad.

In fact, she felt ready to ride another queller. The feeling of the beast moving beneath her was unlike anything she had ever experienced.

But all the people I killed . . . the thought splintered through the exhilaration of the memory, but she tried to reframe it. Turning the pain of it into power.

Yona was watching her closely.

"Are you well?"

Anoor grimaced. "I'm trying to be."

Yona patted her shoulder. "That's all I ask."

"I just wish all your teachings hadn't left my mind, so I could have stopped the queller sooner."

Yona's eyes flashed. "It seems you do not remember everything I taught you."

Anoor inhaled sharply. "I-I'm sorry, the rune just wouldn't come to me."

"Do you remember what I told you about the diffuse rune?"

Anoor wasn't sure where her grandmother's line of questioning was going, so she let Yona answer herself.

"It is irrevocable. Once that rune is drawn, the godbeast can never be used again. That queller is completely useless to us now. *That* was the loss I was talking about."

Yona wasn't annoyed about the people she had killed but the *godbeast.*

Anoor steadied her mind with another sip of tea. "Perhaps I can help make a new one?"

Yona smiled, releasing the tension from her face. "In time, Anoor, in time. But before you train under the master crafter you must be presented to the commune leaders, tonight."

"But they've already met me." Anoor suddenly felt very tired.

"Not formally, not underneath Kabut's eye in the open temple." Yona turned to the window where the half-moon hung in the sky. "He watches us with an eye half closed in scrutiny, assessing his child."

Anoor looked to the window.

Are you watching me, Kabut? Are you watching me, Father?

Whether it was a rush from the sugar in the tea or a missive from the God, she felt a soaring of emotion in her chest.

Anoor smiled as the feeling of elation made her bold. "Take me to the temple. Let the Child of Kabut meet the commune leaders under his eye."

Yona's answering grin was full of teeth.

Anoor felt a calmness settle over her as Yona led her up a rocky path towards a peak on the mountain top.

She looked down on Yellow Commune. Most of the straw huts had already been erected again after the wreckage from the earthquake. The bodies, twenty-five by Yona's count, had been fed to the endless flame in Anoor's name. No—in the Child of Fire's name.

The Child of Fire felt no grief or remorse. The Child of Fire was made powerful by the pain of those around her. The Child of Fire was going to bring down the Wardens' Empire.

Anoor felt herself don the prophesied persona as she walked up the stairs to the open temple. It was easier than she expected to suppress her feelings of helplessness and remorse. As under the half-moon Anoor could not deny the pull of Kabut.

With each step they got closer and closer to the God's gaze. The moonlight was bewitching as it cast shadows across the expanse of the Volcane Isles. Anoor was enamoured by its beauty.

"Oh!" Anoor tripped over Yona's foot and fell forward, her hands flailing outwards to dampen her fall, but they got caught in her sleeves and instead she fell face first into the open temple.

Anoor felt blood trickle down her cheek from the rubble on the ground. Her first instinct was to hide her blood from the onlookers. Her second was to brace herself for Yona's chastisement, for a kick or a slap to hide her embarrassment. But Yona wasn't Uka. Instead, her grandmother helped Anoor up.

"Kabut blesses you with pain as you enter this sacred site." Yona was projecting her voice. Anoor looked up to see the eight leaders, each standing by a temple pillar.

The open temple was smaller than Anoor expected, and much less grand. As the name suggested, there was no roof, and the weather had taken its toll on the stonework. Cracks from earthquakes littered the tiles, though the pattern of a spider was still clear. In the centre of the spider's body was the endless flame.

It started to rain, and the fire hissed and crackled as Anoor and Yona approached.

"Stand here." Yona guided Anoor to the head of the spider.

Yona removed a small pot of salve from her pocket. She turned to Anoor and held her face in her hands. Carefully she began to rub a substance across Anoor's cuts.

"Grandmother, I don't think I was hurt on my forehead."

But still Yona circled the cream into her whole face. "In a moment I'm going to ask you to do something that you won't want to do," Yona murmured. "I need you to put your hands in your pockets and trust me, okay?"

Anoor nodded.

They were closer to the fire than any of the leaders. It licked towards her in the wind and Anoor felt sweat merge with the blood, paste and grit on her cheeks.

"Kabut, I bring before you a child of your blood. A child who will lead us into battle and grant death to the unbelievers. As proof of your regard for her, watch her walk through the flames."

"What?" Anoor whispered to Yona.

Her grandmother threw her a disdainful look. "Walk through the flames. Go, now."

Anoor looked at the fire. The rain had diminished it slightly, but it was still large enough to turn her to cinder.

"Go, it's only four steps across it," Yona commanded.

Anoor hesitated for a second more before putting her hands in her pockets and plunging into the fire.

As soon as Anoor stepped onto the coals, her dress caught fire, the embroidered flowers in the hem exploding into rainbow flames as they burnt. Anoor could hear the gasps from the onlookers when the fire that swirled around her turned multicoloured. She would have marvelled herself if she hadn't been concentrating on moving as quickly as she could.

On her second step her shoes burnt away, baring the soles of her feet. On the third step her hair caught fire and sizzled to the roots.

And on the fourth step there was pain.

Ice-cold pain that made her scream until her throat was hoarse.

She reached the other side of the fire a wraith of ash, blood and burns. Her screams had become a battle cry that the leaders exalted in, shouting, and howling along.

Anoor saw Yona through the flames on the other side. Her grandmother's smile was bloodthirsty and proud.

"The Child of Fire; she who brings the Battle Drum."

Anoor stood naked before them, with coals on her feet and sparks on her chest.

The pain was still there, and her hair had gone, but she wasn't seriously hurt. The dress had been designed to protect much of her body, and the paste her grandmother had used shielded her face from the burns.

She was all right. She was more than all right.

She *was* the Child of Fire. This time she wasn't pretending. The old Anoor was no more.

The Child of Fire looked up to the night sky and smiled a smile of ash and cinder. "To begin, we must end," she cried.

CHAPTER THIRTEEN

Hassa

Rebellion is in the air. Send as many soldiers as you can to the capital. Someone called the Truthsayer is inciting revolution. We will not have it. For the safety of the empire, send all able troops.

—Letter sent by Warden Pura to the twelve
imirs of the Wardens' Empire

"What do you mean, you're my daughter?" Vahi took a shaky step towards Hassa.

Hassa swallowed, took a deep breath, and signed, *My mother was called Dahlia. But I was raised by someone called Marigold.*

"Marigold? They're still alive? I wasn't sure because I hadn't seen them. They were Dahlia's friend . . ." His words petered out when he saw the droop of Hassa's shoulders.

The grief had dulled slightly, eclipsed by the larger emptiness of Kwame's loss.

Marigold died in the tidewind trying to save others.

Vahi blinked slowly. "Are you really my daughter?" He took another step towards her, tears welling in his eyes.

Hassa wasn't sure how to feel, shock had tightened its talons around her mind, arresting her thoughts.

You were the reason my mother died, she signed, her arms quivering.

Vahi shook his head, tears falling down his cheeks.

"No, no, no. Dahli was my life, my beloved. Turin found out she was sneaking out at night to visit me at the plantations."

You were still the reason she was killed.

Vahi fell to his knees sobbing. Hassa watched him with a strange kind of detachment.

"I tried to give her money, but Dahlia refused to take it, she didn't want our love to be a transaction."

A transaction. That's what Hassa had thought she always was. The product of money. But now Vahi was saying that she was born from love.

"Turin told my father about us, and he had Dahlia killed. I didn't mean for it to happen." Guilt racked Vahi's shoulders, and it was an old guilt, gnarled and deep-rooted. Hassa knew that Vahi wasn't lying. But it was difficult to let go the nineteen years she had spent blaming the father she had never known.

But she knew she had to try.

Hassa knelt on the floor next to Vahi. Looking into his dark brown eyes, she saw the resemblance there.

I am your daughter. Hassa signed the words for the first time. The sign for daughter looped her right wrist around her left, before sliding down her forearm.

She signed it again.

Daughter.

And again.

Daughter.

She felt shock give way to raw emotion and she began to cry.

Vahi folded her into his arms. For the first time since Kwame's death Hassa let herself feel something other than rage.

"I can't believe I found you. I can't believe you're alive. You know I wouldn't have left if I knew?" Vahi's words were muffled by Hassa's shoulder as he held her together.

But she was breaking. Tears flowed down her face. Here was her *father*, an Ember, yes, but her father first.

They stayed like that for some time until the coming of the tide-wind shattered their peace and they broke apart.

"I want to know everything about your life."

Hassa considered whether to tell him the truth. But while she hesitated there was a knock on the tidewind shutters, and a piece of paper thrust under the door.

Who could be delivering letters during the tidewind?

Vahi went to pick it up and Hassa read it over his shoulder as he murmured the final words.

"... All blood colours can bloodwerk, and everyone will need to bleed—for war is coming. Meet me where the plantations no longer bloom when the tidewind ends. I am building an army."

Hassa's heart thudded in her chest.

Vahi looked up at her.

"What do you know of this?"

So, it would have to be the truth after all.

They spoke until dawn broke. Neither of them was tired, their curiosity vanquishing all exhaustion.

Hassa learnt that Vahi had led a humble life in Jin-Kutan away from his father and his old life as an imir's son. His family had presumed him dead many years ago and that had suited him fine. After all, the lies Turin had told of her father were small compared to the lies the empire had told him.

"What I don't understand," Vahi said, "is why Turin kept you alive?"

Hassa frowned. It was difficult to summon the words to explain Turin to someone who knew her less well.

Turin is a complicated person. I believe she felt guilt about my mother's death. Despite the number of clients who asked after me, she never made me work in the maiden house. She protected me in ways she didn't have to.

Vahi shook his head sadly. "But she is heinous and only cares about money."

Yes, that is true. But I do not think she is any more heinous than imirs, or Ember business owners. They are all equally corrupt, she just doesn't hide it.

Vahi reached for Hassa and rested his hand on her shoulder. "I'm glad at least that she didn't force you to work in the maiden house."

Hassa broke away from his gaze. There were other things that Turin had her do that were equally as unpalatable, but she didn't tell him that.

Vahi glanced at the leaflet the Truthsayer sent. He seemed to sense Hassa didn't want to talk about Turin anymore.

"So, the Ghostings were invaded?" Vahi asked. Hassa had told him all she knew of the truth and the world beyond the empire.

Yes, four hundred years ago the wardens stole our land.

Vahi put his head in his hands. "And the inkwell you had me make, you'll be able to use it?"

Hassa nodded.

"Show me."

Hassa had been itching to try out the inkwell, and now, set free from the shackle of lies, she could.

She pulled the inkwell out of the bag with her arms. She managed to tug the strap taut herself, with the loop Vahi had made in the leather. Then with a bit of pressure on the stylus, it slipped into her vein.

"Here." Vahi handed Hassa the notes from Turin. "Don't think I'll be needing these anymore. You can use the paper to practise on."

Hassa had only learnt the one rune—*Ru*. She drew it slowly on the paper, trying to ignore the numbers and notes written in Turin's curling penmanship.

Of course, Turin knew how to write, and not just simply, but with style. Always breaking the law with a flourish, she thought.

As soon as Hassa finished the final line on the rune the top page in the pile slipped forward, like it had been pulled by a sudden breeze. The force was so strong the paper ripped into pieces.

"Incredible," Vahi breathed. "You did it, you really did it."

Hassa gave him a look that said, "Did you doubt it?"

"Now try *Ba*."

I only know this rune. I haven't managed to teach myself much more.

Vahi smiled. "Well then, let me teach you."

The last few strikes before dawn were spent learning from Vahi. His bloodwerk was mediocre by his own admission, but he knew enough of the basics to teach Hassa.

As the orange hue of sunrise began to slip through the slats in the shutters they stopped.

People will be gathering to see the Truthsayer now, Hassa signed.

"Yes, they will." Vahi drummed his fingers against his chin. "Do you think the Truthsayer could be this Sylah friend of yours?"

Hassa barked out a laugh. *No, Sylah is only interested in one thing—Anoor.*

"And Anoor is . . .?"

Hassa ran her wrists across her brows before signing, *Gone. We don't know where.*

"Who is this Truthsayer?"

Hassa shrugged, though she suspected she knew: there was only one person who had contacts at a printing press and could mass-produce so many leaflets this easily.

The tidewind had stilled. They both looked to the door knowing that the world outside was immeasurably different than it had been when Hassa had first arrived.

What do we do now?

Vahi sighed. "We should go to the meeting. If what you tell me is true, then none of it matters anyway."

Both hesitated, unwilling to break this small piece of solace and the joy they had found in discovering each other.

Hassa reached for the bag that held her inkwell and mould, and she felt the spell of their evening together end. It was time to face the real world.

Let's go.

Hassa and Vahi joined the stream of people walking to the plantation fields. The air was laced with smoke and the light of dawn cast a spectral glow across the Dredge.

The atmosphere was hushed, and the crowds moved as if they sleepwalked. Perhaps they thought this was indeed a nightmare.

Hassa had never not known about the empire's rotten heart. It was taught to every Ghosting from the moment they could sign. She couldn't imagine finding out that the life you had led had been based on a lie.

"Hassa!" She heard someone call her name and Hassa and Vahi turned.

"Do you know this person?" Vahi sounded worried.

Hassa nodded her head wearily as Sylah pushed through the crowd and stopped in front of them.

She thrust a leaflet under Hassa's nose and said, "Did you see this?"

Hassa surveyed her friend. This was the first time they had spoken since they'd argued in the Nest. She understood why Vahi had been concerned. Sylah cut a terrifying sight.

Shadows hung beneath her eyes and her braids were matted and frayed as if she'd run her hands through them too many times. Dirty clothes hung off her lean frame. Her tongue probed between her teeth as she waited for Hassa to look at the leaflet—of which hundreds were scattered on the ground around them. Sylah's fingers were shaking, blurring the words on the page she held out.

Are you back on joba seeds? Hassa asked.

Sylah frowned. "No. But look, Hassa, this changes everything."

Hassa shook her head and continued walking, Sylah falling into step between her and Vahi.

Now you seem to care about the empire, Sylah? What, your efforts to find Anoor have failed?

Sylah winced and glanced away, and when she looked at Hassa again her eyes were red.

"I'm sorry, Hassa, I'm not ready to give up on her."

Hassa wheeled on her. *I never asked you to give up on her, Sylah. But there are other people here who love you, other people here who need saving. When did you stop fighting for the Ghostings? For me?*

Sylah's eyes widened.

"I'm so sorry, Hassa." Sylah's face crumpled. "Sometimes I wish I hadn't come back at all."

Hassa watched her friend weep, then touched her wrist to her cheek. *Me too.*

The words were harsh, and perhaps a little untrue. But Hassa hoped they'd help Sylah realise that it was time to take her place in the war to come.

But you are here now, and that too is a responsibility, Hassa continued. *Perhaps the Truthsayer will have a place for you, by their side.*

Sylah blinked away her tears and straightened.

"No, I can't let Anoor go. Not yet."

Hassa wasn't angry. She understood the depth of love Sylah felt for Anoor. She'd had it with Kwame. Again, the adage came to her: *if we forget the individual, we forget ourselves.*

But it still felt like a betrayal.

The crowd swelled around them and Hassa felt Vahi's hand tighten around her wrist as they were pulled away from each other. Sylah disappeared in the sea of faces. But Hassa didn't look for her.

Instead, she looked to the plantation fields, where the atmosphere had turned hot with rebellion. A drumbeat of stamping emanated from the crowd, drawing up dust and ash from the charred ground. Chants of "Truthsayer, Truthsayer, Truthsayer!" raised the hair on Hassa's arms.

These were people willing to fight. Hassa pushed all thoughts of Sylah and Anoor from her mind.

It was time for the empire to fall.

CHAPTER FOURTEEN

Jond

"Chief of the Winterlands" is a hereditary title held for the last three hundred years by the Vorman family. They have had a long-standing trade treaty in place with Tenio, as their land has long been rich with oil beneath the snow and ice.

—Excerpt from *Politicking Across Borders,*
written by Rubo Oh-Kinsha

Falling was the opposite feeling to flighting. Instead of Jond's stomach dropping through his ass, it felt like it was coming up through his mouth.

His arms cartwheeled around him in a flurry of snow. His open mouth filled with ice, freezing the scream in his throat until he felt like he was choking, dying, in a white cloud of biting cold.

The impact came sooner than he expected. It brought with it a brief blackness, a respite from all the white, as his teeth knocked together and his head collided with the ground.

"Argh." He'd bitten through the edge of his tongue, the salty copper of blood filled his mouth. He spat, spraying the crimson droplets wide before rolling onto his back, panting.

"What in the name of Anyme . . ."

Above him was a perfect circle of light.

Am I dead?

He tilted his head to the side and that was when the snowflakes caught the light. The perfect circle above him was the sky. The memory of the roof tiles came flooding back.

He pushed himself up and looked around. It took a moment for his eyes to adjust to the dimmer light, but it appeared he was in a cavern, no, not a cavern . . . a room.

Snow surrounded him in the same perfect circle. He and Kara had fallen through a window on the roof into what looked like an office of some kind. Broken slate tiles were scattered on top of a thick white carpet from where the roof had given way. Scrolls littered a spruce wood desk set off to the side. Shelves lined the walls filled with more papers, all flecked with ice.

But he couldn't see Kara.

"Kara!" Her name was like a bolt of lightning in his veins, and he jumped up, much faster than he should have done.

"Monkey's hairy bollocks." He clutched his temples from the sudden burst of pain behind his eyes. Darkness blurred the edges of his vision and he realised he probably had a concussion.

He stumbled forward, searching the shadows for Kara.

"Kara!" he shouted over and over.

"Stop shouting. You could bring an avalanche down on us." Jond located the sound of her voice. She sounded strained and weak.

"Kara, are you hurt?"

She was huddled against the back of the desk. Violet ink spread across the scrolls where she had fallen. Not ink—blood.

"I need to bind my wrist. Help me rip this fabric." She tried to tug on her dress but seemed too weak to achieve anything.

"Where are you hurt?"

She winced as she straightened, revealing the white bone of her wrist protruding from her freckled skin. Pain and fear filled her eyes.

"Oh, that little scratch?" he said.

A small laugh huffed out of her followed by a shout of pain. "I can't get us back to the Academy for healing . . . it's my orb hand."

Jond had already noted that. But that was a problem for a little later. First, he had to make Kara a splint. He reached for her elbow and gently guided up her injured arm. "Hold it above your heart. There you go."

The chair that was tucked into the desk had frozen in place. The ice had made the wood brittle, and it was easy enough to snap off the chair leg.

He spoke soothingly as he reached for her wrist. "Now I'm going to have to set the bone, because we can't bind it up with it sticking out like that, can we?"

"How much is it going to hurt?" The question surprised Jond. He hadn't been sure Kara felt pain, let alone feared it.

"It'll hurt less than if you had two wrists broken," he offered with a grin. She grimaced back.

"Tell me something. Anything. Tell me about back home."

She wanted distraction, so he obliged. "Home, it's a funny concept, isn't it? Somewhere you're meant to belong, right?" He measured the splint across her wrist and aligned it. "But to achieve a sense of belonging you must *not* belong somewhere else. And I have not belonged in three places." He tightened her hand around her forearm, readying her wrist against the splint. "The first place was the Ember Quarter. I was born to noble parents, in a world where Embers rule. But I didn't belong, none of us did. Turns out the land was the Ghostings' after all."

Kara hissed as Jond tied the splint in place.

"I'll never understand the belief that different blood colours are superior," she spat out.

"Hmm, it seems foolish now, but that was the truth we lived by. The second place I didn't belong was the Sandstorm Rebellion. Twelve of us were stolen from Ember homes and raised to take down the wardens . . . 'An Ember's blood, a Duster's heart.'"

"You were a rebel?" Kara asked through clenched teeth.

"Yes, I was."

There was a crunch as Jond push hard on Kara's wrist bone, forcing it back into place. Kara's scream rattled the pain in his head, but he continued with his story until her cries petered out.

"We were a group of children raised to kill, to destroy, to burn down the empire. But Sylah . . . she turned her back on it . . . and I-I couldn't kill her."

"And the third place you didn't belong?" Kara's voice was hoarse from her scream. Her nose was pinched as Jond continued to bind her wrist with fabric.

Jond gave her a lopsided smile. "Tenio. I have never felt more out of place than among the people of the Academy. There, done."

Jond let out a relieved sigh. Kara had been losing a lot of blood and he wasn't sure she would have survived much longer without the wound being bound. Jond made to stand but Kara reached for him with her other hand.

She cupped his cheek drawing him closer, so they shared one breath. He felt his heart begin to race and he wondered if she could hear it thundering in his chest.

Then she spoke. "You're wrong, you know. Home isn't the opposite of *not* belonging. It's *choosing* where you belong. And you chose the Blood Forged. We're your home now."

Though Jond was cold, colder than he'd ever been in his life, her words warmed him. He smiled, his teeth still bloody from the cut on his tongue. "Thank you."

Kara didn't respond. Instead, she was concentrating on trying to stand. Jond reached to help her up. She gasped as she stood and Jond thought he had hurt her.

"What is it? Are you injured elsewhere?" He scanned her with concerned eyes, but she didn't answer. Instead, she stepped forward, her good hand reaching outwards to point. Her words seemed to be stuck in her throat.

"What?" he pressed.

"Look."

His gaze followed her shaking hand.

In the corner of the room, what Jond had thought was a pile of clothes was something more sinister. Perfectly preserved in death was a body.

Kara dropped to her knees and bowed her head in salute. "Takolay, chief of the Winterlands. May this death not be your last."

Jond followed suit, his brain reverberating in his skull with pain.

Takolay's blue eyes were open and unblinking. His dark skin had turned ashen from the dusting of snow. The luxuriant furs he wore fanned out beside him in shades of brown and white. His expression was frozen between a smile and a grimace, raising the hairs on Jond's arms.

Kara was whispering quietly to herself, and though Jond couldn't hear it, it sounded like a prayer. When she was finished, he asked, "I thought religion was banned in Tenio?"

"It's not banned, it's just viewed differently. Once the eight tribes made an alliance under the banner of the queendom, faith and law were separated. Many religions died out."

"And yet, you pray?"

Kara didn't sound like she was going to respond, until her mouth parted, and a breath of fog escaped. "The women in my family have always passed on waxing fables of the Gods."

Niha had taught Jond of the waxing fable tradition in Tenio—how each tale purposefully swelled and changed with each telling. "The prayers comfort me," Kara added. "I hope that words have power."

Jond stood, and walked towards the corpse of the leader who was supposed to have helped them.

"Words *do* have power. Is that not the basis of all religion?" Jond knelt in front of the fallen leader as he spoke. "Anyme, bless this soul, welcome him into your realm in the sky."

There was no fire down here, no smoke to carry Takolay's soul upwards, but the small prayer would have to do.

Jond turned back to Kara who was watching him with troubled eyes.

"Look at the door behind his body," she said. Jond turned and looked. Bloody nail marks scoured the wood. He knew what it meant.

The hole in the roof above them was too high for them to climb out.

"We're trapped," Jond said.

The two of them huddled together beneath the waning light of the broken roof.

"We have one or two strikes of daylight left," Jond said. His head still throbbed, but he noticed it less sitting this close to Kara.

Her head rested on his shoulder. He could smell the freshness of her hair and sweet undercurrent of the perfume she used: mint and something softer like vanilla. He savoured being this close to her. That was, until she spoke.

"Thank you for the commentary," Kara said with a scowl.

Jond was about to retort back but then he noticed Kara's lips were pale and her breathing shallow. He needed to keep her talking.

"Do you think anyone survived the avalanche?" he asked.

"I hope so. We need those longboats to transport our armies."

Jond winced at her callousness.

"What? You think me too cold?" Kara laughed. "Every action, every thought I have is calculated . . . it has to be."

Jond didn't say anything for a moment, and Kara continued, her voice softened, "It was how I was raised. Everything I do or say must have purpose."

"Sounds like quite an upbringing. Were you raised near the Academy?"

"No, a city to the north."

Jond didn't know much about the geography of Tenio.

"Where exactly? All I know is that the Shard Palace is to the north," he asked.

"Not far from there," she said.

"In a village? A town?"

"Yes." Answering both questions evasively.

Jond was about to ask for specifics, but then she spoke again.

"I miss the smell of roses," she said. "The gardens near my home were always full of red roses. I used to lie under the bushes when I was a child. Even though the thorns pricked me, I didn't mind. I thought the beauty was worth the pain . . ." She trailed off with a yawn.

"No, you know we can't sleep. You sleep, you die."

"Mmm." Kara's eyes had closed.

"Why did you decide to be a flighter?" he asked, trying to draw her back to consciousness.

"My mother," she said.

"Ah," Jond said. "I know what it's like having overbearing parents."

Kara shook her head. "No, my mother, she was ill, she fell from a great height and I wasn't able to get her a healer quick enough. If I had been able to flight . . ." Her speech slowed to a stop.

"Kara, I need you to give me your orb."

Her eyes shot open. "No."

"I still have my inkwell, I just need you to teach me the combination to get us out of here."

Her laugh was brittle. "It took me over a decade to learn the combination to flight with an orb."

"But I won't be using an orb, I just need to get the runes right."

"No. It is against Academy law. You cannot learn without becoming a student first."

"Fuck the rules—"

"Fuck the rules? If we didn't have laws then this war would have happened much sooner, the balance would have been thrown off by any commoner who decided to try their hand at deathcraft and bone marrow."

Jond reeled. "Any *commoner*? Tenio is sounding more and more like the empire each day."

Kara was breathing heavily. Good, at least she wasn't sleeping. He needed to keep her angry and alert.

"I didn't mean it like that—"

"You did, and besides, those laws didn't stop the war, did they?"

Kara's mouth flattened into a line.

Jond continued, "Give me your orb. It's the only way we're going to survive. Unless you've given up?"

"I have not given up." Kara's good hand pulled off the strap around her palm. With nimble fingers she withdrew her orb. Jond glanced at the open wound beneath and winced. Their technique might be quicker than inkwells, but he'd never get over the sacrifice it required.

Jond held out his hand.

"No chance," Kara said, holding the orb up to his face. "You will watch and listen to me very carefully."

"Fine, but stop wasting time, I won't be able to draw in the dark."

Two strikes later and Jond still hadn't finished drawing the first combination on Kara's arm.

"You're doing it wrong, you need to create a thicker line in the centre arch," Kara barked at Jond.

"I'm trying but you won't let me hold the orb, so I'm doing it from a distance here." The pain in Jond's head was worse, pulsating with every word he spoke.

"There is no way I'm giving you this orb."

"Will you stop moving? Every time you talk the orb shakes and we've got three more runes to go."

It went on like that until they were straining in the last rays of daylight. The combination was complex, requiring coordinates transcribed into runes that had to be positioned in perfect order. In addition, the distance they could go wouldn't get them directly to the City of Rain, but a few leagues away from it. Kara wasn't sure how strong Jond's blood was, so they were careful and opted for a watch tower that Kara knew was safe.

Kara reached for Jond's hand before he completed the final rune on her forearm. "Are you ready? The last line here will flight me before you. All you need to do is complete the rune on your arm afterwards."

Jond nodded. Blinding pain seared his temples. He grimaced, pressing a hand to his forehead.

"What's wrong?" Kara asked, concern etched in her brows.

"I'm fine. Go. I'll follow shortly afterwards." He completed the combination on her skin.

"Jond . . ." She disappeared before he could answer.

The runes on Jond's own arm were already drying. All he had to do was finish the last shape: a circle around the centre and a line through the middle.

"Argh." The pain was so intense he retched.

The stylus fell out of his inkwell and clattered onto the ground. His knees followed shortly afterwards. Then his head.

Blood loss and a concussion don't go well together, he thought before blacking out completely.

CHAPTER FIFTEEN

Sylah

We have lost over 120,000 rubber trees in the fire, with a further 15,000 damaged beyond use. The fields are, for now, barren. We are in the process of reassigning 80,000 plantation workers while we look at sourcing more saplings. This will have a significant effect on all patrons of the Guild of Duty. Those masters who were appointed to the plantation fields may hang up their whips for the interim. I will send for you anon.

—Message sent to all Embers in the Guild
of Duty from Warden Aveed

Sylah elbowed her way through the crowds with little care. She'd lost Hassa and Vahi early on, but it had come with some relief. Hassa's words had cut her deeply.

When did you stop fighting for the Ghostings? For me?

Sylah winced from the fresh wound.

Nothing had changed, Sylah was still fighting for them, but Anoor came first.

The plantation fields were ash beneath her feet as she moved towards the speaker in the centre. Instead of rubber trees, she wove between rows of charred stumps, some still faintly smouldering. The tidewind had made the blaze surge hot and quick, burning through the trees until there was nothing left by morning.

Sylah was glad to see the plantations go, and so were the Dusters who had toiled in the fields. The mood among the droves of people was festive, despite the world-shattering truth they all clutched in their hands. The leaflets littered the Duster Quarter and Dredge. It seemed Sylah was one of the last to have read the contents, as the crowd was bigger than any Duster gathering she had ever seen.

The Dredge's clockmaster had set up a platform in the centre of the crowd, ready to repeat the Truthsayer's speech so those further away could hear what they had to say.

But Sylah didn't want to listen second-hand. She reached the heart of the mass with brute force, thrusting aside a young couple to get the best view.

"Eyoh, watch out!" one of them shouted at her.

Sylah paid them no heed, because her gaze had focused on the Truthsayer in front of her. They stood in the middle of a copse of smoking stumps, which surrounded their silhouette in an ethereal haze. Clad in bronze armour and a helmet, Sylah could make out little of the person's features.

Who are you? Sylah thought. Though the shape of the armour seemed familiar . . .

A hush fell over the crowd as the Truthsayer's words projected outwards.

And as soon as the Truthsayer spoke, Sylah knew who it was.

"Thank you for coming here today," the Truthsayer said. "We have a little time before the army descends. I forged the Keep's gates together during the tidewind to stall them."

Cheers sprang up from the crowd. The Truthsayer held up a hand. "But it will not take them long to cut through my poor handiwork. Then they will bring runeguns and anger." The gaiety disappeared completely. "You are here because I shared the secrets of the empire with you. Secrets that should never have been kept from us. I have called on you so that we may never let it happen again. The Ending Fire was a lie used to hide the world beyond the empire. How do I know this? Because I know people who have travelled there."

There were murmurs and gasps. Though Sylah heard more than a handful of people muttering with doubt.

"Four hundred and twenty-two years ago, this land was the Ghostings', until a group of Embers and Dusters arrived on the empire's shores and stole it from its inhabitants. Bloodwerk was once a skill used by the native Ghostings of this land and can be used by anyone. Power is not constrained by blood colour."

The mutterings grew louder until someone called out, "Prove it, show us how you bloodwerk."

The Truthsayer removed their gauntlet and brandished their inkwell. They inserted the stylus, letting blood run to the tip.

It was red.

"An Ember . . . an Ember . . . the Truthsayer is an Ember." The whisper swelled through the crowd.

"Yes, I am an Ember, so though I cannot prove that all bloods can bloodwerk, know that what I say goes against everything I was taught."

There were sneers and a few laughs. The Truthsayer was losing the trust of the audience.

Sylah was tugged backwards as someone made their way past her. She recognised the narrow shoulders of the Ghosting winnowing her way to the front.

"Hassa?"

She didn't turn around at Sylah's call and instead moved into the empty space next to the Truthsayer. The two of them spoke for a moment, but Sylah couldn't read the signs from the angle she was at.

Then Hassa turned and faced the crowd. She held one of the Truthsayer's leaflets flat against her wrist. On her other arm was a metal contraption Hassa hadn't been wearing earlier. The cuff sat flush against her scars with a hinged stylus inserted into the vein at her wrist.

Sylah felt her eyes prickle with heat and a wide smile grew across her face.

She made an inkwell that works for Ghostings.

Hassa's blood seeped to the tip, clear and sparkling. Then she drew on the leaflet. The crowd were split, half straining to see, and the other half shaking their heads expecting the experiment to fail.

But Sylah knew it wouldn't. She'd seen Hassa's power at work. The leaflet flew through the air with the speed of a runebullet, shredding apart as it went.

The Truthsayer's words fell like nameday confetti onto the crowd.

There was a moment of stunned silence. Then deafening, mind-racking cheers.

The Truthsayer rode the moment.

"The wardens are ignoring the signs that the tidewind is getting worse. They sit in the Keep with their food and their drink, denying the safety of its walls to the citizens who suffer."

"Then why did you burn down the tidewind shelter?" a man bellowed to Sylah's right.

"The shelter was not helping people, it was killing them. Everyone must have heard stories of people disappearing after going in," the Truthsayer said. "Well, the truth is hard to hear: those people are never coming back."

Someone beside Sylah gasped.

"What would you have us do?" Another person added to the rising cacophony.

The Truthsayer's eyes glittered through the glass of their helmet's visor.

"It is time to fight. We outnumber the army threefold. I know this because I worked within the Guild of Strength. Our numbers will overwhelm them."

"But they have runeguns."

"And you have scythes and your blood. Be ready when I call on you."

The chant started slowly, gaining momentum as it spread, until the ground was shaking with their stamping and the air hummed with rebellion.

"Scythes and blood . . ."

"Scythes and blood . . ."

"Scythes and blood . . ."

It drowned out all other sound, disguising the thunder of army boots on soil.

It was the Truthsayer who saw them first.

"Officers! The army is coming from the north!"

But the Truthsayer's words weren't carrying, so Sylah joined their siren call.

"Run! The army is here!"

Screams pierced the chanting and people began to flee. Sylah heard the first few shots of a runegun and instinctively ducked.

She looked up in time to see the Truthsayer make their way to the right of the plantation fields. Sylah pushed against the panicked crowd, towards the direction the Truthsayer had gone in. Their armour made them easy to spot, and they must have realised that as they slipped into the nearest building in the Dredge.

The villa was a crumbling ruin. The original foundations of limestone—a cheaper material used to build the Dredge—had been poorly patched with whitestone. There were so many holes in the villa's structure that Sylah was surprised that it hadn't collapsed completely.

The Dredge is a risky place to linger, Sylah thought. It was likely the army would do a sweep of the surrounding area.

Sylah followed the Truthsayer inside the decrepit building.

But the room was empty.

Sylah growled, the sound echoing in the dusty room. She walked back outside just to make sure she hadn't mistaken the doorway. But this was the only villa on the street that still *had* a doorway. The rest had caved in long ago. This had to be the building she'd seen the Truthsayer enter.

Thud. Thud. Thud.

The army was close. If Sylah didn't run now, she'd be captured, and likely questioned about her attendance. *Strongly* questioned.

She looked around the room one more time. Blue sand filled every surface and covered every floorboard—

Except one.

Sylah probed the clean floorboard with her toe. It gave way like a seesaw, revealing a ladder into the tunnels below.

Sylah hesitated. Traversing the tunnels without Hassa was risky. Getting lost wasn't Sylah's primary concern—flammable gas grew beneath pockets of earth this far out from the centre of the Dredge.

Thud. Thud. Thud.

The sound of the army's footfall sealed her fate. She lowered herself down the ladder and into the warm glow of runelight below. Sylah looked around as her feet touched the ground.

The room was small but every part of it was covered in notes, with a map of the Keep drawn with chalk on the far wall.

A pallet lay against one side with a chair in the centre where the Truthsayer sat, watching Sylah. Slowly, they took of their helmet off with a sigh.

Sylah looked into the tired eyes of Gorn.

"How's it hurting?" Sylah said with a crooked grin.

"The army, have they passed?" Gorn asked.

Sylah shrugged. "They were moving into the Dredge, but I followed you."

Gorn cursed. "I should have realised the wardens would have called back their troops from the twelve cities. I'd been so worried about the officers in the Keep, I hadn't prepared for those coming from the north," Gorn muttered to herself. Then she looked up and seemed to see Sylah fully for the first time.

She stood from her chair in a rush, knocking it to the ground.

"What are you doing here?"

"That was going to be my first question to you," Sylah retorted.

Gorn didn't smile. The woman's wide face sagged with fatigue. Her eyes were set into deep hollows and her greying hair had grown out in unkempt tufts.

"What of the mainland? Did you find aid?"

Sylah grimaced at the hope in her voice. "It's a long tale."

Gorn nodded before righting the chair and lowering herself back on it. "First, I need to tell you something, Sylah." She looked away. "Anoor is—"

"I know."

"I let her down, she's gone. I don't know where, but she's gone."

Sylah knelt beside Gorn and put a hand on her forearm. "I know where. She's gone to the Volcane Isles. The Zalaam have taken her."

Gorn's head snapped up. "What?"

"Let me start at the beginning."

Sylah recounted the last few mooncycles. When she finished Gorn looked at her with pity. It stung more than Hassa's wrath.

"And you came back, just for Anoor?"

"Of course. The Zalaam have taken her prisoner."

"Sylah, Anoor is not a prisoner. She went with them, with Tanu and the rest, out of *choice*."

Sylah shook her head violently. "No, you're wrong. She would never leave the empire. Not now with everything that is happening."

"She wasn't the same person you left behind. Losing her mother broke something in her that she wasn't ready to fix. She was meeting Tanu and the other disciples for weeks without me knowing."

"No." Sylah refused to believe it. "She wouldn't just leave."

"You have to let her go. I realised this and now you need to as well."

"No, I can't, I won't."

"Everything you've told me has furthered my resolve that the people need to rise up, now more than ever. The wardens need to be ousted. We need to prepare for the final battle—"

"No, no, no."

Sylah's mind was a swirling mess of hurt and anger and pain. That Anoor had gone with the Zalaam by choice had never been a scenario Sylah had considered. She clenched her fists and scrunched her eyes against the truth.

How could Anoor go with them willingly? It didn't make any sense. Her eyes were hot, but tears didn't fall. She released her hands by her side and set her jaw.

No, Anoor wouldn't have. Not without being told lies by someone, somewhere.

And there was only one person who could corroborate this theory.

Sylah made her way to the ladder.

"Where are you going?" Gorn asked.

"To get the answers I need."

"You can't keep her here anymore, Sylah. She's scaring the erus," Tomi said as soon as she appeared. His cheeks looked wan, his expression worried.

Sylah fished in her pocket and withdrew the last of the slabs she'd taken from her mother's stash.

"Here, this should buy your silence and your tolerance for a bit longer. Don't worry, she won't be your problem very soon."

Tomi looked at the white slabs before pocketing them and running out of the stables with haste.

Sylah opened the pen where Tanu was tied up. She brandished her dagger by her side. Tanu saw the intent in Sylah's eyes as she pulled the gag from her mouth.

"Tell me," Sylah said, her breath hot, "what the Zalaam want with Anoor?"

Tanu's lips pressed together. Sylah slid the blade between them, nicking the corner of her lips until blood ran across Tanu's teeth.

When she withdrew the blade Tanu said, "Perhaps you should be asking, what does Anoor want with the Zalaam?"

Sylah let out a sound of frustration. "I'm going to kill you, you know."

"Good. My death is inevitable, now or in the Ending Fire."

There was no winning with a person ready to die. So, what else could she leverage? Tanu had been raised by the Sandstorm, just like Sylah—and who did the Sandstorm hate more than anyone else?

Embers.

"When I kill you, I'm going to deliver your body to the wardens, who will ensure you have a full state burial led by the Abosom."

Tanu shrugged. "I prayed to Anyme all my life. I just never realised it was really Kabut I was praying to all along."

"No, you didn't hear me. *I* will deliver the body. And I'll be sure to tell them the tale of how you saved me from a Duster who tried to take my life. How you thanked the wardens for their guiding spirit with your last breath. Your sacrifice will become a griot story spun by Embers in the Keep. Tanu the pious, Tanu the true. A citizen of the empire. An Ember until the day she died."

Tanu contracted in on herself, smaller and smaller as Sylah spoke. But still she didn't answer Sylah when she asked, "What do the Zalaam want with Anoor?"

So, Sylah pounced, the dagger pressing against the artery in Tanu's neck. The blade was sharp, Sylah had ensured it, but just as she clenched her muscles to make the killing blow, Tanu whispered, "She is the Child of Fire."

Sylah stumbled backwards as if she had been the one stabbed.

"What?"

"She is the foretold one that will bring the Battle Drum." Blood dribbled down Tanu's chin as she spoke, the truth a violent thing between them.

The prophet of the Zalaam had prophesied that the Child of Fire would spark the beginning of the Ending Fire.

That meant Anoor wasn't a prisoner . . . *but one of them.*

Sylah struggled to breathe, her next words coming out in stuttering bursts. "Who . . . t-told . . . you . . . th-that?"

Tanu grinned red. "Yona, the Wife of Kabut."

Sylah felt the cold shower of dread spread over her. Of course, Yona was a key player in the Zalaam. She had instigated the tidewind shelters. She had taken Anoor away.

Sylah felt the world spin as her mind reeled.

Anoor is truly gone.

Not just from the empire. But from her.

It hurt to stand. It hurt to breathe. It hurt to keep her heart beating. For it was shattering within her chest.

Tanu was laughing at Sylah's pain, her head tipped back baring the hairline cut on her neck where the dagger had started to slice.

The tempest of Sylah's emotions hardened into bloodlust.

Tanu sensed the change in her expression, her laugh petering out. When she spoke, her voice was tinged with panic. "You're not still going to kill me, are—"

Sylah lunged.

CHAPTER SIXTEEN

Anoor

I have returned with the Child of Fire. The last battle is nearly upon us. Each commune has a part to play in our preparation for the Ending Fire. Ready yourselves. To win we must begin again.

—Missive from the Wife sent to every commune

"You did well today," Yona said.

They were back in Yona's rooms. Anoor was perched on the edge of a stool. After walking through the endless flame Anoor had spent a strike in the healer's hut. Until she was declared fit to leave.

The healer had covered her in a powder to aid with the few burns she had. Her feet had fared the worst, but even the pain there had already faded. Now she was just sticky and uncomfortable, her head cold from the baldness.

She didn't grieve her hair. Instead it felt like the flame had blessed her, branding her as the true Child of Fire.

"How did the dress burn up like that?" Anoor had caught a few people whispering about the spectacle as they had moved through the Foundry, the rainbow fire hailed as a sign from Kabut.

Yona snorted. "I copied the effect from a griot in the empire. His speciality was performing while on fire. The colour of the flames was caused by different minerals stitched into the hem. A cheap trick, but I knew it would work for those who were yet to be convinced of your worthiness."

Anoor frowned. What if she wasn't worthy? What if the true Child of Fire didn't need a ruse? Her earlier resolve wavered. Sometimes she felt like she was the *only* person who could be the one prophesied. But then at other times, like now, she wondered whether trickery had been used on her too.

The doubt persisted longer than she liked, so she voiced it.

"What if I am *not* the Child of Fire?"

Yona's eyes blazed hotter than the flames Anoor had just walked through. "You are because *I* say. The Wife of Kabut."

Anoor flinched and Yona's voice softened. "Did you not feel his presence today in the open temple? Did you not feel how your heart soared with warmth?"

Anoor couldn't deny she had felt something. Something other-worldly. And when she had walked through the flames, she felt like there was nothing she couldn't do.

Yona stood and walked to her bed. "Tomorrow, you will let the people see you. It is time that the rest of the communes met the one foretold."

Anoor hid her groan, she had hoped she could continue her training in godpower.

"Can't I start work in the Foundry? I'd like to help build the queller I destroyed."

"That will come later. It's important the communes know who they are fighting for."

Anoor felt troubled. They weren't fighting for her, they were fighting for the empire's freedom. For the Ghostings and the Dusters under the wardens' rule.

"I think if they knew what the empire was like, they wouldn't need me."

Yona strode across the room to grasp her chin in her hands. Though her touch was gentle, her nails dug into the fresh burns on Anoor's face.

"Only we have seen how rotten the empire is at its heart. The leagues that stretch between us and them are great chasms to the Zalaam. They cannot fathom the atrocities the wardens commit every day. Do not diminish your importance. The Child of Fire will lead us to war."

Anoor nodded, her thoughts leading back to the empire's shores. *Click—*

"No!" She jerked out of Yona's hands and clutched her temples, pushing the sound of Kwame dying from her mind.

But the thought of his murder had been enough to bring the simmering heat of vengeance back to the surface. Anoor straightened. All doubts had fled her mind.

And Yona watched her from across the room, eyes wide with wonder. "Yes, this is the person the communes need to see. Let them see the flame in you burn, Anoor."

Yona's pride sent Anoor's heart soaring. Uka had never looked at Anoor this way and she revelled in it. Even if Yona's gaze was a little more zealous than Anoor was used to.

She held the intensity of Yona's stare for as long as she could. But it unsettled her after a while, so Anoor looked away, feigning a yawn to break the silence.

Yona laughed, her gaze softening. "Yes, I think it is time for bed. It has been a long and exhausting day for us all."

Anoor went to her cot and collapsed on it. Her mind felt heavy, full of thoughts of the empire and Kabut. It didn't take long for her eyes to shutter closed.

Yona spoke from the shadows of the room. "Sleep now, my child. Kabut will guide you to darkness."

The next morning the Yellow Commune leader, Teta, took the disciples on a tour of the Volcane Isles while Yona caught up on urgent matters with Chah, the master crafter.

"The Volcane Isles are made up of three separate islands. The Yellow Commune and the Foundry are based on the largest of the three. Now to cross to the Green Commune we must travel north by boat."

Qwa groaned under his breath. "Not another boat."

"Hush, be polite, she can hear you," Faro replied.

Teta raised an eyebrow. "Faro is right, I can hear you very clearly, Qwa."

Qwa scuffled his foot on the ground. "Ah, sorry, Commune Leader Teta."

Anoor held back a laugh. It was satisfying to see Qwa chastised. He was so rarely called out for his rudeness.

Teta led them to a small rowboat that shifted gently by the rocky shore. It was one of around fifty that people were using to sail to the other island.

On her journey from the empire Anoor had marvelled at the expanse of the ocean, but here on the Volcane Isles she could appreciate the beauty of water in all its forms. Like the trickle of the streams that ran down the mountainside by the Foundry, and the estuary that flowed from the beach and into the sea.

And now this beautiful bay that spread out ahead of her in a semicircle, blending shades of turquoise and lapis. Fish darted in the shallows below the boat and Anoor smiled as they set the water sparkling.

Anoor took her seat in the bow and dipped her hand into the water. It was warmer than she expected, and she wondered if she might have time to go for a swim later.

A swim? This is not a holiday. Her conscience soured her pleasant thoughts. She was meant to be preparing the Zalaam for war, not enjoying herself.

She clenched her fists. *I need to present myself as the leader I am.*

While Anoor fortified herself, Teta began to row them across.

The journey wasn't far, twenty strokes, if that. So Anoor asked, "Why don't you make bridges?"

"The Volcane Isles are very rich in both copper and iron ore. Copper, we use to trade, it's too soft to make creations with. But iron is precious. Every piece that is mined is melted and shaped into the godbeasts you have seen in the Foundry."

Anoor could understand that.

"And wood? You have trees, don't you?" Qwa really couldn't keep his mouth shut.

Teta's mouth pursed. "We do, but clearly you have never lived by the sea. Saltwater eats away at rope, and in a few years the bridge would be in the depths of the ocean, and we would be exactly where we started."

Qwa didn't ask any more questions after that.

The boat bumped onto the shore of the Green Commune. The

landscape was identical to the rocky terrain of Yellow Commune, but with less elevation from the mountainside. The air too was sweeter here, less sulphuric.

As Teta led them towards the centre of the town, Anoor began to hear a deep reverberation on the breeze.

"Is that an earthquake?" Anoor asked Faro.

But it was Teta who answered. "No, that is the sound of the commune's choir."

Now she said it, Anoor could hear the deep baritone, woven in melody with a high-pitched falsetto.

Teta's lips were twisted in disapproval. Clearly singing wasn't something the Yellow Commune approved of.

As they rounded the corner the choir came into view. The singing procession lined the street on either side of the same straw huts that stood in Yellow Commune.

The song had no words, careening through minor and major chords with seemingly no rhythm.

"Child of Fire, welcome to the Green Commune." The Green Commune leader wore a thin green bandeau across their chest and a lace skirt that pooled at their ankles. "Please enjoy this performance of the song of the sea."

"The song of the sea . . ." Anoor heard it now. The rhythm moved like the stirring of waves and the surging of the tide.

She smiled, feeling her body sway with the music like some of the singers were, their hands lifted by their ears, their hips swirling. She wanted to join them in their dance. But then she remembered what her grandmother had said: "Let them see the flame in you".

The Child of Fire didn't dance. The Child of Fire *burnt*.

She didn't think of Kwame, or Lio, to ignite the fire in her. Today she thought of Sylah.

These people are going to fight for me, Sylah. Would you be proud? The empire must fall, and I will be the one to topple it.

She passed through the Green Commune tour with a stoic expression.

"The Green Commune have always put more stock in the arts than any other commune," Teta said quietly to her. She had watched Anoor approvingly throughout. "The Orange Commune will be less . . . rowdy."

Qwa snickered. He was probably wondering whether Teta knew what rowdy meant.

The Orange Commune was indeed far more sober. Their community specialised in education, housing the only schools on the Isles. Though it quickly became apparent that their education consisted of two things: swordcraft and religion.

The Orange Commune leader gave each of the disciples a mug of bitter leaf tea while they toured the schools. The tea wasn't as good as Yona's.

"Do you want some barknut?" Faro whispered at her side. They pulled out a small packet of the red powder from their pocket. "Yona gave me some last night. Just in case you wanted some to sweeten your drink."

Anoor smiled, touched that her grandmother had thought of it.

"Yes, please."

Faro tipped some of the powder into the tea. Anoor swirled the mug and tasted it.

"Better?" Faro asked.

"Better."

Faro slipped the powder back into their pocket. They both had to run to catch up with the commune leader who had ducked into a classroom.

The school children all watched Anoor with a sense of awe as soon as she was introduced. Some even began to weep.

Anoor drank deeply from her mug, trying to hide her discomfort. She wasn't used to this reverence. She was used to being ignored. Or abused.

The only person who had ever looked at her like that before was Sylah.

Anoor conjured her lover once more to keep the fire in her gaze burning.

Their children are just like the citizens of the empire, Sylah. The people I'm going to save.

Anoor imagined Sylah's response: *Burn bright, my little kori bird, burn bright.*

Her words set the blood in her veins singing like the melody of the song of the sea. The rest of the school tour passed in a daze.

Lunch was had in the Violet Commune upon copper plates made

from the copper ore in their mines. Qwa drank too many glasses of alpine wine, a sweet green liquor made from the region's indigenous grapes.

"So, you're telling me that for years, four hundred years . . . you've just been sitting here waiting for the Child of Fire?" Qwa slurred at the Violet Commune leader.

"Yes," the commune leader replied through tight lips. "Though 'sitting' and 'waiting' are not quite the phrases we'd use. Preparing for war is more astute."

Teta and Anoor exchanged a glance.

"Perhaps it's time we moved on," Teta said, before Qwa could insult anyone else.

The journey to the Indigo Commune required another trip by boat to the final isle. Anoor took pleasure in dunking Qwa's head in the water before they left the boat.

"What did you do that for?" he shrieked. The circle of brown hair around his bald patch had already begun to curl from the water. Anoor wondered where he'd found a hair press in the Volcane Isles.

"You need to sober up," Anoor said.

Qwa mumbled something to Faro, which sounded akin to "says you", but Anoor couldn't be sure.

The tour to the indigo-blooded was Anoor's favourite. For they gifted her something precious.

"When we heard of your arrival, we made sure that our stitchers were put to work. Everyone on the Isles has a set of armour, and this will be yours."

The commune leader pressed the clothing into Anoor's hands. She ran her thumb along it. "What is it made of?"

"Barrel cactus. We mulch and dry it to create this hardened leather. It won't deflect the tip of a sword, but it will give you added protection from falls and blunted attacks."

Faro strode out of the dressing tent in their new armour. "What do you think?"

The armour was a deep shade of green. Four squares tessellated over their shoulder making up the pauldron. A diamond of leather covered their torso, the end of which connected to a wide skirt of panelled material.

"You look wonderful, Faro," Qwa said. His expression always softened for his lover over everyone else. Thankfully his bout of drunkenness seemed to be easing.

"You do look ready for battle," Anoor agreed.

The commune leader turned to Anoor. "Why don't you go and try yours? We styled it a little differently."

Anoor put on the outfit behind the cotton curtain of the dressing tent. She donned the armour quickly before striding out towards the mirror on the other side of the room.

When she peered into the looking glass, she didn't recognise the person staring back at her.

With her hair gone her features seemed accentuated. The deep set of her eyes seemed unfathomable, her high cheekbones striking. The burns from the endless flame had left the skin on her face mottled but the rest of her was covered in armour.

And what an outfit it was.

The breastplate was a panelled corset embellished with studs along the hem. The cactus leather on the faulds had been stitched into a thick weave that draped on either side of her hips. A cape was clasped at her throat, protecting her back.

The gauntlets wrapped around her forearms to her elbows and the gloves, which fitted snugly, were adorned with metal claws at the end of each nail.

And in the centre of her chest woven in silver like threads of the moon was a spider.

She splayed her hand against it and felt the beating of her heart beneath her fingers.

I look like a warrior.

She saluted the commune leader by the waist like Yona had taught her. "Thank you for this gift."

Clad in her new armour, Anoor no longer felt the need to call on Sylah's memory. She was starting to feel more and more like the Child of Fire she was supposed to be.

She strode into the sixth commune of the day with surer footfalls. But then her steps faltered as she looked around.

This commune looked different. The straw huts were sparse and less thickly woven, as if there were not enough leaves to be braided into walls. Not only that but it *felt* different. Less welcoming.

Parents with tens of children huddled in doorways with narrowed eyes. Anoor had seen more than a few flashes of a blade by people's waists. She moved closer to Faro and Qwa.

Qwa gave her a distasteful look as she brushed his forearm with her own. Anoor ignored him. "How do the red-blooded contribute to the Isles?" Anoor asked Teta.

"Metallurgy—they create our weapons. There's a smaller forge in the centre of the town."

Anoor looked to the sky. A cloud of smoke bloomed in the distance, making the air taste bitter.

That must be the forge.

Qwa grunted. "But why do we need weapons, surely the godbeasts are enough?"

Teta shot him an annoyed glance. "There are far more people than godbeasts. Everyone not riding upon one of God's creations will be part of the infantry. We do not know the full might of the army we face."

Anoor frowned. "But we do, I know the details of the Wardens' Army intimately—"

A woman lurched out into the street and spat at Anoor's feet. "You are not worthy."

Teta lunged, pulling the woman by her long braids, and throwing her to the ground. Qwa pushed his body in front of Anoor's as Faro dived onto the assailant's legs, pinning her down.

Teta withdrew a dagger from the folds of her yellow dress and ran the blade through the woman's neck.

As she gurgled on her life's blood Teta said, "I pray Kabut grants you forgiveness in paradise."

It was all over in a few breaths. Anoor stood still, paralysed by the amount of blood that had just come out of one person.

I have seen more dead bodies in the last two days than I have in a lifetime, she thought.

But if Yona had it right, then Kabut welcomed sacrifice and would bless Anoor for being the cause. She swallowed her immediate horror and tried to reframe the woman's death.

She closed her eyes and prayed like Yona had taught her.

"Glorious one up above, you who knows no bounds or boundaries. You, who spins the web of my future, take my pain, and bless me anew," she murmured.

The prayer gave her a flicker of strength. When she opened her eyes, Teta was wiping her blade on the woman's trousers. Then she strode back to Anoor. "I apologise, Child of Fire, the red-blooded were made to believe that one of their own would be the prophesied child. It is perhaps a good idea to move quickly through this commune. I will speak to the leader of what happened here today."

Anoor nodded numbly.

The blue-blooded commune welcomed Anoor much more happily, being one of their own. This commune was the largest, spanning across fields of wheat and corn. But she only half-listened to their commune leader as she discussed their agricultural land—because her mind was filled with the words of someone else.

You are not worthy.

The clear-blooded lived in the final commune. Here Anoor felt herself begin to relax once more and feel at ease. She couldn't help the grin that filled her features and lifted her eyes as she saw Ghostings who hadn't been maimed.

"This could be the empire in the future," Anoor said to Qwa. Faro stood apart from them talking to the commune leader about the healing skills of their inhabitants.

"I don't think there'll be any Ghostings left after the final battle, Anoor," Faro said under his breath.

"What do you mean?"

Qwa snorted. "You think the godbeasts can tell Embers from Ghostings?"

Anoor's grin fell. "No, they'll stop the godbeasts after they destroy the wardens."

"Will they?"

Anoor frowned. No, this was not a part of the plan. She would lead the Zalaam into war against the wardens, not the Ghostings.

But Qwa was right, the queller hadn't known not to kill one of its own let alone to separate Ghostings from Embers.

I won't let it happen. The Ghostings have suffered enough.

Sacrifice was one thing, but murder was something else entirely. And right now, Anoor could still tell the difference between the two, even if that line was blurring by the day.

She jogged to match her pace with Teta's. "Can you take us back? I need to speak to my grandmother."

CHAPTER SEVENTEEN

Jond

Niha Oh-Hasan has been reinstated as a full member of the Zwina Academy under the charter of the third law. Let the record show, all former crimes have been forgiven. Beyond that, Oh-Hasan is granted permission to teach without a licence as outlined by act two, section twelve per the requirements of military necessity.

—Updated ledger documenting
graduates of the Zwina Academy

Flashes of white.

Cold. Ice cold. Sharp cold.

Voices, so many voices.

Then warmth.

Jond woke smothered in fur. He coughed, and the mound of fur meowed.

"Rascal?" His voice was hoarse from disuse. A pink nose and blue eyes filled his vision. "Hello, little one. Though I shouldn't say little, you've grown a whole handspan in the week I've been gone."

"Two weeks," a voice said.

"What?"

"You've been in a coma for a week." Niha's smiling face came into view. His one eye was overfilled with joy to see Jond awake. He lifted Rascal off Jond's chest.

Jond sat up and yawned. He was back in the City of Rain, the fleshy mushroom walls a strange comfort. "Why was I in a coma?"

"You had a bleed on your brain."

"Oh, that's what that was." Jond ran his hands through his hair, glad to feel his head was still firmly on his shoulders. "Zenebe healed me?"

Niha grinned. "Yes, and so did I." He waved his orb at Jond, currently held in place with a leather strap.

"Good to know healing came back quickly to you."

"Yes, or you'd be dead," he said matter-of-factly. Niha took a seat on the chair next to the bed and propped his feet up on the covers. Rascal used his legs as a bridge to get back to Jond. He stroked the kitten as he waited for Niha to tell his tale.

"It was quite dramatic actually."

"Oh yeah?"

"Kara came running into the council chamber requesting aid. She demanded the use of a flighter, the only flighter left in the City of Rain, I might add, to rescue you, *immediately.*" Niha spoke lightly, his eyebrows arched upwards.

"The council said no, of course. So, she threatened to leave the Blood Forged unless someone helped her, all the while refusing healing until you were brought back."

"I'm guessing they listened to her then?"

"You'd be dead if they hadn't. She walked around with that broken wrist for two days as Zenebe and I worked on you. Apparently, when Zenebe did get round to healing her, he had to break the bone again as it had already started healing incorrectly."

Jond winced. He didn't like the idea of Kara in pain, especially if he was the one responsible for it.

Niha watched Jond curiously before saying, "I have a question for you . . . What is going on between you and Kara?"

Jond's laugh was disbelieving. "Oh, nothing, less than nothing. I guarantee you she wanted to save me to ensure there was someone she trusted to lead the army into battle."

"Aha! So, she trusts you!"

Jond gave Niha a sardonic grin. "Barely."

Niha was flipping something across his knuckles. When he saw Jond looking he gave an apologetic grin.

"Sorry, I'm trying to keep my muscles nimble. It's been a while since I wielded an orb."

"What is it?"

"Just a coin. One of the smaller denominations of the money we use."

Niha handed it over and Jond inspected the bronze disc.

"I've never seen Tenio's currency before. Is that the Queen engraved on the back?"

Niha nodded, his lip wavering. He'd been a true royalist, and her death had hit him hard.

Jond looked at the small picture. The coin had been rubbed smooth so all he could make out of the Queen was a hint of curly hair. He passed it back to Niha. "Is that food behind you? Hand it over."

Niha left Jond to eat and wash.

Jond moved around his room slowly. He had never been healed by the third charter before, but he remembered Sylah explaining it: "It's like you're both invigorated and tender. Like your flesh and blood is new, but you need to get used to your body."

He nodded at the Sylah in his memory. It was exactly like that. He felt tired but also felt the itch to exercise.

Rascal refused to leave his side as he washed and dressed. "I missed you too, little one," he said to the sandcat.

She chirruped at being addressed and wove in between his feet. He picked her up and placed her against his chest beneath his coat.

"You really have grown. By the blood, I'm going to have to get a bigger coat." Rascal tucked her chin under Jond's as he went out into the rain.

Everyone turned to look at Jond as he entered the council chamber. He pulled down his hood and greeted them all.

"Not dead yet," he said.

"Jond!" Ads barrelled into him, the hug constricting his ribs uncomfortably. The young Ghosting was laughing with delight. "I thought you were going to die. But you didn't, you survived."

"That I did. Ads, you're squashing Rascal."

"Oh, no."

Jond withdrew the kitten and handed her to Ads. "Why don't you go and get Rascal some food, she looks hungry to me."

"She's always hungry." Ads rolled her eyes but took the hint and headed out of the council chamber.

The temperature in the room seemed to drop as soon as she left. There were no laughter or smiles in the strained atmosphere.

Elder Dew stood nearest to Jond wearing the least hostile expression. They nodded deeply at him, part acknowledgement, part welcome. Jond noticed Dew wasn't using a cane and wondered if they too had partaken of the healing powers of Councillor Zenebe.

Elder Ravenwing stood next to Councillor Sui, a light-skinned woman with green veins. Jond noted the link of runes around their wrists allowing them to speak into each other's mind. Elder Reed sat straight-backed, her blue eyes boring into Jond's, a look of distaste—her default expression—adorning her features.

Kara's face was once again covered, though her eyes looked bored. She hadn't looked Jond's way since he had entered the room. The concern she'd had for him appeared short-lived.

He swallowed his bitter disappointment. She was just an asset to him, someone she trusted to lead the army into battle.

But even when he'd spoken those words to Niha, he'd harboured a small bit of hope that it had been something more. That perhaps her concern had been because she cared.

It is clear she does not.

Councillor Zenebe stepped towards Jond, pulling him from his thoughts of Kara. Recently, his mind had been lingering on her more often than he liked.

"How are you feeling?" The councillor's kind face split into a smile.

"Alive, thanks to you and Niha."

"And Kara," he said with a touch of disapproval.

Jond nodded in Kara's direction. Still, she didn't look at him, but he thought he saw her eyes crease as if she was smiling. It was then that he noticed a stranger flanked by two guards, standing in the far corner of the room. He wasn't sure how he hadn't seen them earlier as they were covered head to toe in furs. "Who's that?"

Before anyone could answer they stepped forward and lowered their hood revealing a delicately boned face, and green eyes lined with thick lashes. "I am Olina, of the Winterlands." She spoke the common tongue like it was poetry. Her red hair, more auburn than Kara's burnt crimson, was short and cropped by her ears.

There he was, thinking about Kara again.

"The Winterlands?" he asked, interrupting his own trail of thoughts.

"She arrived a week ago, with her fleet of longboats, to join our cause," Kara said. She was impatiently tapping her fingers on the table. Jond noticed the skin around her glove was swollen and a little purple.

"Rendering your journey there useless—" Councillor Elyzan grumbled. A knot of vines wrapped around his neck. As a councillor of the first law, he could grow and manipulate plants.

Zenebe raised a placating hand. "Let us not play this argument out again. Kara knows she was in the wrong."

Kara was definitely smiling beneath her scarf. It tweaked Jond's own lips.

"And Jond Alnua, does he know? The Blood Forged do not make individual decisions, we are not a monarchy." Elyzan's eyes flashed to Jond.

"Ravenwing agrees," Councillor Sui voiced on behalf of the elder.

Ravenwing gave Jond a bloodthirsty grin, baring the scarred flesh of his tongue.

"I get it, we did wrong, now can we go back to the matter at hand? Shouldn't we be celebrating or something? We finally have our navy," Jond said.

Kara looked at him for the first time and he felt his skin prickle. Then she laughed scornfully. "We don't have a navy, Jond. We have three ships."

Jond's jaw went slack. He took a moment to gather it up again.

"Three? And they can take . . . ?" he said.

"Thirty people."

"Shit."

"Precisely," Kara muttered.

Olina thumped her heavy boots on the ground.

"I did not brave the warm currents to be disrespected so. My entire family are dead, my chief, as you tell it, perished beneath the snow. I have brought fifty soldiers to fight, and they will fight with the strength of a thousand of yours."

Kara said, with a diplomatic smoothness Jond was getting used to hearing, "Olina, I apologise, I did not mean to disrespect you. Only our outlook is dire—"

There was a movement in the corner of Jond's vision, and he swung his gaze just in time to see the guard beside Olina lunge forward. There was a flash of metal and a spray of orange, then a gurgle.

Zenebe fell to the floor, his hands clutching the gaping wound in his neck.

The room erupted, Kara blinking away from her seat to arrive behind the guard who had attacked. She stabbed them in the centre of their back with a dagger.

The vines around Elyzan's neck grew at speed, branching towards the attacker until they were restrained in a tangle of leaves.

Jond took no chances and ran towards Olina, pulling her arms behind her back. The woman didn't resist. Instead, she seemed frozen in horror at her fallen comrade.

"Zenebe, hold on, hold on. I can heal you." Niha was crouched beside his old teacher, his orb patterning the older man's skin with his blood. But nothing was happening.

Because he was already dead.

A low moan emanated from the corner of the room. It was coming from Sui. She would have fallen if Ravenwing hadn't held her up with his arms. Sui looked to Olina.

"You did this." Sui's grief turned to anger in the space of two breaths. Olina slowly raised her head.

"I—I didn't know," she said with numb lips.

Sui lunged for her, and Ravenwing let the woman go. Sui pulled out what looked like a pen from her waterproof robes and drew it back as if to plunge it into Olina's face.

"Stop. Drop the poisoned dart." Kara's tears had merged with the attacker's indigo blood on her cheek.

She held aloft a letter.

"The assassin was working alone. This was on his body. It's from the Zalaam."

Sui dropped the poisoned dart and reached for it. She read out loud:

"To all the Blood Forged,

We hear you, we see you. We welcome your fight. Honour to Jano Reduo who gave his life to take one of yours. He has passed into Kabut's realm in favour.

We have our Child of Fire. The time for war has come. We bring the battle in two turns of the moon on the shores of the Drylands. And if you do not come, we will find you. For every non-believer must be purged.

To win we must begin again."

The silence was broken only by the dripping of Zenebe's blood on the ground.

Drip, drip, drip.

It sounded like the ticking of a clock.

CHAPTER EIGHTEEN

Hassa

We must reinforce the Keep's gates and increase patrols in the courtyard. Nar-Ruta stinks of insubordination, and without a Warden of Strength to lead us, I, Warden Pura of Truth, have stepped up to take on this holy path. You will report to me going forward.

—Letter sent to General Dullah of the Wardens' Army

Hassa watched Sylah follow Gorn in the chaos after the army's arrival at the plantations. She moved to join her, but someone caught her by the arm.

"Eyoh, Hassa, I've been waiting for you to return all night. You never cleaned my dress." Turin's lacquered nails dug into Hassa's forearm above the inkwell she wore. She held the smoking butt of a radish-leaf cigar in the other.

"Turin, let my daughter go." Vahi appeared by Hassa's side. She wrenched her arm free from Turin and turned to her father.

We all need to go unless we want to be caught by the army.

Officers had begun firing runebullets into the dispersing crowd, as if the small projectiles could do anything to stop the tidewind of truth that Gorn had let loose in the empire.

Nothing would be the same again.

Turin smiled sweetly at Vahi. "Oh, so you figured it out then. Yes, indeed, Hassa is your daughter." Her grin turned to a sneer. "But she is still *my* servant." Turin tugged on the purple and yellow waistband around Hassa's waist.

Vahi hissed.

Vahi, it is fine. Let us go with her, for wherever we go today, she will find us. We might yet use her in the war to come.

Vahi hesitated. His long face pulled down in a frown.

"Are you sure?"

No, but we don't have time to argue.

He nodded. "Let's go."

Turin's answering chuckle was triumphant.

They weaved through the mass of people aided by the ease of Turin's Gummers who had come out of the crowd to flank them. The Purger jogged at the front of the procession, using brute force to carve a pathway through the chaos.

Dusters were flung left and right as they made their way through the Dredge. The army was at their heels, but Turin's Gummers had been trained under Loot, and they knew how to use their muscles.

When they arrived at the maiden house the Purger opened the door for Turin. Hassa and Vahi were cajoled in a little more violently by the Gummers who made up the rear of the group.

"Get off me," Vahi said, pulling away from the grip of a young man who had jerked him forward.

Hassa, more used to being treated like a tool, let them manhandle her until she was standing and panting in the centre of the room.

"Close the tidewind shutters," Turin said to the Purger. There was only a slight sheen of sweat on her upper lip. Her violet dress and woven braids still looked pristine—certainly not like she'd just been chased by the Wardens' Army for half a league.

Hassa surveyed the room. Ala stood passively watching, the coffee already stewed on the table in front of her.

Hassa turned to Ala. *Did you not come to the plantation fields?*

No, there was nothing spoken that I did not already know.

But this changes everything.

Ala raised her immaculately painted eyebrows. *Does it? I am still a servant.*

Hassa growled low in her throat. *You do not have to be.*

No, I do not, but I am not a soldier, Hassa.

Hassa scowled and turned away before taking a seat on the sofa next to Vahi. There was a gasp from Ala at Hassa's audacity, but Hassa had played the servant for too long.

Turin turned to her. "So, you can bloodwerk."

The tidewind shutters clattered into place, rupturing the silence.

Hassa looked at Turin coolly and nodded.

"The empire, is what the Truthsayer said true? It was once the Ghostings'?"

Again, Hassa nodded.

The Purger whistled between her teeth. "This changes everything." Purger gave voice to the words Hassa had just signed to Ala.

And Turin reacted similarly. "This changes nothing," she snapped. "I am still the Warden of Crime and the Dredge is my jurisdiction. This Truthsayer should have come to me first."

The quiet grew tense as the Gummers looked to each other, the floor, the ceiling—anywhere but at Turin.

Vahi rested his elbows on his knees and leant forward. "Turin, nothing is your jurisdiction anymore."

Turin got up and began to pace, seemingly not hearing what Vahi had said. "War . . . war is profitable. Hassa, this Truthsayer, what do you know of them?"

Hassa shrugged. She wasn't about to tell her anything about Gorn.

"Can you get them a letter? I'd like an audience."

Hassa's eyes narrowed to slits. She was done being Turin's lackey. There were no more secrets to glean from being a Ghosting in her employ. The elders would understand that Hassa no longer needed to continue the guise.

"Please, Hassa," Turin said.

Someone in the room choked on their saliva. Here was the Warden of Crime pleading with a Ghosting.

Hassa savoured it while she considered. Turin could be a good ally for Gorn.

Tell her I will get her an audience with the Truthsayer. But it will be the last thing I will ever do for her.

Vahi repeated her words. Turin's gaze didn't leave Hassa's until she nodded.

"Fine, but I want to meet the Truthsayer today."

And that was that. Her whole life Hassa had given Turin a semblance of allegiance—even if it had been a ruse. Now it was over, and Hassa felt no different than she had before.

Maybe a touch lighter, she thought.

Hassa got up to leave.

"I'll come with you," Vahi said, rising too.

"No—" Turin started.

"Your threats no longer hold me here, I will go where my daughter is."

Hassa felt the warmth of his support at her back, but it wasn't until they were outside that she signed, *I think it is best if I go alone. I know the Truthsayer.*

"Oh, all right. Are you sure?"

Yes, and . . . Vahi. This last thing I do for Turin is the last thing I do for anyone. I'm leaving the city tonight.

Vahi took a deep breath. "Hassa, I understand, and I wish I could remove the chasm of years where I was absent from your life. You know I would never have left you here, with her—"

Hassa held up an arm.

I would like you to come with me if you are willing? The Ghostings in the Chrysalis could do with an extra armoursmith, I am sure.

Vahi's wide smile was answer enough, but he said, "Yes, if you will let me, I would like to see the Chrysalis and help the Ghostings in any way I can."

I'll meet you tonight, at the forge. Be ready for a long journey.

"I'll be there."

Hassa suspected where Gorn's lair was. She'd heard pacing in the tunnels a few days ago but hadn't had time to investigate. The sounds had been far enough away that Hassa hadn't been alarmed.

She made her way north through the pathways beneath the Dredge. When she reached a crossroads, she paused, casting the runelight down a tunnel to her right.

Jagged shadows erupted on the wall cast by rocks and the crumbled remains of the tunnel. Hassa felt a sob choke her throat as she looked at the wreckage left from the explosion that Kwame had inadvertently caused. It looked like the broken tatters of her heart.

With a heavy sigh that raked at her throat she turned away and down the opposite corridor towards the flickering light in the distance.

Hassa didn't mask the sound of her footsteps as she approached.

"Hello, is someone there?" a voice called out.

The sound of shifting metal drew closer until Gorn came into view at the tunnel's entrance. She had her helmet off, but the tidewind armour still on. Hassa wondered whether she ever took it off anymore.

"Hassa." Though they didn't hug, Gorn's voice held the same affection as an embrace.

She stepped into the room Gorn had made her own. A straw pallet was tucked away in the corner, almost as an afterthought among the piles of notes and maps. Hassa spotted the edge of a worn zine sticking out from the blanket on the bed and wondered how Gorn was faring since Anoor had gone.

You have been very busy, Hassa signed with a small smile. She always had to sign slightly slower for Gorn. Her lessons with Hassa had often been cut short by her other duties as chief of staff.

"Yes, someone had to start telling the truth."

They did.

"And time is running out. More than I thought. Have you seen Sylah?"

Hassa's eyes flashed. *I have. Though only briefly. Her mind is love-clouded. She cannot see beyond Anoor. We all had to let Anoor go in the end.*

Gorn grimaced and her eyes turned wet. "Yes, we all had to let her go in the end."

Hassa circled the room taking in all the notes and drawings of the Keep. She pulled up a piece of paper between her limbs. It was a detailed map of the Keep's courtyard with the doorways highlighted in red.

Gorn came to stand behind her. "The wardens spent the last few mooncycles sharing with me all the secrets of the Guild of Strength. They did not know how valuable that information would be."

Very valuable indeed. You plan to make an army out of plantation workers?

Gorn sighed. "Yes, it will be difficult and there will be losses, but I think we can do it."

You'll need warriors to lead, to help plan.

Gorn's smile was tight. "I have sent messages to contacts in the Keep who I think will be sympathetic to the cause. But they are all Ember servants, not soldiers."

The Warden of Crime has over a hundred people in her employ. They will not be trained warriors like the Wardens' Army, but they are a start.

"Will she join the rebellion?"

She has asked to meet with you today. Offer her riches, contracts, anything monetary.

Gorn shook her head. "These things will not matter when the Zalaam come to our shores."

Exactly, let her name her price. It will be high, but it will not matter.

Gorn pondered for a moment. "I will meet with her. Here, alone. Sixth strike."

Hassa nodded once and turned to leave.

"Will you come?"

Gorn had always seen more than anyone ever realised. It was why she was the perfect person to lead this rebellion.

No. My father has found me, and together we will be travelling to the Chrysalis.

Gorn didn't ask her to stay.

"Thank you, Hassa, for the years you carried the burden of the empire's secrets. I don't know how this rebellion will go, but I hope I see you again soon."

Scythes and blood. The signs were all angles and sharp movements, but they felt right to part with.

"Scythes and blood," Gorn replied.

Then Hassa slipped into the darkness and traversed the tunnels to the maiden house for the final time.

With her last duty complete, Hassa made her way to Vahi's forge. She had packed light, just some food, water, her hormone herbs, and the inkwell mould. They were lucky that the wardens had called the full might of their army to Nar-Ruta. It meant it was unlikely they'd meet officers on the road. As every single officer was in the capital city.

Hassa had considered stealing an eru, but the creatures couldn't travel in the shortcuts beneath the ground.

Vahi was waiting for Hassa when she arrived. He was dressed in tidewind protection armour.

"I didn't get to show you this before, but I made you one too. We can travel during the night if we need to."

The armour was mirror-polished with far more intricate embellishments than the other pieces he had made for Turin. But though lovely, they weren't what captured Hassa's attention. The gauntlets tapered at the wrist with additional joints so Hassa could still sign when wearing it. There was also a slot for her to attach her inkwell, which would allow her to practise on the journey, because there was no carrying this armour. She was either wearing it all the time, or not taking it at all.

She chose the former and dressed quickly. Even the hinges had been fused with chains so she could clothe herself by looping them through her arms.

"Do you know the way?"

Yes, I have memorised it enough times. There are tunnels we can travel in for the first few days, then we must follow the brightest star in the sky north-east.

Vahi opened the door, but before he crossed the threshold he turned to Hassa and spoke. "Are you ready to leave it all behind?"

Hassa looked past him to the Dredge beyond.

Yes, it is time to go home.

CHAPTER NINETEEN

Sylah

To all Embers who require safety and solace,
The Keep's gate will be open between seventh and eighth strike
tonight. After which we will be sealing and barricading the doors.
The wardens do not tolerate the spread of lies, and once decorum
is reinstated the Keep will open its doors once more.

—Letter hung from the Keep's gates

Sylah stepped into the dim glow of runelight in Gorn's lair.

"I brought you a present," she drawled before throwing a bound and gagged Tanu into the runelight. There was a shriek, too high to be Gorn's. Sylah turned bleary eyes to the other person in the room.

"Maiden Turin?"

The maiden turned to Sylah and scowled. "Warden Turin to you, Sylah."

Gorn went and knelt beside Tanu, who had balled herself into a foetal position. "Sylah, why is Disciple Tanu on the floor?"

"Ransom her. Use her as a bargaining tool, or something." Sylah tore her gaze away from the red line across Tanu's throat in case she finished what she had started.

Gorn pulled Tanu to her feet and set her on the edge of the bed. Her eyes went distant as if she were planning something.

"Has Hassa been here?" Sylah asked Gorn.

"She's gone," Turin said with a sour smile. "Left with that father of hers, going north she said."

"Father?" Sylah exclaimed.

Turin waved a hand. "Oh yes, long story. He didn't know she was alive, I was blackmailing him for information on his daughter, Hassa figured it out . . . you know how it goes." Turin shrugged.

Sylah lowered herself to the ground. There was so much Hassa hadn't told her.

But we weren't really on speaking terms, Sylah reminded herself.

Sylah had wanted to reconcile with Hassa. Tell her what she'd learnt about Anoor. But if she was going north then that meant she was going—

"To the Chrysalis," Sylah whispered to herself.

"Huh?" Turin said.

Sylah turned her question to the warden. "What are you doing here?"

"The Truthsayer." Turin said her name with mockery. "And I were in the middle of negotiating my role in the new government in exchange for my Gummers in the rebellion."

"What are you talking about?"

"I'm to be Warden of Duty," Turin said with a flourish of her hand.

Gorn caught Sylah's eye and wearily nodded her head.

Sylah burst into laughter. "You are going to be Warden of *fucking* Duty?"

Turin shifted her shoulders like a bird ruffling its feathers. "Yes, and I'll run the empire better than any Ember ever could."

Sylah couldn't stop laughing. Here was Turin planning for a future that wouldn't exist.

Turin began to take offence, her plump lips pressing together in a thin line. "Well, what do you bring to the rebellion other than this sacrifice to the cause?"

The word "sacrifice" struck Sylah like a whip, and she jerked forward, the heaviest bead in her hair striking her against the head. She went to unravel it from its binding in her braid. The obsidian orb was cool against her palm. The small runes engraved in the stone bore flecks of the previous owner's blood.

The law of creation could sway the course of the rebellion.

But could she use the runes again?

The last time she had failed in her task of destroying the Tannin. But maybe this was her chance to make a difference in this war.

For Anoor was gone, and Sylah had no other purpose. Except this one.

Hassa had been right all along. This was where she needed to be. Fighting for the Ghostings, fighting to be free.

I wish you were here, Hassa. I should have told you that I stood with you. And I'll use every tool in my arsenal to burn the empire down.

Sylah brought the orb up to the runelight, casting shadows across the ceiling.

"You ask what I bring? I bring deathcraft."

Sylah made her way across the Tongue and into the Ember Quarter. It was her first time in the district since Gorn had condemned Embers with the truth. It had been a long few days.

Fresh graffiti covered the villas, the words illegible. It was the first time most Dusters had ever written words. Litter filled the streets and fires softly burnt in looted buildings.

In the first few days the army had tried to keep the riots in check. But 80,000 plantation workers without jobs meant they had a lot of time to cause mischief. The wardens had called the retreat in the second week, drawing the army behind the safety of the Keep's doors.

Sylah slipped down a side street towards the eru stables.

The barn doors were wide open, the erus inside long gone.

"Fuck." She'd been banking on finding an eru here. She needed one to mimic the movements for her creation.

As she turned to leave, she heard the distinctive trill of an eru. At the back of the barn was another room, where Tomi had lived. It wasn't large enough to hold an eru, so she hadn't looked.

She picked the lock with the piece of wire braided into her hair. It had once been a part of Elder Zero's belt, before he sacrificed himself to the Tannin. The unlocked door swung open.

Someone lunged at her. "You touch her, and I'll kill you!"

Tomi held up a hammer, his face tight with fury.

Sylah cocked her head. "Tomi? What are you doing here?"

He collapsed in relief. "Oh, it's just you. Sorry, I've been hiding here for two days. People keep stealing the erus and I won't let them take her, I won't."

"Her?" Sylah looked past Tomi to see the ruby-red scales of Berry. His room wasn't big enough to fit a full-grown eru, but a juvenile? Just about.

"Tomi, why don't you and Berry come to the Dredge? I'm sure we could find an old stable to house her in."

Tomi shook his head fiercely. "No, no, no. Here we have food, we have shelter."

"But what about the rebellion? Don't you want to fight?"

Tomi looked pained. "I have to look after Berry."

He's just a child. He must have only been branded four years ago, five at the most.

"Fine, but be safe, all right? Here, take this dagger, I've got more where it came from. And untuck your thumb when you stab."

He took the dagger gratefully.

"I need to ask one thing though. I have to draw something on Berry."

Tomi frowned. "What?"

"It won't hurt her, just a couple of runes."

"Why?"

"It'll take too long to explain."

He chewed his lip then said hopefully, "Got any more slabs?"

Sylah shook her head. "I don't think they'll be all that helpful right now anyway."

"Fine. You did give me the dagger."

"Yes, I did."

He moved out of the way of the door and let Sylah enter.

The eru shrilled at her as she approached her. Sylah tried to sound soothing. "Hello, Berry, remember me? I almost stole you."

The great beast grunted, huffing a spray of spittle at Sylah's face, and she laughed.

"You remind me of Boey, an eru I rode once. She had the same temperament."

Sylah ran a hand over Berry's scales. "Now, I'm going to draw just a couple of runes here. They're not going to hurt."

As Sylah's stylus touched the eru, the creature balked. Tomi was there in a moment, whispering softly by her head until she calmed, and Sylah could continue. "There, all done."

Hopefully that rune sequence will help my creation mimic an eru's movement.

Now all she had to do was match the pattern to her whitestone structure.

"Thank you, Tomi. If you change your mind about fighting, come to the Dredge and ask for me. I'll make sure you're looked after."

Tomi's brows knotted together but he nodded.

Sylah left hoping she'd see him again but knowing that she might not.

She walked quickly back the way she had come, not stopping until she reached the old maiden house in the Dredge.

Sylah entered the building to the sound of the Purger and Turin arguing.

"We're going to need more weapons than that if you want to win the war," Turin said coolly.

"I carried as much as I could!" the Purger replied.

"I'm not sure why you're still here, you should have already gone to fetch more. Take more Gummers with you if you must."

Sylah smirked as the Purger stomped past her. The assassin was used to cutting throats, not going on errands. She hissed at Sylah as she passed.

The living room was filled with supplies for the upcoming battle. Maps and papers littered the wall, brought from Gorn's old hideout. And among it all were two glittering eyes.

Tanu sat chained to a chair. She wore no gag, though she hadn't spoken a word since the wardens had refused the terms of her ransom: her life, in exchange for the general of the army.

Turns out the wardens didn't trust Tanu's tale of Anoor's kidnapping either. Despite the unpaid ransom, Gorn had insisted on keeping her alive just in case she could provide more information.

But not one word had passed Tanu's lips. The movement of her eyes as she tracked Sylah walking across the room was the only indication she was alive at all.

Sylah looked away and joined Gorn by a makeshift desk.

"We need a way to mobilise people in the other cities," Gorn said as Sylah joined her. "I can no longer use the printing press, the wardens destroyed the printers there."

Sylah thought for a moment. "What about the griots? Their network is far-reaching. And I'm sure they'll want to help."

Turin overheard and walked over. "I think that's a good idea." She grinned at Sylah. "You can do more than carve stone?"

Everyone thought Sylah's creation was a joke. Some days so did she.

"That stone carving might be the only reason we win this. Did you find another stonemason to help me?"

Turin's mouth twisted. "No, but you can use Ala. Ala, come here." A Ghosting with delicate features stepped forward. Sylah recognised her as one of Turin's former nightworkers.

"Do you have any experience with carpentry or stonemasonry?" Sylah asked her quietly.

No, though I have repaired my limestone villa many times after the tidewind has sought to break it. And I know a good recipe for mortar.

So, not a stonemason, but she could be of assistance. "That would be helpful. Come with me."

Sylah led Ala through the Dredge to a clearing that had once been called the Ring. The fighting competition had been Sylah's salvation for a time, and here she was, in the same place preparing to do battle again.

Ala circled Sylah's creation. *What is this?*

Sylah winced at the mound of whitestone. "It's supposed to be an eru."

She'd decided the eru's form would be the ideal shape and size for a creation of war. The whitestone brick would prevent the tidewind from destroying it and its speed and muscle mass would be optimal in helping break down the Keep's gates.

And you will be able to bring it to life?

"Yes, I will be able to bring this to life to help fight the wardens." *And lose a piece of me in the process*, she thought.

Well then, we'd better make sure it has feet. And a face. And a tail.

Ala laughed and Sylah joined in. But the laughter was brief, and their smiles soon turned brittle.

Anoor's face crept into her mind, as it always did. The Child of Fire, Tanu had named her.

But she was simply Anoor to Sylah. No title was worthy of her. The apparition beneath her eyelids smiled, her curling hair fluttering in an imaginary breeze. The baby hairs that framed Anoor's face were so soft, Sylah yearned to touch them again.

She felt herself lean forward as if to cup her cheek but when she blinked Anoor's face was replaced by the creation in front of her.

Sylah picked up a chisel and cracked through a piece of whitestone, shattering her thoughts along with it.

CHAPTER TWENTY

Anoor

What is paradise? Some have called it the haven of the true. But who is true and who is false? I like to think of paradise as my final rest. The unending sleep full of dreams and joy. Kabut will know when I am worthy of my place in his realm. I await it, and when it comes, I will welcome the last pain. For to win, we must begin again. And I intend to win.

—Last sermon delivered by commune
leader Andu before his death

The journey back to the Yellow Commune was a three-strike walk across land, but less than a third of that time by sea. Teta rowed the whole way while Faro and Qwa spoke quietly to each other at the back of the boat. Anoor sat in the bow, her mind churning like the currents they traversed.

Qwa suggested that the Zalaam intended to kill everyone in the empire, *including* Ghostings and Dusters.

No. Anoor shook her head. *Yona had always made it clear that it would only be the wardens who would suffer.*

But even as she thought it, she wondered if it were true. Had Yona ever specified only the wardens would get hurt?

Yona was waiting by the harbour as their little rowboat pulled in. Anoor resolved to confirm the details with her.

The nose of the vessel nudged onto the sand and Anoor waited for Teta to help her out. She'd learnt the hard way after tripping three times.

Her grandmother held a steaming mug of bitter leaf tea in her hand and held it out to Anoor, who accepted it gratefully. The evenings were much cooler than in the empire, and it was so cold she had lost the feeling in her fingers.

"How was the tour?" Yona asked.

Anoor took a sip before answering, the sweet liquid warming her throat. "Interesting. Do you like my new armour?"

Yona smiled. "You look ready to go into battle."

Anoor lifted her chin and straightened her shoulders as if an army stood at her back. For a moment she imagined they did. She felt the shadows of godbeasts and the fever of the Zalaam as they all looked at her to lead.

Her heart pounded with something akin to excitement.

Then Anoor remembered what Qwa had said about the Dusters and Ghostings.

"How are you going to protect the innocent from the godbeasts?" she asked Yona.

Teta looked from Yona to Anoor then said, "I think I'll take Faro and Qwa back to their hut."

Once they left Yona sighed and looked to the sky. The sun had set, giving rise to the soft cerulean of twilight. "Kabut's eye closes even more today, you see the way his gaze is narrowed. He watches us."

Anoor did not respond. She sipped slowly from her tea and waited.

Yona reached out a hand. "Come."

Anoor clasped her grandmother's hand and let herself be led across the beach. They stopped when they reached a rocky outcrop.

Yona folded herself up on one of the flattened rocks, crossing her legs with ease. The contours of her muscles could be seen through the silk of her dress as the material strained against her knees. "Sit with me."

Anoor joined Yona on the ground, squirming a little until the grit and pebbles shifted beneath her buttocks.

"My brother and I used to come here—" Yona began.

"You had a brother?"

The look Yona gave Anoor was full of pained impatience. She continued, "My brother and I used to come here every evening to share what food we had pilfered from the Foundry's canteen that day. We did not have a lot. We were orphaned young, and though children are cherished, my brother and I were not the easiest to raise."

Yona smiled showing teeth. "Once, Andu, the old commune leader, tried to keep us locked in our rooms at night. My brother faked an earthquake with drums and the stamping of feet. It sent Andu running to the fields so we could escape."

Her smile grew then fell. "The problem was, we weren't true believers, not then. How could we know what riches Kabut would bring us?"

Anoor took another sip of her tea. The hairs on her forearm stood on end and she felt herself become lulled by the story.

"But Kabut knew," Yona said. "He knew that I was destined to be the Wife. Only after the greatest thing had been taken from me—my greatest sacrifice. Inansi."

"Inansi?" Anoor had heard that name before. But right now, her thoughts felt a little hazy and she couldn't recall why the name seemed important.

"Inansi was my brother's name."

Anoor nodded. Yona must have told her that before. She dismissed her concern, only to jump to another. "Did you sacrifice your brother to the endless flame?"

Yona didn't speak for a time. Then she said, "No, perhaps if I had done, I would have been the Wife sooner. Inansi was lost at sea, though it was years later that I discovered his death had actually been in the Wardens' Empire."

Questions upon questions, but Anoor bit her tongue.

"The greatest sin to our God is to doubt, Anoor."

Anoor shivered, her heart racing. *Do I doubt?*

Godpower was very real, so too were the burns from the endless flame. But Kabut? She glanced up at the sky, at his scrutinising gaze. What she felt then couldn't be put into words.

Yona continued, "Those who do not believe do not have the eye

of our God. But through sacrifice they might yet be honoured with
a place in paradise."

"So those who don't believe in Kabut could still be saved—in
death?" She thought of Kwame.

"If we dedicate their sacrifice to Kabut, yes."

"And this paradise—what is it?"

Yona's dark eyes twinkled. "A place where we can be Gods."

The words settled into Anoor's bones and blood. Her veins prickled
with exhilaration, and not a small amount of trepidation.

*Was it better for innocents to die in the war and reach paradise or
survive and rebuild the empire?*

The question fractured her mind. "How am I even considering
this?" Her voice had the tone of Sylah's and it sobered her.
"Grandmother, we cannot kill those who have wished us no harm."

"Why do you doubt today, Anoor?"

Anoor shifted on the ground, her knees straining. "It's not that I
doubt exactly . . ." How could she deny the power of Kabut at work?
" . . . but Qwa said—"

"Qwa?" Yona's head snapped up. Her voice low and contained.
"What did Qwa say?"

"He . . . suggested that the Zalaam were intent on killing Dusters
and Ghostings, too."

"Are there not Dusters in the infantry of the Wardens' Army?
What of them, Anoor? Shall we test everyone's blood before we
strike?"

"No . . . but—"

"And the Ghostings who choose to serve the Embers in the Keep
instead of escaping to their little settlement in the north—oh yes, I
know about that—what of them, Anoor?"

"I . . ."

Yona looked at Anoor with the faintest twist of her mouth. Anoor
felt like she had failed her, and she searched for the words to turn
Yona's disapproval back to pride.

"I just think th-that m-maybe . . ." Her words stuttered to a stop.

Yona's eyes narrowed and she jutted her chin at the mug of tea.
"Finish your drink."

Anoor wanted to retort, but she was too afraid of further invoking

Yona's ire. She imagined how Sylah would have spat and shouted at for being talked to so. But Anoor was not Sylah.

Anoor hid her shame by downing the honeyed tea. The dregs of it left fine bits of red barknut powder on her tongue.

The barknut didn't taste that sweet and she found herself grimacing as she swallowed the last flecks.

When she had finished Yona said, "We must kill all who have served the wardens, Anoor. It is all of them or none. The Ending Fire comes, for we will bring it."

Anoor considered the alternative: the wardens continuing to destroy the lives of the people they ruled.

Click—

"No!" Anoor shouted. She balled her hands into fists, curling the leather of the armour. She would not, *could not*, let the wardens live. She met her grandmother's gaze.

"It is all of them or none," Yona repeated, stoking the fire of Anoor's rage.

She felt Yona's words resound with truth. Her heart hammered against her chest, sending small shocks along her veins. It wasn't entirely unpleasant, like Kabut had blessed her for hardening her resolve.

Anoor nodded once. Yona's displeasure gave way to a grin of triumph. And it felt like her grandmother had blessed her too.

Then her gaze narrowed on Anoor's gauntleted hand.

"The stitching has come away from the seam," Yona remarked.

Anoor looked down to her wrist, where, unbeknownst to her, a rip had formed in the fabric. It must have happened when she had pulled it taut from clenching her fists.

"That is a problem to fix tomorrow. Come, night has fallen around us, it is time to retire," Yona said.

Once more her grandmother offered her hand.

Once more, Anoor took it.

The next day, Yona sent Anoor and Faro back to the Indigo Commune to have the tear in her armour repaired.

"Can't we send Teta, or someone else? I want to work in the Foundry." Anoor itched to hone her skills with godpower.

Yona leant against the Foundry door. "No, it's good for you to be seen travelling through the Isles. I have reports that your tour yesterday was good for morale. But perhaps don't venture into the red-blooded commune."

Teta told Yona what happened, Anoor noted.

Faro shifted their feet and lifted their gaze to Yona's. "Wife," they said, "where is Qwa?"

"I sent for him this morning. He'll be helping me in the Foundry. We're testing some of the elements of the godbeasts. Of the three of you, his runes needed the most work, so I think this extra practice will do him good."

Faro's eyelids shuttered slowly, but they didn't ask any more questions.

"And Anoor, be careful." Yona's warning grated on Anoor. That morning she had awoken in a foul mood. Her skin felt sore and dry. The burn scabs had cracked in places, and she'd needed to call for more of the healing powder before getting dressed. It had made her late for breakfast, though she found she had little appetite.

Anoor turned to Faro.

"Let's go," she said without glancing back at Yona.

The trip to Violet Commune was uneventful. It took less than half a strike to have the garment sewn back together, though the stitcher who had been there the day before was nowhere to be seen.

"Yona probably punished him for the poor stitching. Armour is not supposed to rip," Faro said.

Anoor was about to reply that Yona wouldn't do that. But of course she would.

Faro continued, "They kill with less care than the wardens."

Anoor felt a flash of irritation.

"No, Yona is *not* the wardens."

But she had been, once. Anoor pushed the thought away.

Faro was watching Anoor wrestle with her mind, and their eyebrows quirked.

"Sacrifice is how we please Kabut, it is not senseless killing," Anoor said with more conviction. "In sacrificing the stitcher, she allowed him to find his place in Kabut's realm."

The words echoed with Yona's teachings, rinsed of feeling. For her feelings were complicated in this moment, and it was easier to put them aside.

"Yona is not the wardens," she repeated woodenly.

"No," Faro said, their face impassive. "She is not."

Then Faro smiled, and Anoor felt the tension of the moment ease. "Come, let us make our way back," they said. "If we row around the periphery of the Blue Commune, we will be back at the Foundry by lunch."

Each commune was connected to the sea in some way, though the largest port was in the Yellow Commune. Even then the boats weren't as big as the ship they had arrived in.

As Faro began to row, Anoor asked, "How will we transport the godbeasts to the empire?"

Faro shrugged their narrow shoulders. "How would I know?"

There was a rumble beneath their feet and Anoor leant over the edge of the boat. "What is that?"

The rumble increased in tempo, the waves rippling and swirling outwards. The sea grew murky as the volume of the sound grew louder.

"Earthquake!" Faro shouted. "Hold on to the boat."

They pulled in the oars and huddled together in the hull. The sea vibrated and shifted with the sound.

"What if the current drags us out to sea? We could be lost." Anoor had to shout to be heard.

"Then pray that doesn't happen."

Anoor wasn't sure Faro was being literal, but she called on Kabut. "Glorious one up above, you who knows no bounds or boundaries. You, who spins the web of my future, watch over us, your children, and guide us through this strife. Glorious one up above . . ."

Soon Faro was joining in her chant too. With their backs to the boat and their faces to the sky, not knowing where the currents were taking them.

As her lips moved her mind wandered. *What if I die here?* The thought was less painful than the next: *What if I never get to see Sylah again?*

A tear fell down her face and into the creases of her ear. Sylah was out there, perhaps on these very waters, seeking a solution to the growing tidewind. She was doing her part in this war, and Anoor was running errands.

Kabut, if I survive this then I promise I will not stop until the Zalaam are victorious. I will spend every day in the Foundry helping to bring godbeasts to life.

If Anoor brought an army and Sylah brought aid, then together they could break the empire and heal it again.

Her praying grew in volume and tempo. Her desperation to live surging through her faith.

Eventually the earthquake slowed then stopped.

Anoor sat up first, her eyes widening.

The ocean had pulled them south and they were less than a hundred handspans from the Yellow Commune port.

"Thank you, my God," she murmured.

Faro reached for the oars. "That was lucky."

"No, that was Kabut," Anoor said.

Faro didn't reply, or perhaps they hadn't heard her in the first place—their eyes had narrowed on something in the distance.

"What is that?" Faro asked.

Anoor followed the path of their gaze towards the peak of the mountainside.

The volcano was shrouded in a thick cloud of smoke.

Anoor ran through the streets of the Yellow Commune and up towards the Foundry. Fewer of the residential huts had collapsed this time, and Anoor hoped that meant fewer casualties.

The Foundry doors were open. She expected pandemonium but the crafters there were already back at work. After scanning the workstations Anoor made her way to the back warehouse.

"Grandmother?" Anoor called, searching the rows of godbeasts. She reached the balcony that overlooked the lower storage unit and peered over.

"Can you see her? Or Qwa?" Faro asked, joining her.

"No." Though crafters moved through the warehouse, none of them was Yona. Then Anoor noticed a gap among the godbeasts. A *very* large gap.

"The clawmaw is missing."

Faro raised a tired eyebrow. "Didn't Yona say she was testing a godbeast today? Maybe it was that one."

"Maybe."

Anoor looked beyond the missing godbeast to the door at the side that led to the laboratory. She ran to it and tried the door. But it was locked, as it always was.

"Child of Fire!"

The call came from behind her and Anoor turned to see Teta running towards her.

"What is it? Is my grandmother safe?"

"What of the volcano?" Faro interrupted with a more urgent question. "Is it going to erupt?"

Teta shook her head. "No, sometimes the volcano blows smoke, and though I admit that is more smoke than I have seen before, I do not believe it is something to worry about."

"Then what is it?" Anoor pressed. She was anxious to see her grandmother.

"There was an accident at the testing strip. Qwa—"

"What happened to Qwa?" Faro's voice rose to a volume Anoor had never heard before.

"Perhaps we should go to the open temple and let your grand-mother—"

Faro was already running. Anoor tried to keep pace but the lack of food that day made her weaker than normal.

Sylah would be so annoyed to see my stamina so low.

Anoor dipped beneath the legs of a queller.

But she'd be proud of the army I'm raising.

She ran through the Foundry and up the steps to the open temple two at a time, gaining on Faro. At the top, Yona was chanting over the fire, the shroud of a body flickering between the flames.

"Yona," Faro shouted. "Who is that in the fire?"

Yona finished her prayer before standing. She turned to Faro and Anoor.

"I am sorry, Faro. There was an accident during the earthquake. A godbeast fell upon Qwa and he perished."

Faro froze, their features going slack. "What? He's dead?"

Anoor felt the familiar sharp pain of grief. She hadn't liked Qwa all that much, but the three of them had been a team in this unfamiliar land.

Faro began to run towards the fire as if to plunge themselves into its depths. "Let them sacrifice themselves if that's what they wish," Yona said. But Anoor wasn't listening.

She lunged after Faro and pulled them back from the fire at the last minute. "No, Faro. Do not do this."

Faro was wailing, their cries incomprehensible beyond "love" and "gone".

Yona's words came back to her and she spoke them to Faro now. "Death has power. Let his sacrifice fuel you."

For the first time Anoor believed it. Kabut had saved her today, his touch guided their lost boat back to the Yellow Commune. And she had made a promise then, to fight for the Zalaam until the very end.

Yona watched Anoor from the other side of the temple, her expression full of pride. Faro's sobs quietened to a low drone. Anoor held them until the sun set, repeating Yona's words until Faro too spoke them on numb lips.

"Death has power. Let his sacrifice fuel you."

CHAPTER TWENTY-ONE

Jond

Queen Karanomo, our beloved,
Fair and ever true
See-ee how she rules our land
See-ee how she guides
Queen Karanomo, our beloved
She who serves me and you.

—Song sung during Queen Karanomo's coronation

Zenebe's passing-over rites were conducted the evening he died.

Jond stood on the periphery of the mourners as he listened to the tributes of the council.

It was different to funerals in the empire. No prayers to Anyme, or pyres to carry the soul to the sky in smoke. Instead, each person shared their treasured memories of Zenebe, bringing him to life with fond smiles and watery laughter.

The air smelt of wet earth and plant matter. Zenebe's body had been buried deep beneath the ground.

"To feed the next cycle of life," Niha had explained.

Jond thought the concept morbid and a little creepy. He padded his boots down on the wet mud, wondering how many skeletons were buried beneath his feet. It was raining softly, thankfully not flooding weather, though the lifts were nearby if the skies turned.

Hundreds of people had come out to grieve the councillor. They surrounded the Blood Forged members who stood closest to the burial site.

A beech tree sapling grew from the centre of the overturned earth, grown by Elyzan from a seed. Niha stood next to it sharing his story with the congregation.

" . . . and though I struggled with my final rune . . . Zenebe stayed with me all night until I finished the last carving." Niha's words were choked with sobs as he recollected his favourite memory of his old mentor.

Jond's eyes stung to see his friend grieving. It made him think of Sylah, and what he'd do if she died.

He shook his head, shaking the thought free.

No, Sylah is too angry to let death come for her.

Sylah was a fighter, just like him.

Niha stepped away from the sapling, sobbing. Jond couldn't imagine loving a mentor the way Niha had loved Zenebe.

Was that how I was supposed to feel when Master Inansi died?

Jond thought about what Kara had said about *choosing* where to belong. The Sandstorm had never given him that choice.

But he was choosing now.

Jond straightened his shoulders. They didn't have long. A couple of mooncycles until the final battle. Everything was against them, but still he held on to hope.

But he was worried this wouldn't be their last funeral before the end.

Elyzan stepped up to the sapling. The councillor looked haggard, his olive skin pallid, and shadows gathered beneath his brown eyes.

"For years we have stood by each other's side and there are too many great memories to recount. For you were a *great* man, Zenebe. He saved me more than once." Elyzan pressed his gloved hand to his heart. Jond knew that beneath the fabric roiled the vines that had petrified his hand. An experiment gone wrong.

Zenebe had managed to act just in time to stop the plant taking root beyond his wrist.

"I have always been a man of few words," he continued. "But let my actions here today show my love for you, my old friend."

Elyzan bent over the sapling. Jond saw his orb glint in the light as he inserted it into his hand.

A few moments later, coaxed by the blood-red runes drawn on its branch, the sapling began to grow.

And grow.

Every few handspans that the tree grew, Elyzan drew on more runes as if each pattern pushed the tree through a new season.

Half a strike later and the beech tree towered over them. Elyzan looked even more haggard now he'd lost so much blood, but he patterned the tree one more time.

The beech leaves changed from yellow to orange to a deep coppery brown. Then they started to fall, scattering the crowds in a sprinkling of colour. The wind carried some of the leaves across the rolling hills in the distance and Jond found himself making a prayer of his own.

"Anyme, grant Zenebe a place in your sky. We thank thee for what you give us. We praise thee for where you lead us. We serve thee for how you punish us. The blood, the power, the life."

But the prayer felt hollow. Now he knew that the invaders of the Ghostings' land had been the Zalaam, he could see the way that Anyme had been fused with their ideals.

Destruction and religion ever intertwined, he thought. But there was some good there too. But right now, in front of Zenebe's grave, it was difficult to glean the positives. The Zalaam justified their cause by their God's predilection for sacrifice. But what made Anyme a worthier deity than Kabut?

Jond rubbed his brow. He wasn't used to pondering the deeper meanings of life. It was why he'd always found it easier to follow than lead. Unlike some people who seemed so natural at it.

His gaze swung to Kara. Leaves fell around her, some landing in the kinks of her curls. She looked like an oil painting, her silhouette blurred by the drizzle. He had wanted to comfort her earlier, wrap his arms around her waist and hold her against his chest while she cried. Like he had held her in the Entwined Harbour, the memory seared into his mind. But he was worried she would plunge the assassin's knife into his chest if he tried, so he didn't try. He kept his distance.

And in any case, she didn't look like she needed consoling anymore. Her jaw was set under the face covering she wore. He could tell from the way the fabric contoured around her neck and the shadows it cast against her clavicle.

Still, he couldn't help but imagine his thumb running the length of her collarbone. And imagine her shiver in response.

"What is going on between you and Kara?" Niha had asked. The truth was, Jond didn't know. They couldn't stand each other, that was apparent, but beneath that was something magnetic that drew his gaze to her no matter where they were.

He shook the thought free. Kara *hated* him. Even if he was not entirely sure that he didn't hate her too.

Jond felt the air shift beside him and smelt mint. It sent his heart racing, and he wasn't sure why until he saw who had flighted next to him—Kara.

"I can't believe he's dead," she said. It was the first time the two of them had spoken alone since the Winterlands.

Jond wasn't sure what to say, so he settled on, "I'm sorry."

Kara chuckled as if Jond's sympathy was unnecessary. But he saw the tears in her violet eyes.

He was getting better at noticing when bravado masked her true emotions. Jond reached for her hand and squeezed it. He let go before she could fling him off.

Her breathing turned light and shallow. And the hand he had touched clenched slightly, as if she was squeezing him back, just a little too late.

The silence between them turned strained.

Jond gathered his thoughts and tried to voice the turmoil of emotions he was feeling. Because maybe, just maybe, she felt something too. "Kara, I wanted to say thank you—"

"Have you reviewed the changes Ravenwing put forward regarding personal guards for council members?"

Jond recoiled at the change of tone. Her voice was pitched higher, more formal than he was used to hearing from her.

Disappointment curdled his stomach, but if she wanted to pretend there was nothing crackling between them, then so could he.

"Yes, Ravenwing and I have already implemented the new regime," he said.

"Good, I hear we have received three hundred more refugees."

"Yes," he said through tight lips. "More soldiers."

"More funerals," she countered, the hardness in her voice softening. Grief flickered across her face as she looked at Zenebe's grave.

Jond didn't reach for her this time.

"We'll train them. *I'll* train them. Anyone who has blood in their veins can be a soldier. Bloodwerk will swing the tide of this war. With Sylah removing the threat of the Tannin—"

"The Tannin's not gone, Jond. Olina sighted it on her journey, though she wasn't within range of its tithe."

Jond felt like he was falling into snow all over again. "Sylah . . ."

"Sylah *failed*."

Jond took a step back. That meant Sylah was . . .

"No," he said firmly. "No, I don't believe it."

Kara made a disgusted sound in the back of her throat. "You're a fool, Jond."

Then she was gone.

Jond raised his gaze back to the burial site. The three Ghosting elders were approaching Zenebe's place of rest. A hush fell across the congregation as the elders began to sing.

The deep resonance of their throat-humming sent a shiver across the hairs on Jond's skin. The tune was haunting, their faces solemn.

Elder Dew stepped forward and signed upwards to the sky. Though Jond couldn't understand it he knew they were signing to Anyme.

The song turned to a major key, the elders' hums harmonising into a hopeful lilt. He closed his eyes and listened until it came to a stop.

Sylah wasn't dead. She couldn't be.

He held on to that thought before he turned on his heel and left the mourners among the dead.

The council didn't reconvene until the next day, and Jond was late. He'd only known he was late because he'd asked a passing student in the hall. Though he had a clock in his room, he had no idea how to read it. The knowledge had been kept secret from everyone but a select few in the empire, and he hadn't got round to admitting he didn't know how to read it yet.

He threw on his uniform. During his coma the Blood Forged had finalised the designs of their ranking system. Everyone in the army was given two sets of simple grey slacks and shirts made out of the waterproof fabric that Jond had learnt was called "fiscosa". The material was similar to rubber but had more flexibility so it could be woven into cloth.

As a higher-ranked official of the Blood Forged Jond was given a black boiled leather jacket. Three pins lay above the breast pocket shaped in the Blood Forged's insignia—a drop of blood surrounded by two blades. Lieutenants wore bronze, captains silver, and colonels gold. As major general, Jond wore all three.

He shrugged the jacket on and ran out of his room.

Last night was just a blurred shape of memory. He'd stayed up drinking all evening with Ravenwing. The date wine slipped down much easier than it did when it came back up this morning.

The rain was refreshing as he crossed the bridge, and since he hadn't had a chance to wash, the rain shocked some of the nausea from him.

When he reached the council chamber door, two guards stopped him. "No one enters." The larger guard bared his teeth.

Jond pulled down his hood. "I'm Major General Jond Alnua, I think I'm allowed to enter."

The soldier jumped in response to his command, pressing his wrists together, a new salute Ravenwing had instigated.

"Apologies, Major General, I thought you were already inside."

"Well, I'm not, so please stand aside."

Jond stepped into the thick atmosphere of a heated debate, but nobody was speaking.

He looked down at the table and saw the runes there. Jond took a seat next to Sui and pricked his finger.

"Add me in please?"

Sui frowned, breaking concentration from the discussion in her mind. "You're late," she said, taking a droplet of his blood and drawing a sequence of runes.

Jond was plunged into the mind discussion.

"Can someone explain to me what Sui and Kara are arguing about?"

"Jond Alnua, you are late."

"Too much date wine?"

"I agree with Kara."

"You don't even know what she was talking about."

Jond clutched his temples; the voices overlapped and all he wanted to do was scream.

"Silence!" Dew's voice eclipsed all others and Jond flinched. The telepathy granted by the second law allowed for the Ghostings to seamlessly join all discussions without the use of a translator.

"Kara," Dew said, "will you please illuminate the council? What are you and Sui arguing about?"

Jond looked across at Kara and noticed that there were dark rings around her eyes and the faint aroma of stale wine. Looked like someone else had also had a rough night. He wondered who she had been drinking with.

The flash of jealousy was unwelcome.

"We were arguing about nothing." Kara responded faster than she would have been able to speak.

"If they knew, if they knew you were still—" Sui began to say.

"No, we separated the two roles for a reason."

Jond's curiosity was piqued. "Two roles?"

"Enough of this." Reed's voice cut like being whipped by her namesake. "Speak plainly."

Kara seemed to concave inwards.

"It is our only chance, the only way to bring more people to our cause. More armies. More allies," Sui pressed, a little gentler.

Elyzan spoke for the first time. "Zenebe would agree. The old world is lost, in this new world you can be both."

Kara nodded, more to herself than anyone else. Then slowly, as she spoke, she straightened, her back growing taller, her chin lifting.

"When I came to the Academy to train, I came here under the guise of a different name, a different person. I didn't expect to excel as I did. I should have abandoned my studies . . . but the truth is . . . I loved it more than I had loved anything, other than—"

Her child. The child she lost. Kara swallowed and looked to Jond before continuing.

"When I was offered the role of councillor I refused. It was then that I told the council members why. But still they wanted my advice, my expertise. I was the best flighter in three hundred years, my ability to guide and teach others was second to none. Zenebe convinced me to pursue both roles, that doing good wasn't limited to just the one."

Jond felt a ripple of understanding around the table, but he still didn't grasp the context of Kara's words.

She looked away from him before she spoke again.

"My name is Karanomo, leader of the queendom of Tenio and fourth councillor to the Zwina Academy."

Jond stood, his shock lifting him upwards. "What?"

Kara turned and raised an eyebrow at him.

He slowly lowered himself down, his mind reeling. "The Shard Palace, it was destroyed." If he'd been speaking out loud and not through the mind link, he would have stuttered with shock.

"I survived because I was here, but I lost a lot of my people that day," Kara said.

"Your armies?" Ravenwing asked, his dark eyes glittering with hope.

"Our barracks were wiped out in the earthquake. Some may have scattered, but I expect those that survived made it here."

"They need to know you live. We need to give the people hope. We need to give your allies hope," Sui said, her pale green lips twisted.

"It made no difference, the Entwined Harbour know me as Karanomo, there is no knowledge they don't have, and they didn't come to our aid," Kara said.

Jond placed the truth of Kara's—*Queen Karanomo's*—identity into the context of his memories, knitting together some of the details he'd learnt. Kara said she'd been raised in the north of Tenio where the Shard Palace was. The father of her child had been a diplomatic partnership. She always wore a silk scarf across her face in big crowds. And the ocean guard had *bowed* to her.

"I'm such an idiot." Jond didn't realise the thought had projected out into the collective until Ravenwing agreed.

"Yes, and a lightweight, too." His grin was wide.

"Are there any other hidden identities we should know about?" Dew asked. They were clearly annoyed.

"No," Elyzan said. "But we should announce the Queen's pledge to the Blood Forged as soon as possible."

"We'll need to be on high alert for assassins. The Zalaam won't like that you survived the earthquake," Ravenwing added.

The topic turned to logistics: when would they present Queen

Karanomo to their troops and how best to get the word out to the remaining allies?

Kara was quiet, her mind elsewhere. After some time, she wiped away the runes containing her blood and stepped away from the council table. A few people looked up, but they let her leave, it was out of her hands now.

Jond followed her. "Wait," he called out in the rain, but she hurried across the bridge and into the corridors of another mushroom.

Students filtered out of classrooms with newly forged inkwells and Jond had to weave through them to keep sight of Kara.

"Excuse me . . . sorry . . . would you mind . . . *move!*"

Annoyed glances turned to looks of respect as they recognised Jond. He was the first teacher most of them had had. He only hoped the others who had taken up the helm taught with the same precision.

Kara slipped out of the other side of the mushroom and back across the next bridge. She slowed, eventually stopping in the middle.

"Why didn't you just flight here?" Jond said, panting.

"I wanted to make you run." Jond heard the smile in her voice. He bent at the waist and lowered his chest to his knees.

"What are you doing?" she spat.

"Bowing," Jond replied from his folded stance. He tried and failed to keep a straight face.

"Get up, you idiot." Kara didn't laugh, but her eyes crinkled for a moment.

She rested her elbows on the edge of the bridge and looked outwards.

"It wasn't easy, being two people. But it was easier than being one. As councillor I could be who I wanted to be, as Queen I had to be what people expected of me. Beloved—" She laughed harshly. "Do you know how many times I've heard that? The Queen is *beloved*. But where are my allies now? Where are my people?"

Jond reached for her hand and held it.

"We're here. We've always been here."

She didn't look at Jond, but neither did she shake him off.

"I don't know how to be her again. Not without my regalia, my crown, my staff . . ." She whispered the words into the wind.

"Why don't we get all that stuff then?"

"What?"

"Not everything in the Shard Palace can be ruined. There must be something you can recover."

Kara shook her head. "I can't go back there." Her voice cracked and Jond squeezed her hand.

It was too much for her and she pulled away.

"Do you really believe Sylah survived the Tannin?" The question was sudden, as if it had plagued her for some time.

Jond thought about it.

"I must. Because I can't live in a world that she isn't in."

"You love her very much, don't you?"

Jond inhaled, trying to gather his thoughts on how to answer the question. Everything about Sylah was complicated and messy and—skies above—frustrating. But it came down to one word in the end.

"Yes."

Kara nodded as if to confirm her own thoughts before saying, "I suppose I had better prepare a speech."

She didn't say bye before she flighted away.

The next morning Jond knocked on Kara's door. He smelt of fire and copper, and he was heavy-boned tired.

"Jond? What are you doing here?"

Her hair fell to her shoulders in soft waves. Her nightclothes were white, almost translucent, and he worked hard to keep his gaze above the neckline. He wanted to reach for the soft skin there, to kiss it—

"I made you something." His voice was rough from the smoke in the forge. He held it up to the gaslight.

Kara's mouth parted, her violet eyes widening as she reached for the metal. Her fingers ran over the copper in wonder.

"You made me a crown?"

"I used some of the offcuts from the inkwells. This was my fourth attempt."

She lifted the diadem up. The circlet was oddly shaped, as no matter how many times Jond tried he couldn't get it perfectly symmetrical. The front, however, he was pleased with. He had used a stylus that had been too long for the wearer and braided it painstakingly over strikes.

"A rose vine?" Kara asked, her voice filled with wonder.

Jond smiled. "Yes, I remembered what you'd said about the rose gardens in the palace."

When Kara looked at him her eyes were full of gratitude.

"Would you?" She handed the crown to Jond and dipped her head for him to place it.

The moment seemed significant, and yet he didn't know why. He pressed it onto the softness of her curls.

"How do I look?"

The oblong circlet was disguised by the waves of her hair, the vines came forward in a V in the centre of her forehead.

"Enchanting."

She smiled and Jond wondered if it was the truest smile he'd seen her make.

"Thank you, Jond." She opened the door wider. "Do you want to come in?"

He did, oh, he desperately did. But she was just being kind to him because he had gifted her something.

"I think I'll go get some rest. It was a long night."

"All right." Was that a flicker of disappointment in her eyes? He couldn't be sure, but he couldn't double check because the door closed in his face.

You've got less spine than an earthworm. The voice in his head sounded like Sylah, and for a moment he thought she was talking to him in his mind. Until he remembered she was dead.

"No," he said to himself as he walked away. "She isn't dead."

"Who isn't dead?" Niha appeared in the corridor ahead.

"Nothing, no one."

"Were you just leaving Kara's chambers?" Niha held a hand to his mouth with scandalised glee.

"No . . . well, yes . . . I had to give her something."

"Oh, yeah? Did you give it to her?"

"Yes," Jond said crossly. "Oh, maiden's tits, not like that."

"Maiden's tits? Interesting nickname."

"No, that's not what I meant." Jond grew increasingly flustered, but Niha just laughed as he walked away.

"See you for breakfast . . . King Jond."

*   *   *

Jond wasn't the only one who had been up all night. Elyzan and his students had spent all morning growing another mushroom large enough to house every citizen in the City of Rain.

As Jond entered he whistled low.

"How many people can the stalk take?" He expected his words to echo, but the spongy flesh of the mushroom's cap absorbed it all.

"We grew seventeen oaks alongside its roots to stabilise it," Elyzan said. Though he was very clearly tired, his eyes shone with pride.

"You wanted a spectacle, this is it," Jond said.

"The people need this. Hope can be stronger than any weapon."

Jond understood that. Hope was what had tied him to the Sandstorm. That, and he'd had no choice.

There was an irritated sigh behind them, and they both turned.

"If the Zalaam wanted to strike a blow, all they'd have to do is destroy this one shroom." Kara crossed her arms across her chest and set her lips in a grim line, but it didn't mar the loveliness of her image.

She wore a dress so deep a purple that it was almost black. The neckline was cut low to her navel. Tied at her neck were her water-proof robes, but instead of looking practical they were knotted in a way that made them look like a cape, shimmering like liquid silver. Her hair was loose, except for three braids intertwined with the circlet of the crown.

"What?" she said. But Jond wasn't listening. Her lips had been painted with purple gloss, as if she'd just eaten a bowl of blackberries. And her eyes . . . Anyme above . . . her eyes were lined with copper paint that swirled around to her brows.

She was every bit the Queen.

This time, when Jond bowed to her, he wasn't teasing. "You look incredible."

Elyzan barrelled out a laugh. "Aha, ha! Yes, my dear, you look utterly compelling. Wherever did you find that dress, it becomes you."

"It was actually Jond's." Kara's lips quirked.

"Oh, yes?" Elyzan replied. The councillor was prone to wearing dresses himself and he eyed the detailing with interest.

It was then that Jond recognised it as one of the many garments he'd worn in the Winterlands. It must have been removed when he was being healed.

Jond squirmed as he wondered who had removed it. Kara dipped her chin and looked at him as if she could read his mind.

"When will everyone start arriving?" Jond asked quickly.

"Now, look here come the rest of our collective, citizens won't be long now, let's take our seats."

Elyzan led Jond and Kara towards the raised benches grown from the gills of the mushroom that lined the ground like floorboards. Their seats faced the raised circular stage in the centre.

"Are you ready?" Jond murmured into Kara's ear. She smelt of rain.

"Ready for people never to treat me the same way again? I don't think anyone can ever prepare for that."

"Perhaps not."

Kara raised her hood to cover her face as people filled the room.

Jond said, "I've been wondering one thing."

"Dangerous. You've only just healed that brain, try not to think too hard."

He smiled and continued, "There was this waxing fable I heard of you once. It said you were the kindest woman to walk this earth. How did they get it so wrong?"

Kara laughed and Jond was pleased to see the frown that had shadowed her brow disappear.

He reached for her gloved hand and squeezed it. "I promise to never treat you any differently. Just remember, you're not Kara or Karanomo, Queen or councillor. You're both, stronger as one."

Kara looked at their intertwined hands for a moment before releasing his.

"It's time." She lowered her hood and stood. She took a pace forward, then stopped. Slowly she removed her glove and looked at her orb. With a tight smile to Jond she patterned her other wrist and flighted to the centre of the stage.

There was a collective gasp, thousands of citizens exhaling in a rush. Who was this person who wore both crown and orb?

She was someone magnificent and soon they'd all know it.

Kara walked onto the centre of the stage until someone ran out with a sound projector.

Jond started in his seat. It had only been a few mooncycles since he'd taught his first lesson on bloodwerk and yet his students were already using the runes to make sound projectors. He wondered if they'd come up with anything else.

If the empire had been like the Academy, then the wardens would have promoted innovation, not securing the status quo. The world would have been different.

It could still be.

Kara began to speak.

"Some of you may know me as the councillor of the fourth charter, a few among you might even know me from the Shard Palace. I stand here not as two people but as one. My name is Karanomo, my legacy is to rule this land, my want is to guide this council. I am both Queen and councillor."

The shock of the announcement rendered the thousands of listeners silent.

Kara continued, her voice clear and unwavering. "I am a Queen without a palace. A Queen without a throne. But I have my people and my allies. Fear will not cow me. Hope will sustain me. And it is that hope that the Zalaam should fear. It is our strength in purpose that will scare our enemies. We will bring them low and rise once more. We have sent our flighters to all corners of the world. The Queen of Tenio calls upon all countries to pick up their arms and bring the power in their blood. For the final battle is coming in less than two turns of the moon."

Jond looked around. Fear was written on the faces of all around him. Kara's words were no comfort. This had been a foolish exercise. He was about to say that to Elyzan when he heard the rumble. After a time, it built in volume and Jond could hear the distinct syllables.

"Kara-no-mo! Kara-no-mo!"

Cheers filled the auditorium, shaking the structure as people stamped and whooped with delight. Gone was the fear in the collective and Jond realised it wasn't Kara who had brought the hope, it was them, every one of them: the student who had lost his teacher, the mother who had lost her son, the guard without a leader.

They each chose in that moment to belong.

CHAPTER TWENTY-TWO

Anoor

One of the prisoners overcame their sedation and removed their canula. They succeeded in freeing four more of the harvest before being destroyed. Unfortunately, that means we have lost another batch.

—Nightly report from Faro to the master crafter

Anoor was woken by Teta at dawn.

"Yona has sent me to measure you for a new dress."

Anoor sat up. "Where is my grandmother?"

"She has business in the harbour this morning."

Two crafters Anoor recognised stood in the doorway. Teta waved them over. Anoor didn't ask why crafters, not stitchers, were making her clothes.

Because the Wife had told them to, and no one disobeyed Yona. The crafters prodded at her hip bone and back, jotting down the measurements between them.

When they left there was a knock on the door and Anoor opened it.

In the three weeks since Qwa's death Faro had become smaller. Their eyes had shrunk, their chest grown concave. Even their voice had lost life.

"The Wife asked me to bring you breakfast," Faro said, offering a plate of the sliced yellow fruit they called "pineapple". "She noticed you've been skipping breakfast and going straight to the Foundry every morning."

Faro passed Anoor the plate, but she didn't take it. The tangy sweet smell of the pineapple was making her feel nauseated.

"Could you make me a cup of bitter leaf tea instead? I'm not hungry this morning."

Faro set the plate to the side with a frown. "I will go and make it."

Anoor dressed simply in the garments Yona had provided for her: a skirt that fell to her feet and a loose jumper of some sort of animal hair.

Faro was waiting for her outside her room holding a hot drink. Anoor took the cup from Faro's outstretched hands and took a grateful sip.

"Thank you."

Faro fell into step beside her but didn't reply. They walked the short distance to Anoor's workbench in the Foundry before Faro slipped away to the warehouse at back.

Faro had been assigned a role in the laboratory where the formula was made. It was the only part of the Foundry Anoor was yet to see, but every time she asked Yona, her grandmother always told her it was too dangerous.

"Child of Fire, it is good to see you this morning," Chah, the master crafter, greeted her. He ignored Faro as they left, but it was easy to ignore Faro. They only seemed half present.

The warehouse was already bustling and Anoor relished the sound of it. Hundreds of carvers all working for one purpose: To bring down the Wardens' Empire.

Even the scraping of metal on metal was the sweetest of melodies in her ears.

"How goes your project?" Chah asked.

"All right, but I'm struggling with this sequence. It looks like it should work but it feels like something is missing." She held up the slice of metal.

The older man smiled softly at her as he reached for it. There was something in his nurturing gaze that reminded her of her father.

"I see where you've gone wrong, that rune placement is too high . . ."

The day passed without Anoor noticing. At some point Faro

returned and asked about lunch, but Anoor didn't move, and Faro didn't come back. So, she just continued, carving, moulding and engraving her project.

Yona found Anoor just as the sun was beginning to set.

"Chah says you're a quick study."

Anoor looked up from her work, blinking at Yona with blurry eyes. She scrubbed her hands over her face, willing them to focus.

"Chah is a good teacher," Anoor said.

"He should be, it was I who taught him."

Anoor looked for Chah at their workbench a few handspans away. But he wasn't there. In fact, Anoor was completely alone.

"The day is over, Anoor."

Anoor shook her head. "I'm nearly finished. I was a little slower than the others as I can't carve as quickly. But the time I spend here will save us more on the battlefield. Engravings are incredibly efficient. Letting the blood seep into the grooves of the runes is ingenious really."

Yona laughed lightly. "Yes, we started introducing that technique fifty or so years ago. I, in fact, perfected it."

Anoor was envious of the life Yona'd had in the Foundry. She'd been free to explore, free to create.

I wonder what godbeasts I could have made if I had been born here.

Yona leant over, paying closer inspection to Anoor's project. "Is that a bird?"

Anoor nodded. Yona reached for one of Anoor's notes.

"I haven't seen the schema for this before. Who authorised this?"

"I did." Before Yona could open her mouth to ask, Anoor cut her off with the explanation. "Chah said as my engraving skills don't yet match up to the other crafters, he couldn't assign me to create quellers." Anoor swallowed that old disappointment. "I got to thinking. What could I contribute to the battlefield? And I thought about kori birds, how sometimes they're trained to send messages?"

Yona's expression dipped into boredom and Anoor said in a rush, "So, these last few weeks I've been perfecting this kori bird."

"It won't work," Yona said simply. "We've tried thousands of times to create birds, but they never gain flight. Their anatomy is too hard to capture in any material."

Anoor grinned. "That's why I'm also incorporating bloodwerk runes. See, here? I'm using forces to help keep the bird steady."

Yona tipped her head to the side, her eyes moving back and forth as she read through Anoor's sequence. "That could work. Anoor, that is an impressive development."

Anoor felt pride swell in her chest.

"But why a kori? Why not one of the birds on the Volcane Isles?"

Anoor's smile slipped.

My kori bird . . .

Sylah's words cleaved through her thoughts, leaving her mind raw.

"Anoor?" Yona brought her back.

"I-I thought that it would be best to mimic a kori bird because they are native to the empire and better suited to the environment there." The lie sounded believable even to Anoor.

"How astute."

Yona placed the schema back onto Anoor's workbench. "But it's time to rest now. I've asked Faro to bring you dinner in our rooms."

"Where are you going?"

Irritation flickered across Yona's face but was smoothed away soon after. "Our trade partners from the mainland were delayed by a storm, but they have been spotted on the horizon. I'm to welcome them."

"Visitors from the mainland?" *Where Sylah is.* "I want to come."

In the last few weeks Sylah's love had started to feel more distant, the leagues stretching between them. Even Anoor's memories of Sylah had started to fade as if her mind had only space for battle plans and godpower. Anoor missed Sylah dearly, and her heart soared at the thought of mainlanders visiting the Zalaam. Perhaps they would know of Sylah. The thought was more hope than sense, but Anoor clung to it.

"No," Yona said sharply. "I've been told you haven't eaten all day. And I need you to regain the strength you're expending in the Foundry. Besides, the Shariha don't do well with strangers, and I think it'll be better for negotiations if we don't bring out the Child of Fire quite yet."

Disappointment was bitter on her tongue. She opened her mouth to argue but Yona placed a hand on her shoulder.

"Your skills are required here, Anoor. Look at how much you've accomplished already." Yona gestured to the kori bird and Anoor's pride swelled. But it wasn't enough to completely eclipse Sylah from her thoughts.

"All right, Grandmother. I'll see you later then?"

"Later," Yona promised.

Anoor waited for Yona to disappear out of the Foundry door before slipping out after her. If there was a chance of news of the mainland, then Anoor needed to know.

Yona walked slowly through the Yellow Commune towards the shore. Teta was waiting at the edge of the beach, and together they set off towards the harbour.

The looming shadows of ships filled the horizon. There were hundreds of them—ten times, maybe twenty times larger than the boat she had travelled on to the Isles.

Anoor followed Yona at a distance. Though there was nothing to hide behind, there were enough people on the beach that she didn't look out of place. Without her armour to mark her out, she looked like any of the Zalaam. Even Anoor's baldness helped her blend in— Yona's sacrifice all those years ago had created a fashion for shaven heads.

Her grandmother had stopped at the end of a pier where a group of people waited. Just from their clothing Anoor could tell they were outsiders. Silk fabrics hung from their necks and were entwined in their hair like jewellery. Their flowing clothing was bound and twisted in intricate knots over their skin—which varied from browns to pale pinks. And as Anoor got closer, she could hear the lilt of an accent she had never heard before.

"Short on few. But more then coming," one of the Shariha was saying. From her stance and the way the others deferred to her, Anoor assumed she was the leader. The dress she wore was patchworked in blues and greens. It reminded Anoor of the shallows.

"That's not good enough, we're in the final stages of preparation," Yona said.

"Nah, nah. Counting for picking. Enough there is not." The Shariha rubbed her hands together. "Few, few."

Yona shook her head. "You want the copper? Then you need to bring us more harvest."

The Shariha hissed through her teeth. "Who you, to come here and tell Shariha, eh, eh?"

Yona crossed the pier to stand a handspan from the woman's face.

Anoor could only hear the deep cadence of her grandmother's voice and see the wideness of the Shariha's eyes. Whatever threat Yona had spoken, it had met its mark.

The leader of the Shariha barked orders in a language Anoor didn't understand and soon there was movement as some of her crew opened a hatch in their ship's hull.

Anoor slipped closer to stand ten paces behind her grandmother. Strange sounds of clanging metal were coming from the ship and at first Anoor thought a battle had commenced until she saw what the Shariha were leading out onto the beach.

Not what, but who.

Hundreds and hundreds of prisoners shuffled into the daylight. The noise Anoor had heard was the clattering of the chains around their waists, feet and hands.

"Some of them look sick," Yona said. "We need them to survive until we have drained them of bone marrow."

"Fine they'll be," the Shariha leader snapped back.

Anoor felt the cold claws of dread tighten around her neck. "Bone marrow?" She crossed the pier in quick strides.

Yona turned round as Anoor reached her and let out a short sigh. "Anoor, I told you that you should have stayed in the Foundry."

"Hassa was right, wasn't she? You were harvesting bone marrow, that's what was in the crates in the boat. The pale liquid . . ." Anoor was gasping, trying to get the words out, the truth out, but then she saw something that caught her eye.

"You want to press a scythe to the neck of the empire? Then this is the way, Anoor," Yona said with little patience.

But Anoor wasn't listening. Her eyes were drawn to a flash of metal hanging from the sword of a young Shariha boy. She walked towards him until she was a handspan away and reached a shaking hand forward.

"Eh, eh. Back keeping you," the boy said as he snatched away the sword from her reaching hand. But not before she had touched it and proved it was real.

My sword . . . the sword I had gifted to Sylah for her journey to the mainland.

Anoor began to search the dirty faces of the prisoners, but she knew Sylah wasn't there, she would have been able to sense it. Her presence had always resonated with something deep within Anoor's soul.

"Where did you get this?" Anoor's voice was level, quiet.

"Taken, mine now."

"Where is she? The prisoner you took this from?"

The young boy's gaze flickered to his leader before answering with a smirk.

"Gone."

And in that moment so was Anoor.

Anoor sipped her drink with numb lips. The bitter leaf tea was probably too hot, but she couldn't tell. She hummed as its warmth spread through her body, awakening some semblance of life in her.

"I added extra barknut powder to this one," Yona had said when she handed it to Anoor. And though her mind wasn't able to process flavour, she could feel the grit of the powder between her teeth.

Anoor looked up at the moon and felt the swell of power that she had come to associate with Kabut's gaze.

Is this what you wanted? Kabut? Father? You have taken all from me, my home, my love, my friends. Is this the cost?

"Anoor, you should come inside now, it is cold." Yona stood on the threshold of the Foundry entrance.

"How did you know you were the Wife?" Anoor asked her grandmother without turning.

Yona came to stand beside her. "When Kabut called upon me I knew the truth like the moonlight on my skin. It was the moment between joy and pain. Love and hate. It is hard to describe, but I suspect you know what I mean."

Anoor looked up and assessed her own feelings. She couldn't deny the awe that surged through her as she perceived Kabut's eye in the sky. But she also ached with a deep hollowness that gorged her through the centre of her soul. The space where Sylah had been.

Joy and pain.

"How many more deliveries are you expecting from the Shariha?" Anoor asked.

Yona had taken Anoor to the laboratory beyond the warehouse. Behind the locked door were rows and rows of beds of people being drained of their marrow. The air had smelt vinegary and reminded Anoor of the infirmary. But instead of healing people, the laboratory killed them, draining their bones of marrow.

But it didn't feel as heinous an act as Anoor knew it should. Her conscience was silent, drained of life too.

The bodies were sedated as they were harvested of precious liquid. Not bodies—sacrifices, because Anoor couldn't see them as people anymore.

She had lingered by one of the beds and watched as the cloudy red liquid was drawn from a needle in their hip.

They were an Ember, like Sylah.

Her name echoed in the emptiness of Anoor's mind.

She had taken in the tour of the laboratory passively. She had nothing to live for now, no one to live for anymore. Killing the wardens was her only purpose.

And if this is what it takes, it is worth it.

Then the Zalaam could be welcomed into Kabut's paradise as Gods. And perhaps Anoor could see Sylah again.

She clung to the hope as tightly as she held on to the mug of bitter leaf tea.

"This shipment of harvest was the last, the Shariha claim that the mainland is starting to mobilise their own armies against us."

Anoor turned to look at her grandmother. There must have been something in Anoor's gaze, as Yona's lips trembled, and her eyes widened.

Then Anoor spoke. "The wardens have stolen everything from me. And in turn I will kill every one of them. Ready we will be when the Child of Fire brings the Battle Drum. I am here. And I am ready."

CHAPTER TWENTY-THREE

Sylah

Come now, come now. Gather all to fight,
Wardens trapped behind their walls.
Come now, come now. Let us do what's right,
It is time for the empire to fall.

—Poem circulated by the griot network

Two weeks passed and Sylah's creation soon took shape. Ala had proven her skill in not just masonry but artistry and had taken pride in embellishing the creature with crystal eyes, and engraved scales along its snout and tail.

"There, I think that will do it. The tail is sufficiently long enough that it won't be off balance, and the claws sharp enough to tear through the army."

Ala smiled before removing the chisel strapped to her wrist. *You must finish the runes now, right?*

Sylah nodded and chewed her lip.

She didn't admit to Ala that she wasn't entirely confident in her ability to wake the beast. She'd been practising on smaller creations every evening but most of the time they hadn't worked.

Ala brushed her wrist over the stone eru and grinned. *I used to help Elder Dew with the carvings in the Nest's walls. This project has brought me peace.*

Sylah frowned, wondering whether to voice the question that had itched at her mind since she met Ala.

Ask, Ala signed, seeing the confliction on Sylah's face.

"Why is it you haven't left Turin's employ and gone to the Chrysalis?"

The Ghosting's eyes twitched. It was as close to rolling her eyes as Ala would get.

I haven't the strength to fight.

Sylah frowned. "Fighting is never really about strength. It's about stamina, tenacity, and a great deal of determination. Because it really depends on what you fight for. What are you fighting for, Ala?"

Nothing.

Sylah laughed, and then regretted it as it sounded cruel, and she said more kindly, "We're all fighting for something."

Ala looked pensive but she didn't speak on it again.

When Sylah returned to Turin's house later that day there were three new people in the living room. Which wasn't unusual. As the headquarters of the rebellion many people drifted in and out. But there was one Sylah recognised.

"How's it hurting, Griot Sheth?"

The griot bowed his head, the beads in his locs tinkling. "Well, Sylah, very well indeed."

The other two Sylah didn't know. Both women were middle-aged but only one had a brand on her wrist, marking the taller of the two an Ember.

"Who are they?" Sylah asked Gorn, who hadn't looked up from her desk since Sylah had returned with Tanu.

"Huh? Oh, that's Zuhari and Ren. Zuhari was once a part of—"

Sylah lunged across the room and wrapped her fingers around Zuhari's throat.

"You are the reason she went into hiding, you are the reason—"

"Sylah, get your hands off her now!" Gorn shouted. But it was the Purger who took pleasure in throwing Sylah to the ground.

Despite being winded Sylah scrambled to her feet ready to tackle the woman again. Zuhari rubbed her throat and tried to speak, but Gorn cut her off.

"Sylah, Zuhari never meant for Anoor to be accused," Gorn said in a tone clearly trying to be soothing but just came out cold.

"But she didn't stop it either, Hassa told me what you did," Sylah spat.

"Zuhari will be leading a big portion of our infantry. Her skills gained in the Wardens' Army have already earned her my forgiveness."

"Not mine!" Sylah shouted.

"And Ren, her apothecary has powders and potions that will be invaluable."

Ren spoke for the first time. She took a step towards Sylah, leaning heavily on a cane. She had a pleasant face, a trusting face. But Sylah knew she would never trust her.

Sylah tensed her muscles, ready to fling Ren out of the way.

"I know what Zuhari did was wrong," Ren said softly.

"Wrong?" Sylah couldn't take this. She looked past Ren to Zuhari, who was still rubbing the red marks on her neck from Sylah's hand.

"I'm sorry," Zuhari said as Sylah's eyes landed on her. But Sylah couldn't hear the words over the sound of her blood pounding in her ears.

Sylah lunged forward, intent on pushing Ren out of the way, but then Turin barked, "There will be no violence under this roof, not anymore."

It wasn't the volume that had Sylah pause in her attack, but the tone in which Turin spoke. Sylah turned to the Warden of Crime.

Turin's eyes were watery, showing Sylah for the first time the buried memories that she too had endured as a maiden. Her lips shook, but she stood straight-backed, her jaw lifted. As if she was ready to throw Sylah out herself.

Sylah wasn't going to let that happen. Though Turin's pain had tempered some of her anger, Sylah felt stifled by the passivity of everyone in the room.

"Zuhari is the reason Anoor is not here, with me," Sylah said, gruff with emotion.

She was about to storm outside into the night air but then the tidewind let itself be known. She was trapped.

If I stay here, I'm going to kill Zuhari. The thought was one of the truest things Sylah had ever said to herself.

She marched away from the main chamber and into one of the back rooms. Then she slammed the door and leant against it.

"How dare she show up here? After everything she did to Anoor? How fucking dare she?" she said to herself.

There was a sound of chains clinking and Sylah spun.

Tanu looked up at her in the red runelight. "Oh, I forgot they moved you here."

Tanu didn't respond.

"Whatever."

Sylah paced the room for a quarter of a strike before she was calm enough to sit. She couldn't go back out there, not tonight.

Anoor would tell me to forgive her. Even Hassa had said Anoor had wanted her to go free. But I am not as forgiving as Anoor.

Sylah withdrew one of the smaller creations she'd been practising on from her pocket and began to draw. It stilled the rage a little while.

"You should swap the last two runes." The voice was raspy from lack of use. It took Sylah a minute to realise Tanu had spoken. The disciple looked back at her with a bored expression.

"Because they trigger right to left," she continued. "You're currently instilling life before you protect the blood from drying out. Unless you draw quickly, the power will have waned before the runes begin."

"How do you know this?"

Tanu shrugged. "Yona was teaching us."

Us. Sylah wondered if that included Anoor, but she couldn't ask how deep Anoor's loyalty to the Zalaam ran. It would break her already bleeding heart. For every day Anoor was with the enemy, Sylah felt herself losing her a little more. Drop by drop, ebbing away from the beating heart of their love.

"Will you help me? Finish the creation?" Sylah asked instead.

Tanu blinked slowly.

"All Kabut wants is sacrifice. And I think it might please my God very much if I help you. Because the wardens will be the greatest sacrifice of all."

Then she smiled and it chilled Sylah to the marrow.

*   *   *

Tanu circled the stone eru, her shackles clinking.

"And the material, it has not had any prior use?" Tanu asked.

When brought to life, creations took on a semblance of the material they were made from. It was why the Tannin had become a beast of sacrifice because the Academy had made it from the stone of Kabut's temple.

Sylah had been careful with every element of the eru, ensuring the whitestone was freshly mined, and bore no previous wear. "Straight from the quarries in Jin-Dinil. Brought in with the other ore supplies."

They were lucky that it was the time of year that whitestone could be readily harvested. For two mooncycles of the year the Jin-Dinil lakes grew shallow from the sun's heat, leaving the terrain a bog. Though the swamps were unpleasant, they did allow for miners to harvest whitestone beneath the lake beds.

Tanu pursed her lips and peered closer at the red blood patterning its underbelly.

"You have already drawn the mimic runes onto the real eru?" she asked.

Sylah nodded. "Yes. There's a stable on the other side of the Tongue, which I think houses the only eru left in the Ember quarter. I drew the runes and copied the combination here, so when the creation awakes it will mimic the movement of the eru."

Tanu scrutinised the runes before giving her verdict. "Thankfully that sequence is correct. About the only rune combination that *is* correct."

Sylah had doubted Tanu's intentions—after all Sylah had almost killed her—but that day she made more improvements to the whitestone creature than Sylah had made in a mooncycle.

For five more days they worked on the eru. Sylah didn't attend the nightly meetings at the maiden house anymore, she had decided that avoiding Zuhari was safer for everyone.

But that day, when she locked Tanu back in her room, Gorn pulled her to the side and said, "I think you might like to stay for this meeting."

Sylah scowled and tucked herself as far away from Zuhari as she could. The room had filled with more people Sylah didn't recognise.

The griot network had drawn in Dusters from other cities, and those given leading roles were housed here.

"I'd like to introduce you all to Rohan," Gorn announced to the room. An old man stood up and nodded to the congregation. Sylah would have dismissed him if there hadn't been something familiar in the way he tilted his head.

Gorn continued, "Rohan is Kwame's father, the Ember who was murdered on the rack."

Sylah inhaled through her teeth, and it came out as a hiss.

Rohan cleared his throat and addressed the rebellion. Sylah noticed he was breathing heavily. "I have amassed a group of Embers who will fight on your side. A thousand, more or less."

Turin snorted. For it was a paltry number compared to the masses of Dusters and Ghostings ready to storm the Keep.

Rohan looked at Turin with bloodshot eyes. "They all have the ability to bloodwerk. Some have their own runeguns that they have kept after retirement from the army. All I ask is that you let me lead them."

The Purger rolled her eyes. "Retired Embers led by an old man? Surely this is not what it has come to."

Rohan didn't balk. "They took my son from me. I have only a few weeks, perhaps a mooncycle to live, and I would see the wardens pay for what they have done."

Griot Sheth crossed the room, his locs swinging by his waist. "Revenge sheds the years on any man. I say we let Rohan lead his Embers in this battle."

Turin looked to Gorn and nodded.

Gorn unravelled a map. "Now let us lay out where best placed you will be when we attack."

Sylah watched Rohan from afar, her throat bobbing. *I wish I'd had a chance to say goodbye to you, Kwame. You showed me kindness when I showed you none.*

"Sylah?" Zuhari stepped towards her.

Sylah bared her teeth. "What do you want?"

"I just want you to know how sorry I am, I never meant for Anoor to be blamed. I sought revenge for what Uka had done to my child, to those involved in the revolt of the hundred. I thought you might understand."

"Why would I understand that?"

Zuhari tilted her head. "Are you not one of the Stolen?"

Anoor must have told her. Sylah didn't answer. Revenge hadn't been her calling in a long time.

"Well, that settles that," Gorn said, drawing Sylah and Zuhari's attention back to the meeting at hand.

"What did we miss?" Sylah asked.

The atmosphere in the room had turned feverish with energy.

Turin gave Sylah an irritated glance. "Rohan's people can help bring down the Keep's gates. It's been the last piece of our operation unaccounted for."

"And?" Sylah said.

Gorn smiled. "We go to war tomorrow."

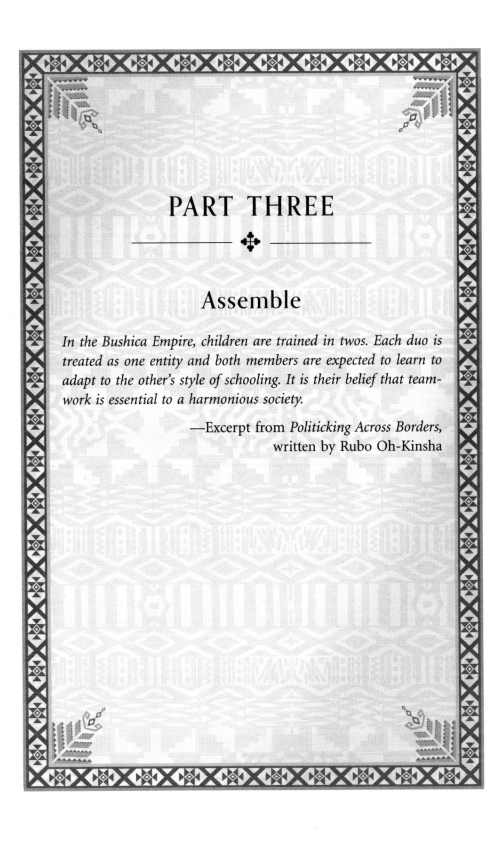

PART THREE

✛

Assemble

In the Bushica Empire, children are trained in twos. Each duo is treated as one entity and both members are expected to learn to adapt to the other's style of schooling. It is their belief that teamwork is essential to a harmonious society.

—Excerpt from *Politicking Across Borders,*
written by Rubo Oh-Kinsha

Story told by Shola, former captain of the Entwined Harbour, during the full moon when one cleric is nominated to recall a tale to the city

Seven hundred years ago, our ancestors sailed from countries unknown, a fleet of five ships. They sought a new land where they could raise their families away from the structures of government they'd known. But it wasn't land our forebears found, but the ocean.

The Ica Sea was more beautiful than any mountains, any desert, any forest. For it had all of that and more beneath its turquoise waters.

So together they tethered their boats and our country began. And though the Ica Sea gave us many things, it could not give us one: books.

And so we began to trade, knowledge becoming the most important attribute among our people.

Twiners have never hidden away from current affairs, we have proudly cited our novels and our histories—always ready to condemn or support on the morals we hold so dear to our chest.

So, today I ask you a question. Do you wish to be the clam or the shark?

The clam must be placed in hot water before it opens its shell. But then, only death awaits it. We must be like the shark, quick to attack our prey.

We cannot wait for the hot water before we take our place in this war. For then, only death awaits us all.

CHAPTER TWENTY-FOUR

Anoor

I think I have completed the final schema for the clawmaw. All it requires are the measurements of the rider. Now for me to build it.

—Notes by Nayeli Ilrase during her first year as master crafter

Anoor watched the ships loll on the waves. The Shariha's fleet was large enough to carry the thousands of godbeasts, along with the Zalaam's army. Which it turned out, was most of the population. Only those too young or too old to hold a sword would stay behind.

Anoor paced the shore, weaving between the throngs of soldiers boarding the ships.

One last journey before I join Sylah in Kabut's realm. Three weeks living without Sylah in the world should have been an unbearable amount of time, but she had turned that grief into hope. Soon she would see her again.

Anoor sipped on the bitter leaf tea and felt herself marginally relax. The drink was the only thing she could stomach at the moment.

She couldn't remember when she had last eaten or bathed. Her days were spent in the Foundry making adjustments to the kori bird. She'd have to wait until they were in the empire to mimic it to the real species.

Anoor spotted Faro lingering in the shadow of one of the great ships. They seemed to blend in with the blurred edges of darkness. She had seen Faro less and less over the last few weeks.

"Faro, how are you under Kabut's eye?" she asked.

Faro raised their slight shoulders. "I am fine, Child of Fire."

Anoor couldn't remember when they had stopped calling her Anoor. Perhaps when she had stopped being her. Anoor had died when Sylah had, and all that was left were the flickering flames of the Child of Fire.

She looked at Faro. "You seem troubled."

Faro glanced at the crates of bone marrow being loaded into the hull of the ship, a frown upon their brows. "No, I am just anxious to leave."

Anoor could tell it was more than that. "Walk with me."

Faro's frown deepened but they did as Anoor bade and fell into step next to her.

"We don't speak as much anymore," Anoor said.

"My work in the laboratory has kept me busy." Their steps had led them to the Foundry and Anoor nodded as crafters saluted her as she passed.

"I hear there have been quite a few accidents of late," she said to Faro. "Broken vials, missed sedations . . ."

Faro's lips pressed into a thin line before they spoke. "It has been . . . difficult."

"Tell me then, what is on your mind, perhaps I can ease it?"

Faro hesitated, the words forming on their lips.

"Tell me," Anoor said, softer.

"How are we going to get past the Tannin?" Faro whispered.

Anoor drained her tea and left the cup on a workbench. "Ah, the Tannin, the godbeast you lied to me about on our journey here?"

Faro swallowed. "The Wife told us we—"

Anoor waved a hand. "I know, I know. I'm not chastising you, merely stating the facts."

She had grown accustomed to speaking her mind. There was a part of her that enjoyed brandishing her thoughts so sharply, she had little patience to pander to people's feelings.

They had reached the warehouse door. Anoor nodded to the guards there who let them through.

The godbeasts had all been loaded onto wheeled trollies to transport them across the beach to the ships. The sight made Anoor's heart soar. "Incredible, isn't it? The power we have just in this one room."

The clawmaw was still missing, but Yona had assured Anoor that she was making some necessary changes to the creature.

"Careful," Anoor barked as some of the workers tipped one of the quellers to the side. "If you put too much pressure on that rune, you'll render it useless. Keep them upright, like I requested."

No longer was she meek. No longer would she cower.

I am the Child of Fire. And I will burn those near me.

Anoor continued down towards the laboratory.

She pushed open the door and stepped inside. Faro shivered as they crossed the threshold.

Thousands of beds filled with sedated sacrifices were lined up for as far as her eyes could see.

"I come here sometimes, after your shift is finished, when the Foundry is empty," Anoor said quietly. "Every time I look at them, I feel Kabut's presence. Our God is pleased with us, Faro." Anoor paused by a bed and looked down at the sleeping woman in it.

She wondered if Sylah had died this way, or in the Shariha's hold.

"Gone," the boy with her sword had said.

The memory stirred feelings of grief, but Anoor had become proficient at letting that emotion fuel her.

Death is power.

Faro stopped by the foot of the woman's bed, their expression slipping, giving way to the roiling emotions within. "How do you do it? How do you see them as sacrifices and not people?"

Anoor shrugged. "Think of them like iron ore. They are an important component in the final battle. It is Kabut's will. Unless you doubt his will?"

Faro's eyes closed slowly. When they opened them, their face was once again neutral.

"Tonight, all bone marrow harvest will be stopped. For this final batch of ore has another purpose yet," Anoor said.

"What do you mean?"

Anoor spread her arms wide. "You asked how we were to get past the Tannin's tithe? This is how."

* * *

The next day Yona called on Faro and Anoor at the port. "Faro, the ship you're assigned to is the *Grove*. You'll be overseeing the harvest for the Tannin. Anoor, you will be on the *Cleaver* with me. It's the largest ship of the fleet. We are awaiting the clawmaw which will be stored in our hull. Ah, here it is."

It took twice as many people to push the clawmaw across the beach than it did the quellers. As it drew near, Anoor noticed the changes Yona had made in the godbeast.

A cavity was carved into its shoulders where a rider would sit. Four thin blades, which seemed too randomly placed to be unintentional, branched towards the rider's seat.

Faro noticed too, their mouth moving softly. "Why are the blades facing inwards?"

They seemed to come to some realisation because their eyes went wide.

"Faro? What is it?" Anoor asked, prompting them.

They swung their gaze to Anoor's, but the expression of shock was gone. Instead, their jaw was set, their nostrils flaring.

"Nothing."

"Why don't you go to your ship, check out your cabin?" Yona said, her voice sharp with command.

Faro nodded and left. But Anoor was sure they were going in the wrong direction to where the *Grove* was docked.

She looked to the clawmaw one more time and tried to connect Faro's thoughts, but her mind felt hazier than normal.

Too much barknut powder in my tea. The sugar is surging in my veins.

"Come now, the *Cleaver* is this way," Yona said, guiding Anoor towards the gangplank. "We'll lead the charge into the Tannin's lair."

Anoor let herself be led by the elbow onto the deck of the ship. She stumbled on a loose plank and found the ground rushing up to meet her. She lay there dazed for a moment, the world spinning around her.

"Anoor, get up," Yona said, but her words felt like a dream, far away and blurry.

She felt her limbs begin to quiver with exhaustion. The days of not eating or sleeping were catching up with her. She pushed herself to her elbows. All the crew on deck were watching her.

"What are you all looking at?" Her voice came out high-pitched and irritated. Part of her barely recognised the sound of it.

But the crew just averted their gaze and continued working as if she wasn't there.

Yona's face appeared in Anoor's vision, her eyebrow cocked. "You'll be pleased to know I've brought a tin of bitter leaf tea with me. Shall we go brew some?"

Anoor felt herself relax at the thought. She gave her grandmother a watery smile. "Yes, I think I'd like that."

She pulled herself to standing by leaning on a metal canister set into the boat's edge. As she stood, she examined it closer. "What's this?"

Yona turned to where she was looking.

"That's a cannon, it's part of the amendments I made to the ship over the last few weeks. Those metal balls over there are triggered to release with bloodwerk. Like a runegun, only larger."

"Will it destroy the Tannin?"

Yona's mouth twisted. "The cannons are not for destroying the Tannin. Remember the beast is our God's own. The sacrifice it requires is a blessing and will grant us further favour in the eyes of Kabut. Remember, to win, we must begin again."

"To win we must begin again," Anoor said with numb lips.

"Come, let us—"

There was the sound of grinding metal and crunching wood.

Anoor pressed her chest to the railing of the boat and looked out towards the sound.

A queller without a rider had been brought to life and was smashing its way out of a ship's hull in the distance.

"What has happened?" Anoor murmured.

Yona shook her head. "Divine's web, someone must have fed the beast a vial. We've lost a ship," she said, her face flushed with fury. She removed a small metal plate from her pocket.

"What's that?"

"A last resort. We cannot wait for the marrow to wane, it may be a strike before that happens, and if it destroys more ships, we'll have no army at all. This disc will diffuse the life within the beast. I have used bloodwerk and godpower in tandem, inspired by your own work."

"So, the disc will magnetise to the queller's body," Anoor said.

Yona nodded. "But I must get close enough to the beast without getting hurt."

The queller had crushed the ship and was making its way across the beach in a path of destruction. People were scattering towards the centre of Yellow Commune.

A soldier appeared. "Wife, the clawmaw, we need your bloodwerk power to secure it."

Yona growled and pressed the disc into Anoor's hand. "When it draws near, throw this. And Anoor, aim true."

The cold bite of metal felt like an awful lot of responsibility.

Anoor spotted Faro in the crowd. Thankfully they were close enough to their ship to board and get to safety. If the queller didn't choose their boat next, that was.

But then the earthquake began.

It was the loudest one yet, rattling Anoor's eardrums and shaking her feet. Even the queller stumbled, falling onto its back, and kicking its legs to the sky.

Anoor thought she was seeing things as orange blood filled the horizon.

Lava.

The volcano was spurting red and orange liquid like a ruptured artery. Lava ran thick and fast down the mountainside smothering everything it touched.

The open temple was swallowed in a spray of sparks—the endless flame given a righteous death.

The ground rumbled once more, and the Foundry doors were crushed beneath a rockslide of boulders. The lava followed, sealing the doors forever more.

The Yellow Commune was next, the huts burnt quickly in a river of molten rock and fire. Plumes of smoke permeated the air, shrouding the Isles in ash.

Yona reappeared, her expression one of resignation.

"Cast off!" she called. "Cast off!"

The message was passed from ship to ship, each second precious. The air turned hot and stifling as the lava reached the shore on waves of flame.

Those who had run in the opposite direction of the harbour, away from the queller, had changed direction. Now they screamed from the beach for succour.

With a lurch their ship moved away from the shore.

Anoor didn't move from the railings for some time. She was pleased when Yona appeared with a mug of bitter leaf tea. "Extra barknut powder."

Anoor pocketed the diffuse disc in her hand and took the tea. The Volcane Isles were just a speck in the distance. The horizon was now filled with their fleet.

"Everyone left on the islands, the children, the ancients . . . they're dead now?"

Yona met Anoor's eyes so she could see the honesty there. "Yes."

Anoor took a sip of tea and smiled. "A worthy sacrifice to start our voyage."

CHAPTER TWENTY-FIVE

Hassa

Jin-Laham has been liberated. All those who seek to live in a society built by the people, in service to the people, Dusters and Ghostings are welcome. Embers who wish to settle here must undergo extensive checks, and their crimes tallied as an act of restorative justice.

—The people's council of Jin-Laham

On the second week of their journey north, Vahi's blisters grew so bad they had to rest in Jin-Laham a while to let the wounds dry out or risk infection.

The soles of Hassa's feet had hardened over years of traversing the empire, often without shoes. So, though she didn't understand the pain, she could tell from the tightness in Vahi's face that it was uncomfortable.

I'll go and see if I can get some valerian root. If we add it to warm water, you can soak your feet in it, she signed to Vahi. *The herb will help with the discomfort and aid healing.*

He looked up from the bed. The room they had rented for the night was small but clean. "It'll delay our journey."

It'll delay our journey even more if it gets any worse. Do you really think you can walk for another week?

Vahi winced at the thought, but he still hesitated before he nodded. "Fine, but don't go far, the city is in turmoil."

Hassa smiled; it was nice to have someone to care for her. She darted forward and pressed a kiss to Vahi's whiskered cheek.

Her father laughed. "What was that for?"

But Hassa had already slipped out of the room and to the city beyond.

It had been a long time since Hassa had been around so many people. The first few days of their journey had been spent beneath the dunes of the Farsai Desert.

Though the days had been long and dark, Hassa had cherished the time she had spent with her father beneath the ground. In some ways, nothing had existed beyond the sound of their footsteps and quiet conversation. They were not Ember or Ghosting, simply father and daughter. It was almost as if the war to come was unfathomable.

But then they left the tunnels and their reality had shifted once more.

With the army all called to the capital, Dusters and Ghostings moved freely between cities like never before. Most of the people travelling were going south to Nar-Ruta to join the Truthsayer's army.

It had taken the griot network a mooncycle to successfully dismantle four hundred years of the empire's lies. They met many griots on the road, all intent on sharing the one story that they called "The Ghostings' plight, the wardens' flight".

From then on, Hassa and Vahi had camped each night with caravans of travellers. Some who shared the hearth of their carriages so that Hassa and Vahi wouldn't have to sleep in their armour outside.

Each shared the same news from the cities they had travelled from: revolution had begun.

There were tales of Embers being chased out of their homes, and Dusters running households. Some villages had burnt to the ground and others had reassigned property to Dusters and Ghostings.

But it was the stories about Jin-Laham that had piqued Hassa's curiosity.

Within a week of the truth breaking, the imir of Jin-Laham was sequestered in their home. The imir and their family were held prisoner by their own farmhands who had spent years rearing cattle under punishment of whips. The farmhands had then formed a council with the other Dusters and Ghostings in the city.

Each Ember in Jin-Laham was then put under investigation for the crimes they had committed before being tried in the old Guild of Truth courthouse. The tales spun a picture of peace and prosperity with justice at its heart.

So, when they needed to stop for supplies, Hassa set their course for Jin-Laham.

Hassa stepped out of the inn and into a changed world.

Music filled the streets as she wove through the dancing crowds. She passed a school and what she saw nearly made her stumble: a Ghosting standing at the front of a room filled with Dusters, *teaching them how to sign.*

This was what the whole empire could be like.

Hassa continued with lighter footsteps. As she turned a corner, she passed a square full of people. They surrounded something large in the centre of the clearing. Hassa could just make out a spinning metal device from her vantage point. She concluded that it could only be one thing—a ripping.

Her heart began to pound, and her eyes grew hot. Images of Kwame began to flicker beneath her eyelids. She pressed her wrists to her eyes trying to staunch the flow.

I cannot watch another person suffer like this, I won't. She steeled her nerve to confront the crowd, but then someone tapped her on the shoulder.

"Would you like some goat? It's free for all." The Duster brandished a bread roll full of glistening roasted meat. The crowd parted ahead of Hassa, and she could finally see into its heart.

The contraption she had glimpsed wasn't a rack but a spit, and spinning on its needle was a goat, not a person.

She let out a laugh that sounded more like a hiccup.

The Duster in front of her smiled and passed her the sandwich. "Enjoy."

Hassa chewed the meat slowly and watched the bustling square. No one went hungry. Everyone who passed was given a hot meal.

Hassa swallowed the last bite with disappointment. It was one of the best things she had ever tasted.

She set off on her task once more. On her way back she could grab a sandwich for Vahi too.

There was an apothecary on the next street. She pushed open the door to find the smiling face of a Ghosting, perhaps a year or two older than Hassa.

Hello, what can I get for you? they asked.

Why aren't you in the Chrysalis? It was a rude question, but Hassa was curious. It was usually older Ghostings who refused freedom—those too tired or comfortable with routine to change.

They laughed, such a rare sound from a Ghosting. *I was, but it wasn't for me. Too many rules.*

Too many rules? Hassa was astonished.

Yes. They scrunched their nose. *I think we should all be mindful of complete reign.*

What do you mean? Hassa asked.

I think everyone should get a say on how a city is run. Like in Jin-Laham every Ghosting, Duster and approved Ember is going to be given voting rights on all changes made to the city. I'm even going to nominate myself for the people's council—they're the people who put forward the legislation to vote on.

Hassa's eyebrows shot up. *That is an interesting concept.*

She thought through the ramifications of a society run by collective vote and how that would work in Nar-Ruta. If the end product was a city like Jin-Laham, then the future was a peaceful one.

The other Ghosting watched Hassa with a glint in their blue eyes. *What can I help you with today?*

As much as Hassa wanted to learn more about these new politics, she needed to get back to Vahi, she'd been gone too long already.

Can I get a jar of valerian root and hormone herbs? Hassa needed to stock up.

The Ghosting pulled the items down from the shelves. Hassa delved in her pockets for what remained of her slabs.

No, no, your money is useless here. We're looking at introducing a bartering system, but I'm assuming you're not local. So free it is.

Hassa nodded gratefully. *What's your name?*

Vine.

It was nice to meet you, Vine. Good luck with the people's council.

When Hassa got back to their room—with two more sandwiches—she filled in Vahi on everything she had learnt while he soaked his feet.

"It's the perfect case study for how the wider empire could one day function," he said.

I don't think a voting system is in the elders' plans, she thought but didn't say.

"While we're sitting idle, you should continue practising your bloodwerk," Vahi said.

Hassa had wanted to start working on her bloodwerk half a strike ago, but she'd been politely waiting for the valerian root to lessen Vahi's pain. Now that he had prompted her, she sprang forward, her stylus poised and ready to go. She withdrew another of the Truthsayer's old leaflets.

"Okay, so today we'll practise trigger runes . . ."

Vahi's blisters only delayed them by a day and the next morning he was up and ready to leave. They left the inn as soon as the tidewind stopped, leaving the rest of their slabs on the counter. Even if they had no use here, Hassa couldn't leave without giving them something.

As Hassa pushed open the door to the street one of the innkeepers came down from their upstairs room. "Wait, you, are you not an Ember?" the innkeeper asked.

Vahi turned, unsure whether to answer.

Hassa hesitated on the threshold of the villa. People were looking in.

"Show me your brand." The innkeeper's voice was starting to draw a crowd.

Hassa began to feel uneasy.

Tell them you're my father, Hassa said.

But when Vahi spoke the words there was doubt on the innkeeper's face.

"All Embers are being held in the gaol while we assess their crimes. Those that have been freed have been given papers. Where are your papers?"

We need to run, Hassa signed quickly to Vahi. *We cannot afford the delay of being processed through their system.*

Vahi nodded to her and said, "Are you ready?"

The innkeeper's nose pinched upwards. "Ready? For what?"

Hassa ran. She wasn't as light on her feet as she would have been without her armour on, but she was still faster than Vahi. He stumbled through the city after her, both his lack of coordination and his wounded feet putting him at a disadvantage.

A few Dusters swiped at him, but his stumbling gait helped him lurch out of their way.

They were close to the city's walls, with the expanse of the Farsai Desert beyond. No one would follow them there without the right supplies. The gruelling heat, deprived of a water canister, was threat enough.

Hassa directed them down a side street away from the main thoroughfare that was already full of drums and dancing.

A platoon of officers barred their way. She blinked, then realised they weren't part of the Wardens' Army. They were Dusters, all brandishing scythes. They were not the Wardens' Army, but still soldiers, nonetheless.

"Halt," they said to Hassa. "We've been informed the person you're travelling with is an unregistered Ember."

"We're just passing through, we mean no harm—" Vahi said.

"No harm? What about the oppression of our people for four hundred years? What about the needless murder and colonisation of her"—he nodded to Hassa—"people? No harm. I think not."

Shadows shifted on the sand dunes beyond the soldiers. And Hassa peered around them to see closer.

"You'll need to come with us." Two of the soldiers flanked Vahi, letting Hassa see the full extent of the sand dune behind him.

What she saw made her fall to her knees.

Vahi stopped struggling.

"Hassa? What is it?" But his gaze, and that of the soldiers, followed the shaking path of her wrist.

Thousands of soldiers crested the horizon, peppering the blue sand of the Farsai Desert with glints of metal. She thought the thumping she had felt was the thud of her heart, but now she recognised it, the footfall of soldiers marching in formation. And they were intent on one destination—Jin-Laham.

Vahi gasped beside her, but it seemed such a small sound for such a great sight.

Hassa took a shuddering breath in. Her vision was set alight from the sparks of sunlight gleaming from the metal gazelle pins on the soldiers' breasts.

The Ghosting army had arrived.

CHAPTER TWENTY-SIX

Jond

Though I have attended classes of all the charters, I am drawn to the first law. The runes come easier to me, perhaps because my mother had always loved plants. I am learning quickly. Elyzan has allowed me to stay behind after class to conduct my experiments. So far, they have yielded good results.

—Ads' journal

With Queen Karanomo rising from the dead, all training was paused for the whole day—much to Jond's chagrin.

It was a delay Jond didn't think they could afford, especially with more and more people flocking to the City of Rain who all needed training. Teaching gave him a purpose, one he enjoyed. But anywhere was better than here.

The auditorium was noisy, *very* noisy. An instrument called a "lyre" had been brought by a spritely older woman, and she was playing it with gusto in the centre of a ring of dancers. They twirled in and out in a complicated organised dance that gave Jond a headache just to look at.

He hated the manufactured joy of a party. The forced conversation, the overindulgence of food and wine. He'd never been one to socialise, or really have friends. Just Sylah.

He winced as her name rang hollow in his mind.

"Jond." Niha waved as he spotted him in the crowd.

Niha is a friend too, he supposed. There was a chirrup by his ankles and Jond scooped up Rascal, pressing her fur to his nose.

"And you as well, sweet girl."

The sandcat wriggled from his arms until she perched on his shoulder, her tail curled around his neck.

"Too big to fit in my shirt now, aren't you?"

She rubbed her cheek against his beard before settling down.

Niha thrust a platter of food beneath Jond's nose. "Have you tried these fried courgettes? Absolutely delicious. Elyzan grew them overnight, and I swear I've never tried anything better."

Jond shook his head. "No, I'm fine."

How he longed to go to bed and return to the world of the novel he was reading, *Beneath the Coral*. Shola had given him the book when he left the Entwined Harbour. The romance at the story's centre reminded him of Shola's parting words: "Stories nourish the mind and feed the heart."

Jond's gaze turned to Kara. She wove between the throngs of people like a lustre eel in the shallows. Some of her hair had fallen from her fringe, across one of her violet eyes. She didn't seem to notice, and Jond's hand twitched by his side, knowing how soft her hair would feel between his fingers.

Kara was generous with her time, moving from group to group with a rare grin on her face that nevertheless didn't quite light her eyes. Two guards trailed her around the room. From the moment she announced her true identity, she had revealed a target on her back. The Zalaam would be after her now.

Niha jostled Jond's shoulder. "You haven't taken your eyes off her all evening."

Jond rubbed his brow but didn't look away. How could he when she looked like that? All grace and power, soft smiles and sharp frowns. "I don't think two guards are enough. She's just walking around. Anyone could stab her."

"They're her people, Jond."

"Olina didn't know that one of her own had turned to the Zalaam. Zenebe wouldn't be dead if we'd had more guards."

Niha flinched and Jond opened his mouth to apologise for his careless words.

"No, it's all right." Niha waved his apology away with a grimace. "We all must get used to losing loved ones. You never know, it might be me next."

Jond frowned. "What do you mean?"

Niha gave a small smile. "I'm the new councillor of the third charter."

"What?"

Niha shifted his feet. "I was voted in by the councillors last night. There hasn't really been a right time to tell the rest of the Blood Forged, but I'll be taking over the logistics of our healing centres for the war."

Jond smiled with genuine happiness and clinked an imaginary glass against Niha's. "Congratulations, this time last year you were exiled . . . now look at you, councillor of the third charter."

Niha dipped his head in thanks, then said a little sadly, "Life is too short to look backwards." He reached up and gave Rascal a scratch behind the ears. The kitten stretched out her toes down Jond's chest, her claws clinking on the pins of his uniform.

"Why don't I take Rascal home with me tonight? Give you a night alone?" Niha didn't meet Jond's eye, but the meaning was clear.

"That's not necessary," Jond said through clenched teeth, but still his gaze was fixed on Kara's across the room. She noticed him staring and inclined her head. His felt his pulse quicken.

"Those who play with a mistbear will finds its claws," Niha muttered.

"What?" Jond hated Niha's endless proverbs.

Niha's eye twinkled as he lifted Rascal from Jond's shoulder. "I'm taking Rascal, I could do with the company. Do what you want with the rest of the night."

Jond gave Rascal an affectionate pat on the head before waving Niha away. "Fine, go. But I'm just going to go to bed myself."

"Sure, you are. Good night, Jond."

The crowd in the auditorium was thinning, with people beginning to make their way back to their rooms with full bellies and hope in their hearts.

A few still lingered around Kara. Even though Jond could see that she was exhausted, still she gave them her full attention.

"What time is it?" Jond asked the guard stationed behind Kara.

"A quarter past three in the morning, Major General," they responded.

"Skies above," Jond muttered, then he shouted to the dregs of the crowd. "The Queen needs her sleep. Time for bed, everyone."

Kara turned to him.

"And who are you to give orders to the Queen?" Her voice was playful.

"The major general of the Blood Forged army," he said, his voice rough.

Something hot sparked in her expression as she grazed her eyes over his jawline, down his neck and to the pins on his chest.

Then she turned to the crowd and said, "Perhaps I am a little tired. I thank you all for your stories and your kindness. It has been a long day."

Kara said her final goodbyes and departed. Jond joined the guards at her back and escorted her to her rooms.

"Why are you following, Jond Alnua?" Kara said, when she noticed him.

"Two guards are not enough. It could be dangerous."

Kara raised her jaw as she appraised him. "Are you telling me you are not a danger to me, Major General of the Blood Forged?"

The heat in her eyes scalded him, turning his heart into a mass of glowing embers. One of the guards choked on his saliva, reminding Jond that it wasn't just him and Kara in this corridor.

Jond quirked his lips. "I did not say that, Queen Karanomo."

He thought he saw her shiver before she continued on down the hallway.

At the threshold to her chambers Jond ordered the guards to stand outside while he searched the rooms. Though they had ample soldiers patrolling throughout the night, he couldn't be certain someone hadn't infiltrated Kara's bedchamber.

Kara gave him a bemused glance as he entered.

The room smelt like mint and vanilla. Both sharp and sweet. It was as simply furnished as his, with a bed in the centre and a washbowl set on a table. He was surprised to find a stack of books by her bed, and he found himself reaching for one before he could stop himself.

It was called *The Wounded Tailor*. He cracked open the spine at the bookmark, his eyes glancing over the page.

She ran her hands along the grooves of his torso, ending where the skin turned coarse with hair. He groaned softly in her ear as her fingers danced across the length of his—

Kara flighted next to him, making him jump. "Interesting way of getting yourself into my chambers, Jond Alnua."

"What? That's not . . . I didn't . . ." He felt the blood rush to his face.

She spotted the book in his hands. "Learn any tips in there?"

Jond cleared his throat. "I didn't know you read."

Kara's laugh was a little scornful. "In seven languages, actually."

Jond ground his teeth. "I meant—"

"I know what you meant." She took the book from his hands, her fingers brushing against his. Her eyes widened at the contact.

"Kara . . ." He said her name on the wisp of a breath. He stepped towards her until he could feel the heat of her skin.

The book tumbled out of her hands, but she didn't move. Her lips parted softly before she spoke one word.

"Kneel."

"Kara . . ." His voice came out strangled.

"Queen Karanomo," she corrected him, then said again, "Kneel."

The order was hungry, demanding. How could he disobey?

He lowered himself to the ground in front of her.

She closed the gap between them, her breasts grazing the roughness of his beard. She grabbed the back of his head and grasped at the root of his hair until he looked upwards into her violet eyes. It was blissfully painful.

"Do you want me?" she asked.

"Yes," Jond breathed. Because it was true. He wanted her, badly.

She released her hands from his hair and reached behind her neck to remove the clasp holding the bodice of her dress. It fell to her waist.

"Kara . . ."

She didn't take her eyes off Jond as she removed the rest of the dress, followed by her underclothes. Then she was standing before him, with nothing but her crown.

Every bit a Queen.

Jond pressed a kiss to her navel, his hands weaving around the smoothness of her lower back.

"No." She pranced backwards before returning and resting her hand on his chest.

Jond felt a shudder of desire as her hand slipped under his jacket. He didn't realise what she was doing until she pressed the three badges from his uniform into his hand.

"You can kiss me in three places," she said, her smile mischievous.

Jond had never desired anyone more.

He stood up from his kneeling position and pressed a pin to her lips.

"One," he said. No sooner had the badge fallen to the floor, than his mouth replaced the coolness of the metal.

She tasted like a storm. Wild and fierce.

Her breathing was shallow, her lips glazed. "And where else, Jond Alnua?"

Jond held up the silver badge and placed it on the quickening pulse of her neck.

"Two," he whispered.

His tongue stroked over the contours of her clavicle and up towards her ear, until she shuddered and stepped away.

"Where will you spend your final badge?" Her voice was rough, thick with desire.

Jond's placed the cold gold metal on the tip of her breast.

"Three."

He lowered his lips to her nipple and gently sucked until he could feel her tremble. He realised in that moment that he had wanted to incite the thrums of her desire for a very long time. Like the strings on the lyre, she hummed beneath his touch and he revelled in it, his own desire swelling.

He listened to the panting of her breath and followed the rhythm of it as it quickened.

"Stop," she commanded. "Undress and get on the bed."

He released himself from his underclothes and did as he was bidden. The game had so far yielded him good results, though he was out of pins and wasn't sure what exchange would be made next.

"Lie down." Her eyes slid over the expanse of his body.

"Kara . . ." Her name was a tortured sound on his lips.

The Queen strode over to him, cloaked in the beauty of her nakedness. Her eyes blazed hot with desire and he knew they reflected the same heat in his own gaze.

Kara lowered herself onto him, and he gasped. Then she was moving, faster and faster.

No longer was she the lyre, and he the musician. Now she was the conductor setting the rhythm of his beating heart as she drove him closer and closer to oblivion.

Her panting turned faster then she stopped and quivered around him, her hips dipping forward, her eyes scrunching closed. He wanted to hold on, he wanted to savour it, to enjoy this moment, but . . .

Ecstasy burst in sparks across his body, and he pressed her hips down on his as he shuddered. The ripples of bliss as exquisite as each kiss he had given her.

When the waves of pleasure had abated, he opened his eyes.

Kara was watching him with a satisfied smile on her face. Her crown was lopsided, her hair entangled in the vines of the metal.

She hummed low in her throat and ran her hands over the coarse hair of his chest. He felt his breath go short once more.

"Where did you get that scar?" she asked, her fingers dancing on a raised bit of skin above his rib.

Jond smiled as he recalled the memory.

"Throwing knives. Sylah and I were practising and it went wrong." He chuckled. "Well, it went more than wrong. She nearly nicked my akoma."

"Akoma?" The word sounded strange on Kara's lips and his smile slipped. It had been his nickname for Sylah for so long.

"It's what we call the largest artery in the body. It's the reason why our heart keeps beating." Like Sylah had been. Once.

Kara's expression turned carefully blank.

A breath later she had lifted herself off the bed and padded to the privy. Jond lay there for a few moments, utterly speechless. The warmth in the room had plummeted and he wasn't sure why.

"You don't have to stay," Kara said, her nightclothes already on. "In fact, I'd rather you didn't."

Jond's mouth dropped open. "Was that it?"

Kara cocked her head. "Were you not satisfied?"

"I—but—I thought—" Jond spluttered.

"You thought what? That this was the start of a love story? This isn't a novel, Jond." Kara's lips twisted cruelly and Jond found himself getting up.

He dressed with weary arms. How could he have been so stupid, to fall for yet another person who didn't want him back . . . not in the way he wanted.

"I'll see you tomorrow. Good night, Queen Karanomo," he said.

Kara bared her teeth at her title on his lips. But he was too resigned to spar with her. The evening had been everything he had wanted. Until it was not.

That night he slept without the soft purring of Rascal by his side. Loneliness crept in from the shadows and lay heavy on his chest.

As he tried to sleep under its weight, Niha's words came back to haunt him. "Those who play with a mistbear will find its claws."

Jond rose early and headed down to the ground. The training barracks in the city was large and well equipped but Jond didn't want any company today. He took a set of armour and a sword and shield before leaving the other trainees to their lessons.

He strode to the top of the nearest hill and donned the metal armour. It was raining, as was the norm, but there were no floods. Still the mud made the terrain difficult to train on.

Blue bloodwerk glinted on the shield and Jond examined it.

"By Anyme . . ." he breathed in wonder. The bloodwerk combination on the shield was built to repel other weapons.

It was genius.

Jond picked up the sword. It too had etchings, but instead of repelling, it attracted with the rune *Gi*, pulling on items around it. Though it wouldn't work on people, it would work on the armour, magnetising them towards the blade.

These were innovative techniques that could really change the tide of the war. He moved into Nuba formation three with a wide grin on his face and a lighter heart.

"Last night didn't go well then?"

Jond moved from Nuba formation three to four before replying. "What are you doing down here, Niha?"

The new councillor of the third charter wasn't an especially stealthy man and Jond had heard his firm footsteps from fifty handspans away.

"I think the question is, what are you doing here? I come down here every morning and am yet to meet a soul."

"I needed space . . ." Jond exhaled and dropped formation four. "I needed air."

"That, I understand. I'm a man of the earth and need to feel the mud beneath my feet."

Jond looked down and saw Niha was barefoot. He grimaced. "Your toenails are like eru claws."

Niha laughed through his nose. "All the better for climbing."

"Erus don't climb, they're giant lizards."

Niha shrugged.

Jond sheathed the sword and wiped the sweat from his brow.

"Did she turn you away then?" Niha pressed with gentleness.

"No, she didn't," Jond replied a little too sharply. "I was a task that she completed. She doesn't care for me."

Niha frowned. "I knew Kara when I was training at the Academy, and she has always, always placed responsibility before her feelings. She does what is right and just. Makes sense now that it turned out she was Queen. But my point is, that woman never *ever* panics."

Niha reached forward and squeezed Jond's forearm. "But she did the day you collapsed in the Winterlands."

Jond was shaking his head. "No, you're wrong. That doesn't mean she cares."

Niha refused to hear it. "I think the question you should be asking is, do you care about her? And if so, have you shown her that?"

Sylah appeared in his thoughts unbidden. Sylah whom he loved.

But *how* did he love Sylah? He wasn't sure. He had thought she was the only person for him. The only one who could ever truly understand him—his akoma. But he wasn't the man she had known anymore.

Besides, she's dead now. The thought tore open the wound of her loss and he felt his eyes burn.

"This is foolish, we have a war to win." Jond pulled out the sword again and lunged into nuba formation five.

"Jond—"

"If you say another proverb, this sword's next destination is your chest."

Niha laughed at Jond's very real threat. "Do you know why I speak in proverbs?"

"Because you like to give me a headache?" Jond said, moving into formation six.

"No." Niha shook his head at the periphery of Jond's vision. "My partner was from Bushica, and his first language wasn't the tongue you and I speak. He was from the nomad tribes of Bushica, whose understanding of the world was vaster than I could ever imagine."

Jond fell silent and listened to Niha's tale. It was rare he spoke about his partner.

"They don't tell stories in his homeland, not in the way our waxing fables swell and grow in Tenio. Instead, their knowledge is held in adages. I keep a part of him alive by sharing those he taught me."

Jond wanted Niha to get to his point.

"Do you know what the most poignant proverb he ever told me was?" Niha continued. "A chick must break the egg to live. Do not close yourself off from love, Jond. There is a life worth living beyond the shell."

Jond didn't reply. How did he explain that it wasn't him that was closing himself off, but Kara? Couldn't Niha see that?

His thoughts broke his concentration and he fell out of his formation and face down into the wet mud. He was about to curse at Niha, but the councillor was ambling away, barefoot and whistling as he went.

Jond growled and went back to his routine.

After two strikes of training, Jond returned to the council chamber for a strategy meeting with Ravenwing. His afternoon was then spent teaching bloodwerk—or rather being taught new formations in blood-werk—and then a few strikes with his captains and lieutenants overseeing the training of recruits.

Strikes turned into days and still no new allies appeared following Queen Karanomo's resurrection. Even the refugees, which had arrived in droves before, had slowed to a trickle of fifty, twenty, then none.

Elyzan remained the most hopeful of the Blood Forged leaders. He had grown three more mushrooms for the new, as yet non-existent, soldiers to live in. But time was running out.

The letter from the Zalaam had said two turns of the moon, and already a fortnight had passed.

On the fifteenth day after Zenebe was killed, Jond left the City of Rain to train on the ground in the sunrise. Mercifully it wasn't raining for once. But he did get wet from the sweat that ran down the back of his armour. It only made him feel more alive.

Eventually the rain started, it always did. It began slowly, one fat droplet here and there, smacking the ground with wet dollops. Then the cadence of the rhythm changed as it grew heavier, splattering flecks of mud onto Jond's shins. Soon it fell like sheets of water from the sky, a constant downpour that obscured the world beyond.

Though the hill he was training on was unlikely to get swallowed in the impending flood, he didn't want to take the risk. He began to collect his things and make his way back to the City of Rain above. But as he turned to pick up his shield, he saw watery dots moving in the fields below the Truna Hills in the distance. It was difficult to pick them out in the mist and rain, but as he looked closer, he realised they were people, hundreds of them. No, *thousands* of them.

The allies had arrived.

But so had the floods.

CHAPTER TWENTY-SEVEN

Sylah

To the Truthsayer,
We beseech you to reconsider your stance. Anyme grants no forgive-
ness to those who seek to destroy the wardens' holy place in this
world. If you turn yourself in, we will not prosecute those who
have aided you. If these terms are agreeable, then come to the
Keep's gates unarmed.

—Torn pages of a letter found by Gorn's desk

The griots spread the word across the city that besieging the wardens would commence at dawn. Those willing to fight would meet at the plantation fields before being assigned their regiments—each led by a different Gummer.

The following morning the field echoed with the pounding of scythes.

"There are more people than we could have ever imagined," Gorn breathed.

Sylah and Gorn stood at the edge of the plantation fields. The ash from the burnt ground lifted up from the beating of the army's feet. The black haze spread through the sea of Dusters and Ghostings. The atmosphere crackled with energy and the heady anticipation before a battle. Though the soldiers had no uniform, most had streaked soot across their cheeks, drawing out the hollowness of the cheekbones that the empire had starved. But no more would they allow the slow death of their people. The glint of determination in their eyes was the one thing that united them all.

"This is the second most beautiful thing I have ever seen in my life," Sylah said, surveying the fields. Gorn didn't ask what the first was, because she knew the answer.

Anoor.

Sylah pressed her hand to her chest to ease the pain that had suddenly sparked there.

"Are you all right?" Gorn asked.

Sylah nodded, but she wasn't sure she was. With every day that passed Anoor's image in her mind seemed to blur, as if seen through tears. She was Zalaam now, and that fact would never cease to hurt.

There was the sound of heeled boots on sand and they both turned to the triumphant smile of Turin. "Aren't they magnificent?"

It looked like Turin was already imagining them as her subjects.

Sylah cast her gaze back to the row of soldiers. She spotted Zuhari's stiff gait in the distance. She was moving between the Gummers' factions ensuring that their orders were clear.

Sylah had to begrudgingly admit that the woman's experience in warfare had been beneficial. Ren too had proved invaluable. Her apothecary powders had contributed to the creation of runeflares— an easy signal for the army—and her stock of sleeping herbs was a lynchpin in their plan to storm the Keep.

"Was Ala successful in deploying the drugs into the barracks' rations?" Sylah asked. The wardens' inability to let go of their basic pleasures meant that Ghosting servants were still expected to attend to the Keep. It was a foolish security risk that the Truthsayer had taken full advantage of.

Gorn nodded. "Yes, she said that Sami, another Ghosting in the kitchens, had agreed to add it to the groundnut stew that evening. The sleeping herbs would have taken effect by now."

Groundnut stew. The words roused the aroma from Sylah's memories, and for the first time in a long while, she thought of Lio. How she would rejoice to see the wardens ousted at last. Lio hadn't been the best mother, but the Sandstorm had twisted her to their needs, just as they had Sylah.

"So, the Keep's soldiers will make easy pickings for the Purger then," Sylah said.

The Purger's regiment of Dusters would be the first into the court-yard. They were the best equipped of the other fighters in the army, wearing stolen daggers and swords at their waists.

Sylah watched as the Purger strode towards her faction. She wore the night armour Vahi had made for her, all except the helmet. A foolish decision for combat, but the Gummers weren't trained in the way Sylah had been. Their techniques were fifty percent bravado, fifty percent brute strength. But the bravado instilled confidence in them as leaders, and the strength instilled faith in them as warriors.

Turin had offered Sylah a faction to run but she'd shaken her head.

"I am not a leader or a teacher." She'd learnt that quickly in the City of Rain. Sylah had been trained to kill quietly and effectively. She was not collaborative—she'd never had to be.

The Sandstorm had ensured she only knew two things: how to win, and how to kill.

Besides, Sylah's role in the war for the city was already cast.

"Truthsayer." Griot Sheth appeared behind them. "Rohan's people are in place ready to break the gates with bloodwerk. They await your signal."

Gorn took a deep breath. "It is time. Sylah, go now. When you see a runeflare in the sky, let loose the creation. We will ensure none of our own is in the courtyard to receive it."

Once the Purger's faction had stormed through the gates, any of the Wardens' Army not drugged would be lured into the courtyard. It was Sylah's job to release the creation when a runeflare lit the sky. The stone eru would then make quick work of the enemy. If it didn't kill them, it would at least send them fleeing. Either way, the Keep would be theirs.

But first Sylah needed to finish the final runes.

"I'll await the flare." Sylah nodded to Gorn. The bigger woman held her gaze for a moment, her eyes flint sharp. "It is time the wardens faced the consequences of their actions," Gorn said, her proud jaw set in defiance.

"Burn it all down. For Anoor." Sylah's voice broke on her name.

Gorn's nostrils flared and a wicked grin spread across her cheeks. "Oh, I intend to."

Then Sylah was running, weaving through the crowds that spilt out from the Dredge. The streets grew quieter the further she got from the plantation fields, but not still. The silence was fraught, like the split second between an inhale and an exhale. It turned Sylah's skin into the pebbled texture of eru leather. She shivered and continued on until she reached Turin's house.

She unlocked the door and entered the villa. It was empty, save for one person.

Tanu sat quietly in the shadows of the living room. The chains around her hands clinked as she raised them to wave at Sylah.

"It's time," Sylah said. She opened the door and waited for Tanu to trudge through with her shackles.

Together they made their way east through the Dredge. The Truthsayer's army had started their descent on the capital, and the marching of footsteps cleaved the silence of the city with the drumbeat of war.

Sylah led them through backstreets away from the flow of soldiers until they arrived at the Ring. It was no longer a fighting arena, but it was where Sylah had waged her own war on the empire with the orb of creation.

The eru stood in the centre of the clearing. The statue was a monstrous and beautiful thing. Erus were large beasts but seeing one carved in whitestone made the lizard's presence loom larger. Engraved scales scored across its back and tail. The legs were strong and muscular, ending in talons that Sylah had spent four days sharpening—the claws needed to be sharp enough to cut through skin.

"The changes you have made are impressive," Tanu murmured as she regarded the creation.

"I know. Now I need it to move." Sylah's mouth twisted on the next words. She hated that she had to ask Tanu for help. "You said you could show me how to finish the final rune combination?"

Tanu didn't reply at first. Her bound hands ran over the dried black-red blood of Sylah's runes. Then they stopped. "Here, you need to change this rune, as it is triggering out of sequence. And this one here is drawn incorrectly."

Tanu's expression was feverish, her eyes wide. Sylah knew that Tanu was only helping because she saw the wardens as a worthy sacrifice to Kabut.

"Why do you believe in Kabut?" Sylah found herself asking.

Tanu swung her gaze to Sylah's, a smile spreading across her face. "How can you not believe in him, as you stand there bringing stone to life?"

Sylah shook her head. They didn't have time to debate faith. And perhaps, deep down, Sylah knew that it could easily have been her in Tanu's place—if she hadn't had the strength to turn her back on the Sandstorm and all they stood for.

"Show me how to finish the sequence," Sylah said.

With Tanu's coaching, Sylah drew the last runes across the back of the eru. It took about a strike to finish the combination, and Sylah realised there was no way she would have completed it without the disciple's help.

"This last stroke will bring the godbeast to life, so only complete it when you are ready," Tanu said.

"That's it. That's everything," Sylah breathed. She couldn't believe it, this was going to work.

It was time to bring the wardens to their knees.

She thought of Hassa then. How her friend had left thinking Sylah had given up the cause in order to search for Anoor. Her brows knitted together as she thought of the hurt she must have caused.

When did you stop fighting for the Ghostings? For me?

Sylah leant her head on the stone eru.

"I will not stop until this land is the Ghostings' once more," Sylah whispered against the cool whitestone.

When she looked up, Tanu was gone. Sylah whipped her head left and right, searching for any trace of the disciple but Tanu had disappeared down a side street. Sylah had been too immersed in her thoughts to notice the absence of Tanu's tinkling chains.

Sylah growled low in her throat. "Maiden's tits, where did that woman go—"

The bright red of a flare shot into the sky.

"Shit." It was time.

She was forced to abandon her search for Tanu and finish the final rune on the eru.

With her hand flat on the forearm of the lizard she added the last line of her blood. For a second nothing happened, and she was worried all was lost.

Then the stone beneath her fingers rippled, ever so softly. Like it had moved from solid to liquid to solid again in less than a breath. Suddenly the stone began to groan and creak, and Sylah took a step back with a gasp.

Her creation shuddered to life.

Sylah whooped as the eru pounded across the Dredge. The creature was magnificent, and she cherished running in the dust of its wake. The tail swung as if made from flesh and bone, and not whitestone. Its snout dipped up and down as it lunged forward with an agility that had Sylah marvelling.

I made this creature of grace and destruction, she thought. *Is this how Azim felt when he created me?*

Like a God.

They had balanced the stonework perfectly and the creature moved just like an eru would, even its claws clattered with the same cadence.

It crossed the Tongue in eight strides but as it reached the other side it seemed to stall, its footfalls growing haphazard and its tail swinging wide. The eru careened across the district until it crashed into the side of a villa and was still.

"Fuck!" Sylah sprinted towards the creation, but it was beyond saving. And though its legs kicked wildly, the villa's roof had collapsed on it, pinning the eru to the ground. Soon the power in Sylah's blood would run out and it would be still for good.

Something must have gone wrong, she thought frantically.

But it had worked, it had worked *perfectly*.

There was the sound of a dry chuckle in the distance. Then Sylah saw her. A shadow at the far end of the Tongue where the Duster Quarter met the bridge.

"You did this!" Sylah screamed at her.

Tanu waved, the metal of her shackles cleaved through with whatever tool she had found. Her hands were stained with blood.

"Why?" Sylah asked.

Sylah couldn't understand it; Tanu had wanted the wardens to suffer. It didn't make sense.

Tanu cocked her head. "I decided your suffering would be pain enough, for now."

Sylah began to make her way towards the disciple. Moving slowly as she spoke. "Then why did you help me with the creation?"

When Tanu smiled Sylah recognised something in her expression. "I wanted to see if I could do it." Tanu had felt like a God too.

Sylah was halfway across the Tongue now, she'd soon be within reach of Tanu's neck.

At this distance Sylah could see that the disciple's hands were wet with blue blood.

But Tanu was an Ember.

"Sylah?" The call was weak and filled with pain.

Sylah whirled around to see a figure stumble across the Ember side of the Tongue.

It was Tomi, the stable hand.

Maybe the old Sylah would have hesitated and chosen vengeance over helping a friend. But not today. She ran back the way she had come, stretching the distance between her and Tanu.

Tomi knelt in the dust of the street, his hand pressed to a wound in his stomach.

"She killed Berry, Sylah, I tried to stop her . . . with the dagger . . . but she killed her . . ."

Sylah shook her head wearily. *Of course. Tanu killed the source of the mimic runes.* She cursed her own stupidity for telling Tanu about the eru.

Tomi was sobbing, causing the wound on his stomach to seep all the harder.

"Shush now, you're all right. I'm going to put some pressure on the wound, okay? Then I'm going to carry you towards a healer."

Tomi whimpered as she picked him up. She stole a glance at the bridge, but she knew she'd find it empty.

I'll find you, Tanu. And when I do, I'll kill you.

CHAPTER TWENTY-EIGHT

Anoor

This agreement seeks to reinforce the partnership between the Zalaam and the Shariha. The signatories herewith establish that in exchange for the Shariha's services and fleet, their community will be acknowledged as a subsidiary of the Zalaam and granted the same religious, political and economic standing. In addition, they will be fully recompensed with land that is mutually agreed, upon success.

—Pact between the Zalaam and the Shariha

Anoor gripped the engraver's tool until her knuckles turned pale brown. She scoured the last rune on the kori's wing and held it up to the light. The lamp swayed with the lulling of the waves on the open sea.

The kori's shadow flickered on the wall as her hand shook. Tremors had plagued her since they'd left the Volcane Isles. Nothing seemed to calm them except bitter leaf tea, but she found that the sugar from the barknut powder left her feeling queasy and her mind hazy. So, she avoided it while she worked.

She narrowed her gaze, trying to focus on the small godbeast in front of her. Runes ran along the bird's wings, each connected to a shallow irrigation system of grooves that would flood with bone marrow from the catchment on its back. The creature was delicately small, no bigger than her hand, and intricately made. Feathers crafted from thin sheets of iron were marked with the bloodwerk runes of the Wardens' Empire, to guide it in flight.

But it was godpower that would bring it to life.

"I think . . . I'm finished," she said to herself. All she needed now was to place the mimic runes onto a kori bird.

"Indeed?" Yona stood by her cabin door as she so often did with food, water, or tea. This time it was the latter.

Anoor had struggled to remember to care for herself during the journey, and sleep was still fleeting and brief. "Here, Anoor, take this."

"I don't want any," Anoor said, sharper than she'd intended. Yona just stood there with the steaming mug of tea held out, her face impassive. The liquid inside sloshed close to the brim as the ship moved.

Anoor sighed and reached for the drink. "I'm sorry, I think I've been in this cabin for a bit too long."

"Two weeks. We should see the Tannin any day now," Yona said.

Had that much time passed? The days, like her mind, were blurry.

"I think it will do you good to come outside. Kabut's eye is shining beautifully today."

Anoor nodded. Seeing her God always soothed her.

"Yes, I think I'd like that." As Anoor stood she became painfully aware of a pressure in her belly. When was the last time she had relieved herself?

"I'll meet you on deck," Anoor said to her grandmother, who nodded and left.

Anoor stumbled as she made her way towards the bowsprit where the washrooms were located. Her legs weaker than they'd ever been.

I should practise my Nuba formations. Anoor's own voice was distant in her mind, and it held no conviction. *Sylah would be ashamed of how I have lapsed.*

Sylah's name held a spark still, though that too was flickering, threatening to gutter out completely.

Once she had relieved herself, she washed her face with the urn of water that sat on the counter. She took a shuddering breath as the cold bit into her skin. When she opened her eyes, she gasped.

In front of her stood a spectre.

It had dark skin that had gone ashy and dull. Its short hair faded into fuzz, blurring the ghost's edges. It wore clothes streaked with dirt and flecked with metal shavings.

Her fingers reached out and touched the cloudy mirror.

"It's . . . me," she said in disbelief. When had she let herself fade so much?

Sylah won't even recognise me in Kabut's realm.

The thought scared her. It was time she took better care of herself. She needed to eat and drink more. And wash, she definitely needed to wash.

Anoor picked up the bitter leaf tea she had left on the side and downed the warm liquid.

She made her way to the deck of the boat on unsteady feet.

The moonlight shone down on Anoor's brow, glinting the sweat that beaded there. When she reached the railing, she gripped it gratefully, her breathing unsteady.

Since coming aboard Anoor had rarely left her cabin. There was no one she knew on the *Cleaver* except for the master crafter, Chah. Once she had asked him if he knew how to play shantra. The withering look he had given her had stopped any genial conversation. She only went to him now when she had questions about godpower.

But now the kori was done.

A smile spread across her lips, and she felt her heart swell with pride. She took a deep breath in, revelling in the feeling as Kabut's eye looked down on her.

"You feel Kabut's blessing?" Yona said as she came to join Anoor.

Anoor tipped her head and looked up at the moon. It was waxing, its edges ebbing into nothingness. Just like she had been in the mirror. She knew then that it was a sign from her God, that he took what she gave. And in the end, he would require all of her.

Her grin turned manic, but sometimes that was how she felt—wild and frenzied.

"He is proud of me today," Anoor said, her voice thick.

Yona smiled beside her. "You are his daughter if you feel it so."

They stood quietly side by side as the ship moved through the night. The Zalaam's crew called softly to each other as they manned the sails as the sea got rougher.

Anoor stumbled as a wave crashed into the side of the boat. Yona caught her by the elbow and guided her back to the railing.

"Are you hurt?" Yona asked.

Anoor shook her head. No, she was the opposite of hurt, she felt whole, she felt free.

Rain splattered against her cheek, but then she smelt it—both crisp and earthy, sharp, and salty.

She raised her hand to the growing wind until she felt it. Small particles of blue, as intrinsic to her soul as her blue blood.

Sand.

"The Tannin is here," Anoor breathed. And with it, the godbeast brought the tidewind from the Wardens' Empire. She felt her heart begin to race and flutter, her God's will surging through her veins.

"Flash the lanterns," Yona shouted to the crow's nest above.

The code was a signal for the ships harbouring the harvest of people to move into formation and prepare for the sacrifice.

Anoor smiled as the familiar glitter of the Farsai Desert began to swirl around her.

Shadows cut through beams of moonlight in the distance as the *Cleaver* was overtaken by the ships carrying the Tannin's tithe. Only half of the fleet carried prisoners for the godbeast, while the other half carried godbeasts, like the *Cleaver.*

The sea churned below, and Anoor caught flashes of a white tail patterned with her God's beautiful runes. In the distance, screams, like the sweetest of melodies, cut through the clashing of waves.

Yona watched through her telescope. She growled low in her throat. "The *Grove* isn't sacrificing their harvest."

The number of prisoners had been calculated to mirror the number of the Zalaam's warriors. If the *Grove* wasn't throwing them overboard then the Tannin would take one of the other ships instead.

Like this one.

Anoor frowned. Then she remembered. "The *Grove.* Isn't that Faro's ship?"

Yona let out a sharp exhale and thrust the spyglass into Anoor's hands. "See for yourself."

Anoor looked through the telescope. It took a while for her eyes to focus, but when they did, she could make out the silhouette of

Faro on deck. They stood with their arms crossed looking out into the sea. The crew of the *Grove* stood behind them in similarly defiant stances.

"What are they doing?" she murmured.

"Nothing at all. It appears we have a mutiny on our hands. But we cannot risk losing one of the other ships. Faro needs to sacrifice the harvest *now*."

Anoor lowered the telescope and met Yona's eyes. They both knew what had to be done, but it was clear Yona wanted to hear Anoor say it.

And Anoor did. "I think it's time to use those cannons."

Yona nodded once before barking orders to the crew.

Anoor welcomed the pain as the tidewind swelled and began to cut her cheeks, blue blood drenching her like rain.

The Tannin crested the waves and she laughed, revelling in the monstrosity of her God's power. As the cannons struck Faro's ship Anoor felt euphoria swirl like the waves within her chest.

And when it sank and the storm abated, she tipped her head to the sky, blood-soaked and blissful. "Take this sacrifice to light the spark of my flame. For I am the Child of Fire, and I shall burn it all down."

CHAPTER TWENTY-NINE

Jond

*Three large courgettes, sliced into thin rings—ideally ripened by
 the first law for best flavour*
½ teaspoon of cumin
½ teaspoon of turmeric
¼ teaspoon of salt
¼ cup of flour
Dust the courgettes with the spices and flour
Roast in an oiled pan for twenty minutes until golden

—Elyzan's crispy courgette recipe

Jond rushed to the nearest lift and gave orders to the guards there.

"Our allies have arrived. And the water is rising. We need help.
Flighters, camels, carts. Anyone who can swim. We need to get
everyone to the top of the hills as fast as we can."

Jond didn't turn around to see if the guard followed through.
Instead he went back down to begin the rescue.

The hordes of people had moved closer since he'd gone for help.
There were thousands of them, some in armour, some without, but
all were ready to fight. Though joy swelled in his heart, it was tainted
by the approaching danger. If they didn't make it to the foothills soon,
there'd be no allies left.

The rain was so heavy it pummelled his skin as he headed down
towards the oncoming allies. They were running too but they were

weighed down with supplies and weapons. Murky water lapped at their feet.

Jond knew how quickly that water could rise.

"How far?" said the first person he came across. They were panting, their face flushed.

"The top of this hill, not much further at all, keep going." He repeated the words as he ran to support the most vulnerable. "Keep going, everyone! You're so close now!"

He spotted a heavily pregnant person. "I'm going to carry you, okay?"

They nodded. Jond lifted them and began to run. He deposited them at the top of the hill and pointed towards the lifts where people were already on hand to help.

By the time he returned to the fields, the water was already at his shins. And getting higher with each breath.

Up and down Jond ran, helping tens of people. His armour slowed him and so he began to shed pieces of it as he went. More and more people from the City of Rain had joined the rescue. He saw someone with violet eyes flight in and out of the fields more than once, but he didn't have time to look at Kara today. Ignoring her presence had proved difficult in the council chamber, but here, where there were so many people who needed his help, he couldn't let her distract him.

The flood had now reached his hipbones and rainwater had begun to seep into his undergarments through the waistband of his slacks. The waterproof material had weathered well, but even it had its limitations in an all-out flood.

"Help him, please!" Jond heard the cry and ran towards it.

A man in his later years held aloft a young boy of six or seven. Tear tracks left clean lines down the old man's mud-streaked face.

"My grandson, he can't swim." The water was already up to the man's waist.

Jond didn't waste time replying. The last dregs of people were already swimming to succour. He scooped the child from the man's outstretched hands and lugged him over his shoulder. The boy was crying something, shrieking out into the wind, but Jond couldn't hear him.

The crowds around the lifts were already thinning. Jond jogged up to a soldier who was helping direct people and handed over the child. As soon as the boy's feet touched the ground, he turned on Jond, slamming his little fists into Jond's stomach.

"You left him, you left my grandpapa, and he can't swim either. He can't swim!"

"Oh, maiden's tits," Jond said under his breath. Then clutched the boy's hands in one of his and said more gently, "I'll go and get him."

The water had risen another three handspans to the top of Jond's shoulders. Jond knew he had to be quick.

"You can't go down there," the soldier who had taken over the crying boy said. "It's too dangerous, Major General."

"Yeah, well. I'm going." Jond set off towards the field. But as he looked out at the water, he couldn't see the old man anywhere.

"Fuck." The man must have drowned in the time it took Jond to rescue his grandson. Jond was getting ready to dive into the water to blindly search when the water swelled ahead of him. Two bedraggled people emerged onto the muddy bank.

"Take him," Kara said, pushing the grandfather into his arms. She was breathing heavily, like she'd been holding her breath for a long time.

The elderly man clung onto Jond and fell to his knees, coughing up water. Jond patted him on the back.

"My grandson, is he okay?" he croaked.

There was a cry behind them and then the young boy was hurtling towards his grandfather's weak arms. The soldier who Jond had assigned to look after the boy followed soon after and helped both the old man and his grandson into a lift.

Once they were safe, Jond turned to go back to the field. A hand clasped around his arm just as his foot breached the water.

"He was the last," Kara said. She looked as wan and as exhausted as Jond felt. Her words hit him like runebullets, and he felt himself slide to the ground. He let out a weak sigh as she slipped down next to him.

They lay there on the muddy bank of the Truna foothills looking up at the sky. The rain was already lessening, the clouds growing brighter. Though the flash floods had only taken a strike to arrive, it'd be half a day before the fields stopped being lakes.

"My bones feel like they are made of concrete," Jond said.

"So, he finally speaks to me," Kara muttered. But she didn't sound bitter, more relieved.

Nonetheless, Jond chose to ignore the comment. Kara had made her feelings clear, but that didn't give her the right to deny him his.

"Thank you for saving that man," he said. "I promised his grandson I'd bring him back."

Kara snorted, but even that seemed weak in mettle. "Stupid promise, Jond Alnua."

"No, I don't think it was. If I hadn't have saved him, I knew someone else would have."

Jond didn't look at Kara, but he thought he heard her chewing her lip.

"The allies came," he stated.

"They did."

"We should probably go join the other councillors, to discuss next steps. I imagine people are looking for us."

"Jond, I guarantee there are at least five soldiers standing behind us right now. I have rarely been truly alone in my life." Her words were stark and bleak. It gave him a rare glimpse into what she thought about being a monarch.

"You don't like it much, being Queen?"

Kara sighed. "I have no choice, Jond, so it doesn't matter whether I like it or not."

"Can you not just . . . give it to someone else?"

She chuckled. "No, the title is hereditary. Besides, my name called all these people here today. Though the crown may be heavy, it is worth something."

"Maybe after the war. You could give it all up."

Kara hummed, and her tone turned wistful. "What would you do if you could do anything in the world?"

"I'd own a bookshop. A free one," he said confidently.

She laughed. "You would own a bookshop that gave away free books? I don't think that would be very profitable."

"Well, you said anything in the world, you didn't ask for a business proposition," he said a bit defensively. When she only laughed harder, he added, "What would you do?"

"I'd like to be a gardener, not like the first law, but the natural way. Pruning and nurturing the land."

He turned his head to Kara to find her already looking at him. Her rose-vine crown was flecked with dirt and rainwater. He could imagine her among the plants, her hair loose and free.

"You'd grow roses, lots of roses," he said softly.

Her smile was warm. "Yes, just like the gardens in the palace." An image of her wearing *just* the crown appeared in his mind, and he pushed it away.

The rain had stopped now and the chill of the mud at his back seeped into his skin.

"We should go, I don't think the major general and the Queen of Tenio should really be lying on the ground," he said. But he didn't make a move to leave, her gaze still held his so completely.

Kara's mouth began to twitch, her expression turning conflicted.

"Jond—" Kara started, but then her eyes moved past his to something . . . no, *someone* who had entered her vision.

"Queen, Major General." The soldier bowed and saluted above them. "Ravenwing sent me with a message . . . erm . . . he said, 'Tell them to get their asses up to the council room before I send Ads down to drag them up.'" It was a threat the elder knew would hit home. Jond didn't have the strength to manage Ads' inane chatter.

Jond got up first and offered Kara his muddy hand. She grasped it and he eased her to her feet. It was the first physical contact they'd had since he'd left her room last week.

He wanted to keep her hand in his, but he knew the pain of holding on to an unrequited love. Sylah had taught him that.

And he wanted so much more than Kara could give him.

She had asked him that night, "Did you think this was the start of a love story?" And the truth was, yes. That was exactly what he had hoped for. He wanted the feelings that he'd read about in ink and paper.

He looked down at their entwined hands then up into her gaze. Kara's expression was guarded, her jaw set on the offensive.

It was not an expression of love. But she'd told him that already.

He untangled himself from her grip and didn't look back as he walked away.

*　*　*

"Fifteen thousand, three hundred and seventy-two people. Half of them are part of Tenio's disbanded army, either from Sea Lord or Earth Lord realms. About a quarter are refugees seeking shelter, but we've appointed those with useful skills to our supporting staff for the battle. We have also received words from the southern harbour that the navies from both the Grasslands and Bushica have arrived with an additional twenty boats from the Winterlands. This brings our total to just over three hundred ships," Jond announced through the mind link.

There were smiles and nods in the room. Hope unfurled from the shadows for the first time in a long while. Jond felt the tendrils of that hope move through his mind. It had taken them three days to process and assign all the new recruits.

"It won't be enough."

Everyone turned to the speaker. Jond hadn't heard Olina say a word since one of her own murdered Zenebe. She lifted her head and surveyed the room with bloodshot eyes before continuing.

"My comrades had to make a detour during their journey to the City of Rain due to an iceberg in the north of the Marion Sea. The Tannin still roams the ocean around the Wardens' Empire and we do not have the numbers to fight it and the Zalaam."

"Then we wait for the Zalaam here," Metteh, a Sea Lord, said with a dismissive wave. "If their goal is to destroy everyone in this world, why make it easy for them? Why must we travel to the Drylands to fight? Let them brave the Tannin and destroy half their armies to get to us."

There was an explosion of anger through the mind link and more than one person winced and held their temples. Jond didn't notice, though, as his was one of the voices.

"You cannot sacrifice an entire nation, you cannot abandon them," Jond shouted.

His anger was fuelled by one thought: *if there's any chance Sylah is alive, she's there and I will not let the Zalaam kill her.*

Kara's eyes snapped to his and he wondered if he'd let the thought leak into the mental room they shared. But there was no way she could have heard it because Dew was shouting now, too, their mental voice so loud it vibrated Jond's skull.

"That is not an option," they said, silencing the other elders and Jond. Dew stood, signing along with their mental speech. "The final battle must be fought on the empire's soil or the blood of every murder there will seep into our soul and poison our future. There is no winning if we let them take our land."

The silence was heavy with guilt.

"Then what do you suggest we do? We no longer have the orb of creation, so we cannot even destroy the Tannin," Sui muttered.

"I have an idea." Ads' voice was uncharacteristically tentative.

Be quiet, child, Ravenwing signed to her. Jond recognised the signs as he'd seen the elder so often chastise her with that exact phrase.

"Let her speak," Dew said.

Ads nodded gratefully and stood. She held a thin leaf in her hand. The hue of it seemed familiar.

"I've been working with Elyzan in the greenhouses, developing ways in which we can manipulate the first law for battle purposes. The problem with the first law is that it is nature dependent, and nature is difficult to manipulate. But, if we combine bloodwerk forces with it, we can, for example, make an oak sapling into a dagger by pushing it horizontally."

"Girl, reach your point before nightfall," Ravenwing grumbled.

"We could bind the Tannin . . ." She slapped the leaf on the table.

"With steelweed," Jond finished the sentence for her. He'd seen the plant being used in the Entwined Harbour. Fully grown it had the strength of its namesake metal.

As he leant forward, he saw the wet shimmer of translucent blood patterning the frond. Ads inserted her stylus into her inkwell and finished the combination on the leaf. When complete she held out her hand. The steelweed began to grow, spinning faster and faster around her wrist.

She made a squeal and Elyzan reached forward with his orbed hand and released the steelweed from her wrist.

Metteh scoffed into the silence. "It's effective on a little girl, but on a sea creature, like the Tannin? A creature of deathcraft? How can we be sure?"

Elyzan was rubbing his jaw in a pensive gesture. "With enough steelweed we might be able to crack the stone, rendering the runes on the Tannin useless."

"Might?" Kara asked. She had watched the proceedings with little input. But with one word she made known her worries.

"Exactly, we need certainty here," Metteh said.

Jond looked to Metteh, then to Kara, and said, "There are no certainties in war."

"Says the boy who's never been in one," Kara muttered.

Jond stood on legs shaking with anger.

"I have seen more violence and bloodshed than you could ever imagine," he said roughly. Then his eyes narrowed in on Kara's. All the voices in his mind went silent as he said, "I was born of a rebellion to tear the wealthy from their thrones."

"People like me, Jond?" Kara said as if no one else could hear them. He was about to retort but then she said something that rendered him speechless. "I will never be your precious Sylah, Jond."

His brows knitted together. He had never expected her to be Sylah, not once.

Niha coughed, bringing both Kara and Jond back to the meeting at hand. Ravenwing was smirking, but most people looked either bemused or annoyed by their outburst.

Jond sat back down. "I think the potential outcome is worth the risk." He was talking about the Tannin, but Kara flinched as if his words cut deeper.

"The risk is smaller than you think," Ads insisted, drawing all stares away from Jond, to his relief. "All we need to do is send out a small barge with a few students of the first law to the edge of the Tannin's lair. We need to make sure we're in an area of thick steelweed which might take some mapping with a flighter beforehand. The rest of the ships can be on standby. Flighters can be used to confirm our success."

"And if you're not successful?" Metteh asked.

Ads shrugged. "We die, but it's a chance I think we'd all take."

"Who is *we*?" Elyzan asked.

Ads shuffled her feet. "I've already trained a few students in the right combination of runes." Ads lifted her chin. "We are going to do it whether you agree to it or not."

Olina and Metteh were nodding, coming around to the plan. Niha,

Reed and Dew looked supportive. But Kara's face had turned to stone and Jond couldn't parse her thoughts.

Jond looked to Ads. She had changed in the mooncycles they'd been in the City of Rain. She spent most of her days with Elyzan and his students, and it reminded Jond what the world could be like if inquisitive people like her were free to innovate. If they survived the war, Ads would be one of the world's future leaders.

Jond cocked his head. He could see it. Of course, the council would have to curtail her incessant chatter, but she was warm, and curious. Two things some leaders lacked. His gaze glossed over Kara's once more.

Ravenwing stood abruptly, drawing attention to himself. As the commander of their armies, his opinion mattered. The elder looked between Ads and Elyzan and down again at the steelweed.

"No. Too many Ghostings have already been lost to the war that this continent started. We find another way." Ravenwing wiped away the link of blood runes on his wrist and left the council chamber.

There were mutters around the room. Some took umbrage with the blame being placed at Tenio's feet, others, like Jond, were frustrated that Ravenwing denounced the plan.

"I'm going to do it anyway, he can't stop me." Ads' jaw jutted out as she spoke.

Dew sighed with the tiredness of a person who had lived too long and slept too little.

"Of course you must do it, Ads. This is not the Wardens' Empire. We do things by vote, and I don't even need to call for a vote to know what the answer *must* be. It is our only chance to subdue the Tannin." Dew rubbed their brow and said to Ads, "Ravenwing will come around. He lost Zero and he doesn't want to lose you too."

"He doesn't even like me."

Dew's response was fierce. "Like? *Like?* You are a Ghosting. A free Ghosting at that. That supersedes like."

Elyzan cleared his throat, and Dew and Ads slipped into the Ghosting language, continuing their conversation privately. "All in favour for Ads' plan to go ahead?"

Every arm in the room was raised except one. Kara met Jond's gaze before nodding once and pointing her hand skyward. He supposed it was some sort of apology for her earlier words, but he couldn't be certain. Her words about Sylah had baffled him and he wasn't sure he understood her at all anymore.

"The plan goes ahead," Elyzan said grimly. "We have a lot to be getting on with. The safest route has been ascertained to avoid the floods. We move west tomorrow." Elyzan stood up, removing himself from the connection.

Jond felt Kara's eyes still on his, but he didn't turn. His mind churned like the roiling sea, and his feelings for Kara were like the Tannin in its depths. But he couldn't let himself get distracted.

Because tomorrow the march begins.

CHAPTER THIRTY

Anoor

I don't think I can be complicit in the murder of the prisoners in the hull of the boat. There are five hundred of them, all chained together. Some still bleeding from the holes in their bones. I had thought the Zalaam would liberate the empire, but I see now how wrong we have been, how foolish. Fighting atrocities with more atrocities does not make peace. If only I had seen it sooner. Then perhaps Qwa would have lived.

—Last words written by former Disciple of Duty, Faro

Anoor had removed her shoes before she stepped off the gangplank. So when her feet touched the ground, they sank into the sand. She closed her eyes and revelled in the feeling of the Farsai Desert between her toes. The sand was hot, warmed by the midday sun. It was a dry type of heat, one that parched the throat and peppered the brow with sweat.

How she had missed it.

I'm home again.

And though the words echoed in her mind, she didn't entirely feel at home. *Home* was an idea that belonged in the past. Where Sylah was.

But Sylah will be in my future. If I bring all the non-believers to their knees.

Anoor tipped her head back and opened her eyes to the burning orange of the sun. She had been cold for so long, she had forgotten how hot the rays of the Wardens' Empire could be. But though they warmed the surface of her skin, they still didn't melt the ice in her core.

"Will you get me some bitter leaf tea?" Anoor said to the nearest soldier. Her voice was hoarse from lack of use.

The soldier startled at her words, as if they hadn't even noticed she was there. And maybe she wasn't wholly present. Since Faro's death she felt as if she were diminishing. Her part in the sacrifice of her friend—though righteous—had left a deep scar. Too deep ever to heal.

"Pardon?" the soldier asked.

Anoor repeated herself though her voice still came out weak and frail. The soldier heard her this time and slipped away to do as she'd asked.

Anoor lifted her gaze to the sky once more. Too quickly it seemed, as the edges of her vision turned black.

Even my sight is going.

Anoor was disappearing.

She blinked away the black spots in her vision and checked her body. She was whole, that she knew, but her spirit was ebbing. Like Kabut's eye in the sky, she felt herself slipping away into the darkness of a new moon.

She ate when food was put in front of her and she drank when tea was brought, but there had been no improvement in the tremors that had started on the ship. One evening she had steeled her will to practise her Nuba formations. But as she tried to hold the first position, her muscles shook until she collapsed onto the floor sobbing and shaking.

Yona had roused her strikes later with a mug of bitter leaf tea, the only thing that seemed to bring her back to life.

But she only had to live for a little longer. First the wardens had to be sacrificed to Kabut. Then she could leave this life for the next one, where Sylah awaited her in Kabut's realm.

And there they would be reunited once more.

What if Kabut hasn't granted Sylah a place in paradise? The thought drenched her in cold sweat.

"No," she murmured softly to herself. "I am the Ch-child of Fire. And the sacrifices I make will ensure Sylah has a place by my s-side."

Stuttering the words fatigued her, and her breathing grew laboured. She lowered herself to the ground and thrust her hands into the sand by her feet. The warm granules calmed her beating heart.

Yona strode into Anoor's view. "Anoor, get up. We have a long walk ahead of us."

Anoor didn't reply, sometimes it was just easier to do as her grand-mother asked.

They had docked just south of Jin-Laham where the shore was wide and flat, allowing their army to disembark more easily. Their journey would take them north of the Jin-Dinil lakes, then south down to Nar-Ruta.

A long march of three or four days on foot. But it would be even longer with the godbeasts.

Anoor shivered and wrapped her arms around herself. She noticed there was less to hold on to than there had been a few weeks ago.

"Are you cold?" Yona asked.

Anoor nodded, and Yona exchanged a few words with one of her soldiers, and a few moments later Anoor felt something settle on her shoulders. The cloak was heavy, and when her hands went to touch it, she discovered that it was the cape from her own armour. Made from the thick cactus leather that was native to the Volcane Isles. The stiff material wasn't quite the blanket she had envisioned, but it would do.

Anoor struggled under the weight of the cloak but didn't take it off.

She turned her bleary eyes to the city of Jin-Laham. Or what was left of it. The first ships to come into port had released five quellers into the city. The massacre had been brutal. Equipped with bladed legs, the mechanical spiders had run amok, destroying people, build-ings and plants. Fuelled by the bone marrow vials in their metal bodies, the quellers had survived for three days, far longer than any blood-powered godbeast normally would.

That is, except the Tannin that had been fed by thousands of souls.

Smoke drifted up from the wreckage of Jin-Laham. It was Anoor's first taste of the destruction the godbeasts could reap.

"I-I want to go into the city," Anoor mumbled. She wanted to see the glory of her God's sacrifice.

Yona's nose pinched upwards. "It will delay our march."

Anoor felt her head begin to nod in agreement, but then a flicker of her old spark came back to her.

"It is Kabut's will," Anoor replied, lifting her chin. She had come to realise that the words worked as a key, unlocking doors and opportunities that would have otherwise been withheld.

Yona's eyes narrowed as if she knew *exactly* what Anoor was doing. But what could she say?

After all, I am the Child of Fire, Kabut's will is my own. The thought fanned the flames of her spark of strength.

Yona called for an escort and soon Anoor was smothered behind the deep green of the Zalaam's army.

The unit moved as one towards the smoking ruins of Jin-Laham with Anoor hidden in its midst. She could see nothing of the landscape around her until the circle of soldiers surrounding her parted, revealing the destruction beyond.

The roofs of the villas that lined the streets were gouged with holes from the quellers' legs. Bodies punctured with wounds the width of Anoor's hand lay where they had fallen. Fires smouldered and spread across the city, destroying any building that was still habitable. The smoke choked the last breath from the few citizens who still lived.

Here was her God's power at work.

Anoor dropped to her knees. The soldier closest to her tried to catch her, but then they heard her prayer:

"G-glorious one up above, you who knows no bounds or boundaries. You, who spins the web of my future, take this s-sacrifice as your own." Her finger sank deep into the ground where the soil was tacky with the blood of non-believers.

She tried to stand but struggled to summon the strength. The soldier to her right helped lift her. And as Anoor stood she noticed a piece of paper lying on the side of the road. It was unblemished, a stark white thing among the blood and ash.

She picked it up and read. "Vote for Vine for the people's council of Jin-Laham. N-no more will we let the Embers sow dissent. V-vote Vine: Ghosting, fighter, leader."

The people in this city had overthrown the Ember imir and were forging a new path for their government.

Ghosting, fighter, leader.

Something on the edge of her conscience seemed to crack. The smallest of fissures.

"Child of Fire, it is time to move out," Chah said. She hadn't noticed that the master crafter had joined the group of soldiers. But she rarely noticed much anymore.

She let the leaflet fall to the ground. It fluttered until it landed in a pool of water. She watched the liquid seep into the paper until the words were completely marred. It was only then she realised that it wasn't water on the ground.

It was Ghosting blood.

"Let us go," Anoor whispered. But she didn't have the strength to say more. Her thoughts were a storm rolling in on the horizon. She knew something was wrong, but she couldn't put her finger on what.

When she returned to Yona, a cup of bitter leaf tea was waiting.

"I thought you might need it," Yona said.

Anoor gratefully took the drink, a part of her knowing it would help numb her troubled thoughts.

She had noticed that the tea did more than soothe. It relaxed her so completely that she often found herself hoping she'd have access to it in Kabut's realm.

"Were you satisfied by the quellers' power?" Yona asked.

Anoor nodded, euphoria singing through her veins. "Kabut is happy."

Yona's smile was slow, but wide. "I am glad you think so."

"Are we ready to depart?" Anoor asked softly, her words only a little slurred. Once the initial taste of oblivion from the tea ebbed, a weariness settled into her bones.

"Yes, the clawmaw was the last godbeast to be unloaded. We are ready."

Anoor turned her gaze to the army at Yona's back. She let out a quiet, "Oh", surprised to see the sprawling sea of soldiers and godbeasts. It was no easy thing to forget the existence of an army so large, but Anoor had done it, and seeing them now made her heart sing.

The infantry stood shoulder to shoulder on the shore, the emblem of Kabut's eight-legged form on their armoured breasts. Rows of sentinels were loaded onto carts behind them, the wolf-shaped creatures glinting menacingly in the sunlight. The cone-shaped heads of the hollowers sat further back. The quellers loomed at the rear on even larger carts. The vast number of their bladed spider legs, one after another, was a sight to behold.

But the godbeast that drew Anoor's attention was the clawmaw. The only creature to stand on two legs, its height and bulk overshadowed the rest of the army. Even though Anoor had never been close enough to inspect the runes on the clawmaw, she knew that crafting it was a feat of creativity and genius—and so it could only have been Yona who had made it.

Her grandmother's arm shot skyward, the signal for the army to advance. Wheels turned with a grinding sound as the crates were pulled across the sand.

Their journey to Nar-Ruta would not be a quiet one, no slinking in during the night to take the wardens unawares. They also had to assume that those who had fled Jin-Laham during the attack would spread the word of the Zalaam's coming.

Let them talk, Anoor thought. *And each day the wardens' fear will grow until they too would begin to feel some semblance of the dread their citizens have lived with all their lives.*

As the army began to move, Yona turned to Anoor. "Lead the way, my Child of Fire. We must arrive at Nar-Ruta before week's end."

Anoor straightened her back and took a step forward. Though her legs still trembled, she felt the strength of the army at her back.

The tempest in her mind had calmed, and only one thought remained:

Wardens, the Child of Fire is coming. Embers you may be, but I will not stop until you are tinder and ash.

CHAPTER THIRTY-ONE

Sylah

Someone once told me that we are all fighting for something. I think our passivity may be our downfall, not just for this rebellion, but for ourselves. Our ancestors have laid the path for our future. The time to act is now. The shackles we now wear are of our own making. Let us shake them free.

—Signed message sent from Ala to Sami,
a Ghosting in the Wardens' Keep

Sylah ran through the streets with Tomi in her arms, his life blood soaked into her tunic.

"She killed Berry," he murmured against her shoulder.

"I know," Sylah soothed. "But hush now, save your strength."

Every time he spoke, more blood gurgled up from his stomach. She had bound a torn piece of her sleeve across the wound, but it was already soaked through, loosening the knot of the fabric. Tomi wasn't going to make it. "Tomi, I'm going to stop and try and bind the bandage tighter, all right?"

Tomi didn't respond.

Shit.

She ran into the nearest Ember villa and laid him down across the kitchen counter. It was clear that the house had already been looted, so she didn't waste time looking for supplies.

"Tomi?" She ripped off her other sleeve and tied it around his waist, but the blood had already stopped flowing.

Because his heart was no longer beating.

Hot tears splashed onto her cheeks.

"I'm so sorry, Tomi," she whispered.

This was her fault. If she hadn't told Tanu about Berry, then Tomi would still be alive.

For a little while Sylah sat paralysed with shock and grief. She mourned not just for Tomi and Berry, but for the empire too. Without the eru creation being let loose in the courtyard, then the rebellion had probably failed. She couldn't bear to leave this villa to find out.

When she could finally summon the strength of will to stand, she went straight to the flint stone by the villa's stove and struck it against the wooden counter where Tomi lay.

She couldn't abandon his body for the vermin. The wood sparked and the fire crackled to life.

He will not be the first who will die from my actions today.

A sob threatened to consume her, but she knew she couldn't linger here much longer. Smoke had already filled the villa. The fire was moving quicker than Sylah had anticipated.

Sparks stung her eyes as she stumbled to the front door. Smoke filled her lungs, and she began to choke. She tried to stabilise herself by holding on to the wall but in the haze, she tripped, falling heavily on the ground.

You can't die here, Sylah. Anoor's voice in her mind was as sweet as a kori's song.

Why not? I failed, I bring nothing to this war except my longing for you.

Anoor would be so disappointed to see Sylah die this way. But it would be so easy. So simple. All Sylah had to do was inhale deeply, letting the smoke strangle the air from her.

If I let go now, I will never have to face Anoor on the other side of the battlefield. The thought was too painful to imagine.

A wraith of soot and smog moved ahead of her.

"Anoor?" Sylah coughed.

Strong arms wrapped around her wrists and hauled her out into the blissful relief of fresh air. Her knees grazed the ground as she was dragged across the threshold of the burning villa and to the street opposite.

She wiped ash from her eyes and looked into Zuhari's concerned face.

"Thank the blood," Zuhari breathed.

Sylah would have scowled at her saviour, but in that moment, she needed to concentrate on breathing.

After a minute of hacking coughs, she turned to Zuhari. "How did you know I was there?" Sylah rasped.

"Gorn was worried you hadn't shown up. I was passing through when I saw the fire. I would have walked right by if I hadn't looked through the window and seen you falling. What were you doing in there?"

Sylah didn't want to voice Tomi's death just yet. It was her burden to carry. "You know just because you saved me doesn't mean I forgive you for what you did to Anoor."

Some feuds were destined to last.

Zuhari broke Sylah's fierce gaze and looked away. "What happened to the creation?"

Sylah's cheeks flushed with shame. "It's over there."

Zuhari glanced towards the end of the street. Now that it lay still, the eru's body was so well camouflaged among the fallen whitestone that it was hard to make it out.

"Thankfully we won't need it after all," Zuhari said.

"What?"

"The wardens have handed themselves over to the rebellion."

"*What?*"

Could it really be this easy? Her hands shook as a memory flooded her mind.

"*You are the Final Strife, the last frontier before freedom for all,*" Azim preached to the Stolen, and they listened with the stillness of complete faith. "*Win the Aktibar and infiltrate the Keep, then the empire will be ours to mould. Never again will the wardens' rule break us. It is time for us to break* them."

The Sandstorm hadn't had her loyalty for a long time, but something in her chest loosened—something that had been planted as a seed and fostered with fervour by the Sandstorm.

Her purpose.

Now it had been fulfilled, and she too felt free.

Zuhari watched Sylah grapple with her shock, until she tipped her head and said, "Come and see. Today is the beginning of a new world."

Sylah had expected blood to be running through the streets the closer they got to the Keep. She'd seen in the drawings of the Siege of the Silent etched into the Nest how brutal a battle with the empire could be. But there was no blood marring the Ember Quarter as they drew closer to the Keep's gates. Instead, the city seemed like it was sleeping.

But then she heard the screams.

She withdrew her dagger as she started to run. The Keep's gates were wide open, and she flew through them, a snarl on her lips.

But what she had heard weren't screams, but cheers.

The courtyard was full of people celebrating. A group of Dusters had linked arms and were crooning a nursery rhyme whose last lines they'd changed:

One, two, three, four
All the wardens in a row
Ruling us never more
Freedom for all below.

Sylah recognised the labels of the Keep's Jin-Eynab wine as the bottles were passed from hand to hand. Ghostings and Dusters revelled beneath the great joba tree. Sylah watched in awe as people tore pieces of their clothing and added them to the branches. The multicoloured decorations were more beautiful than any trinkets the wardens had ever used.

A lump formed in Sylah's throat. Not only had they broken the wardens, but the citizens had started to heal too.

Zuhari caught up with Sylah as she stood dumbfounded among the celebrations. "I tried to tell you, you don't need your blade—the Keep is ours."

"How did it happen?" Sylah asked.

Zuhari smiled. "The servants," she said simply. "They were led by Sami, a Ghosting. Even the Ember servants joined our cause. This morning, when news of our movements reached the Keep, they locked all the wardens in the courtroom and barred the doors. After that, the Keep surrendering to the rebellion was just a formality."

Sylah shivered as she stepped through the Keep's doors. The last time she had been there she was saying goodbye to Anoor.

No, I will not let memories of her ruin this moment, she thought to herself.

"And what of the army?" Sylah asked.

"The sleeping herbs Ala laced the food with were stronger than anyone expected. Only a few hundred soldiers were in a state to fight. The Purger's regiment dealt with them."

"Casualties?"

"Fifty, mostly their side."

Sylah shook her head in disbelief. "So, the Wardens' Empire is finally liberated."

The Final Strife had been fulfilled—and without the help of any of the Stolen. It seemed fitting that the Sandstorm's dream had come to pass without the aid of those they had exploited.

Sylah laughed. "The servants. Of course it was them."

Hassa had taught her that servants had a quiet strength that was often unaccounted for. She wished her friend was here to see the Keep like this, full of laughter and cheer.

"Gorn, Turin and Ren are in the courtroom," Zuhari said.

Sylah knew the way. She lengthened her strides so she didn't have to walk alongside Zuhari.

The door to the courtoom was open. Inside, the room was a stark contrast to the festivities in the courtyard. Sylah's wide smile of triumph faltered as she sensed the tension. Gorn, Ren and Turin looked up as she entered.

"Sylah." Gorn let out a sigh of relief. "When the creation didn't appear, I was worried."

Sylah didn't embrace Gorn—she wouldn't even know how with the amount of armour the woman was wearing—but she nodded deeply. "Tanu sabotaged the creation and it failed. And she escaped."

"What?" Ren and Turin said together.

"She stopped the eru by killing the source."

"Whose blood is on your arms?" Gorn asked.

Sylah shook her head. She still wasn't ready to say his name aloud. "Where are the wardens?" she asked.

"Locked in the old Nowerk Gaol along with all the imir officials who refused to surrender. The soldiers who succumbed to the drug have been stripped of their weapons, and when they awake, they'll be given the same choice. Gaol—or fight the Zalaam under our command," Gorn said. "Because time is running out."

Ren passed Sylah a worn piece of paper and she knew that this must be the source of their worries.

Sylah ran her eyes over it:

We have our Child of Fire. The time for war has come. We bring the battle in two turns of the moon on the shores of the Drylands. And if you do not come, we will find you. For every non-believer must be purged.

To win we must begin again.

"When was this sent?" Sylah asked. But when no one answered she asked again, an octave higher. "When was this sent?"

"We don't know, but it must have been before they closed the gates, because no messengers could come in or out," Gorn said.

"What of the duty chutes? They were still in operation?" Sylah asked, hoping, pleading for more time.

Gorn shook her head.

"I destroyed them the night I left the Keep, sent fireballs into the joints so the wardens had no easy means to commune with the outside world. The letter was delivered over a mooncycle ago. We must assume that we have but a few weeks until the Zalaam arrive."

"Or days," Turin added.

That means Anoor could already be at the empire's shore. The thought set Sylah's heart racing. She found herself reaching for an imaginary joba seed between her teeth.

How she wanted to escape to oblivion. And if she'd had a joba seed right then, she wasn't sure whether she would have been able to refuse it.

She was burning with a need to see Anoor, but a fear troubled her. *What if Anoor no longer wants to see me?* Sylah had to assume she didn't. Anoor had *chosen* the Zalaam.

But maybe, if Sylah could see her, she could convince her to defect?

Her thoughts were cleaved by the sound of shouting.

"Truthsayer!" The call was frantic, and they all turned to see the Purger run into the room.

"An army's been spotted at the plantation fields."

Turin let out a manic laugh. "Or mere minutes."

CHAPTER THIRTY-TWO

Jond

Major General Jond Alnua will be leading a specialised squadron of soldiers who have all received bloodwerk-altered armour. As our resources are limited in this area, please speak to him if you would like to enlist in this operation. The squadron will be highly exposed, with an increased risk of injury or fatality.

—Message left in the army barracks of the City of Rain

Two weeks after Ads' demonstration they were ready to set sail. The Blood Forged met for a final time at the western shores of Tenio. The air felt thick as soup, hot with anticipation and spiced with more than a little foreboding.

They stood beneath a temporary canopy on the shingle beach, south of the City of Rain. The sky was grey, and rain pattered down on the roof, setting an uneven tempo.

Dew was talking logistics. "I have coordinated with Commander Ravenwing to ensure each vice admiral leading our fleet has a Blood Forged member, a healer and a flighter. Every ship is equipped with supplies to last two mooncycles. I will circulate the details showing your ship assignments now." Dew nodded to Ads, who removed a scroll from her bag and handed it to Elyzan, who noted his allocation before handing it to the next person.

Jond watched as the scroll worked its way around the room, all the while wondering who he'd be travelling with.

Then Dew said, "Now I will hand over to Olina, who has the final naval configuration." Dew took their seat.

After some shuffling, a map of the Marion Sea was unfurled in the centre of the table. The room was so crowded that Jond had to push his way through to see it. Yesterday the Tsar of the Wetlands had arrived with six of her warwomen, each leading a regiment of soldiers.

"As you all know, I will be leading the fleet as admiral of the navy," Olina said. Despite the humidity she still wore her thick furs from the Winterlands. "In addition, I will be overseeing the Tannin operation. Elyzan, Ads and their team of students will be travelling with me. All other ships will be stationed two leagues south and will remain there until our flighters have confirmed it is safe to pass. There have also been some small changes to the rear squadrons . . ."

Sui, the councillor of the second charter, tapped Jond's shoulder. The scroll that showed the ship assignments had made its way around to him. She handed it to him and he scanned the page to find his name scrawled under the ship named *Helwa*. His stomach sank as he saw whose name was below his.

"Assign me a different ship," Jond said loudly, interrupting Olina. She stopped mid-sentence.

It took Jond a moment to identify Dew's gaze among the sets of eyes staring at him.

"No," the elder said simply. "My role is to manage operations, yours is to manage soldiers. I don't question your choices, so do not question mine. Every person's skill has been carefully weighed to ensure the best possible outcome for survival. I have made my decision. Accept it."

Kara was sitting on the periphery of the circle. They had barely spoken since the flood at the bottom of the Truna Hills. Her eyes settled lazily on his. There was a question in her expression, but he didn't know how to answer it.

Jond scowled and looked away. Olina glanced at him, then back at Dew, before continuing. "As I was saying . . ."

Three weeks at sea with Kara was a torture he did not want to endure.

Jond pressed the scroll into the next person's hand. He wiped the blood from his wrist, marring the runes that connected his mind to the room. Olina went blessedly silent.

Then he left the council meeting. The rain cooled his flushed skin, made hotter by the memory of Kara's gaze on his. He hated that with one look she had brought to the surface all his frustrations. A reminder that she felt nothing for him, while he . . .

Jond let out a long breath. Despite only exchanging greetings for the last two weeks, she hadn't been far from his mind. Every time she passed him in the corridor, her scent would linger in his thoughts. Once, her foot had brushed against his under the table. The touch sent a jolt of fire up his legs to his groin. The brief caress of her skin a reminder of the night they had spent together.

Jond ran a hand through his hair. He had shaved it close to his skull so that his helmet could fit more snugly. He also knew that the style suited him in a dangerous sort of way, drawing attention to the sharp lines of his jaw and the muscled contours of his neck.

The harbour sprawled out ahead of him. Ships of all sizes swayed on the gentle waves. The long riverboats from the Winterlands were tied closest to the shore. A row behind them the wide sails from the Wetland ships flapped in the breeze. Anchored further out were the largest vessels; made from Bushica wood and steel they blotted out the horizon. Five hundred ships all told, but Jond couldn't help thinking they weren't enough.

"Major General." A soldier stood to attention as Jond neared the shore.

"At ease," Jond muttered, wondering when *he* would ever be at ease with his title.

Jond identified the *Helwa* among the ships moored. His stomach sank as he inspected it. It seemed more decrepit than any of the others in the fleet. Then Jond smiled. Of course Kara had insisted on giving the best ships to her subjects. The main mast looked to be constructed out of three different types of wood nailed together, the crow's nest was crooked, and the sails hung tattered and frayed in the breeze. Not that the sails mattered now. The students that had learnt blood-werk runes had used them to create metal propellers much like the ones that had powered the *Baqarah*, the ship that Jond had travelled on to Tenio. The propellers would make their voyage much quicker.

As Jond neared the ship, the sickly-sweet aroma of robi oil grew stronger. The substance, derived from a tropical nut, coated the decks of the ships, protecting them from the acid rain they might encounter as they circumnavigated the east coast.

Soldiers boarded decks and filled the hulls with supplies.

"Did you have to make such a scene?" Jond turned to find Kara flanked by two guards. She was wearing well-worn leather armour in a deep purple. How he wanted to peel it off.

Jond shook off the intrusive thought and met Kara's gaze. Since she had announced her identity, she had stopped wearing the slip of silk across her face, exposing her smile. And right now, that smile was sarcastic, and more than a little condescending.

"I thought it would be better for both of us if we weren't trapped on the same ship for three weeks," Jond said.

Kara snorted. "My request for Commander Ravenwing was ignored."

He knew that she'd been avoiding him as much as he'd been avoiding her, so the barb shouldn't have stung as much as it did.

They both stood for a moment in tense silence. Jond's gaze drifted back to the fleet. The sea licked up the sides of the ships, the waves an obsidian black.

Are you down there, Sylah? He found himself wondering.

He reminded himself that it was unlikely she had survived the Tannin. He had to come to terms with that.

"You were thinking of Sylah just now, weren't you?" Kara said, her voice cold.

Jond started, worried for a minute that their minds were linked. When she saw him look for the second charter runes on his arm she laughed bitterly and said, "Your face softens whenever you think of her."

Pain flashed across Kara's face and Jond couldn't understand it. He was about to ask, when Kara turned to go, but just before she left, she said, "I'll keep out of your way, if you keep out of mine."

She waited for his response. Jond wished it could be different, but he couldn't force someone to love him. So he simply nodded and said, "Fine."

One of the guards shot Jond a sympathetic look before running after her. Jond exhaled through his nose and turned back to the horizon.

Not a second later there was a nudge against his leg. He looked down to find Rascal gazing back up at him.

"Where have you been?" he chastised her as he picked her up. She chirruped and rubbed her head under his chin. "Have you been helping Niha with the patients?" The march from the City of Rain to the coast had presented the councillor with his first casualties.

Niha's booming voice followed a rough clap on Jond's back. "Jond, thank the good-hearted twist of fate, you're assigned to this ship!"

Though his voice was filled with cheer, his stocky frame stooped with the weight of fatigue. "One healer, one flighter, one fighter and a cat." Niha tweaked Rascal's nose.

"Trapped on a boat together for weeks . . ." Jond added, grimacing in Kara's direction.

Niha rubbed his one eye and said, "The dog's tail remains crooked even after fifty moulds."

"What?"

"The two of you. You're stubborn. Stupid, too, I might add."

"Thank you," Jond said sardonically.

"You know what I mean."

"No, actually I don't."

"She wants you. Do you deny it?"

"I am not a meal to be wanted."

Niha recoiled, then laughed. "I can't stop thinking of you on a plate with an apple in your mouth. Ha! What a sight that would be."

Rascal squirmed in Jond's arms, Niha's laughter startling her. The older man held out a hand to soothe the kitten as he spoke. "All right, all right. Look, all I'm saying is, you two need to talk. If you don't want her because of your love for Sylah, then tell her that, and we can all move on. Because I am bored of *this*." Niha flicked a wrist across the space between Kara and Jond.

"Sylah has nothing to do with this."

Niha's eye bulged. "If she has nothing to do with this, then what is the problem? Either enjoy yourself or don't."

Jond ground his teeth before he said with some reluctance, "I want more. I want more than just pleasure. I want it all, the hurt, the pain, the excitement. All the facets of it. Why can't I want that?"

The smile dropped from Niha's face, and he nodded a little sadly. "Are you sure she doesn't want that too?"

"Yes—"

"But are you *sure*? She might think Sylah was the person you wanted that with."

Jond had never said that to Kara. And he was just about to explain that to Niha, but the sound of a horn cut him off.

"Time to set sail," Niha said with finality.

Jond looked towards the shore and wondered if he'd ever come back to Tenio.

Niha looked forlorn as he too took in the sight of his homeland.

"I think I'm going to go rest my feet," Niha said quietly after a moment. "Did you get your cabin number from the council meeting?"

"No, I must have missed it." Jond hadn't read the scroll in detail. All he had seen was *her* name next to his.

"This way," Niha said. Rascal jumped from Jond's arms and plodded after Niha as he led them up the gangplank and onto the deck of the ship.

They weaved between soldiers who offered up hasty salutes as they passed by.

"The vice admiral of our squadron is a Bushica native. We will dine with them tonight in their chambers, along with Kara. That's their great cabin." Niha pointed sternward to the room that spanned the width of the ship.

"My room's next to the infirmary, across the hall." Niha pointed to a much smaller room on the other end of the corridor. "You have been assigned this cabin."

They stopped in front of a door that croaked on rusty hinges as Jond pushed it open. A small bed, a bedside cabinet and wash basin were the only things in the room. It was simple, but peace and quiet was all Jond really needed.

"I don't have to share my cabin?" Jond asked dubiously.

"You're the major general. Of course you don't have to share. The soldiers are in dormitories on the next level down."

Jond nodded and looked at his cot, suddenly very tired despite the time of day.

"I think I'm going to rest my feet too. Rascal, you staying with me? Or do you want to explore some more?"

The white cat flicked her tail in goodbye before trotting off back down the corridor.

Niha laughed and waved as well before shutting the door and leaving Jond to darkness.

"The very darkness will be your only friend." Sylah's voice drifted up from his memories as it so often did.

"Even in death you still chide me, Sylah." He fumbled for the gas-lamp switch. As it flickered to life, he breathed easier. Though loneliness still made his chest ache, the light cast a little warmth, easing the feeling. He dropped his pack to the floor and collapsed on the bed.

He thought of what Niha had said: "She might think Sylah was the person you wanted that with."

Did Kara truly believe that? How could she? He had never even spoken to her of Sylah. Or had he?

"Your face softens when you think of her." That's what she'd said earlier.

Jond growled in frustration, and buried his face in his pillow, smothering his turbulent thoughts.

The mattress was a little hard and the sheets rough, but the Blood Forged had few resources and it was impressive that they'd managed to assemble a fleet so vast.

After a strike the ship, propelled by bloodwerk, lurched forward, and Jond let out a shaky breath. He reached into his pack and withdrew the tincture of ginger tea he had brewed for the journey. He swallowed a healthy dose and sat back, wiping his hand across his mouth.

"I fucking hate ships."

Jond woke with a lurch. Disoriented and with no indication of what time it was, he stumbled out of his cabin and into the corridor. He tripped over the lip in the doorway and fell heavily to the floor.

The cabin door next to his head opened. "Are you drunk?"

Of course, Kara's cabin was *right there*.

"No, I fell." Jond spoke through gritted teeth. His cheeks flamed with embarrassment as he stood.

"All right then," Kara replied before stepping out into the corridor with a lot more grace than he had. She wore an azure silk dress so long it pooled at her feet. Jond recognised it as another one of the dresses they had stolen from the Souk. It looked much better on her than him. "Are you coming?"

"To where?" Jond asked.

"Dinner? In Vice Admiral Lawha's cabin."

"It's dinner time?"

Kara didn't deign to respond. Jond scowled at her back as he followed her down the corridor. She stopped at the stern of the boat, where a set of double doors opened to a dimly lit room beyond.

Jond could smell the food before he saw it. He'd got used to having a primarily vegetarian diet in the City of Rain. Elyzan's greenhouses kept the city fed on a steady supply of beans, courgettes and cauliflower. Jond had found himself partial to the latter, especially when the cauliflower was glazed with honey and roasted until golden like the platter in front of him.

He barely noticed Lawha or Niha as he took his seat in front of the food.

"Jond, this is Vice Admiral Lawha," Kara said dryly. Jond looked up into the warm brown eyes of the vice admiral. They wore a type of wide-brimmed hat that Jond had never seen before, and a doublet with brass buttons so large they had Jond wondering about their functionality.

"Hello, Vice Admiral Lawha."

The vice admiral saluted. "Welcome, Major General, Queen."

Lawha was a shy musawa who said very little during the course of the dinner. Every now and then they'd smile and run their hand over their bald head with a nervous gesture. Thankfully Niha had the ability to fill the silence with story after story.

" . . . and I said, 'the camel's dung points to the camel, of course.' And can you believe what he said? 'No, the dung pointed to me.' *Me*, if you'll believe it?"

Kara laughed politely and Jond rolled his eyes. If every evening was to be spent like this, he'd launch himself into the sea now and let the Tannin take him.

Eventually the talk turned to the operation at hand. Lawha perked up then. "It'll take us a week to reach the rendezvous, at which point the admiral's ship will then lead the assault against the Tannin. If successful, we will proceed to the Drylands and set up camp."

"It sounds so easy," Jond muttered into his drink. Perhaps he had drunk too much. Bushica wine was thick and potent.

"Of course, it won't be easy. War is not *easy*." Kara's lip curled as she replied under her breath.

Oh, how I vex her so.

Jond laughed at the thought that this woman could possibly want anything from him other than pleasure.

"What's so funny?" she asked. Niha was amusing the vice admiral with another tale, completely ignoring Jond and Kara's conversation.

"You. Us. All of it," Jond said.

Kara's mouth set into a line, but she didn't respond.

The evening wore on. Jond got drunker, and Niha's stories got funnier. But eventually even Niha grew tired of his own voice.

"I think it might be time to retire," Niha said, and the room seemed to collectively sigh in relief. "I for one need to check on my patients. We had a couple of mishaps before we left . . ."

They all drifted off to their quarters. Kara slipped away without saying bye.

On his way to the comfort of his bed, Jond hesitated by her door. He was feeling wine-brave that night, so he rapped his knuckles three times.

She opened the door with a sigh. "Jond, I'm tired, what do you want?"

It was clear she was in the middle of getting ready for bed, as the top buttons of her dress had been unfastened. Jond's gaze lingered on the open seam. She saw where he was looking and ran her fingers over the buttons there.

"Oh, is it going to be that type of visit?" she asked softly.

Jond found himself leaning in, his heart pounding as his hand went to the back of her neck. She arched into him until their lips were almost touching.

"Is this what you want?" he asked roughly.

She looked into his eyes as if searching for something.

"Is this what *you* want?" she countered.

Yes, desperately, yes.

But he found himself breaking away, the pain of their last coupling was still too fresh. He couldn't let himself be used like that again.

Kara stiffened and then drew her arms around her chest like armour. "Go to bed then, Jond. You're drunk."

He was, but that didn't mean he couldn't get to his point. "I don't understand . . . why is it th-that one day it's like this . . . but I'm not a thing you can use . . . you know? A-and there are feelings here . . . but hidden . . . I think sometimes you're with me and then gone. Understand?"

Only nonsense was spilling forth.

Kara's lips lifted in a scowl. "What?"

Jond tried to distil his thoughts into a single question. Then it came to him, as thick and as potent as the wine: "Why can't you give me more?"

Kara's lashes fluttered against her cheek. "I don't think that's the question you should be asking."

Then she shut the door in his face.

Jond didn't remember getting back to his cabin. But he must have, as he woke strewn across his bed with a dry mouth and a pounding headache.

He dressed slowly, his freshly laundered uniform hanging from the back of the door. It disturbed him that a servant had managed to get in and out without him waking.

Sylah would be ashamed to know him. The badges that denoted his rank lay on the bedside cabinet. As he began to pin them onto his shoulder he thought of Kara and the exchange they'd made that night in her room.

One for her lips. One for her neck. One for her breasts.

Then the memory of going to her room last night flooded back to him.

"You fucking idiot," he growled. The woman had made her intentions clear. And yet . . . hadn't she shown she desired him last night?

But desire is not love. The thought was salt in an open wound.

He needed breakfast, and something to punch.

So Jond fled his cabin and his thoughts and went to train with his soldiers.

*　*　*

"No, drop your shoulder, you're hunching it and taking the tension between your ears instead of in the thrust of the sword. Try again," Jond barked.

His regiment stood in rows on the upper deck of the ship, practising their form.

The midday sun was strong, bringing heat and perspiration. But it comforted Jond, making him feel closer to the home he had left.

One of the soldiers lunged forward, her sword aiming directly at Jond's heart. He blocked it with his axe. She fell backwards on her ass, eliciting a few laughs and titters from the watching crowd.

Jond offered her a hand up. "You did well. You could have killed me with that blow."

"I was terrible," she growled.

"How long have you been training?"

"Three weeks, Major General. I was a carpenter before enlisting."

"I've been training since I was four years old. What you just did was brilliant."

"But the Zalaam . . . What if they're all like you?" she asked.

"They won't be. And remember we have something they don't." Jond tapped the bloodwork on her armour and shield. Then he raised his voice, addressing the entire squadron as he spoke again.

"This training isn't about winning and losing rounds. It's about preparing you for the battlefield. And no matter what we do, no one can truly be prepared. This will be a war like no other. It isn't about winning or losing, it's about surviving. We have something to live for, but the Zalaam, they don't. They welcome death, they *seek* it. And that is the true advantage we have over them. I want you all to remember that."

There were nods and some fearful glances, but Jond felt his soldiers' demeanour change from apprehension to determination.

"Now come at me with all that you've got," he said to the soldier who'd fallen before.

And she did. Again and again.

That evening Jond sent a note to Vice Admiral Lawha to let them know that he'd be dining with his soldiers in the mess hall.

When the supper bell was rung, Jond filed into the mess hall along with everyone else. He was handed a bowl of lumpy vegetable soup and directed towards the rows of tables. Not quite the same quality of fare as yesterday, but he'd take it over sitting next to Kara for another evening.

Most of the soldiers had developed friendship groups or factions and Jond didn't want to intrude. Many had already noticed his presence and were acting differently because of it. At the back was a small table, where one person was seated facing away from him. They wore the grey slacks and tunic of the Blood Forged's army, but he saw no badge on their shirt. Their hair was tied up in a scarf at the nape of their neck.

Jond sat on the empty bench opposite and looked up into the violet eyes of the Queen. His eyes flickered to the nearest escape route.

"Jond, are you following me?" Kara said lightly.

"What are you doing here? And dressed like that?"

He wasn't sure how he hadn't recognised her. The disguise might work on some of the soldiers, but up close, she still carried herself like royalty.

She cocked her head and surveyed him. "*You* came to sit here. And besides, I quite like being incognito."

"You look ridiculous." She didn't. She looked wonderful, she could wear a sack and still be the most exquisite thing in the room.

Kara just raised an eyebrow. "So I assume you also excused yourself from dinner with the vice admiral."

"By Anyme, this is ridiculous." Jond stood and surveyed the room, but now every single seat was taken. He was about to leave and retreat to his cabin when Kara said, "Stay. We can eat in silence."

"Fine," he muttered and sat down.

After his third mouthful, Kara asked, "How long were you and Sylah lovers?"

Jond almost choked on his soup. The question had fractured the silence like an earthquake.

"Excuse me?" he said.

Kara's voice was light. "How long were you lovers?"

Jond frowned. "We weren't, not really."

"But you loved her?"

"Love," Jond said automatically. He couldn't think of her in the past, not yet.

Kara nodded deeply.

Jond was about to explain, that his love for Sylah was different . . . it was complicated with deep roots that gnarled in knots. But then Kara stood.

"You asked why I couldn't give you more, Jond. But the truth is, you never gave me anything in return." Her expression was frank.

Jond reached for her wrist but stopped short of touching her. He didn't want to be burnt again.

"You're the one who rejected me, Kara."

She shook her head, and when she spoke, her voice was bleak. "Every relationship I have ever had has been a transaction, a political token on a board game I don't know how to play. And I've spent my life teaching myself the rules. But I don't want to play a game with you, Jond."

Then she left, leaving Jond more confused than ever before.

For the rest of the week, he ate his dinner in his room.

CHAPTER THIRTY-THREE

Hassa

They've trapped us in, sealed the doors. Wern is hysterical, apparently she hadn't yet fed her pet kori birds that day. But animals are the least of our worries. The truth crushed us all in the end. I can hear them at the Keep's gates. It won't be long now. I pray, let it not be long.

—Last journal entry by Aveed, former Warden of Duty

Hassa stood on charred ground. The city of Nar-Ruta sprawled out ahead of her, the Ghosting army to her back. The Wardens' Keep thrust up from the landscape in the distance, the five hundred steps a matchstick on the horizon.

But who ruled behind the Keep's walls?

The city streets were quiet—deathly quiet, but without the death. If the citizens had indeed risen up—like the griots on their route had claimed—then Hassa expected there to be more evidence of violence.

A plume of ash bloomed up from the dirt as she shifted her feet. She never thought that she would live in a world where the plantation fields were no more. A smile spread across her lips as she took in the burnt rubber trees.

The ground will be more fertile now, Memur signed next to her. Her silver hair trailed down the back of her leather armour. She stood beside Hassa as the interim general of the army in the elders' absence.

A new beginning, Hassa replied, hope sprouting in her chest like the plants she imagined growing anew in this field.

The seed of hope had been sown the moment the Ghosting army had arrived in Jin-Laham and saved Vahi from the people's council. It was then that Hassa had begun to think they might have a chance against the Zalaam.

She looked back on the rows of soldiers behind her. Three thousand Ghostings, all armed with blades at their wrists and gazelle pins at their chests.

It was a sight to behold.

"I can't hear any fighting," Vahi said by Hassa's side.

No, me neither. Hassa frowned, scanning the empty streets.

Can we infiltrate the Keep through the tunnels beneath the city? Memur asked Hassa.

Yes, there is an entrance in the dunes. Sometimes the shifting sand conceals it.

Go find it, Memur signed.

Hassa positioned herself north of the Dredge and used landmarks to home in on where the hatch would be. As she moved through the rows of soldiers a few nodded to her in reverence.

Some saluted and signed, *Watcher, may Anyme bless you.*

Though Hassa and Vahi never reached the Chrysalis, she was glad to be back with her people. The army's arrival at Jin-Laham had saved Vahi from certain imprisonment. The troops had been travelling for two weeks by the time they'd reached the city. Memur had ordered the army south after hearing about the Truthsayer's plight. Hassa and Vahi had joined them, retracing their steps back to Nar-Ruta.

Now they were here, Hassa felt her heart pound with anticipation. There was something in the afternoon wind that felt different.

She weaved through the Ghostings, searching for the hatch that would lead her to the tunnels below.

Each soldier wore a sheet of metal on their back that during the night tessellated together to create a tidewind shelter large enough for the army to sleep in.

The first time Hassa had seen them build the tent, she had been mesmerised by the synchronisation of their movements. Grunts from squad leaders' throats directed them in different movements. The metal sheets slotted into place in an intricate dance. The army had been thoroughly trained.

Hassa stopped at the base of a small dune. She removed her sandals and pressed her soles into the ground. Her toes probed through the warm sand searching for the texture of wood.

When she felt it, she hooked her foot through the handle and pulled. Her muscles strained until the hatch gave way. She waved Memur over.

This will take us to the Keep. I can lead a scouting party to see what has become of the capital.

Memur frowned. *No, I will come with you.*

It might not be safe, Hassa countered.

A Ghosting has never been safe in this empire, Hassa. Not under the wardens' rule. Today will be no exception.

Hassa dipped her head at Memur's words.

The older woman touched her wrist gently before signing, *Lead the way through the tunnels, Hassa. If the fighting has ended, then it is time we made our move.*

A shadow stretched on the dune ahead, and the two Ghostings turned to find Vahi had followed them.

"General Memur, will you allow me to accompany you? I would like to stay by Hassa's side," Vahi asked as he joined them around the hatch.

As an Ember, Vahi was only tolerated because he was her father.

Yes, you may come, Memur replied, and Hassa let out a sigh of relief. She had encouraged Vahi to stay near her for his own safety. She'd seen the flashes of violence in some of the soldiers' eyes. This battle was a long time coming and they were ready to confront any Ember in their sights.

As Hassa began to climb down the ladder there was a sound of running footsteps. A scout appeared in the sunlight above her, signing frantically to Memur. Hassa couldn't read the signs, so she continued her way down. If it was important, Memur would tell her.

Hassa breathed in. Though it had only been a few weeks, she'd missed the darkness and the damp of the tunnel network.

She felt for the groove where a torch should be, the scent of oil guiding her arms until she found it set into the stone. With the torch in the crook of her elbow she reached for the piece of flint that hung from the wall with string and pushed it against the rough whitestone until it sparked.

By the time the torch was lit, Vahi and Memur had reached the bottom of the ladder. Memur looked like she was catching her breath from the effort.

This tunnel will lead us under the Ruta River to the Keep? Memur asked.

Hassa nodded.

The firelight flickered across Memur's face. *Let us go then.*

Hassa led them through the tunnels at a steady pace. They walked for over a strike until Hassa slowed beneath the cracks of a flagstone. She could hear movement coming from the kitchens, and the smell of bread pulled thoughts of Kwame to the surface of her mind.

She hadn't been to the kitchens since he'd died.

"You know what the trick is to making the best bread?" His twinkling eyes shone brightly in her memory.

She shook her head from the kitchen counter she sat upon. It was early morning, the tidewind still wreaked havoc outside. Kwame's hands kneaded the dough in a slow rhythm.

"Some people think it's the kneading, or the shaping, but the truth is much simpler." Then he turned to her and put his floury hands on either side of her face. Hassa began to squirm away, but before she could, he pressed a kiss to her smiling lips.

"Patience," he whispered as he pulled back. "The best things are worth waiting for."

She swallowed down the grief that threatened to choke her.

"Are we here?" Vahi whispered.

Hassa nodded. She doused the torch and set it back into the wall just in case the smoke drew unwanted attention. Then she climbed the last few rungs on the ladder and pressed her wrists against the flagstone. Usually, the stone would give way with a click from the hinge that lined one side of it. She tried again but something heavy was weighing it down.

Hassa flipped her stylus into position and pushed against the stone until she felt the pinch of the needle entering her flesh. When she felt the wetness of her blood beading at the tip she began to draw.

Bloodwerk had come easily to her, as if she had always known it and was just remembering the specific strokes. Every day she had practised for one or two strikes, Vahi guiding her with his knowledge. But it was clear that she was innately talented at replicating the runes. She learnt she could easily recreate them, with or without light.

The flagstone flew open, pushed by the rune *Ba*, and the strength of her blood.

Hassa scrambled out into the light, prepared for anything, or anyone, she might find.

The pantry had been decimated, flour, salt, sugar all strewn on the floor. Even the herbs that used to hang from the ceiling to dry had been ripped down and trampled on.

Vahi shook his head. "Stupid, we could have used all of this. What a waste," he murmured.

Memur made a sound behind them and both Vahi and Hassa went to help her up the last step of the ladder.

Thank you, she signed when she'd regained her balance. *I have not climbed that many ladders in a very long time.*

She pressed her wrist to her beating chest where the gazelle emblem of the Ghosting army adorned her jacket. Then she looked around and the wrist moved to her mouth.

What happened here?

I don't know, Hassa replied.

The pantry door was ajar, and after a quick look through the gap, Hassa slipped out into the kitchen.

A group of Dusters were drinking from the bottles of some of the finest vintages of wine. They turned when they saw Hassa.

"It's a good day for you Ghostings," one slurred.

"But a bad day for the wardens," another added. They burst into snickering laughter.

The drunk Dusters were not a threat to the Ghostings, so Hassa led Memur out and towards the west side of the Keep.

The corridors were full of celebrating Dusters, some drinking, some looting, some dancing.

They did it, they managed to overthrow the wardens, Hassa signed, then laughed abruptly. Vahi joined in until their eyes were wet with joy.

But Memur's lips stayed firm, and when she signed, she sobered them. *We still do not know who is in charge. I will not tolerate one poor ruler for another.*

Hassa hadn't considered that those now in power would be anything other than good. She assumed Gorn would have led the rebellion, but it had been over a mooncycle. There was no evidence that Gorn was still at the helm.

When they reached the courtroom Hassa felt herself sag with relief. Gorn was there, her form looming over a table with Zuhari, Ren, Turin . . . and Sylah.

Hassa was surprised to find her old friend here. Last time she saw her, Sylah was planning on travelling to the Volcane Isles to rescue Anoor. Abandoning the fight.

Abandoning me, Hassa thought.

Sylah jumped up when she saw Hassa and crossed the distance between them.

"Hassa?" Sylah said her name tentatively as if she couldn't believe she was really there.

I didn't think I'd find you here, Hassa signed into the silence. Memur and Vahi still stood in the doorway. Gorn looked like she wanted to speak, but she respected the moment between Sylah and Hassa.

"I . . . I didn't go after her." Sylah's lips quivered as if she'd been about to say "Anoor" but couldn't manage it. Then she exhaled, started again. "I'm sorry, Hassa. Sorry that I ever made you feel like my sword wasn't yours. I fight by the Ghostings' side, always."

Her words rang with the cadence of someone who had practised them before. Like she'd been waiting for this moment to heal the cracks that had formed.

Hassa crossed the rift between them and wrapped Sylah's body in an embrace. Sylah stiffened before relaxing into it with a relieved sigh.

Hassa leant her chin against Sylah's shoulder and breathed in her familiar scent: the saccharine of firerum and the sharpness of lemon rind. Bitter and sweet.

"I had lost sight of what was most important," Sylah murmured into Hassa's shoulder.

Hassa broke away and signed, *I've seen you make many mistakes, Sylah. The Ring, the drugs, the drink, the Aktibar—*

Sylah scowled. "Okay, okay, you don't have to list everything."

Hassa smiled then signed more seriously, *This mistake hurt me, but I'm glad you were here to make it right. Thank you for taking back our country.*

Sylah dipped her head, and when she looked up again, she noticed Vahi and Memur.

"Memur, it is good to see you again."

The older Ghosting nodded in greeting, a faint smile on her lips.

"And that is your father? The armoursmith?" Sylah asked.

Gorn must have told her. Hassa beckoned Vahi closer.

"Hello, I'm Vahi." He gave Sylah a tight smile.

Sylah clasped his forearm. "How's it hurting?"

Gorn strode forward. "Hello, Hassa. I presume the army at the plantation fields are yours?"

Yes, the Ghostings have come to reclaim our home, Memur signed.

Gorn frowned. Hassa was about to sign the words slower in case she had missed them, but then Gorn spoke. "I don't think it is perhaps the time to discuss this." Her eyes flickered to Turin who sat back in a chair looking at her nails.

I think this is the perfect time, Memur continued. *The Wardens' Empire it is no longer. The Zalaam are coming, and we will be in control of our homeland when that happens.*

Turin cleared her throat, and everyone turned to her. "Can someone explain what is going on?" she asked.

"The Ghostings lay claim to the Wardens' Empire. We are under their rule now," Sylah said with a nod to Memur.

Hassa felt a swell of pride towards her friend. Sylah made clear that the Ghostings claim on the land was irrefutable.

Turin sat up in her chair. "No, I think not. For I am the Warden of Duty and I vote no."

Hassa scoffed at her old master. *You are nothing and no one. The land has always been the Ghostings'.*

This land has never been truly owned and cannot be bartered, Memur reprimanded Hassa. *It belongs to Anyme and those who walk on this hallowed ground must understand the ancestors' souls upon which we rise. The land has always been our home, whether the Embers preached it or not. Now we will govern it as we see fit.*

Turin couldn't understand the Ghosting's words, but they left a chill in the air—just a hint of a threat. And that Turin understood. She sprang to her feet. "We had a deal, Truthsayer. My Gummers for the title of warden."

Gorn inclined her head but didn't reply.

You can remain warden. But we will not acknowledge your power, Memur signed.

Sylah took pleasure in translating Memur's words for Turin.

The maiden scowled. "I'll take my Gummers and leave. See how you fare then."

No one replied, so she stormed out in a cloud of radish-leaf smoke. Hassa watched her go.

"She can't go far," Sylah muttered.

Hassa wasn't so sure. Turin's ambition was as dangerous as any blade at your throat. She knew it wasn't the last she would see of her.

Gorn let out a slow breath. "With the Zalaam so close, we cannot afford to fight among ourselves. They are expected at our shores in mere weeks. I too believe that the empire is home for the Ghostings, but I do request that you keep me abreast of your plans. It may not look like it right now, but I have an army too. And we will need every single person in this fight for our lives."

Memur's pale eyes glittered. *I see the sense in your words.*

Hassa felt the tension in the room ebb only to tighten again with Memur's next words. *But we do not have weeks until the Zalaam arrive. They are here already.*

What? Hassa signed.

A scout informed me they have destroyed Jin-Laham. They move west.

Hassa choked. *Destroyed?*

Memur nodded sadly. *The city is gone.*

Hassa thought of Vine, the Ghosting she had met there—the hope they had for the people's council. Then she thought of Vahi, and where his place would be in a country run by Ghostings.

Gorn's expression shuttered into one of helplessness for a few brief moments before hardening again. "Well then, we have much to prepare, you and I."

Before the talk turned to battle plans Hassa signed, *We should be a republic. With voted-in leaders. Of any blood colour. We cannot afford to become just like the wardens.*

Memur's eyes narrowed. *An interesting concept, but I'm afraid we do not have time to vote.*

No, perhaps not, but everyone here has proven their ability to lead. Would it not be prudent to work in collaboration? For the sake of survival? Hassa pressed.

Memur looked around the room, then settled her gaze back on Hassa. *Dew always told me you were far wiser than most elders. Regarding the voting procedure, this is not a decision I can make. However, for the sake of survival I see the sense in collaborating. In times of war we must lead as we see fit.*

"As a republic?" Gorn asked.

Memur considered then signed, *As the Dryland Republic.*

The Drylands had been the country's name before the founding wardens invaded. Memur invoked it in honour of their ancestors.

The Dryland Republic, Hassa signed again.

"The Dryland Republic," Zuhari said. Ren reached out and clasped her partner's hand, and they shared a small smile between them. The laws against mixed-blood couplings would be a thing of the past.

The grin carried around the room until everyone felt the joy of this momentous occasion.

Gorn's gaze moved from Ren, Zuhari, Hassa, Sylah, Vahi and then settled on Memur, her next words threading them all together. "Leaders of the Dryland Republic, shall we get to it?"

Memur took her seat opposite Gorn, and the atmosphere shifted from joyous to focused.

You need to discipline your soldiers. Looting and sating their vengeance must be brief, Memur signed.

"Yes, I agree, the celebrations will stop at sundown. Zuhari and Ren are already implementing disciplinary proceedings. Though I'm loath to overthrow one set of rules for another."

We will need obedience in the war to come. My captains can help, Memur said.

"Is there a forge in the Keep? I can continue production of the inkwells and armour," Vahi added quietly. Gorn nodded and directed him to its entrance.

Hassa looked to Sylah, who hadn't spoken since the news of the Zalaam's arrival. Hassa saw she was shaking. She led her to the corner of the room, away from Gorn and Memur's fevered planning.

"Hassa, do you think . . . do you think Anoor is with them?"

I don't know, Sylah.

Hassa saw then that though Sylah had decided to stay, she was still tortured by her choice. She touched her friend's shoulder in a sympathetic gesture. Sylah had helped break the empire, but all the while her heart too had been breaking.

"If they got past the Tannin, maybe they managed to destroy it?" Sylah whispered on dry lips.

If they destroyed it, wouldn't the tidewind have stopped, or slowed? As you tell it, the Tannin drives the cyclical nature of it.

"Yes . . . maybe? I don't know." Sylah's eyes squeezed tight. "Tanu said that the Zalaam believe Anoor is the prophesied Child of Fire. That she went willingly across the sea with Yona."

Hassa felt shock slacken her features. It was rare that she didn't know the truth of things. Everything shifted into place. It made sense now why Yona had shown such interest in Anoor—because she was Zalaam.

It was Yona who had organised the tidewind shelters. It was Yona who had drained the Dredge of bone marrow. Hassa felt her lips draw up in a snarl.

The Zalaam would pay, and so would Anoor. Because the former Disciple of Strength hadn't just defected, she had betrayed them all.

But then Hassa looked into Sylah's tortured eyes and her lips relaxed into more of a grimace. *How would I feel if this was Kwame?* she asked herself. And she could only settle on one word.

Broken. So she resolved to help put her friend back together again.

She touched Sylah's cheek that had become wet with tears before signing, *If this is true, Sylah, then you need to let her go. For she will be on the other side of the battlefield in this war.*

Sylah's voice was bleak. "I know."

CHAPTER THIRTY-FOUR

Anoor

Kori birds have a unique sense of preservation during the tidewind. Instead of fighting the tide of its gales, the birds retract their wings and allow themselves to freefall to the ground. Though they may sustain injuries in the fall, they are less likely to be destroyed by the debris lifted by the tidewind's wrath while sheltering low to the ground.

—Extract from the essay on "The Flight
of the Kori", by Master Fidel

Every night on their journey to Nar-Ruta, Yona would instruct Chah to bring to life the hollowers.

The cone-shaped godbeasts would dig into the sand of the Farsai Desert, creating a network of burrows where the Zalaam could then shelter.

The first night Anoor had been worried about sleeping under the dirt. But when she'd stepped into the tunnel she'd been astounded by her surroundings. Soft pallets had been rolled out for each soldier, with silks separating each room. Gas lamps glowed down a central corridor, banishing the darkness of the underground passageways.

Anoor had revelled in the ingenuity of the burrows. She had told Chah the very same.

He had snorted. "You forget how long we have planned for this war, Child."

Four hundred years, Anoor remembered.

The tunnels were not as comfortable as her cabin on the ship, but it didn't matter, for Anoor rarely slept anymore.

For three weeks their routine was the same. Walk all day, then sleep beneath the ground at night. Yesterday they had finally come within sight of the city. And by that time Anoor could barely tell night from day.

"I need tea," she said to Yona, a voice barely above a whisper. The two of them were standing on the periphery of the army surrounded by guards.

"The hollowers are building the final burrows, Anoor, be patient," Yona snapped.

When Anoor flinched, Yona softened. "I'm sorry. I have a surprise that I was saving for later, but given we're idle while we wait, now seems more pertinent."

Yona spoke to a nearby soldier who slipped away and returned with a dome covered in cloth. Anoor was disappointed it wasn't bitter leaf tea.

"Here we are." Yona removed the cloth, revealing a small cage. "We caught her this morning. Now you can test your kori bird."

Anoor took the cage in her hands. The kori bird's iridescent wings were more beautiful than she'd remembered, its tail vibrant with blue plumes. It turned its dark eyes to Anoor and trilled.

The old Anoor—the one she had thought she'd buried too deep to ever hear again—listened with joy.

"Thank you," Anoor said.

She wasn't sure where she'd placed the godbeast kori, she hadn't seen it since it had been finished on the *Cleaver*. And when Yona had it brought to her with all her tools, she couldn't help but feel like a child being sent to play with a colouring book.

But she didn't mind being tucked away. Anoor had come to realise her role as the Child of Fire wasn't as taxing as she'd expected. Yona rarely called for her anymore, and when she did it was just to lead everyone in prayer. A task that Anoor enjoyed as it made her feel closer to her God. And more alive.

Besides, night was falling fast and soon she'd be trapped beneath the ground with only the thick smell of earth and the sound of Yona's snores.

Anoor held the cage close to her chest as she moved away from the army camp. Two guards followed her, but she didn't notice them anymore. She'd grown used to being watched.

She crested a sand dune. They were five leagues or so from the plantation fields. Though Anoor squinted at the horizon, she couldn't see the trees in the distance. But the Keep, *that* she could see, the tower of five hundred steps thrusting up into the sky like a dagger towards Kabut's eye.

Once her whole life's purpose had been to climb them. Now her purpose was to burn them down.

Anoor turned her gaze to the army behind her. The sentinels were primed and ready for their night's watch. The wolf-like godbeasts were activated every night before the tidewind came. The sentinels were their only defence if they were attacked during the tidewind, weaving between the rows of quellers like dogs sniffing out trouble. Given their small size, only one vial of bone marrow was needed to last a whole night.

Anoor lowered herself to the hot sand. "Hello, little kori bird, I'm going to draw a few runes on you now. It shouldn't hurt, all right?"

But drawing the runes was much more difficult than Anoor could have imagined. The kori squirmed and fluttered in the cage so much that Anoor had to hold it in one hand and draw on its crest with the other.

When she was done, she turned to the godbeast. "Now it's your turn."

She pressed the nib of her stylus to the beak of the creature. From there the blood would flow towards the etching of her runes.

When the final rune was saturated with her blood the godbeast came to life. It didn't fly exactly the same way a kori bird did. Buoyed by the bloodwerk runes, it didn't flap its wings but simply glided as it spun around Anoor's face.

"By the blood, you actually work."

"*My kori bird . . .*" The words were whispered on the winds of a memory.

"Sylah?"

Anoor had heard her, she was sure of it. She jumped to her feet, the godbeast kori spinning with her.

A shadow stretched on the sand below, growing larger as a figure drew closer. Anoor's heart began to race, and she felt dizzy with longing. She hadn't thought of Sylah for many days, but being in the city where they had loved brought the blurred edges of her memories to the forefront of her mind.

"Sylah? Is that you?" she murmured.

Her eyes struggled to focus, perhaps because her hopes and reality were not matching up until the person stood a handspan from her face.

The figure smiled sardonically.

"Tanu?" Anoor said with half relief and half disappointment. It was the first time Anoor had seen her friend since she'd left her on the shores of the empire.

"The very same," Tanu said, and opened her arms.

Anoor folded herself into them.

"Nice armour," Tanu said through the embrace.

Anoor pulled away and looked down at her clothing. She hadn't even realised she was wearing the armour and she wondered when she had donned it. Her mind was a murky thing, and the morning's memories were deep in its depths.

"I didn't know you'd arrived," Anoor said.

"Just now. Yona sent me to get you. The hollowers have finished with the campsite. Time to bed down for the night."

"Did you come from the city?" Anoor asked.

Tanu nodded, a shadow crossing her features. It was then that Anoor noticed the blue blood on her arms.

"What happened?"

Tanu shrugged. "Kabut required a sacrifice." She didn't elaborate further.

There was a clatter and the godbeast fell to the ground. "Oh no!" Anoor picked it up and cradled it.

"Is that a godbeast kori bird?" Tanu asked.

"Yes. Or at least, it was."

Tanu peered over her shoulder to look at the damage. "It just ran out of power. Blood doesn't last long."

"I should have used bone marrow."

Tanu made a sound in her throat. "So, they finally told you about the bone marrow."

Anoor nodded, too weary to be irritated by her friend's deception.

Tanu swept a hand over her brow. "I didn't see Qwa or Faro in the camp. Where are they?"

For a second Anoor wasn't sure. Then the memories grew shapes in the haze of her mind.

"Kabut required a sacrifice." Anoor repeated Tanu's words woodenly.

Tanu's eyes shuttered closed and tears escaped them. She didn't ask any more questions, and Anoor was glad, as her own grief had callused over and she wasn't prepared to open the wound.

They made their way back to the army camp, where they found Yona scrutinising a scuff on one of the queller's runes.

"Have this mended by the morning, we must be ready to fight at any moment," Yona said to Chah.

The tidewind was rising around them, a ribbon of sand shifted in its current. A thought occurred to Anoor as she drew level with Yona.

"Why are we waiting? Why didn't we go straight into battle today?" Anoor asked her grandmother. Yona's eyes widened at Anoor's interruption. But Anoor was beyond caring about manners.

"Tanu," Yona said quietly, too quietly. "Will you please brew the Child of Fire some bitter leaf tea? The herbs are in my possession. Two scoops of the red powder. And please be quick about it—"

"But, Grandmother, I don't understand, the battle will be over in one or two days," Anoor interrupted.

Yona grabbed Anoor by the elbow and steered her away from Chah. "Anoor, please do not question me in front of the others. If you have concerns, then speak to me privately." Yona's breath was hot and angry on Anoor's cheek.

"You sound like Uka." The thought slipped out of her mind and into her mouth before she could stop it.

Yona's expression wavered.

"I need you to understand that you and I must never contradict each other. Half of the army's loyalty lies in their concept of you and I as the Wife and the Child of Fire—and so we must be obedient to the roles Kabut has called us to. Do you understand?"

Anoor fingered the hem of her sleeve. "Yes. But—"

"Anoor, we cannot begin the battle now, because we are waiting for the mainlanders to arrive. This sacrifice must be greater in number than any that has come before. We must purge all the non-believers. So first, we must lure them. And they are on their way."

Mainlanders. Of course. All the more to sacrifice.

Anoor bowed her head. "To win we must begin again."

Yona patted her cheek. "Yes, exactly. Oh, look, here comes Tanu with your tea. Go now to the burrows. The tidewind comes."

Anoor sipped the tea and all thoughts of the war fled her mind. She didn't remember getting into bed.

When she heard the familiar whirring of the tidewind above she felt herself relax for the first time in a long while. She tested the word one more time.

Home. But this time it stung like she stood in the tidewind's heart, the sand ripping skin to flesh to bone.

Until there was nothing left of her, except dreams and memories.

PART FOUR

✛

Brace

There are few things you and I need in this world. Food, water and rest to nourish the body. Joy, love and truth to nourish the mind. And let me tell you we have been starving for too long. It is time to sate our appetites at the wardens' table. This is the story of how the empire truly came to be.

—The beginning of the griots' tale entitled "The Ghostings' plight, the wardens' flight"

A traditional folktale told by Winterlanders to aid the rhythm of their rowboats

A left stroke of the oar is represented by L, a right stroke R.

In a land hidden by waves stood a loaf of bread

L

Thick with crust, seeds and salt, there was no greater bread

R

Your grandmother, your father, your sister, your friend

L

All swam the seas to try and taste its yeasty flesh

R

And died on the rocks, never making it ashore

L

One high tide you find a way to cross the sea

R

And you reach the sandy beach ahead of breakfast

L

You see the plump bread and already know the taste

R

Alas it is dry, alas it is too bitter

L

Oh! You wish you had not tasted it, clean your mouth

R

Know a thought can sustain you far more than the truth.

CHAPTER THIRTY-FIVE

Jond

First, we must each withdraw a young branch of steelweed while keeping it attached to the seabed. It is important that you follow the exact order of the rune sequences. Ads is circulating the final combination among you now. It is crucial that we allow the plant to reach maturity before applying the bloodwerk runes—the plant must be at its full strength. Only then do we have a chance of trapping the Tannin.

—Final instructions shared by Elyzan
to the students of the first law

"It's time. The admiral's ship has moved into the Tannin's waters. They will proceed to bind it at nightfall." The flighter gave the message and disappeared a moment later.

Kara, Jond and Niha stood at the bow of the boat. The navy spread out across the horizon ahead of them. There in the distance, where the sun met the water, were Ads and Elyzan, ready to fight the Tannin.

Jond gripped the railing. He could barely hope for a world without the Tannin, without the tidewind. The Tannin's absence was too hard a concept to grasp. And yet, here they were, about to bind the creature until its body broke into the rubble and stone it once was.

The wind had been picking up for some time, each day bringing stronger gales that whipped the ocean into a frenzy. Sea spray had long soaked through his shirt and slacks, but he didn't mind.

"Do you think they can do it?" Jond asked Niha, but it was Kara who answered. Though they had been avoiding each other, the lure of watching the Tannin being destroyed was pull enough to draw them both to the railing.

"Yes." Her response was resolute. "For there is no alternative."

Jond looked at her sidelong. An errant curl clung to the hard set of her jaw as she gazed out over the ocean. Though it had been three days, he was still parsing the words she'd said: "You asked why I couldn't give you more, Jond. But the truth is, you never gave me anything in return."

He thought he'd been clear about his feelings, but now she'd cast his thoughts in doubt.

Jond pulled his eyes from hers and back to the inky depths of the sea below.

This was where Sylah must have died. The thought was an unwelcome intrusion and it gutted him like a knife. He wasn't sure when he'd accepted Sylah's death as a certainty. But now that he realised he had, grief punctured him through the chest, draining away the breath in his lungs.

He took in a ragged gasp and stepped away from the group, crossing the ship to the port side.

When he was alone, he looked down at the swirling black sea and spoke softly to himself.

"Stolen, sharpened, the hidden key,

We'll destroy the empire and set you free,

Churned up from the shadows to tear it apart,

A dancer's grace, a killer's instinct, an Ember's blood, a Duster's heart."

The chant was an ode to another time, a tribute to all they were and all they had been.

And a goodbye to the woman he had once loved.

"Are you all right?" Jond didn't turn at the sound of Kara's voice.

Jond laughed, and it was a haunted sound, full of the ghosts of his memories.

"No, not really."

Kara's mouth parted, and she seemed to be grappling with her next words. It was so unlike her, but Jond's gaze didn't slip from her lips. Then she spoke.

"It must be hard . . . knowing the creature we face is the one . . . who killed Sylah."

"No," he lied.

Kara reached for his face and wiped away the tear he didn't know had fallen. "You love her very much."

"Yes, and I always will."

There was a flicker of hurt in Kara's face and her hand fell from his cheek.

"No," he said thickly. "Not like that, I don't think I've loved her like that for some time."

Kara's face was impassive as she said, "Oh?"

The sea swelled up, knocking the boat, and causing them both to stumble.

Jond's hand went to Kara's waist, at first to stabilise her, but then simply to touch.

"I haven't loved Sylah like that for some mooncycles now. Not since . . . not since she left." He tugged her forward until their hipbones were touching.

But the tidewind could rage around her and Kara's expression would not have changed. She was waiting for something.

For him.

All this time Jond had not seen it. She had been ready give him everything and he hadn't been ready to do the same.

"It isn't you or her. It's just you," he said.

Kara tipped her head up to his, still waiting. But this time for something else.

With his back to the sea, and thoughts of Sylah's death, he lowered his lips to Kara's.

Jond took his time parting her mouth, exploring the taste of her. And with every stroke of his tongue, she responded, her hands tightening around his arms, her back arching into him.

There was a slow clap behind them and Jond broke away from Kara with a scowl.

"Finally," Niha said.

"Go away, Niha," Jond growled.

The councillor didn't even have the gall to look sheepish, he just stood there basking in their reunion, his one eye glinting.

Niha shrugged. "Well, you can't expect me not to appreciate the good show you're putting on over here—"

Jond felt Kara's hand on his forearm, then a familiar swipe across his wrist. The lurch of flighting followed seconds later, and when Jond blinked again they were in Kara's room.

She appeared a moment later.

"Sorry," Kara said in a way that said she wasn't sorry, not even a little bit. A small smile spread across her face as they watched each other.

In a few strikes the Blood Forged would battle the Tannin, and they could lose, condemning half of their fleet. By nightfall they could be dead.

Jond crossed the distance between them.

"No more waiting," he said as he lifted her up and laid her on the bed.

The look she gave him was hungry.

"Undress me," she said.

Jond obliged, unbuttoning her dress until it lay like a blanket beneath her. She shivered at his touch as he pulled her underwear down over her legs. He discarded the lace in the corner of the room.

She watched him with glittering eyes as he too undressed.

"You are all I want." His voice was a deep rumble in his chest, thick with desire.

"Then, Jond Alnua, you shall have me, as I shall have you." She pushed herself up and wrapped her legs around his waist, until the heat of her desire brushed against the length of him.

The spike of pleasure set his blood boiling.

One of his hands wrapped around her lower back and the other slipped downwards from her navel. She trembled, baring her neck for his tongue.

"You are all I want," he repeated against her throat.

He opened his hand, coaxing pleasure from the molten core of her. Her breath was hot against his neck. That maddening aroma of mint and vanilla. He crushed his lips against hers as she shuddered against him.

Through the aftershocks of her pleasure, Kara guided Jond towards her, gasping as he eased into her.

She matched the cadence of his rhythm, until there was nothing between them but the heartbeat of their desire.

"You are all I want," Jond said as the movement between them grew towards a crest of ecstasy.

And when the moment came, they cried together, traversing the river of pleasure until it slowed to eddies. And eventually was still.

Kara laughed, a breathy laugh, full of wonder.

"I'm glad we had a chance to do that again, before the end." Though her words were solemn, they warmed Jond.

He moved to her side and held her against his chest.

"At least if we go, we go together."

"Together," she repeated as if savouring the word. Then she slapped him against the wrist, startling him from the serenity of the moment.

"What was that for?" he said, pushing himself to his elbows so he could see her playful smile.

"For taking so long to realise it was me you wanted," she said. And though she grinned, there was something hard in the tone of her voice.

"I'm sorry," Jond said as sincerely as he could. Then he kissed her, and all the sharp edges of her softened.

He was just settling back down when there was a knock on the door.

"Jond? Kara?" Niha called through the locked door. "You'd better head to the deck. The Tannin—it's here."

The wind swirled around them against a blood-red sky. It was barely sunset, but the Tannin had already made its presence known.

Jond stood looking out over the sea, where he had been two strikes ago, but this time Kara was in his arms.

"I can see it," she whispered.

Jond could see the Tannin too as it surged out of a wave in the distance. Even this far away it was enormous. Its scales glittered white under the darkening sky.

Niha was leaning over the railing, as if the extra few handspans garnered him a better view.

"I think I can see the steelweed, Elyzan and Ads must have—"

The three of them gasped as the Tannin's tail struck the mast of Elyzan's ship. Though they couldn't hear screams, they knew that the force of the Tannin's weight had done significant damage.

A second later, the flighter that had shared the message before reappeared. Orange blood splattered his arm, and Jond realised he was bleeding from a deep wound there.

"Two of Elyzan's students have been struck down," he spluttered. "I fear there are not enough people to complete the binding."

The crashing of the waves sounded like the rushing of Jond's blood. He looked down at Kara and saw the same resolute expression in her gaze.

She nodded.

Their entwined arms were a barrier against the fear, but for now they had to drop the shield. It was time to be the leaders their people needed.

"Take me to the ship," Jond said to the flighter.

The flighter nodded, relief overcoming the pain and shock he was feeling. Jond held out his wrist for the man to pattern the runes onto and turned to Kara.

"Follow with any others of my squadron who have been fitted with an inkwell and are proficient in runework."

She nodded, her brows knotted in worry. Jond pressed a kiss to where the skin crinkled before the ship fell away and he was transported into the centre of chaos.

"Pull the steelweed towards you!" Elyzan shouted.

Half the deck was in splinters, blood of all colours seeped from wounds and dripped from the railing. Steelweed coiled across the sky as Elyzan finished another rune combination. Jond watched as the plant, driven by bloodwerk and the runes of the first charter, spiralled into the sea.

The waves were too dark to see whether the steelweed had been successful in binding the Tannin. And Elyzan didn't wait long before picking up another frond and beginning the process again.

The wind this close to the Tannin was laced with blue sand— the soil of the Farsai Desert, pulled by the tidewind and out to the ocean.

Jond couldn't let them fail, they were too close to the Wardens' Empire.

Ads was struggling with a ribbon of steelweed between her hands. Jond ran to her as the leaf bucked and twisted in her grip.

"I drew it on wrong," she cried as he joined her. Ads' hair was plastered to her face from the sea spray, and red blood—not hers—dripped from her arms.

Jond swiped the bloodwerk from the leaf, and it went still. She let out a gasp of relief that sounded more like a sob before she began drawing the runes again.

"How can I help?" he asked.

Ads thrust a piece of paper in his hands. It was covered in a thin sheen of waterproof material, but he could still read the runes.

"Draw this on any steelweed that is lying on the deck."

Jond went to do as Ads had said, but as he did, the ship was thrown to the side, sending him careening across the boat.

The ship surged skyward on a wave as the Tannin lurched upwards. Sea water rushed down from its teeth as it opened its mouth in a silent battle cry. The creaking and groaning of its stone jaw was more terrifying than any scream.

Jond could see strands of steelweed wrapped around its body and fins, but there was too much slack, the creature still had space to lunge.

"Fuck, that's bigger than I thought," Kara said beside him. She had flighted in with another volunteer to help bind the beast.

Jond's stomach sank when he saw her. Because they were all about to die.

The Tannin dived for the centre of the ship, but just as it did a slither of steelweed flew through the air and wound through the Tannin's lower jaw.

Jond's gaze followed the path the leaf had taken.

Ads stood beneath the crimson sky, her hands splayed outwards as the steelweed moved from her grip to the Tannin's mouth. Her expression was defiant, her inkwell dripping blood onto the deck.

Tighter and tighter the steelweed spun, urged on with the bloodwerk Ads had drawn. Until there was a resounding *crack* and half of the Tannin's jaw fell into the sea.

Jond stood there awestruck.

"We managed to hurt it," he breathed.

"Stop standing there and come and help, this is just the beginning," Ads screamed.

Gone was the petulant child. In her place stood a woman, a leader.

And she was right, though the Tannin had lost its bite, it still had the bulk of its body.

Jond ran up to join her.

For the next two strikes Jond bled.

Rune after rune after rune, they kept binding the Tannin with threads of steelweed. Not all of them landed and not all of the runes worked. But when they did strike, the Tannin became crushed beneath the steelweed's knots. Bit by bit they chipped away at the great beast.

Until it was only rubble at the bottom of the ocean.

Jond stumbled as he reached for another leaf.

"Jond, stop, you need to stop, you've lost too much blood." Kara's voice seemed far away.

"No, we have to stop the Tannin," Jond mumbled. The steelweed in his hand was slick with his own blood.

"Jond, it's done. The Tannin has been broken."

Jond looked around. The sea had stilled, and night had fallen. The moon hung low in the sky, lighting Kara's hair copper. He reached for her, and she folded herself into his arms.

Tears fell from his eyes. He grieved for all the citizens who had lost their lives to the deadly hurricane. And he rejoiced for all the quiet nights to come.

He spoke the words he never thought he'd say. "The tidewind is no more."

"Yes," Kara said. "The first battle is done. Now let's go win a war."

CHAPTER THIRTY-SIX

Hassa

I think this notebook was once used for my creations, but I'm finding it harder and harder to concentrate now. Tanu says I slept for three days, but I don't remember sleeping. I feel like my eyes are always open.

—Anoor Elsari's notebook

Hassa slipped through the tunnels, her footfalls silent. She walked without a torch. She didn't need the light when travelling alone. And even if she did, she could create her own runelight now. She had perfected the combination for one last week.

The tidewind howled above her.

The Zalaam had arrived last night, their creations swarming across the sand dunes in the distance. But Hassa wasn't satisfied seeing them from the Keep's tower. She needed to get closer.

She reached the hatch that was north of the plantation fields. Sand filled the crevice in the hinges and for a moment she was worried that her bloodwerk wouldn't have the strength to shift the dirt above her.

Then the hatch gave way and for a few brief moments she was swallowed by the tidewind. Sand buffeted against her armour. The wind threatened to pull her away, but she planted her legs deep within the sand and braced herself.

She had told no one where she was going. Except Vahi: more and more often she found herself confiding in him. He'd wanted to come. But it was risky, more than risky, to infiltrate the army camp. And she'd be quieter travelling alone.

Though the Ghostings had used telescopes to view the creations, it didn't prepare Hassa for the sheer size of them when she saw them close up.

They stood thirty handspans above the ground in rows that stretched out for half a league. The warren of tunnels that the Zalaam were using as protection from the tidewind curved in a semi-circle around them. The dirt displaced on the surface was the only indication of the burrows beneath.

Hassa pushed through the tidewind towards the closest creation and peered through her visor at the runes marring the spider's bladed legs.

Sylah had shown Hassa the runes of creation but Hassa didn't want to learn them. With Sylah's failed creation lying broken in the Ember Quarter, they had decided to make smaller, more effective objects using bloodwerk, like crossbows that triggered automatically. Sylah was in charge of making the new weapons and though she'd said she'd given up on the creation runes, every now and again Hassa would find her tinkering with the orb, trying to make something which she thought would improve them. But the changes always failed.

Ever since the Zalaam had arrived Sylah had seemed more distant from the goings-on around her. Perhaps not distant, but taut, like every movement was an effort, because all she really wanted to do was go to Anoor. But holding herself back from the effort was wearing her thin. Hassa could see it in the way she hunched her shoulders, as if she cradled a wound in her chest, in her heart.

It was part of the reason Hassa steeled her will to scout out the enemy. If she could bring back news of Anoor, then perhaps Sylah could begin to move on.

Hassa weaved between the spider's legs.

The Zalaam's creation army were far more sophisticated than anything Hassa could have imagined. The runes were flawless, the construction precise. These spiders were killing machines and once let loose they would destroy the entirety of the city.

Unless Hassa could figure out a way to destroy them first.

She looked for a weakness in the joints, but even the hinges had been carefully hidden behind metal panelling.

The only way to stop these creations was to diffuse them with the rune. But that required getting close enough to the creature without dying first. Sylah had tried etching arrows with the rune, but their supplies of iron were low and wooden arrowheads merely splintered on impact. She'd even tried etching iron rune bullets, which they had plenty in stock, but the size of the projectile proved too difficult and time consuming.

Hassa sighed into her helmet, fogging up the glass. When it cleared, she spotted that one of the creations seemed wider than the others, but as she got closer, she realised it was an entirely different type of machine altogether.

It stood on two legs like a bear rearing up to strike. Its claws were the size of Hassa's thighs, and its thighs the size of Hassa's body. There was a recess where a head should have been. Hassa knew that was where the rider would sit, feeding it vials of bone marrow.

How can we fight something like this and win? Hassa wondered.

Suddenly, there was silence. It took Hassa a moment to realise why it perturbed her so much.

The tidewind had stopped. *In the middle of the night.*

Hassa's heart pounded in her chest. She needed to get back to the Keep.

There was movement ahead of her and Hassa pressed herself against the leg of the nearest spider. Her armour gave her some camouflage against the metal, but it wouldn't fool anyone looking closely.

"If the tidewind has stopped, then the mainlanders have destroyed the Tannin. In less than a week the war will begin."

Hassa knew that voice. She peered around the spider's leg towards the shadows moving towards her.

Yona.

The woman wore no wig, and her skin across her scalp was marked with scars in the shape of a web that shone silver in the moonlight. The person next to her wore a yellow tunic that hung to their ankles.

"Teta, did the hollowers capture any intruders in the early nightfall?" Yona asked.

"I'm waiting for a report, but I do not think so. The pack have a final patrol left in them before their marrow runs out."

"I'll warn the crafters to stay out of their path," Yona said.

The one in yellow, Teta, seemed to hesitate before she spoke next.

"Wife, will the Child of Fire be ready? I've heard reports she has not risen from her bed for three days. I worry about the stability of the Battle Drum."

Anoor, they are talking about Anoor.

As the pair drew closer, Hassa pressed herself further into the legs of the spider.

"I have just come from her shelter," Yona said.

So Anoor was nearby.

Yona continued, "The Child of Fire's Battle Drum still beats. She will ride the clawmaw and lead our soldiers to war. The final needles have all been positioned according to her measurements."

They passed without spotting Hassa. And when they were far enough away Hassa stepped out from the clawmaw's legs and looked up.

In the recessed section where the clawmaw's rider would reside, she could see the glint of sharp blades. What she had thought was a form of weapon were in fact fine needles that would carry blood to the grooves along the creature's body.

Badum—badum—badum.

Hassa felt her blood pumping in her ears as understanding turned her skin to ice. Hassa had heard the prophecy that spoke of the Child of Fire:

When the Child of Fire brings the Battle Drum,
The Battle Drum,
The Battle Drum,
Ready we will be, for war will come.

They had all assumed the Battle Drum was the war drum that would lead the Zalaam into conflict.

But "brings" suggests it's a part of her, Hassa thought.

Her mind reeled as she put all the pieces together in her mind.

"The Battle Drum" is Anoor's heart.

Anoor was going to be sacrificed by the Zalaam.

* * *

Hassa burst into the courtroom. Despite it being past midnight, the council members had been called for an emergency meeting given the tidewind's end.

Anoor is going to be sacrificed at the start of the war, she signed.

"What?" Sylah stood and strode towards her.

The Zalaam, they've made a creation that will drain her bone marrow as she rides it.

"No, you must be mistaken." Sylah was shouting but Hassa knew it wasn't at her.

I am not, I heard it from the mouth of Yona herself. Anoor is being guarded in the burrows that the Zalaam have made their camp.

Gorn, who had risen at Hassa's words, sat heavily back down in her chair. Her lips were bloodless as she mumbled quietly to herself. Hassa couldn't quite hear it, but it sounded like, "Not like this."

With Turin and her Gummers fled from the city, Ren, Zuhari and Memur made up the final three people in the room. Zuhari wrapped an arm around Ren. It was easy to forget that their love had been as fraught as Anoor and Sylah's: one Ember, one Duster, one officer, one shopkeeper. Despite it all they had come together and had had a daughter, only to lose her in the revolt of the hundred.

Memur, who chaired every council meeting, drew everyone's attention to her with a slice of her wrist. *We cannot afford a rescue operation for one person who for all we know does not want to be rescued.*

Sylah looked to Gorn with eyes wet with unshed tears. "Please . . ." she whispered.

But Gorn shook her head, the effort seemingly painful, as her face contorted in anguish.

Sylah took a step back as if she had been punched. "They are going to *sacrifice* her."

Zuhari cleared her throat, drawing attention her way. Ren gave her a warning look but Zuhari powered on. "Is there nothing we can do? Even send in a small team covertly?"

Sylah twitched, and Hassa wondered whether it galled her that Zuhari had spoken in Anoor's defence, but she didn't reply to her. She was watching Gorn.

The Truthsayer met Sylah's eyes. The grief was deeply etched into the lines of her face as she said, "Memur is right. With the tidewind ending so abruptly we must assume the mainlanders have destroyed it and will be here soon enough. We cannot afford to send any soldiers into the army camp, covertly or not."

Sylah looked like she might fall. Hassa reached out to her, pressing her wrist to her lower back. But Sylah didn't seem to notice her friend's comforting touch.

Hassa could hear her panting heavily, but then she straightened and her breathing steadied.

"I understand," Sylah said woodenly. Then she sniffed and rubbed at her eyes. "I'm going to go back to the forge. I want to finish up the bloodwerk crossbows I was working on."

She was already walking away as she spoke, leaving Hassa's arm empty and cold. She shut the door quietly behind her.

Hassa turned to Memur.

Are you sure we can't send even one or two platoons? I can lead them through the tunnels. Abducting the Child of Fire may do more to the Zalaam than runebullets would.

No, Hassa. One life cannot be valued above another.

Hassa frowned then she signed back her own words that she had once signed to Sylah a year ago. *If we forget the individual, we forget ourselves.*

Memur looked at Hassa, her eyes pinched in disapproval.

I know you are wise, Hassa, but do not presume to understand the burden of a leader in battle. Two platoons, you say? That is fifty soldiers. Fifty parents, siblings, friends. Do you want their deaths on your conscience over the plight of one woman? A woman who defected? Who betrayed us?

Hassa winced. Memur's words rang with truth.

She bowed her head and signed, *I understand.* Because she did. This reasoning had been the catalyst of her anger towards Sylah in the first place.

But now the Zalaam were *sacrificing* Anoor. It seemed . . . wrong.

Hassa moved to the door. *Please excuse me while I go and check on Sylah.*

It was strange walking through the Keep at night without the tidewind swirling outside. Those who had woken from the silence had wandered out into the open air. Smiles as bright as the crescent moon in the sky, both lighting the courtyard.

Hassa picked her way through the crowds towards the forge.

Vahi was still awake, working on a new set of runeguns. Hassa touched his shoulder.

Did you even notice the tidewind had stopped?

"Hassa, you're back. Wait, did you say the tidewind's stopped?" He put down his anvil and stepped outside.

"Oh, you're right."

They think the mainlanders have destroyed the Tannin.

"That would be helpful."

Hassa nodded.

"Did you find out anything useful about the creations?" Vahi asked.

No, they have no weaknesses that I could see. Using the diffuse rune looked like the only way to stop them.

Hassa watched as Vahi pulled out a molten orb of iron from the forge with a smelting ladle, the metal ready to be manipulated into a weapon.

If only we could melt them with fire.

Vahi laughed. "You'd need temperatures hotter than a regular fire."

Hassa's mind went to the Chrysalis.

Temperatures hot enough to melt sand into glass?

"Oh yes, that would do it. But I'm not sure how you'd go about doing that."

He began to hammer the cooling metal then stopped. "You're thinking about the Chrysalis, aren't you?"

Yes, if I can figure out how the Chrysalis was made, maybe we could make a fire hot enough to melt the creations.

Vahi shook his head. "I'm not sure how that would work, Hassa."

It frustrated Hassa that so much knowledge had been lost to history.

Where's Sylah? Hassa suddenly realised her friend wasn't here.

Vahi's brows knitted together. "Sylah? I'm not sure, I haven't seen her for a few strikes."

If Sylah wasn't here . . . then where was she?

Hassa thought about how quickly Sylah had given up the fight in front of the council. How she had grown resolute before striding away. She looked to the Keep's gates.

"What is it, Hassa? You look worried," Vahi said, touching her shoulder.

Sylah, she signed. *She's gone to rescue Anoor.*

CHAPTER THIRTY-SEVEN

Sylah

We have counted two thousand spider creations and roughly sixty tunnel-making creations. There is one other that stands tall in the centre of them all. We have named it the "Destroyer", as we are sure there is no surviving it.

—Notes made by Gorn

Sylah made her way through the Ember Quarter. The clockmaster hadn't yet called second strike in the morning.

This is the first time I have ever been outside in Nar-Ruta at this time.

Usually, the tidewind would be at its strongest, ready to rip flesh from bone. But now it was gone, and so was the Tannin.

Sylah swallowed the guilt that grew in her throat. That had been her task, and she had failed. Just like she had failed with the eru creation.

What have I contributed to this war except problems?

She had spent the last few days working in the forge, making bloodwerk crossbows that triggered on command. But it wasn't enough, so sometimes she tried to make creations once everyone had gone to sleep.

Most people had been in their beds when the emergency council meeting had been called, but Sylah had been in the forge with Vahi, trying to bring to life a mechanical sword. It had been unsuccessful like everything she tried to do.

But tonight, she would not fail in her mission. She could not.

Sylah weaved through the city's streets, revelling in the novelty of walking in the moonlight. The city seemed to glow brighter at night, the whitestone glinting silver, the cobblestones sparkling.

Every villa had been seized by the rebellion army and housed all the soldiers willing to fight the Zalaam. The Embers who had refused the Ghostings' terms had been locked in the old Nowerk Gaol with the wardens. Once the threat of incarceration had been made clear, many had defected to the rebellion army. And as much as it galled Sylah to see Embers, who had so readily followed the wardens, fight by their side, she knew they needed every person they could get.

Including Anoor.

Sylah had considered not going after her, but she knew she wouldn't be able to fight against the Zalaam if Anoor led them into battle. For three days the Zalaam had made camp on the edge of Nar-Ruta, and every day Sylah had had to stop herself from running into the heart of it to search for Anoor.

But today her resolve had wavered. She wouldn't let Anoor die entombed in metal.

Sylah passed her eru creation. It lay where it had fallen, half submerged by the fallen roof of a villa. Though Gorn had offered soldiers to help her move it, Sylah had given up on the experiment.

Sylah heard footsteps behind her. She expected it to be a platoon of soldiers from the Ghosting army, but when the shadow came into view, she recognised it.

"Hassa, what are you doing here?"

No, Sylah. That is my question for you.

Sylah thrust her tongue between the gap in her teeth. A hot flash of joba seed cravings rushed through her. She stumbled as her legs spasmed in response. It had been a few weeks since she'd had any physical withdrawals from the drug. Though they had lessened over time, she minded them less than the mental toil of the cravings.

Her mind was her own personal battleground. And at times like these it felt so much harder to hold the line.

Are you all right? Hassa asked. Her brows were furrowed with an expression of concern Sylah had rarely seen in her friend's face. The last few mooncycles had changed Hassa in subtle ways. She walked taller than she ever had, without the tell-tale hunch of someone who was used to walking through tunnels. Her hair had grown out too; instead of the shaved head required of servants, the first kink of a curl had begun to show. And, instead of signing her emotions, she let them show on her face. Like she did now as she scowled and signed, *Why are you looking at me like that?*

Sylah smiled. "Freedom looks good on you."

Hassa's grin was wolfish until she turned serious once more. *Where are you going, Sylah?*

Sylah didn't want to admit to Hassa that she was going after Anoor. Not after they had argued about the very same thing. She continued walking across the Tongue, her footsteps heavy, but Hassa tugged on her sleeve.

You're going after Anoor, aren't you?

Sylah said miserably, "I have to, Hassa. I know you don't want me to, but I can't—I can't—" Sylah became choked with tears.

Hassa gently wiped at her friend's cheeks. The soft flesh of her scars warm on Sylah's face. Then she said, *Memur said to me that no one life can be valued above another.*

Sylah felt her stomach drop. "I can't let her die like that, Hassa, I won't—"

Hassa held up her arm. *But I still value life, each and every one. Let's go get Anoor.*

Sylah felt her knees tremble as she flung her arms around Hassa. "Thank you," she whispered into the Ghosting's short hair.

Hassa pushed away and signed, *Yona mentioned something about patrols. We'll have to be careful.*

Sylah pulled out a dagger from her jacket and twirled it with a bloodthirsty look on her face.

"That won't be a problem."

Sylah and Hassa walked in silence, their only accompaniment the echo of their breathing down the tunnels.

Then Sylah spoke. "The Zalaam's burrows . . . is there a way to access them underground?"

Hassa shook her head. *No, the Ghosting tunnels are much further below ground, in the whitestone sediment of the soil. The Zalaam's tunnels are much shallower and there is no point at which they intersect.*

Sylah frowned. "We'll be easy to spot above ground."

Hassa nodded. *Yes, though Yona mentioned patrols, I didn't see any earlier. It was very quiet.*

Sylah didn't like the sound of that. Quiet didn't mean they weren't there. She preferred to know the threat before it killed her.

Eventually they reached the ladder that led to the hatch below the Zalaam's camp. Hassa went up first.

Moonlight spilt into Sylah's vision as Hassa slipped out and into the night. A moment later Hassa's face appeared above, and she beckoned for Sylah to follow.

She lifted herself out of the tunnels and looked around. The sight of the spider creations set her heart racing.

We won't survive this, she thought.

But Sylah couldn't worry about that right now. She had to find Anoor.

The military camp was quiet. Those asleep probably weren't aware the tidewind had stopped. Hassa gestured towards the burrows.

They slinked across the desert towards the mound of dirt which indicated the location of the Zalaam's underground network. When the Zalaam arrived, Sylah had watched the cone-shaped creations build the warrens beneath the earth.

She shivered as she looked over the results of their labour—thousands of enemy soldiers all slept beneath her feet. At least half the size of the army in Nar-Ruta, but their creations more than made up for the shortfall.

"How do we get down there?" Sylah whispered.

They searched the landscape. In the end, it was the moon that granted them a clue. As Sylah scanned one last time, she saw the moonlight glimmer on a piece of metal out of place amidst the sand.

"It's a lever," Sylah whispered.

Hassa stepped forward and cradled the metal panel in the crook of her elbow before pulling back.

A hidden panel slid beneath the soil, showering sand on a staircase below them. The hairs on Sylah's neck stood on end.

Something wasn't right. It was too easy.

Four hundred years of planning and the Zalaam simply leave a hatch open to their sleeping quarters? No, this isn't right.

Sylah turned and saw movement beneath one of the spiders in the distance. "Hassa, what is that?"

Shadows stretched across the sand towards them. Sylah narrowed her eyes, trying to make sense of what she was seeing. As they drew closer, she could just make out the shape of the shadows cast by the beast at the head of the formation. It moved on four legs, kicking up sand as it gained on them. Then the creature moved into a beam of moonlight.

It was a creation, not a creature.

Sylah gasped. "They've been mimicked to *wolves*."

Fuck, Hassa signed.

As the beasts loped towards Sylah and Hassa, their clawed feet barely touched the ground. Though Sylah couldn't hear their footfalls, the rhythm beat like the blood in her ears—pounding faster and faster the closer they drew.

I've never seen creations like this before, Hassa signed.

"They must patrol only at night, during the tidewind. So our telescopes won't have seen them until now."

Hassa's lips went thin. *We need to move, now.*

The wolves had got close enough for Sylah to see their faces. Their snouts were long, the metal blunted at the nose. The jagged ears that pointed skyward looked sharp. But not as sharp as the fangs that hung from their jaws—those were made for ripping throats.

"Go down the stairs, Hassa," Sylah hissed, urging her friend first.

The creations didn't growl. The only sound they made was the grinding of their metal gears, which was even more sinister.

Click-raah, click-raah, click-raah.

Hassa scrambled down the stairs into the tunnel below. But she wasn't quick enough. There were more wolf creations than Sylah realised, about fifty or sixty. They swept through the area in a V-formation towards her.

They were twenty handspans away now.

Sylah looked to the stairs. Hassa was nearly at the bottom.

Ten handspans away.

Sylah dived into the opening, slipping down the stairs as fast as her feet could take her.

"Close it, close it," Sylah whispered desperately. She wasn't sure how Hassa was going to close it, but thankfully the Ghosting was one step ahead and was pulling back a similar lever that had been on ground level.

The metal sheet slid closed.

They breathed heavily in the dim light.

"That was close," Sylah murmured.

Hassa nodded wearily.

They looked around. The burrow was lit by hanging gas lamps. The tunnel echoed with the soft grunts and snores of people sleeping. Fabric was draped from wall to wall to make tents, providing privacy.

Sylah tensed as she saw shadows moving through the corridor that ran the length of the burrows.

There was no way she and Hassa could traverse the warren without being spotted.

Sylah was about to whisper as much when Hassa ducked into a nearby tent. Sylah's heart went into her throat. *What was Hassa doing?*

Her friend's silent footfall led her back to Sylah a few moments later. *Here, wear this.*

Hassa passed Sylah a pile of stiff green clothes.

"Did you just steal this?" Sylah whispered.

Hassa gave her a look that said, "Stop asking stupid questions and do as I say."

Sylah held up a hand in response and quickly changed into the armour. The material was as thick as leather but more supple. On the chest plate was an embroidered spider.

Sylah's hand lingered on it. *So much pain wrought in your name, Kabut. And the only people who will suffer are* your *people.* She spoke to the God in her mind, as if he could hear her.

Why are you holding your boob? Hassa was wearing a matching outfit of her own, having stolen one from the tent next to the first. It was so large it drowned her, but from a distance the camouflage would do.

"No reason. Let's go. You check the tents on the left, I'll check the tents on the right."

Hassa walked with her wrists in her pockets to hide her Ghosting heritage. But her walk too had subtly changed, the footfalls staccato and regimented.

"You really know how to blend in," Sylah said quietly.

Hassa lifted her wrists from her pockets and signed quickly, *If you've been raised like I have, then you get used to becoming different people every day.*

"Not to me though. You were always yourself with me," Sylah whispered.

Hassa turned to her, her gaze thoughtful. *Yes, I have always been my truest self with you.*

Sylah turned and hugged Hassa tight. Despite their circumstances, Sylah didn't want to let the moment pass. Death could be around the corner for both of them.

"Thank you. I want you to know how much your friendship has meant to me over the years. I truly don't think I would be here if it wasn't for you."

Hassa laughed softly and pushed her away. *You're going to get us caught. I doubt the Zalaam are the hugging type.*

Sylah's smile was sad. "I just needed you to know. If anything happens to me—"

Sylah.

"I know what you're going to say, I'm not going to die here—"

Sylah. Hassa gestured with her arm. *Is that radish-leaf smoke?*

Sylah turned to where Hassa was pointing. If she hadn't recognised the red curls of smoke, she would have soon smelt its distinctive woody aroma.

Turin is here, Hassa signed.

"Could it not be someone else?"

I have to check.

As Hassa moved forward, Sylah stopped. Something sounded out of place among the snores of the troops.

"What is that?"

Sylah held her breath as she listened. It was faint at first, but the more she strained the clearer the melody became.

"It's a kori bird. But what is a kori bird doing down here?" Sylah's voice was thick with hope.

Who from the Zalaam would even keep one as a pet?

Hassa was still watching the trail of radish-leaf smoke, her expression troubled. *Go investigate. I will check if it is Turin. I'll follow shortly after.*

Sylah tried to keep her pace leisurely and unsuspecting. But as she got closer to the kori's cry, she found she was running. When she located the tent, she pushed the material aside and entered.

The air was stale and sour. A kori bird sang in a metal cage beside the bed, its warbling increasing in pitch as soon as it saw Sylah. Its feathers cast sharp shadows across the burrow's walls.

The person sleeping on the pallet was too slight to be Anoor. Sylah swallowed the bitterness of disappointment.

But as she turned to leave, she realised that the soldier wasn't sleeping—their hazel eyes were open. Sylah reached for her dagger, ready to plunge the blade into their throat to stop them from crying out in warning.

But then their gaze drifted drowsily to Sylah's.

And then the wraith spoke with a voice that was unmistakably Anoor's. "Sylah?"

"Anoor?"

It was her, it was really her.

Tears fell from Sylah's face as she gathered Anoor into her arms. She was so light. "Anoor, oh, I'm here, I'm here now."

"Sylah, am I dead?" Anoor's voice was barely a whisper.

"No, you're not dead, you're very much alive."

Only just, Sylah thought.

Hassa appeared at the tent's entrance. *It was Turin, we need to leave now.*

Then her eyes widened as she took in Anoor. *Can she walk?*

"Can you walk?" Sylah repeated to Anoor.

Anoor nodded but it looked like it took a lot of effort.

"Okay, lean on me. Come on, I've got you." Sylah helped Anoor to stand. The armour she wore hung from her emaciated frame.

"This way."

Anoor took quivering steps towards the tent's entrance.

"Did Kabut send you to me?" Anoor asked. She was breathing heavily.

Sylah felt a fresh flow of tears run down her cheeks. "Save your strength now. We'll talk later."

"The kori bird, Sylah, will you release the kori bird?"

I've got it. Hassa held the cage between her limbs.

They shuffled through the tunnel as quickly as they could. Sylah could hear people rising from their slumber and she knew that at any moment they could be spotted.

When they reached the steps, Hassa put down the kori cage and signed, *What of the wolves?*

"Anoor, do you know how we can stop the wolves?" Sylah asked Anoor urgently.

"The sentinels?" Anoor said weakly. "In my pocket, there's a disc that will diffuse the life in them. Press it against the godbeast to stop it."

"Will it only stop one?"

Anoor shrugged and mumbled, "Should be able to use it on all, but you'll have to retrieve it each time."

And not die, by getting too close, Sylah thought.

She pulled the disc from Anoor's pocket. "Hassa, you go up first."

Hassa nodded, running up the ladder with ease.

"One step at a time now, Anoor," Sylah said, guiding Anoor up.

"Did you bring the kori?" Anoor asked.

"I've got it. I've got it. Faster now."

Sylah could hear the trudge of boots getting louder behind her.

The sky was on the cusp of dawn, still dark, but growing lighter as the minutes passed. It was the first time Sylah had seen the world in this shadowed realm—where the blue of the Farsai Desert bled into the blue of the sky. Normally the tidewind ate through the early strikes of morning.

No longer was it the stillness of deep night, but the expectant moment before a new day. Like a bud about to bloom, the air felt charged with energy.

Sylah looked for the sentinels, but the pack were nowhere in sight. Though Sylah wasn't stupid enough to think they weren't out there.

The three of them stepped away from the staircase and towards the hatch that led them to the network of tunnels beneath Nar-Ruta.

Someone moved between the bladed legs of a spider ahead of them.

"I didn't think you'd actually manage it."

The voice turned Sylah's belly to fire.

Tanu stepped out into the half-light of not-quite-dawn, dragging a sword through the sand beside her feet. Her dark eyes shone like fathomless pools as she walked towards them.

Sylah's eyes flickered to the hatch, fifteen handspans away.

"Can you carry her?" Sylah asked Hassa.

The Ghosting nodded. Sylah transferred Anoor's weight to Hassa. "Go now, I'll follow."

"Sylah, don't leave me," Anoor whimpered as Tanu circled them.

Sylah cradled Anoor's cheek before pressing her mouth against her cracked lips. A warmth blossomed between them and even as she felt herself falling apart, she could see Anoor's eyes had more life in them than they had before.

"Never again. Go now." She pressed the kori cage to Anoor's chest. "I won't be far behind."

With Hassa and Anoor safely making their escape behind her, Sylah withdrew her dagger and turned to face Tanu. It was then that Sylah realised the disciple wasn't alone. Three of the Zalaam's soldiers slipped out of the shadows and flanked her.

Sylah's eyes widened as she recognised one of them. The boy had been a part of the Shariha who had captured her, Ina he was called. In his hand was the sword he had stolen from her.

She would have recognised it anywhere. The joba tree gilded hilt that grew into a blade shone beautifully in the weak moonlight. It had been Anoor's once, won in the Trial of Stealth, then it had been gifted to Sylah for her journey east.

From the smirk on Ina's face, he recognised her.

Tanu spoke, drawing Sylah's gaze away from her stolen weapon. "When I saw you and Hassa arrive, I thought to myself . . . let's see how far they get before one of the guards notices. A test, for our defences. One we clearly failed . . . well, almost," Tanu said lightly. She flicked the sword up from the ground, showering sand in Sylah's direction.

Sylah saw the feint for what it was and didn't flinch. "You forget, Tanu. I am one of the Stolen. We were both trained to kill, but I was trained to also win the Aktibar for Strength."

Tanu's smile faltered, just a tiny bit. But then she looked to her side where the other soldiers stood. "It's four against one." Tanu's muscles tensed and Sylah knew she was about to lunge.

But Sylah needed to give Anoor and Hassa more time to escape. She interrupted Tanu's movement with a question. "What did you do to Anoor?"

"It was a kindness, Sylah."

"Starvation? A kindness?"

"No, the Wife didn't starve her, Sylah. She merely blunted the harshness of the world. It was a kindness to lace her tea with joba seeds."

Joba seeds. Sylah's heart constricted and her next words were a tortured whisper. "You've been *drugging* her."

Tanu nodded. "We just eased some of the harder truths. Truths that you and I were both raised to understand."

Sylah felt her throat burn with grief and rage. All this time they had been poisoning both Anoor's mind and body.

Tanu continued, "I can't let you take the Child of Fire, Sylah."

"Her name is *Anoor*," Sylah shouted before lunging towards Tanu's heart.

Tanu rolled to the right before contact, but Sylah had anticipated it. She used her free hand to grasp Tanu's forearm as she spun, sending the smaller woman sprawling.

Ina tried to disarm Sylah but she had a dagger in his neck before he could scream. She revelled in the rain of his blood before pulling her sword from his dying grip.

"Goodbye, Ina. Thank you for looking after my sword."

The boy was no longer grinning.

Sylah felt her breathing steady as the weight of her old weapon settled into her hand. Perfectly balanced. Perfectly deadly.

The moment was gone as Tanu barrelled onto her stomach, winding her. But Tanu hadn't been trained by Azim's sadistic techniques. She didn't know that she'd need much more than that to stop her.

There was a scream behind them but when Sylah realised it wasn't Anoor's she ignored it.

Tanu's sword glanced over Sylah's chest plate, the spider emblem deflecting the brunt of the force.

Sylah laughed at the irony, a manic sound that sent Tanu skittering backwards. But Sylah wasn't about to let Tanu go this time.

She pounced, her blade finding its mark deep within Tanu's thigh. Tanu cried out and stumbled to the ground. Sylah retrieved her sword and stood over her.

"Tomi did nothing to you. He was just a stable hand, he didn't deserve to die," Sylah said.

"Glorious one up above, you who knows no bounds or boundaries. You, who spins the web of my future, take this sacrifice as your own," Tanu murmured, her eyes looking past Sylah to the sky.

"No, this death is not for Kabut. This death is for Tomi." Sylah drove the sword through Tanu's chest, crunching through rib and cartilage until she found her heart.

During her fight with Tanu, Sylah hadn't noticed that the other two soldiers hadn't joined the melee. Now, she wheeled around, worried that they'd slipped past her to follow Anoor and Hassa.

But what she saw made her stumble backwards. The pack of sentinels had arrived behind her and were tearing the two soldiers limb from limb.

Their screams had long been silenced because their throats had been ripped to ribbons. Indigo and orange blood spurted across the sand.

"Oh, shit." Sylah's hand went to the rune-covered disc in her pocket. But if she managed to diffuse the life from one, what would stop her from being mauled to death before she could retrieve the disc?

One of the sentinels looked up, its muzzle dripping with blood. It opened its mouth in a silent howl, just like the creature it had been mimicked from. The others turned to Sylah.

The sentinels rose from their hindquarters and charged.

Sylah began to run.

She launched herself in the direction of the tunnels' hatch, pulling it open just in time for the first snap of jaws to pass her by.

Sylah slipped down the ladder, her hands burning as she slid along the metal.

One of the sentinels lunged above her, lodging itself in the opening.

Sylah knew it wouldn't be long before the creation was free.

Hassa had lit a torch and Anoor lay slumped against the tunnel wall, the kori bird cage clutched in her arm.

Sylah knelt beside her and pressed a kiss to her brow. Her hand slipped up from the nape of Anoor's neck to her shaven head. Sylah suspected her curls weren't the only thing the Zalaam had taken from Anoor, and the deepest scars would be the ones she couldn't see.

"Told you I wouldn't be long," she said, but Anoor had drifted into unconsciousness. Sylah scooped her up in her arms.

Hassa passed Sylah the torch. *We need to collapse the tunnel*, she signed. *Or they'll follow us back to the Keep.*

Sylah winced. Memur would not be happy that the one secret entrance to the Zalaam's camp had been compromised.

"I know."

Hassa clicked her inkwell in place.

You go ahead. I'll do it.

"Are you sure?"

Stop talking, start running.

Sylah did as she was bidden.

"Hold on, Anoor, we've got you now. You'll survive this. We all will."

Stone collapsed behind her, and a plume of dust rushed down with what remained of the tunnel. The torch guttered out.

"Hassa?" Sylah screamed. "Hassa?"

She jumped as someone touched her arm. From the coldness of the metal, she knew it was Hassa's inkwell.

"Maiden's tits, I thought you were back there. Thank you for not dying."

Though she couldn't see Hassa's reply, the soft laugh was enough to let Sylah know she wasn't hurt.

A moment later, Hassa was lit by the warm glow of a runelamp.

"I didn't know you'd learnt how to do that."

Last week. The lamp swung from her wrist as she signed.

They set off at a brisk pace back to the Keep. With Anoor asleep in Sylah's arms, her mind was in turmoil. She thought of the rows and rows of creations and felt her heart begin to race in panic.

"Hassa, how are we going to stop the creations?" Sylah whispered, the question too terrifying to voice loudly.

She hadn't considered the consequences of simply not being able to win. She wasn't afraid of death, growing up in the empire under the Sandstorm's teachings meant she understood the fragility of life more than most people. But the concept of losing in a fight? In a war? No, that she hadn't considered before.

Hassa met her troubled gaze, her signing tentative. *I was thinking about fire. Hot enough to melt the iron.*

"How?"

With bloodwerk, maybe. I'm not sure yet, I need to experiment.

Sylah felt hope flicker to life in her chest, but then Anoor groaned in her arms and the hope turned to fear once more.

"Hold on, Anoor, we're going home."

But the only response was the chirping of the kori bird in its cage.

CHAPTER THIRTY-EIGHT

Anoor

I passed through Jin-Laham on my return from Jin-Sahalia. There are no survivors in the ruins of the city that used to be.

—Griot Holi's report to the griot network

Anoor's dreams were full of shadow and fire.

Then the nightmare had turned peaceful as Sylah appeared, a beautiful mirage that had swirled in on mist and wind.

She let her eyelids flutter open and looked around her. She was in her old room.

I'm still asleep, she concluded.

But if she was dreaming why were things different? The room was bare of any trace of her belongings, even the bed felt different, the mattress harder than she remembered. A kori bird chirped sweetly in a cage by the window. She pulled her gaze closer to the bed and noticed a bucket sat beside her. She felt queasy looking at its contents.

Though she was thirsty, she couldn't stomach drinking from the water jug on her bedside table—a table she had never seen before.

It was nighttime, but there was no tidewind in this strange dreamworld. The moonlight poured in from her open window. Something glinted against the wall—a sword. Anoor swung her matchstick legs out of the bed and made her way across the room towards the blade.

She didn't attempt to lift it, her muscles felt weak, almost incorporeal. But she recognised the weapon. It was the one she had given to Sylah before she left for the mainland.

Anoor smiled. She was glad it had made it to Kabut's realm—because that must surely be where she was.

But would I feel pain here? Her bones ached with a weariness that made her want to crawl back into the strange new bed.

Maybe she could conjure some bitter leaf tea? Saliva flooded her mouth as she concentrated on creating the tea in her hands. But despite how hard she yearned for it the tea didn't appear.

Perhaps there was someone in the kitchens of this realm.

She made her way to the door on tottering legs and pulled it open. The hallway was dark, the tiles cool on her bare feet as she crossed the living quarters of her chambers.

"I don't care what Memur says, Anoor is not a threat. She hasn't even woken for three days. How can she be a threat when she's in a coma?"

That voice. It set her heart racing, yearning harder than she had for the bitter leaf tea. Anoor tried to quicken her pace.

"I know, Sylah, but that doesn't matter, Anoor is sequestered here. We cannot risk her defecting on the battlefield."

Anoor sighed. She was glad her mind had dreamt up Gorn too, she missed the woman fiercely.

"And so, what now? Anoor stays locked up here forever?"

Anoor smiled. Sylah sounded so angry. So fiercely loving.

She pushed open the door to the living room and the three people inside turned to look at her.

"Anoor." Sylah ran to her. Like in her bedroom, this realm had conjured a slightly different version of Sylah too. Her braids were a little longer than the last time Anoor had seen them, and thinner too. Baby hairs grew around her parting, where Anoor was sure there'd been more braids before. Her skin was dull, her cheeks hollow. It was like looking back at the assassin who had entered her rooms all those mooncycles ago.

But this Sylah's eyes were clear, not clouded by the lure of joba seeds, and they were fixed on Anoor with such longing, Anoor felt her own eyes burn with tears.

Sylah's touch was warm as she helped guide Anoor into a seat.

Then Sylah knelt beside her and peered into her eyes with a frown. "How are you feeling?"

Anoor smiled and pressed her fingers into the crease between Sylah's eyebrows. "You don't need to be sad, Sylah. It's all going to be okay."

Sylah grasped Anoor's hand and pressed it against her lips. "I was so worried you wouldn't wake up." A tear spilt from Sylah's eyes and Anoor watched it roll down her cheek and onto her top lip. Anoor leant forward and kissed it.

"I'm not sure I ever want to wake up again." Anoor leant her head against Sylah's chest and breathed in her familiar scent.

Hassa moved into Anoor's line of sight and signed, *She thinks she's dreaming, Sylah.*

"Hassa, I'm so glad you're here too." The changes in Hassa were subtle, but they were there. She moved with more assurance, and her hair was longer.

"Kabut's realm treats you well," Anoor said to the Ghosting.

"Anoor." Gorn stood over her and spoke in a stern voice. "This is not a dream, and this is certainly *not* Kabut's realm. Sylah and Hassa rescued you from the Zalaam three days ago. Yona was drugging you with joba seeds. You are back in the Keep, and we are preparing to go to war."

Anoor felt the ground swallow her up. She looked to Sylah for confirmation. "This . . . isn't Kabut's realm?"

"No." Sylah's voice broke as she spoke.

The world was spinning. "I don't understand. Sylah, how are you alive?"

Sylah frowned. "Who told you I died, Anoor?"

"The Shariha, they had my sword . . . they said the prisoner they had taken it from was gone . . ." Anoor's breath came out in big, shaking gasps.

"The Shariha did capture me, and they did take the sword," Sylah said gently. "But I escaped."

"The sword, it's in the bedroom."

Sylah's lips curled over her teeth. "I got it back."

"How?"

Sylah turned to Gorn. "Do you think you could get Anoor some verd leaf tea? I think there's still a hidden stash in the larder. And Hassa, maybe some wet cloths to bring her temperature down?"

Anoor had begun to shake now, her whole body trembling. "Is Kabut punishing me?"

"No, Anoor. It's the withdrawal symptoms from the joba seeds."

"Joba seeds?" Anoor whispered.

Sylah's expression was grim. "Tanu confirmed it. Was there something that they were giving you? A food or a drink, perhaps?"

Bitter leaf tea with a red powder Yona had called barknut.

Anoor began to sob.

Sylah gathered Anoor in her arms. "You've got through the worst of it now. You weren't on it for as long as I was, so your recovery should be swifter."

"I thought you were dead. I thought you were dead. I thought you were dead." Anoor's sob turned into a wail. Sylah stroked her hair and whispered soothing words in her ear. She held her until the tears subsided, but the pain remained.

Softly, Sylah began to tell her the tale of the last few mooncycles with shuddering starts and stops, though Anoor suspected there was even more to tell.

Strikes passed and still they stayed intertwined on the sofa. Sometimes Anoor found herself crying with the truths and impossibility of what Sylah told her. Other times she found herself laughing. "A camel? What an odd creature!"

Food and drink passed Anoor's lips but the only thing she was hungry for was Sylah. She reached for her now, trailing her fingers along her jaw. Sylah leant into her touch and let out a sigh.

Day had come and night had fallen again, a whole day gone. "Come, let us go to bed," Sylah said. She reached her hand out to lead Anoor away. For a second her silhouette blurred, turning into Yona. Anoor flinched away from her.

"Anoor, what is it?"

She squeezed her eyes tight, only opening them again to slits to make sure the vision had passed. "I saw Yona."

Sylah stepped towards her but didn't touch her. "Yona won't be able to hurt you again, Anoor."

Anoor reached a shaking hand outwards and clasped onto Sylah so tight that she knew it would be painful. Sylah led her slowly back to her bedroom.

"Why has everything changed in here?" Anoor murmured.

"Gorn let the tidewind in before she left. The wardens had to repair the whole tower." Sylah's grin was mischievous.

Anoor smiled. "Gorn the Truthsayer."

They lay together still wearing their clothes. "I missed you," Sylah murmured.

Anoor shuddered, whether it was from the joba seeds withdrawal or Sylah's words, she wasn't sure. Sylah's arm slipped around Anoor's waist, and she pulled her closer.

"If I had known what Yona was doing to you, I would have come sooner," Sylah whispered, her breath hot on Anoor's cheek.

I wouldn't have come to you. The thought sat heavy in Anoor's mind. Even now it was hard to ignore the sense of purpose the Zalaam had given her.

"But now we're together and we can make the Zalaam pay," Sylah continued. She pressed a kiss to Anoor's collarbone.

Anoor moved away and stood. When Sylah reached for her she said, "I'm fine, I can walk."

Anoor moved to the window and looked out on the empire—no, the Dryland Republic, as they told her it was now called.

Once this had been her only view of the world. How it had changed since she'd been gone. No longer did the rubber trees run along the horizon. Instead the landscape there was blackened and burnt. The Ember Quarter was bustling, despite the time of night, as volunteers helped to crate supplies from different areas of Nar-Ruta. Even the Keep's courtyard was unrecognisable, filled with temporary structures and soldiers carrying out drills.

And beyond it all was the Zalaam's army. Godbeasts—no, *creations* as Sylah called them—pockmarked the desert in the distance. Anoor couldn't help the swell of awe that accompanied the vast sight of the Zalaam's force.

Anoor pressed her hand onto the cool glass. "We won't survive it, you know."

"I think we might," Sylah said, joining her by the window.

Anoor looked to the moon. "What if the Zalaam were right? About the God, and the prophecy?"

Sylah scoffed, but then she saw the sincerity in Anoor's face. "Anoor, they're not right. They're fanatics, praying to a false God."

"It didn't feel false," Anoor whispered.

"That was the joba seeds," Sylah said.

Despite what Anoor now knew, she couldn't forget what it felt like to be a part of it, to feel the power of a God thrumming through her. Even if it was just the drugs.

But a piece of her still wanted to believe in some of it. "If Kabut's realm is not real, then what happens to us when we die?"

Sylah grimaced, then wrapped her arms around Anoor. Her grip felt like armour, protective and strong.

"I don't know. But all I do know is we will be together."

Anoor tipped her head backwards and looked into Sylah's eyes. The love that shone in them burnt like fire and Anoor found herself flinching at the heat.

Sylah let her arms drop to the sides, ending their embrace. Her gaze slipped to the ground. "I'm sorry, it must have been difficult being a prisoner for so long."

"I—I wasn't a prisoner." A silent sob racked her chest and she let it pass before continuing. "I was there willingly, and I did some terrible, terrible things. I knew they were using bone marrow . . . maybe not at first but then I knew. And Qwa and Faro—" Anoor's cries were no longer silent as she gasped and shuddered to the floor.

Sylah was there holding the pieces of her together, but Anoor wasn't sure she'd ever be whole again.

After her tears subsided a little, Sylah tilted Anoor's chin up until Anoor could see the braid she held in her hand. It was intertwined with a piece of patchwork material.

"My friend Petal was on the *Baqarah* with me. When my attempt to kill the Tannin failed, she sacrificed herself. And I let her." Sylah swallowed. "We all did what we had to do." Her voice was grim.

Anoor pressed her lips against Sylah's cheeks where the salt of her tears flowed freely. "I'm sorry about Petal. I'm sorry about all of it."

Sylah leant in, until Anoor could feel her breath on her lips. "I'm not, because in the end I found you, and that's all that matters."

When she kissed her, it was the old Anoor that kissed her back.

Sylah broke it off as Anoor's lips grew hungry.

"To bed now. All will be easier in the morning."

Anoor slept cradled in Sylah's arms. She woke once from a nightmare that left her screaming. Sylah had been there, her hand rubbing soothing circles on Anoor's lower back.

Now in the light of day she couldn't remember what the dream had been about. But the echo of the terror she'd felt sent shivers down her back.

She untangled herself from Sylah's sleeping form and padded across the room, leaving her to sleep. The corridor was dimly lit by natural light—no longer would they need to close the tidewind shutters.

Anoor tried the front door to her chambers, but they were locked. She tried one more time, but the door wouldn't give.

She rested her head against the cool wood. There was a sigh behind her and she turned to find Gorn watching her from the doorway of her old bedroom.

"I didn't know you were staying here," Anoor said.

"Yes, I've been sleeping here since we reclaimed the Keep."

"I suppose it was always your home."

"No, Anoor, *you* were my home," Gorn said simply.

Anoor hung her head. "I don't think sorry will ever repair the rift between us. I have made so many terrible mistakes."

Gorn watched her for a moment, her eyes unreadable before opening her arms. Anoor went to her. The embrace was full of hope and memories.

"There will be a time for healing," Gorn said. "But first must come the time for bleeding."

Anoor nodded. "You did it, Gorn, you told the truth and ousted the wardens."

"I did, with quite a bit of help."

"I want to fight too. I don't think I'll be much use with a sword, but maybe I can work on bloodwerk."

Gorn nodded and looked to the locked door. "The Ghostings

weren't all that happy with your arrival. Your rescue compromised the tunnel network that we could have used to our advantage. Beyond that, they do not trust you."

"I'll tell them everything I know about the Zalaam, everything."

"That would be a start."

There was a bloodcurdling scream from the bedroom.

"Sylah?" Anoor found energy she didn't know she had and ran as fast as she could across the hallway.

CHAPTER THIRTY-NINE

Hassa

The Aktibar arena has been stocked with all the supplies we could gather from the looted houses across Nar-Ruta. Two thousand pallets have been laid out, with more being added every day. I still fear it will not be enough.

—Report sent to Memur from Sami

Hassa had been sequestered in the forge with Vahi for the last three days. The Zalaam were yet to attack, with the primary theory being they were awaiting the mainlanders' arrival. Hassa harnessed the extra time.

Memur had been so vexed at Hassa compromising the tunnel network that she had been banned from the courtroom. Hassa didn't mind because she'd been busy testing ways to harness fire.

The idea had come to her the night they'd rescued Anoor. Though the thought had been fleeting, it had made roots, and she couldn't stop thinking about how fire might be the only way to defeat the creations.

She'd shared her thoughts with Vahi, who had been willing to indulge her experiments.

Could we increase the surface area of the runeflare? Hassa signed. *We need it to get as hot as possible to melt the iron.*

Ren frowned over the small sphere in front of her as Vahi translated Hassa's words. Hassa had enlisted her help as soon as she'd had the idea. The runeflare had been her invention, and Hassa thought that the trigger in it could be the first step in creating a fire hot enough to melt metal.

"I'm not sure how, Hassa, if we're using bloodwerk to trigger the release of the catalyst, then we need the runes to be close enough together to release the catchment."

But the fire is not getting hot enough. Hassa gestured to their hundreds of failed experiments that lay in charred remains around them.

And they were running out of time.

"Why don't we just create a forge and circle the Dredge with it?" Vahi suggested. Sweat ran down his face mingling with the soot that streaked his skin.

Hassa shook her head. *We don't have the resources. All imports from Jin-Hidal have stopped and you're already running out of coal for the weapons you're making.*

"We could use wood?" Ren suggested.

Vahi shook his head. "The amount we'd need would be impossible to source."

No one acknowledged the burnt plantation fields. Felled, those trees would have been enough. But rebellions are like fires, something needs to burn to make a flame.

No, there must be a way to use bloodwerk to create fire. My ancestors managed to do it.

Ren shrugged. Her expertise was in potions and powders, not bloodwerk.

Hassa looked to the ceiling where a runelamp swung above them. *Runelamps create light from the friction of two opposing runes. Surely that friction could create fire?*

"Half of the combination in a runelamp is to temper the heat that the friction creates. If you remove those parameters, I'm not sure the runes won't burn away before sparking."

Hassa thought it was worth a try. She rummaged through their discarded experiments before finding an intact sphere. She drew the runes *Ba* and *Kha* on opposite ends.

"Here, put this underneath it, just in case it sparks." Vahi shovelled a few cold coals and brought them over. Hassa lowered the sphere onto them and triggered the runelight.

There was a sharp white light as the two forces competed with each other, creating the brightness that would usually sustain the flare of a runelamp.

Then smoke rose up and Hassa felt hope swell in her ribcage.

Could this be it? Could this be the answer to destroying the creations?

Then she smelt it—the aroma of sizzling iron and copper. Her blood was burning away.

The light flickered and guttered out.

Vahi laid a hand on her slumped shoulders. "I'm sorry. It was worth a try though. Perhaps we should concentrate on making more blood-werk crossbows instead?"

Ren looked dejected as she began to pack away her herbs and powders.

Hassa reached for a vial of clear liquid on the side and held it against her inkwell and limb. It was labelled "sharj oil".

Ren had suggested it as a component for the runeflares as it burnt hotter than any other fuel in the empire. But it was in lower supply than coal.

An idea came to her. *Why don't we mix the oil with blood?*

Vahi shook his head. "It wouldn't work. Blood cannot conduct power. Embers have tried for years—something about the properties of the blood blocking the transition to the new material."

Hassa smiled. *Embers have tried, Embers, not Ghostings. Our blood is clear, so perhaps the power can be transferred.*

Vahi's eyes widened slightly. That was when Hassa knew there was potential to the idea. She moved into action.

"What is going on, Vahi? Can you translate? Hassa, why are you mixing your blood with sharj oil . . . oh. I see." Ren leant in and watched as Hassa repeated the runelamp experiment with the mixture of her blood and the oil.

This time Hassa completed the full chain of runes including the protection ones that would stop the blood from burning. Because this time the blood wouldn't burn, but the oil would.

When she finished the sequence, she pushed herself away just in time for the runes to burst into flame.

Then flicker out.

She put her limbs against her forehead and turned away. She wanted to scream and shout and cry. But Hassa had learnt over the years that those actions did nothing to help her solve a problem.

But she wasn't going to be able to solve this one.

A tear escaped her eyes despite her attempts to stop it.

"Hassa, I think you should see this." Vahi was standing over the runes. His voice gave nothing away.

Hassa dragged her feet back over.

"Look." He pointed to the runes.

For a second Hassa saw nothing. But then she realised the blurring around the runes wasn't her tears but heat waves.

And around the base of her blood was a blue flame, in the perfect shape of the runes.

"Blue and clear, Hassa, the hottest type of flame," Ren whispered.

Vahi knelt in front of the table and looked up at the flame with wide eyes. "The bloodwerk has enhanced the size of the fire. Sharj oil doesn't burn for long, but the energy generated from the bloodwerk is keeping it going."

There was a beat of silence as they all basked in the warmth of the fire.

Then Hassa signed, *We should test it, get some iron.*

Vahi ran to his scrap heap and returned with a small piece of metal between tongs. He lowered it into the flames.

Hassa couldn't take her eyes away as she watched the iron melt. And even when the droplets of molten metal fell onto the runes the flame continued, her protection runes holding strong.

Hassa had made fire with bloodwerk. She had a way of mass-destroying creations. Her smile was grim as she signed.

The Zalaam wanted the Ending Fire. And I think we might be able to provide it.

CHAPTER FORTY

Jond

Ghostings who wish to learn bloodwerk, please attend nightly sessions in the great veranda. You are needed.

—Notice pinned to the barracks' doors by Hassa

Sylah screamed as Jond appeared in the room.

"Jond? Kara? What the fuck are you doing here?" Sylah leapt from the bed and ran towards them.

Jond froze. The breath escaped his lungs in a *whoosh* like he'd been winded.

"Sylah?" he murmured through bloodless lips.

She crossed the room and hugged him. It was only then that he realised she was alive, well and truly *alive*.

He embraced her back fiercely.

"I thought the Tannin had taken you," he whispered into her braids.

She stiffened beneath his grip and pushed him to arm's length. When she spoke, she didn't meet his eye.

"I failed at killing the Tannin—"

"We noticed," Kara drawled behind them. Sylah looked to the Queen and nodded a greeting.

"Hello. We thought you were dead," Kara said in a way that made everyone know that when she said "thought", she meant "hoped".

The two of them had never got on, and Jond wondered if it was just because they were both too stubborn to recognise their similarities.

"Very much alive, I'm afraid," Sylah smiled, showing all her teeth. Jond laughed, looking between Kara and Sylah.

Sylah turned to him with a bemused expression on her face. "What's so funny?"

He shrugged. "I've never been happier to see the two of you argue."

Because Sylah was *alive*. Her smile slipped a little and he wondered if she had remembered his words from their parting argument.

"You're not choosing anything but self-destruction. I look at you and I see a flame, the same fierce and loving woman I have known nearly all my life. But fire's nature is to burn those around it."

He winced as the memory came back to him. But then her hand was on his and she squeezed it.

"I'm glad we're *both* still alive."

"Sorry we scared you." Jond's grin was lopsided. "I couldn't remember many details about the Keep but I knew the coordinates of Anoor's chambers."

It was as if saying her name conjured her and Anoor ran into the room. She wasn't the same person she'd been when Jond left. Her cheeks were sunken, her hazel eyes deeply set, and the depth of them seemed devoid of life. It raised the hairs on Jond's neck.

"Jond?" Anoor said incredulously. Even her voice was frail.

"And who is this?" Kara asked.

"I'm the Ch—" Something hot blazed in Anoor's eyes only to cool a second later. "I'm Anoor."

"Hello, Anoor, I'm Queen Karanomo."

"Queen?" Sylah spluttered. Then her eyes widened in realisation. "Of course, that's why you've always had a rod up your arse."

Kara dragged her gaze to Sylah's. "Helps with my posture."

Her response was so dry that Sylah couldn't help but laugh, and soon Kara joined in.

But all joy left the room with Jond's next words.

"Our ships are less than a day from the empire's shores. We're here to discuss military strategy with the wardens," Jond said.

"That might be a bit tricky." A newcomer stood in the doorway to the bedroom. She was stockily built and filled most of the doorframe. "We don't really allow visitors in prison."

*   *   *

Kara flighted in the rest of the Blood Forged to the courtroom, so the tale only had to be told once. Even Rascal had insisted on joining the party—it was then that Jond discovered animals could be flighted too. She'd cried and scratched at his legs until he'd picked her up and placed her on his lap. Now she was curled up, snoring faintly.

The Truthsayer—Gorn—mediated the meeting once all introductions had been made.

Still Jond couldn't believe it—the Wardens' Empire had been liberated. He was glad to see it in his lifetime.

As the sun reached its zenith, it cast its light on the centre of the joba wood table. The only table of its kind, made from the sacred tree. Jond ran his hands along the grain. It was a symbol of so much more than just the God Anyme. It represented the wardens' impunity and their total authority.

And here they were discussing war across the table. Elbows rested on the wood with little care as military information was shared. Some of the blood of those who were connected by Sui's mind link had dripped onto the table. Purple, indigo, orange, yellow, green: blood colours that had never existed in the wardens' histories. Maps were scattered like graffiti over the white wood, while more notes were made and shared.

The Wardens' Empire was no longer. It was the Dryland Republic now.

When he'd heard that the wardens and their supporters were locked in the old Nowerk Gaol he'd felt the stirrings of bloodlust.

How dare they live, pacing in their cells upon the bones of all they have murdered? he'd thought.

But justice would have to come later.

Jond patted the wood one final time. He had faith for the first time in a long while. Not in any one God, but faith in the future of the world. Even if they failed in this battle, the empire was no longer. His people would die free from the tyranny of oppression.

Soon the discussion turned to strategy and military might. Ravenwing led the conversation through the communication link.

"We have twelve regiments arriving on the shores of the Drylands within the day. It will take us three days to cross the empire. With the Zalaam's army between us and you, we will look to disembark in Jin-Kutan, following the estuary of the Ruta River to the Keep."

Gorn tapped her pen nib on the table. "What if you didn't come here? What if we split the army?"

Ravenwing frowned. "How is that advantageous?"

"The Zalaam had to circumvent the Jin-Dinil lakes because their creations couldn't travel through them."

Jond raised his eyebrows. "Neither can we, unless you all learnt to walk on water while I was gone?"

Part of him wouldn't be surprised, the empire had achieved what he had thought was impossible by simply removing the wardens from government.

Ravenwing's mouth curved into a smile, understanding Gorn's point. "The lakes are swamps this time of year. No more than a handspan of water. The creations wouldn't be able to pass them, and they'd be forced to battle us with foot soldiers."

Gorn leant back in her chair. "The more foot soldiers we kill, the fewer riders can power the creations."

Ravenwing nodded. "Yes, I think this will work."

Jond looked to Sylah. She stood quietly in the corner of the room. Anoor had not been allowed into the courtroom and Jond could tell that in turn Sylah was only half present.

There was a sound at the door and a small Ghosting slipped in only to stop and gawk at the congregation. Jond recognised her, but it was only when Ads cried, "Hassa!" that he remembered her name. The mind link was removed as the elders and Hassa reunited.

Jond moved towards Sylah. He noticed she was pressing her tongue through the gap in her teeth.

"Is Anoor going to be all right?" he asked softly.

Sylah let out a breath. "Physically, yes. The withdrawals are easing, as she wasn't on the drug long. She's even started to gain weight again. But the Zalaam . . . they broke something in her. Sometimes she slips away to somewhere I can't reach."

"Give her something to concentrate on," Kara said, making them both jump. They hadn't realised she'd been listening. "She is grieving her community, her God. Give her a project, like helping out in the medical tent or something."

Sylah frowned. "She's locked in her chambers for defecting to the other side."

Kara cleared her voice and raised herself up. She had the uncanny ability to draw all eyes to her at will. "The time for tallying crimes will come. But now we need every person who is willing to fight. Allow Anoor to leave her chambers. After all, Sylah here stole the orb of creation, and yet we've let her live."

Sylah bristled at Kara's final words but didn't reply.

The Ghosting elders turned to each other and began to discuss between themselves. Ads translated Dew's words. *Anoor can be released from her rooms. Though we remind Queen Karanomo that she does not govern the Dryland Republic.*

Kara's smile was more of a smirk.

Dew continued, *Hassa's interruption here today will have a significant effect on our strategy. She has discovered a way to create fire through bloodwerk.*

"What?" Jond joined the chorus of exclamation.

"Well, that changes things indeed," Kara said quietly.

The discussions continued into the night. Anticipation filled the courtroom, bringing with it a fevered energy. The feeling itched at Jond's skin, and he sought fresh air.

Kara found him in the courtyard looking up at the joba tree.

"Big tree," she said.

Jond smiled and looked at her. Her red curls framed her heart-shaped face and he found himself leaning forward to brush one away from her lip.

Kara started at his touch, then softened and leant in. The two of them were learning how to navigate their newfound intimacy. They had resisted it for so long that the muscle memory of keeping themselves apart needed to ease.

He looked back to the joba tree. "I used to tell Sylah that I'd live in this tree when she was warden." He shook his head, the smile dropping away. "The world was so small back then."

Kara said nothing for a time, letting him linger in his past. When he turned back to her she spoke. "I've flighted the other councillors back to the boats. Do you want to stay here tonight?" Her expression was expectant.

"No. I'd like to spend our last night at sea with you." Jond never thought he'd ever prefer to stay on a boat than on land, but the solace the sea gave them was something he couldn't take for granted. Tomorrow, when the march began, he wasn't sure they'd have another chance to be alone.

Rascal he'd left in the care of Niha and his healers. The kitten would follow Jond to the battlefield—and she'd put up a good fight, he was sure—but he didn't want to see her hurt.

Kara withdrew her orb and took Jond's hand. Gently she drew the purple runes on his wrist. They blinked into Kara's cabin a second later.

Jond slipped his hand around the nape of her neck and kissed her, his hip bones pushing her back until she was pressed against the wooden panelling of the boat. His other hand slipped under the hem of her dress.

The gentle lull of the waves gave his caress a soft rhythm. Kara's hands pulled desperately at his clothes until he laughed and obliged, pulling them off quickly.

There was a hunger to their movements as they sought pleasure in each other knowing it was the last time they might ever get the chance. Knowing that what came next was pain and fire and death.

But tonight, each other's arms were enough to keep the fear at bay.

Jond didn't sleep that night. So, when the empire—no, the Dryland Republic—came into view he was already on deck watching the raw colour of dawn stretch across the blue sand.

His hands clenched and unclenched with impatience. Now the day had begun he was ready. He had his orders once they hit land. Hassa's invention had charted a new course for the Blood Forged.

His veins sparked with the excitement he always experienced before a fight. He was scared too, but he'd learnt how to temper fear into something more practical—like rage.

And by Anyme, was he angry.

He was angry for all the Stolen children manipulated by a dangerous organisation. He was angry for all the Dusters and Ghostings who had been drained of their bone marrow. He was angry for all the displaced people whose homes had been destroyed by extreme weather.

And the anger that wove between it all and grew hotter and more potent with each verdict was the rage he felt towards the Zalaam.

The chant of the Stolen came to him then, but altered:

"Stolen, sharpened, the hidden key,

We'll destroy the Zalaam to set Ghostings free,

Churned up from the tidewind to tear them apart,

A dancer's grace, a killer's instinct, an Ember's blood, a Duster's heart."

He felt the names of all the family he had lost flutter through his mind like sheets of paper.

"Mia, Hala, Bola, Khadid, Yota, Hussain, Ali, Isa, Abrar, Otto, Fareen, Lio . . ."

Each name fed the fire of his rage. Though it had been years ago, the grief of their massacre still took him unawares. Now, knowing that Yona and the Zalaam had manipulated the Sandstorm to weed out the Child of Fire only made him angrier.

His hands clenched so tight his nails left marks in his palm.

"This might be our last dawn." Kara joined him by the railing and rested her head against his shoulder.

He felt himself relax marginally, despite her morose words.

"No, I think you're too stubborn to die," Jond said with a smile.

She was wearing her battle armour—black boiled leather with a silver chest plate that clipped in a sheer gold cape across one shoulder.

She wore no helmet nor mouth covering. The only thing to adorn her face was the crown he had made her, interwoven with her red curls.

She looked magnificent and dangerous.

"You'll stand out dressed like that. That gold cape is a target on your back," he said.

She patted his hand. "I know, but my presence will also bring hope to our troops more than anything else."

Jond set his jaw. He hated that she had to sacrifice her safety in this way.

"Jond," she said gently. "I know how to take care of myself."

He nodded and turned back to the shore.

"I'm going to flight to the beach. Sui thinks it'll help morale for when the soldiers disembark," Kara said.

Jond reached for her. "This can't be the last time I see you. I won't let it be," he said fiercely.

Kara grasped his chin and drew him close. "Then don't let it be, Jond Alnua."

Her kiss left him breathless but as he leant in to grip her lower back she winked out of existence.

He smiled wryly at the space she had occupied.

"I'll see you soon, my Queen."

CHAPTER FORTY-ONE

Anoor

They may have taken the Child of Fire, but her sacrifice remains the same. Our God is sated and calls on us to start the final battle. The Ending Fire is almost upon us. Be ready to ride.

—Words spoken by the Wife to the Zalaam army

Anoor ran her hands over the stone eru and shivered. "You made this?"

Sylah nodded. "With help. It was trapped underneath a villa, but I had some soldiers move it to here."

They were in an empty eru stable. Not entirely empty: two guards stood by the door as Anoor was not trusted, not yet.

"It's ridiculous, you don't need to prove anything," Sylah had seethed. "The information you've given us has been crucial to our approach. And now what, they want to babysit you?"

She'd thrown a rude gesture to the two guards.

Anoor put a hand on her forearm. "I don't mind. If it means I can be useful, then let them watch me."

And perhaps part of Anoor still didn't fully trust herself yet.

Even now, with the stone eru in front of her she couldn't help but shiver from the godbeast's divine presence. The stark brightness of the whitestone was at odds with the wooden stable, marking it out as otherworldly.

But unlike the oppressive monstrosities made by the Zalaam, the eru was statuesque, with embellishments that indicated care over purpose. Even the eye sockets had been fitted with glass orbs.

Anoor was surprised at the delicacy of Sylah's carving, and she voiced as much.

"No, it wasn't me," Sylah said, shamefaced. "It was Ala who did all the decorating. Before she helped me carve, it looked like three blocks of stone."

Anoor laughed, circling the creature. Her freedom was newly earned, and it felt good to be outside of the four walls of her chambers. Touching the stonework, she felt the grain of blood patterned into it and shivered.

It felt like touching a memory. No, a nightmare. The shape of it was familiar, the smell too: iron and copper.

Without warning, she was there again, standing at the bow of the boat as the volcano erupted, burning all those unable to join the Zalaam's war campaign.

But it wasn't the memory of the volcano that had her gasping for breath, but the reminder of how she had felt seeing all those people die.

That they had made a worthy sacrifice.

Suddenly it felt as if lava and smoke burnt up her throat, and she found herself struggling to breathe.

"It's all right, Anoor. I've got you." Sylah's arms wrapped around her waist, bringing her out of the nightmare with her soothing words.

Anoor took a shuddering breath. "Thank you." She moved out of Sylah's embrace. Despite the warmth of Sylah's love, it did nothing to abate the chill from deep within Anoor's bones. She feared she'd be cold forever.

Anoor stepped towards the eru once more. "The runes are perfectly drawn. You learnt quickly," she said, circling the creature.

Sylah cleared her throat. "Tanu helped me finish the combination."

Anoor nodded, ignoring the sharp stab of loss Tanu's name brought. Despite knowing everything Tanu had been complicit in, it was difficult divorcing the person she had come to know from the lies of the Zalaam. She wondered if it was similar to how Sylah had felt at Jond's betrayal.

"How did you ever forgive Jond for all the lies the Sandstorm fed you last year?" Anoor asked her. The question seemed to take Sylah unawares, but Anoor's thoughts had carried her there.

Sylah frowned and thought for a minute. Then she said, "I don't think I ever did. Not really. What I think was more important is that he came to forgive himself. He isn't the person he was back then." Then she smiled wryly. "Don't get me wrong, he's still a pain in the ass, but now I know he knows it too."

Anoor tried to smile back but she failed. Tanu would never have changed. She wasn't like Anoor or even Faro and Qwa; she had never doubted the Zalaam's truth.

But I didn't doubt enough. The thought was laced with guilt.

Sylah added gently, "But I also understand how easy it is to be pulled into a web of lies. How a simple recipe for purpose and belonging can also be used to brew something poisonous and deadly."

Anoor nodded, not trusting herself to speak. She looked back to the eru, ignoring the tears on her cheeks. Then she said, "Without an eru to mimic, we'll have to think of something else."

Sylah didn't question the abrupt change in topic as she asked, "Do we *have* to mimic something?"

Anoor shook her head. "No, but it's difficult to know how the godb—creation will react. They might walk on their hands or run backwards. Mimicking a creature gives you greater control. The fifth law is all about control . . ." Her words drained out into a whisper once she realised she was repeating Yona's words back at Sylah.

Anoor swallowed and continued her assessment, looking beneath the eru's belly. "Did you embed something of purpose in the creation?"

"No, I made sure that the whitestone was freshly mined, since I know the beast would have taken on an echo of its former objects."

"Exactly, that's what you can use to your advantage. Remember how the Tannin was made from the stonework of a Zalaam temple? That's why it was a beast of sacrifice. The Zalaam still embed every new creation with a piece of coal from the endless flame. Again, *control.*"

Sylah was smiling faintly. "I've missed this—you teaching me things."

For a second, they were back there on the floor of Anoor's room leaning over sketches of bloodwerk runes. The runelight flickering on Sylah's face, screwed up in frustration as she tried to learn.

If only I could go back there now. Before I had become the very thing I fought to overthrow.

Sylah drew her back with her voice. "Maybe we shouldn't use it. With Hassa's fire tactics the creations will be molten metal."

"Even if the fire runes work perfectly, we're not sure we have enough sharj oil to destroy them all. We need to use everything, Sylah. Everything." Anoor's voice dropped to a rasp. "Because they will use *everything* against us."

Sylah frowned and looked away. "With the mainlanders on the march, we are not sure when the Zalaam will attack. I don't think we have time."

"When is the next full moon?" Anoor asked.

"Three days."

"That is when they'll strike." When Kabut's eye was brightest.

"How do you know?" Sylah asked.

Anoor looked at her with deadened eyes. "That is when they'll strike," she repeated with more conviction.

Sylah broke her stare. "I'll tell the council."

"Three days is enough time for me to adapt this creation." Anoor ran her hands over the stone once more.

Sylah hesitated. "I promised Vahi I would go back and help with the bloodwerk crossbows. Ala was helping me but she's now assigned to Hassa's operation. I can see if someone else is free to help?"

"No, I'd rather work alone." Anoor no longer enjoyed company like she once had.

Sylah slipped her hand around Anoor's waist, her grin turning sly. Then she pressed a kiss to Anoor's lips.

This time Anoor's shiver was all pleasure. She leant her forehead against Sylah's and said, "I'll see you later, tonight."

Once Sylah left Anoor stared at the creation for a long time.

"You should have a name."

The stone beneath her fingers was cold and hungry. Just like her. And in that moment, she knew exactly what to name it.

Retribution.

* * *

Anoor stood by the open window in her room. Three days had felt like one. Her muscles were gently aching with the work she'd spent on the creation. But it was still not finished.

The changes she'd made were taking longer than she'd anticipated. She hoped it would be ready to use in the fight. Though she wanted to fight on the battlefield herself, she wasn't yet strong enough to wield weapons like she once had. But if she managed to complete the creation that wouldn't matter. It would fight with the ferocity of a hundred Anoors.

The sun was setting; soon nightfall would come, and the full moon along with it. The kori bird trilled in the cage next to her.

"Soon, sweet one, soon."

Anoor slipped her hands through the bars and stroked its crest. The runes there had cracked and faded long ago. She opened the cage door and cradled it in the palms of her hands, removing the creature from its prison. Then she turned back to the open window.

There was a scoff behind her, and a voice called out, "Wait, after everything we went through to save it, are you just going to let it go free?"

Anoor turned and met Sylah's eyes. She had just returned from the courtroom that Anoor was still banned from attending.

"Kori birds should never be caged," Anoor said.

The kori dipped its head in the wind before launching into the twilight.

"Farewell, little bird, thank you for your company. May Kabut's eye shine bright on your flight."

Invoking the God's name was second nature to her, and she hadn't realised she'd done it until she saw Sylah's expression.

Anoor closed her eyes and took a deep breath. "The change is still difficult," she said.

Sylah lingered five handspans away. "Memur thinks the Zalaam will launch their attack tonight."

Anoor nodded. "During the full moon, it makes sense."

"We have a few strikes left before I'm needed on the front line."

Anoor held out her hand to Sylah and drew her close. "Shall we spend it together then?"

Their kiss couldn't sate the need they both felt. Anoor matched

Sylah's rhythm with the same anguished longing. Her teeth ran across Sylah's jaw to her ear where she trailed her lips down to where her clavicle met the collar of her shirt. With hasty movements Sylah's clothing was shorn and Anoor could continue her journey down her body.

Sylah gasped as Anoor's fingers found the tender part of her. Playing the rhythm that only Anoor knew. Soon Sylah's breath was quickening, sweat sheening her brow.

And when the melody reached its crescendo Sylah shuddered, her back arching towards where Anoor's hand had slowed to a stop.

Sylah's grin was feral as she turned her attentions to Anoor, tugging at her nightgown. But Anoor clung to the hem. She felt as though her body had lost all the curves that had made her desirable. "You won't like what you see."

Sylah shook her head. "I love you, Anoor. No matter what you look like. I love *you*."

Anoor began to pull the nightdress over her head, Sylah guiding her when she began to struggle.

Sylah didn't balk when she saw Anoor's protruding ribs. Instead, she splayed her hands against her chest and pulled her near.

At first Sylah was gentle, her kisses soft and soothing. Anoor reached for Sylah's cheek. "The Zalaam couldn't break me, and neither will you. Love me how I want you to. How I need you to."

Sylah showed Anoor her teeth before circling her breast with her tongue and biting down.

But Sylah hadn't finished tasting Anoor. She coaxed small sounds of pleasure from Anoor's throat with each stroke until oblivion blurred her vision.

And for a brief time, all thoughts of war and sacrifice fled their minds.

PART FIVE

✛

Conquer

Archery, swordcraft, shieldwork and hand-to-hand combat make up the four disciplines required by every soldier in the Zalaam's army.

—Additional schooling requirements introduced by the Wife thirty-five years ago

The story of the Wardens' Empire as spoken by Griot Sheth on the eve of battle

The spoken word has been transcribed onto the page; the ✧ symbol represents the beating of the griot's drum.

We have come far, you and I. When we began we only saw in red, blue and clear, but now the world has bled yellow, orange, indigo, violet and green too.

And it bleeds still.

But we cannot forget what has come before.

The Wardens' Empire was an ugly thing, gnarled and twisted by the lies the wardens told. But as our scars fade and the plantation fields turn fertile once more, let us not forget what came before.

We were once a land of blood, let us repent.
We were once a land of violence, let us repent.
We were once a land of pain, let us repent.

We must remember this feeling. This seed at the beginning of it all.

We are the Dryland Republic now, and we do not forget, we do not cower. Let our memories be long, and our feelings great.

Tomorrow the Ending Fire comes, a battle like none of us have known. But we go into the fight a unified people.

They say the Zalaam have come to conquer. But conquer what, I ask?

For they will not overcome the land or the seas, or the rivers or the trees.

And they will not take you or me.

For we live in stories.

And words and memories.

Heroes we will be.

Living free.

CHAPTER FORTY-TWO

Ravenwing

The first day of battle

Ravenwing sat at the head of the table in the courtroom. His dark eyes scanned the map in the centre, lingering on the tokens that represented the Zalaam's army.

He expected the enemy to strike at any moment. It was why he had taken this brief moment of solace in the courtroom. But when he had arrived, the Truthsayer was already there.

He looked at her sidelong. Gorn was standing by the window looking out on the courtyard below. He wondered if she ever left the courtroom, and if she ever slept. He'd asked her once, and she'd replied, "Sleep is a privilege of the dead." Which had elicited a rare laugh from him. He respected her tenacity; after all, she had done what so many Embers had refused to do—she had questioned the wardens' truth and by doing so had begun to dismantle the false thrones their rulers sat upon.

It galled Ravenwing that an Ember had been the spark for the revolution he had spent his whole life dreaming of. But he also knew that it *had* to be an Ember, for they were the only ones with a voice in the Wardens' Empire.

Not any longer. His thoughts brought with them a swell of pride. *If we die now, we die free.*

Ravenwing brought his gaze back to the joba wood table—a garish, costly piece of furniture that was too big for the room. They'd had to bring in more chairs to account for the amount of leaders within the Blood Forged, and he moved some of them away to get closer to the edge of the map.

The Zalaam's position presented the Blood Forged with an opportunity to attack them from two angles. One battlefield in the west where the plantation fields were situated, and the other in the east where the muddy lakes of Jin-Dinil would make it difficult for the creations to cross.

But in doing so they were stretching their resources across two front lines.

The eastern battlefield had been a risk, but drawing out the Zalaam's infantry without creations was an advantage they could not let pass. The Blood Forged were banking on this tactic, as all of Hassa's plans relied on it.

Ravenwing pressed his wrists together and prayed. *Anyme give me strength to guide the success of this battle. Ancestors use me as your conduit of vengeance. Let us claim our homeland one last time—*

His prayer was interrupted by the patter of footsteps.

Reed rushed in, the veins on her neck bulging. *Windal has returned.*

Windal was the leader of the flighters scouting the battlefield. He stepped into the doorway beside Reed. He looked haggard, his greying hair unkempt and flecked with sand.

"Commander, Truthsayer." Even Windal's arms seemed fatigued, moving through syrup to salute.

Gorn turned and said, "What's the report, Windal?"

"The Zalaam are moving," he continued.

Ravenwing looked to the window, where the outline of the full moon shone at Gorn's back. The Zalaam would start fighting at night, just as he had thought.

Gorn looked to Ravenwing, deferring to his authority as the Commander General. "Is it time?"

Yes, Windal, flight in Sui, it's time the communication link is in place. As soon as Gorn translated Ravenwing's words, Windal was gone.

Ravenwing turned to Reed. *Tell Hassa to deploy her operation.* Reed nodded and made her way out. In that second, Windal reappeared with Sui in tow.

The councillor of the second charter pulled up Ravenwing's sleeve without asking and began to pattern the runes that would allow them to communicate. Ravenwing was used to the coolness of Sui's touch, and if her fingers lingered on his bicep more than they should have, he didn't mind.

"Windal tells me the Zalaam are marching." Sui's voice sounded like running water in his mind as the connection fell into place.

"Yes," he replied. Though Ravenwing had never spoken with a tongue before, he imagined it must be similar to the mind link. It was liberating to be understood so easily, though he found himself often signing along with his projected thoughts.

"Windal and I will complete the connection with the other leaders," Sui said. "As discussed, only you and Major General Jond will be able to directly commune. I don't have the power to maintain the vast distances for everyone."

Ravenwing nodded as Sui went to complete the rune combination on Gorn.

Jond would be leading the charge on the eastern battlefield, while Ravenwing would have sight of the west. The others would simply have to listen to their thoughts.

"Right, I'm going to go silent now, but know that I'm listening, Commander General." Sui smiled tightly. "We all are."

Then Windal flighted them both away.

Ravenwing strode out of the courtroom, Gorn by his side.

"The troops are ready in the courtyard," she informed him.

"Good, get in position. We march at my command." He spoke through the mind link.

Ravenwing couldn't help the growl that erupted from his throat when he came within sight of the courtyard. Thousands of soldiers looked back at him. He located his regiment of Ghostings near the Keep's gates.

"Are you ready, Truthsayer?" Ravenwing asked.

Gorn was behind him somewhere in the sea of faces. Though he couldn't hear her reply, the chant of "Scythes and Blood" erupted from the soldiers she led.

The Ghostings in turn stamped their feet and hummed low in their throats. He joined their chants with a bloodthirsty cry that started deep within his chest.

The Zalaam might have creations, but the Dryland Republic had its own power: the will to survive.

And this would just be another thing they'd overcome.

Ravenwing looked to his regiment of Ghostings and signed, *It is time to bring the Zalaam to their knees.*

Then he said down the mind connection that projected his thoughts to all the other leaders, "Blood Forged, advance!"

CHAPTER FORTY-THREE

Turin

The first day of battle

Turin smiled as she walked the length of the front line. The air was thick with anticipation and smelt of the sweet aroma of bone marrow. She located her squadron and sauntered towards them, her hips swaying. She drew the eyes of soldiers with every dip.

The Zalaam had offered her armour, but she'd turned it down. She wanted her former allies to recognise her as she rode her creation into battle.

As I destroy them.

Turin wasn't a disloyal person; she was simply opportunistic. Her ambition didn't stop at the founding of the Dryland Republic. No, she was made for greater things than the allies she had made there.

She pursed her lips as if tasting something unpalatable. The Zalaam had been less welcoming than she'd hoped to her and her Gummers, but once she'd pledged herself to Kabut and shared intelligence they'd accepted her into their army.

With one condition of course.

She stopped in front of her platoon of Gummers, all dressed in the deep green of the Zalaam's armour.

"Commander Turin." The Purger splayed her hand against her chest in greeting. Turin savoured her new title. Along with the promise of the Keep and its lands, a deal had been struck.

"Perhaps you can settle a dispute," the Purger said. "Julash says that my queller is smaller than his."

"It is," Julash replied. "And mine has sharper blades."

Turin laughed lightly as she joined them. It was a little insincere. Even her smile was touched with malice as she spoke. "Stop swinging your dicks around like an Abosom on Ardae."

The Gummers laughed at her joke because they had to. She didn't mind that they felt obliged, only that they did.

A horn blew out across the desert. It was time to mount their creations. Turin's skirt caught on the edge of her sentinel's bladed leg, splitting the seam up to her hip.

"Fuck," she growled. But she didn't have time to go back to her tent to change. The skirt would have to do.

The second horn sounded, and she reached into the pouch at her waist. Milky vials of bone marrow lay nestled within. She selected a red one and poised it above the catchment, waiting for the third horn.

When it went off, she pressed the vial into the slot and watched the liquid seep into the etchings of the runes.

The queller shuddered to life, and with it so did the wind. Turin had heard that in the Volcane Isles the use of bone marrow had caused earthquakes, but here in the desert it pulled up the sand in a hurricane. The wind swirled around them like an ethereal being and for a fearful moment Turin thought the tidewind was back to end it all before the battle started.

But then the quellers moved and she had no more time for fear.

"Here we go!" the Purger cheered beside her.

Turin joined the screams of the Zalaam as they lurched towards Nar-Ruta.

The feeling was incomparable. It wasn't just riches and power that fuelled her exhilaration. Turin knew she was a product of the empire. It had broken her time and time again, and she had forged what she could from the rubble.

But here was her chance to break it in turn.

CHAPTER FORTY-FOUR

Ala

The first day of battle

The sunrise beat down on Ala's back as she stood and waited. Sweat ran in rivulets down her shoulder blades, but she didn't remove her jacket. The emblem of the gazelle was pinned proudly on her chest.

Hassa paced along the front line of Ghostings ahead of her. The charred ground of the plantation fields left her legs soot-stained.

Our scouts have returned. The Zalaam are moving, Hassa signed.

Ala didn't need Hassa to tell her. As soon as the Zalaam activated their creations the wind began to rise.

The tidewind has returned, a Ghosting next to Ala signed with fearful motions. But Ala shook her head.

No, this is caused by the creations, not the Tannin.

Why? the Ghosting asked.

They knew little about the law of creation—Ala least of all—but she did know one thing: *Bloodwerk tips the balance of the world. But marrow makes it worse,* she signed.

Thankfully, the sandstorm wasn't as deadly as the tidewind but it nevertheless affected their visibility.

Ala noticed some of the other Ghostings were watching her exchange. There were a hundred and fifty of them in the regiment. All personally selected by Hassa for having the best mastery of blood-werk runes. Though Ala had been late to the cadre, she had worked twice as hard to learn the bloodwerk runes required.

She rolled the vial of sharj oil in her pocket. Vahi didn't have the time to make significant amends to their inkwells. Instead, he'd drilled a hole into the stylus where they could pour the sharj oil as they drew. It was difficult to master, and they'd all practised with water for a few strikes. But time was not on their side, and they'd have to make do.

Ala, you take your squadron to the western field. Start drawing, but don't trigger the runes until you see my signal, Hassa signed.

Ala crossed her wrists together in salute before turning to her troops. *Let's move out.*

Most of the soldiers under her command had been Ghostings left in the city. The people like Ala who hadn't wanted to leave.

But sometimes the threads of comfort must be pulled apart before you can see the knots. Ala hadn't realised how tightly those knots had bound her until her routine was shorn away.

They picked their way through the carcasses of burnt trees. The ground was thick with ash, and it lifted in the wind.

Ala stopped when they reached the edge of the western field and directed her squadron to begin their designated sequence of runes. Though the rubber tree husks were difficult to traverse, they were helpful surfaces for the Ghostings to draw their runes on.

Ala took her time drawing. Patience had always been a virtue that aided her precision.

There was movement beside her, but Ala didn't look up, not until she was finished. Completing her sequence was more important than anything else, so she ignored it until the final flick of the rune was drawn.

Only then did she gaze up to find Sami, another Ghosting who she had drafted into the army, signing next to her. *There's a flaw in my sequence. Will you help me?*

As he signed Ala saw Hassa's runeflare go up in the sky. That was their signal to retreat. The Zalaam were half a league away.

But any flaw in the sequence could cause an entire section of the fire to fail. It could mean ten, fifteen, twenty quellers would get through.

Go, Sami, I'll finish your combination.

He hesitated, but Ala didn't have time to argue. She ran to his section and began his work again. That was the thing with Ghosting blood—it was impossible to trace, so she'd have to redo the whole sequence.

Ala felt the wind pick up around her as the bone marrow abominations made their way towards them.

Again, she didn't look up. She had to concentrate.

But there was no way to block out the sound the quellers made. Like a knife sliding in and out of a sheath a hundred times over, the giant spiders sliced their way across the desert. The Zalaam's screams caught on the wind, pulling their bloodthirsty cries towards her.

Just one final rune.

Someone shouted and she recognised their voice. It broke her concentration, and she looked up. Flecks of blue sand immediately struck her in the eyes. She rubbed them, partly in disbelief.

Because riding one of the Zalaam's creations was Turin.

Her locs ran wild and free behind her, and the blush-pink dress she wore lifted in the wind like ethereal wings. Turin's lips were drawn back in a snarl as the spider surged forward, fifty handspans from Ala.

Thirty handspans.

Fifteen.

The fire runes would be activated any second now. But the sequence still wasn't complete. Ala knelt down and steadied her breath.

One final rune.

She sought the stillness in her mind, which had been her only defence in this world. Her hindrance too, for why fight when you could find peace within? But now she used her stillness as a weapon.

She finished the last dash of the rune and stood back.

Turin was so close Ala could see the dimples on her cheeks from the smile she directed just at her.

Ten handspans.

It was too late for Ala to retreat. The runes had been drawn in a circle in order to create the required friction of opposite runes. Just like a runelamp.

And Ala was in the heart of it.

She turned and saw the Ghostings in the distance. She raised a limb in farewell before turning back to Turin and her lackeys.

Eight handspans.

Master, let us have a reckoning.

There was a whoosh and a crackle as the runes set alight, triggered by Hassa's final rune far away from the front line of battle.

Turin, at the head of the front line, was caught in the fire first. Her creation stumbled, its bladed legs turning red before pitching forward and throwing her into the heart of the flames until both lay still.

The smoke and smell was putrid: burning flesh and molten metal.

More creations joined the first, but Ala wouldn't be around to see how many of them she had destroyed.

She felt nothing, even as the flames licked at her ankles and climbed her clothing. For Ala, all was blissfully still until the end.

CHAPTER FORTY-FIVE

Kara

The first day of battle

The Blood Forged had brought only two camels with them across the sea and unfortunately one had passed away on the journey.

But one was all Kara needed to be seen by her troops. She mounted swiftly, pulling the reins to command the camel to stand. A cheer rose from the soldiers.

She smiled at those who could see her, though her grin was brittle and forced. Her heart thumped beneath her leathers, and she clutched the reins tightly so no one could see them shake.

Kara had always known that one day she'd die in service to her people. Though she'd thought it would be the endless taxation reports that would end her, not war.

The Jin-Dinil lakes stretched out ahead of her. Though "lakes" was a misnomer—they were so small and shallow, "puddles" would be more accurate.

There was still no sign of the Zalaam.

She searched the lines of troops ahead of her for Jond. As major general he was personally leading the foot soldiers into battle. She felt her stomach churn with acid at the thought. The fool had the gall to worry about her, but there he was, standing at the very front of the formation.

His regiment were all armed with inkwells and enhanced bloodwerk armour. As they'd be the first to engage in combat.

Though Jond was no more than a speck on the horizon, Kara found her gaze being tugged his way.

The man had scoured his way into her heart, and it frustrated her. She shook her head.

I'm about to die on a battlefield, my worries should be reserved for my citizens, not a man from a distant land.

But there was something about his quiet resilience that warmed the core of her, and she realised that she wasn't ready to give that up.

All I have to do is not die.

She was pulled from her thoughts as a violent wind blew in the direction of her troops. It swirled in blue flourishes, given colour by the sand of the Farsai Desert.

"The Zalaam have activated their creations. Hassa, prepare for contact on the western battlefield." Ravenwing's voice rang out in her mind. Though mind communication wasn't really a sound, more an image of Ravenwing's intent that she could somehow translate into words. Ravenwing's "voice" always sounded like metal being struck together.

Kara waited. If the creations had begun their march to the west, then the infantry would be with them soon enough.

A growling sound in the very bones of the earth made her camel balk. She was thrown from her saddle, falling hard on the wet ground.

Her guards rushed to her side. She waved them away and got to her feet, but not before her camel had bolted through the troops.

"Well, there goes that," she muttered, rubbing a grazed knee.

The ground started trembling again.

"Commander General, there's something not quite right here. The ground is shaking," Jond said down the connection to Ravenwing.

Kara pushed her way forward, but she was still thirty lines of people away from Jond. It frustrated her that only Ravenwing and Jond could commune, and all Kara could do was simply listen.

"Could it be the creations?" Ravenwing asked.

"Negative, no enemy spotted," Jond replied.

But something was happening, Kara could feel it. Then Jond's words burst across her mind like the splattering of torrential rain.

"They've used their diggers to create tunnels. The sound is the creations reaching the surface. The enemy is below us—"

But then his words stuttered to a stop.

And Kara didn't think, she simply *moved*.

In two blinks she had arrived in the spot where Jond's regiment had been. It was pandemonium. The enemy was pouring out from a hole in the ground. Swords clashed and rebounded from Jond's soldiers' enhanced armour.

One of the Zalaam lunged for Kara with a jambiya, but she ducked and rolled out of the way, only to land in front of the swinging axe of another.

This time she managed to flight a distance away, just behind the tunnel opening.

A second wave of Zalaam emerged from underground, each brandishing weapons. One was a young boy, perhaps fifteen or sixteen. His eyes were wide with fear as he took in the slaughter around him.

He was just like one of Kara's citizens, following the wiles and whims of his leaders. The thought sickened her, and she realised that blood and death wasn't the most horrific part of war—it was the loss of humanity. Of no longer seeing the enemy as people worthy of life.

How did we get to this point? she thought.

But she didn't have long to linger as a sword took the boy in the gut and he fell to his knees. Though he wasn't dead, not yet.

Kara stepped towards him and tilted his head up to meet hers. Fear still shadowed his expression, but pain too.

He began to murmur a prayer. "Glorious one up above, you who knows no bounds or boundaries—"

Kara slid her knife through his ribcage to his heart. A quick death was all she could give him.

"I'm sorry for the paths that have led us both here," Kara whispered as she pulled her dagger free.

The whole encounter had taken half a minute, and in that time more Zalaam had surged out of the tunnel. They fought with less skill than the Blood Forged army, but there was a fervour to their movements that made them more difficult to predict.

A chant began to swell up from the attackers.

"Purge the land of non-believers,
In Kabut we trust.
Cleanse the world of all deceivers,
His realm will welcome us."

Their cries raised the hair on Kara's arms as they hacked their way across the battlefield. She could see it perturbed her soldiers. Already they were breaking formation. But discipline was their strength.

"Hold ranks," she called, running into the melee.

"The Queen fights among us," was shouted to her left and she felt the soldiers close in around her.

She rushed forward with her dagger high.

Blood and brain matter splattered across her face as she took the eye from her first assailant. She flighted to the right in time to drive her blade into the neck of another who had pinned a soldier to the ground.

In and out she blinked, bringing death and destruction.

But still the enemy poured up from their burrows underground.

Then Kara heard a scream so thick and full of anguish that she had to pause and look. It was a foolish mistake, of course. A glint of metal was the last thing she saw before the sword came flying towards her. She didn't have enough time to flight—she barely had enough time to move.

Suddenly she was pushed to the ground. And the sword struck the back of her saviour's armour.

She looked up and recognised Jond, immediately breathing a sigh of relief.

"Still alive, Jond Alnua?" Kara said, his face a hair's breadth from hers.

"Still alive." He grinned before jumping up and swinging his axe at their attacker. Red arterial blood sprayed in an arc across the battlefield and Kara was about to congratulate Jond on a great hit when she saw it.

A blade, lodged in his throat.

He fell to his knees, and she screamed.

CHAPTER FORTY-SIX

Niha

The first day of battle

Niha wasn't sure when he'd last eaten or drank. But he couldn't stop, not when so many people needed his help.

"Can someone get me more gauze!" Niha shouted.

A student ran over, stumbling as they did. As she handed Niha the bandages, he grabbed her wrist. "You need to sleep, Zed."

"I—"

"No arguments, you're useless to me in this state."

Zed slumped, her hair falling over her face.

Niha said more gently, "I'll wake you in half a day." He turned away and back to his patient. "Press this gauze to the laceration on your arm. I'm going to heal the wound in your abdomen now."

The soldier nodded. He had taken a blade to the gut. And it would take the last shreds of Niha's concentration to heal it.

He cleaned the skin around the wound as best he could before beginning to pattern runes with his orb.

The patient began to scream as his skin was knitted together. Unfortunately, they'd run out of sedatives in the first strikes of the battle.

When the screaming stopped Niha knew that the pain had been enough for the soldier's body to pass out on its own.

Once he was almost healed, Niha had to move on.

"Keep the wound clean, and when he wakes move him to section two," Niha said to one of the Keep's healers.

They had stationed the hospital in an open arena. Niha had been told the empire had once used it to hold games to decide the next rulers. A primitive and brutal technique that Niha could barely fathom. It made him understand the brutalities of his friend's homeland, and perhaps the effects it had had on him.

Niha moved to another patient. This one only needed stitching, which would give him a moment to rest and recoup the lost blood he had shed in doing deathcraft.

Flighters darted in and out of the arena. It was their job to carry the wounded in from the field. Once arrived, the wounded went through a triage system, the very worst being seen by Niha and his team of Academy students.

So, when a flighter blinked into existence in his peripheral vision Niha said, "Head to section one where you'll be directed with the wounded, this area is for healers only."

"Niha." The voice was ragged, and he spun towards the sound.

"Kara?" The Queen was lifting up an injured soldier, her hands holding together the ragged edges of his torn throat. Blood covered the soldier's features, but Niha knew who it was. "Jond," he breathed.

"Save him, please, Niha." Tears were falling down Kara's dirt-speckled face. She looked as if she was holding Jond up with sheer will alone.

Niha didn't hesitate. He guided Kara towards an empty pallet and helped her lower him onto it.

"I don't have time to disinfect the wound," he muttered. He could tell Jond only had minutes, maybe seconds, left. The blade had severed his artery, and if there was any chance for Jond to survive this, Niha had to heal him *now*.

"Remove your hand from the wound when I say," Niha commanded. He'd have to be quick. The pressure from Kara's hand was the only thing keeping Jond alive.

Niha pressed the orb into the open wound on his hand and took a deep breath.

His friend's life was in his hands. Literally. And though he was prepared for the loss this war would bring, he wasn't ready to lose this particular person just yet.

I will fight for you, Jond. I will give it everything I've got, he promised.

"Now," he said to Kara. She withdrew her hand, letting Jond's life blood pour freely. Niha instantly pressed the orb to Jond's neck and began to work.

He shifted his hand in increments, rotating the orb so the right combination could be achieved. He knew any mistake would result in Jond's death.

Two minutes passed.

Then ten.

But still Niha worked, trying to stitch Jond's artery back together with slow, careful movements.

He heard a forlorn meow from Rascal. The sandcat had been keeping recovering patients company since the battle began. But Niha couldn't break his concentration to pet her.

Twenty minutes after Jond had arrived, the blood at his neck began to stop flowing.

Niha drew in a ragged breath and withdrew his orb. He couldn't do any more for Jond. Though there were more smaller wounds beneath the skin, Niha could feel his own blood loss depleting his strength.

Kara's face blanched with fear. She stood as still as a statue as she looked down on Jond's unconscious body. "Will he be all right?"

Niha didn't want to lie. "I'm not sure. I've healed the artery, which was the most immediate problem, but he lost a lot of blood. And unfortunately, I cannot replace blood—only his own body can do that."

"Why isn't he awake?"

"His body is protecting him. He just experienced severe trauma. All we can do is wait and let him rest."

She opened her mouth to argue but he cut her off. "Go, Kara. Jond has much to live for."

His tone seemed to jolt her back into the present and she nodded, her back straightening. She gave Rascal a scratch behind the ears. "Thank you, Niha, I will check back on him soon. Look after him, Rascal." The sandcat, who had curled up on Jond's chest, chirped at being addressed.

Once Kara flighted away, Niha turned to the unconscious Jond and said, "You have too many people who love you to die now, Jond."

Then he turned away to begin another healing, because war waited for no one.

CHAPTER FORTY-SEVEN

Chah

The second day of battle

Chah led his regiment through the tunnels their hollowers had made.

The idea to use the godbeasts had been his. When they realised that the non-believers were attacking across the Jin-Dinil lakes—a swampland their quellers would not be able to cross—he knew they had to do something to give his forces the advantage.

They thought they could best us? He saluted skyward. *They do not know your power, Kabut.*

Chah had unshakable faith in his God's plan for him. Since the moment he had met the Wife in the open temple all those years ago and she had found him a place in the Foundry.

Her words from his first day came back to him now.

"There is no balance in this world. It must be burnt down. Balance comes later once death has taken its fill. The world must be sacrificed so that we can live as Gods."

"Indeed, it is time for death to take its fill." He gave breath to the Wife's holy words in the darkness of the tunnel. The sound of the hollower drowning out his whisper.

The godbeasts dug beneath the sand, gliding through the layer of clay and limestone. Their mechanisms had been designed to compact the excess dirt to create enough space for them to camp in. Which was ample space for his soldiers to travel beneath the enemy's army and ambush them.

Thanks to the ground assault, the first day of battle had resulted in significant casualties for the other side. Chah had been personally responsible for at least a hundred and fifty deaths. He hoped to double that count today.

"Contact in two minutes," Chah whispered to his second in command.

The hollower stuttered to a stop as the bone marrow powering it ran out. The godbeast's range was two leagues, and if Chah had calculated it right, they should be beneath the enemy battalion. But by now, the sound of the rumbling of the hollower had probably alerted the Blood Forged army to their location. It was why they had to move quickly.

"Now!" Chah said, instructing those around him to begin digging the final few metres to the surface.

That was the issue with godbeasts: they were difficult to manipulate. It was simple enough to command a hollower to dig—the animals they were mimicked from burrowed quick and fast. But if and when a hollower resurfaced was difficult to predict. It was why this technique would only last as long as they had hollowers in excess. For where the godbeasts stopped would be where they would forever stay.

The soldiers digging to the surface had let through the first rays of sunlight above them.

Dirt covered Chah's face as something moved across his vision. "Divine's web," he swore as he saw what it was—hundreds of worms were moving in the mud in front of him.

Then the screaming started. At first, he thought the sounds were the enemy and he savoured it, but then the worms reached his forearms and gripped tight.

They weren't worms but roots.

He'd heard of the talents of the Blood Forged, how they had been granted different knowledge than godpower. But the power of the Blood Forged was toxic, a poor attempt to parry the gift Kabut had granted the Zalaam.

Faster and faster, the roots grew until they blocked out the sky above. They wound around Chah's head, and he hacked at them with his blade. But there were too many, and soon they filled the tunnel like a spider's web. They wrapped around his throat, his torso, his hands. The cries of his comrades let him know they were dying too.

Chah tried to reach for his blade one more time. *Kabut grant me strength to continue your legacy.*

With one final lunge, he reached for his sword and hacked at the plant matter. He managed to free his other hand and then reached towards the sunlight.

The ground shifted beneath him, and the tunnel collapsed on the rest of his regiment.

He said a silent prayer. "Take their sacrifice and carve me anew."

Chah stood and looked around, spotting the instigators of the growing plants. The non-believers stood in a ring ahead of him, throwing seeds imbued with their powers.

He withdrew his sword and stalked towards the enemy.

CHAPTER FORTY-EIGHT

Ads

The second day of battle

Ads scattered seeds like bullets. The plants sprouted as soon as they touched the ground, triggered by the runes on the terracotta she had laid in the dirt.

To her left, Elyzan was planting a barrier of ivy across the field whose tendrils hindered the soldiers who had made it out of the tunnels alive.

The first day they had been caught unawares by the Zalaam's underground movements. But not today.

A man emerged from the tunnel closest to her, his lips moving as he murmured a prayer. His gaze narrowed in on the group of first law students and began to move towards them.

Elyzan's ivy stood in his path. He hacked through it, his sword moving faster than the vines could grow. Ads dashed forward, using the delay to her advantage.

"Fall back, Ads, too many of them have escaped," Elyzan shouted at her.

She shook her head. For too long people had treated her like a child. They forgot the empire didn't foster innocence, only violence.

She withdrew a ring of terracotta. Those of the first charter called them incubators, as they were the vessels used to draw their runes. She inserted her stylus and drew.

When the sequence was complete, she pulled out a packet of yellow seeds from her pouch. She pinched one of them between her fingers before pressing it into the dirt in the centre of the incubator.

The plant began to sprout immediately, the roots bursting through the seed husk before webbing downwards into the soil. The stems grew next, a deep luscious green against the mud of the Jin-Dinil lakes.

"Elyzan, I've planted venom glaze, move downwind!" Ads shouted.

The councillor of the first law nodded in her direction, letting her know he had heard her. But still he wasn't retreating.

The plant had grown two handspans already, and buds began to swell along the stems. It wouldn't be long before its deadly flower bloomed.

"Elyzan!" Ads called out again.

He was kneeling in the dirt planting more ivy, trying in vain to stop the soldier who was charging towards them.

Ads saw the flash of orange petals as the venom glaze started to blossom. She lunged for Elyzan and dragged him backwards.

A plume of pollen burst from the flowering venom glaze just as they passed it.

Ads searched Elyzan's face for any trace of the poison, but he wasn't coughing, and his eyes were clear.

"That was too close," Ads said.

Elyzan nodded.

They turned back to the battlefield just in time to see the Zalaam who was charging them escape the vines and walk straight into the cloud of orange pollen.

Ads didn't have time to linger over the soldier's death. When she'd accelerated the plant's growth, she'd also shortened its lifespan. Ads would need to plant more in order to keep the poisonous barrier in place.

She bent over another terracotta incubator and began to draw the next rune combination.

She looked up when she heard coughing. The enemy soldier that had made it past their vines emerged from the venom glaze's fog. His eyes bulged in their sockets, his saliva frothing at his mouth.

Venom glaze wasn't a poison you could survive. Once being exposed to the pollen your death was inevitable.

This man was clinging onto the last few moments of his life. Ads would have ignored his dying breaths if she hadn't seen the intent in his eyes as he staggered forward.

Elyzan was kneeling on the ground again. He hadn't seen the soldier make it through.

"Ely—" Ads cried out.

But it was too late. With the Zalaam's final breath, he plunged his blade into her teacher's heart.

CHAPTER FORTY-NINE

Teta

The second day of battle

Night was falling on the second day of battle. The Zalaam had taken more losses than anyone had expected. The Wife was not pleased. She paced in front of Teta, the hem of her dress balled in her fists. Nayeli was the only person who didn't wear armour.

Our God protects her until it is time for the Wife to take her place beside him, Teta thought.

The Zalaam's camp was quiet, the air in the tunnels thick with anticipation and a touch of fear.

The war was meant to be a quick one, but the non-believers had fought back with more ferocity than they had expected.

Teta looked down the long corridor that ran along the burrows. Shadows moved against the gas light, and she wondered if the enemy's camp was as quiet as this one.

The Zalaam had no infirmary, any injured soldiers unable to fight were sacrificed—an end they all welcomed.

Most of them anyway.

Teta had seen how some of the soldiers' faith had wavered in their final moments. But those were the moments that mattered. When her God called for her, Teta would welcome the blade on her neck and the peace that would follow.

"Have the changes been made to the clawmaw?" the Wife barked at her, bringing her back from dreams of paradise.

"Chah was leading those amends, but he fell this afternoon on the eastern battlefield."

The Wife stumbled. Teta reached to catch her. Her wrists wrapped around Nayeli's, helping her upright.

The Wife shook her off. "I'm fine."

But it was clear she was not. Though Nayeli was thirty years her senior, Teta had known her when she'd been master crafter of the Foundry. Teta had been too young back then to join as a crafter, but she remembered Chah being in Nayeli's shadow during ceremonies and temple prayers.

Teta had been jealous of the years Chah had been mentored by the Wife, and he'd often used it as a suggestion that he should have been commune leader. She couldn't say she mourned his loss, but grief was a complex emotion for one of the Zalaam. Death was a celebration and a source of power, and Teta took from his death all that she could.

She felt herself stand straighter, held her chin higher.

The Wife met her gaze and for the first time, Teta didn't cower from it.

"We took significant casualties today," Teta said.

"Do you think I don't know that?" the Wife snarled.

Teta didn't avert her eyes despite the fierceness in the Wife's expression. Anger was a useful emotion, but not now, not when their soldiers needed a leader.

"We're out of hollowers, too," Teta added.

Some might say she was salting a wound too harshly, but Teta was laying the foundations of her plan.

Nayeli let out a shallow breath. "Not only have we lost the ability to surprise them, but we only have one more wave of quellers left."

The Wife looked dejected, a rare emotion to see on the powerful woman. And Teta couldn't let the expression linger for long.

"I have an idea, Wife," she said with a slow smile.

Teta waited until the Wife waved for her to continue. Her interest was enough to cause Teta's chest to swell with pride. "The harbour to the west is unmanned. Tonight, while the non-believers sleep, we should send a regiment of soldiers in ships around the southern shore. We can then ambush the army from behind. There'll be no reason for them to be looking to the beach."

The Wife frowned. "I've seen those boats. They're mere fishing vessels. You won't be able to take any quellers."

"No, but we could take the sentinels. We only have enough quellers and riders for a final assault, and so tomorrow will conclude the battle. What use will the sentinel patrols be during the night? Either we win, and we storm the city, or we lose and our camp lies empty."

The Wife nodded, a small smile of her own quirking her lips as the plan came together. Teta's grin grew to see it.

"So you'd travel around the southern shores until you reached the beaches of Jin-Laham. It is not a short walk from there to the Jin-Dinil lakes, though."

"The sentinels would cross the distance in the day. If we leave now, we might yet cause some damage come morning."

The Wife nodded. "Yes, I can see the logic in this approach."

Then the Wife looked at Teta with an intensity that felt like Kabut's own gaze on her skin. "You shall lead the operation. Leave as soon as you are able."

Teta knew then that her God was pleased. For the Wife had listened and chosen her to lead. The years of wishing she'd been mentored by the Wife had amounted to this moment. And it felt just like she'd hoped—a searing joy of finally being *seen*.

She saluted the Wife with quivering hands. Teta's voice was thick with emotion as she said, "It will be as you say. Shine bright under Kabut's eye, Wife. I hope we shall meet again in Kabut's realm."

CHAPTER FIFTY

Griot Sheth

The second day of battle

Sheth was not a soldier, he was a liar. "You'd tell me the sun had fallen from the sky and I'd believe it," his mother used to remark after every far-fetched rendition of his day.

Oh, how he could spin and twist the truth like threads of cotton. He knitted together stories like a weaver sewed fabric.

Every day after school he'd hold court in the playground, drawing crowds of his fellow classmates. How he revelled in making them laugh or cry.

But at ten years old school was over. He was branded with the sigil of the guild of duty and sent to the plantation fields.

For many years he never told another story. Until one day, on his eighteenth birthday, his comrades took him to the Maroon for a drink. And there in the corner sat an old woman. It was rare to see a Duster make it past sixty, rarer still to see one so full of life and laughter.

"Listen well, listen close . . ." she crooned, and the whole tavern went silent. "Too close!" she shouted, startling the crowd into laughter.

She continued, "Today I will tell you the story of the lizard and the bird . . ."

Sheth was utterly captivated by the power of the story. He felt the welts on his back ease, and the tension in his shoulders loosen. And it was then that he realised stories could heal.

Griot Ama she'd been called, and after Sheth's insistence she had inducted him into the griot network. Though he still worked the fields, his evenings were spent in the Maroon healing with stories.

How time has passed. Like the pages of the book, we reach the apex of my tale, he thought, drawing his mind back to the present.

He stood on the roof of the very same tavern that had become his solace. Its sticky floor laden with piss, firerum and memories. But instead of healing with words, he was killing with arrows.

It had been a long, arduous journey from there to here. Though the griots observed no one leader among their rank, Sheth had been the most ardent collector of information. He had guided his fellows to convey as much truth as they could in their stories. A small rebellion.

But small rebellions don't change the world.

Some truths were too big to hide among the pauses of a soliloquy. They needed to be shouted. They needed to be confronted.

He loaded another arrow into the crossbow and waited. The bows were an ingenious bit of engineering. They were triggered by the enemies' movement on the ground, aiming towards where the rune was activated.

Thwum.

The crossbows released on the infantry moving through the Dredge. The first row of Zalaam soldiers fell to the ground and didn't move again.

The arrows always hit their mark.

"Movement on the horizon!" Sheth's comrade shouted to his right. Griot Twia was a nervous fellow who had volunteered with Sheth in the early days of the Truthsayer's army.

"I see them," Sheth replied. He didn't need the warning, he could feel the wind drawing closer.

Over the years Sheth had woven many stories about the tidewind and its cruel nature, so he knew what it was like to fear a hurricane. His fear only grew when he glimpsed the creations that moved beneath the wind's currents, their metal burnished bronze in the light of the setting sun.

"They're not supposed to have passed the fire wall," Twia said, his voice thick with terror.

"The sharj oil must have burnt out," Sheth replied as he loaded another arrow.

Thwum.

Another soldier dead.

"Sheth, they're not stopping. We need to retreat." Twia was already moving, scrambling towards the ladder that would lead them to the ground.

But Sheth knew it was too late. By the time they got down from the roof they'd make easy targets for the spiders' bladed legs.

But his comrades were already retreating.

"Stop! Hold the line!" Sheth shouted. "Shoot at the riders, shoot at the riders!"

"But we'll die!" Twia said, his foot paused on the rung of the ladder.

"We'll die either way, at least this way we'll make sure that more people survive."

All fear fled Twia's face and a peaceful expression smoothed his features. He had accepted death quicker than most people could have. For like Sheth, he was a Duster and he knew what it was like to fear for his life in a world that wanted him dead.

When Sheth turned back to the crossbow, the Zalaam's creations were nearly upon them.

Sheth coughed as the sand raised by the wind lodged in his throat. They were in the heart of the sandstorm now, and all he could see was metal.

The creations were terrifying beasts. They were both spindly and powerful all at once. The way they moved through the streets made Sheth's skin crawl. The Dredge became filled with the sound of falling stone as villas turned to rubble beneath their bladed legs.

Thwum.

Sheth's arrow struck the Zalaam rider who rode at the front of the formation. Though the rider died, the creation moved on. It would only stop when the bone marrow powering it died out, which Sheth prayed wouldn't be long.

It was difficult ignoring its impending assault, but he had to move onto the next rider.

Thwum.

Another gone.

Thwum.

And another.

Thwum.

Twia's arrows joined Sheth's and soon the first wave of riders were all dead.

But the creations were not. Soon they filled his vision, blocking out the fire-red sky.

Sheth released his final arrow.

Thwum.

The creation's leg struck him through the chest as it drove the blade down through the roof of the Maroon.

It was a blessing to die upon the ground he had loved so fiercely.

Griot Sheth died with a smile on his lips, and one thought: *What a tale my life will make.*

CHAPTER FIFTY-ONE

Sylah

The second day of battle

The second day of battle had been worse than the first. Hassa's operation had destroyed another wave of creations, but the fire they'd
conjured hadn't lasted the day, and soon the Zalaam were able to
cross the molten remains of the quellers and make their way into the
city.

Sylah's squadron fought bravely against the onslaught of Zalaam.
She oversaw two platoons made up of soldiers formerly of the Wardens'
Army, equipped with runeguns. They held the main line across the
plantation fields, and even gained ground as the day wore on.

But then the sun set, and another wave of creations struck.

They lost a thousand soldiers in ten minutes. It was only because
Sylah had been checking on the supplies of runebullets that she hadn't
been caught beneath a queller's bladed legs.

The attack had been brief and vicious, forcing the Blood Forged
army to retreat through the Dredge.

A strike after the attack started, Hassa and her team managed to
activate another fire circle within the borders of the city, putting an
end to the creations' activity for the night. But in doing so, they'd
had to sacrifice the Dredge entirely.

Sylah looked down at the smoke, made silver from the moonlight,
as it rose up from the circle of fire in the Dredge. The area had been
the grubby underbelly of Nar-Ruta for so long, trading in sex, drugs

and drink—a trifecta of pleasure that Sylah had indulged in more than once. Despite its flaws, the community there had been the only family Sylah'd had for a long time. It was a bitter blow to watch it go up in flames.

"We'll make another Dredge, in the new city that's to come," she said under her breath. She spoke to no one but the land, the promise warming her chest.

Sylah stepped away from the window and turned back to the meeting.

During that evening's pause in fighting, the Blood Forged had gathered in the courtroom—that is, those of the Blood Forged who had survived.

With Elyzan dead and Jond close to it, grief permeated the air like the smoke from the Dredge, stinging their eyes and making their breath laboured.

We only have enough sharj oil for one more attack, Hassa signed to the room. Her friend looked tired, her face soot-stained and streaked with tears, or perhaps blood. At least the blood couldn't have been hers as Hassa looked blessedly whole. It was a small relief to Sylah amid so much pain.

"They can't have that many creations left. We've destroyed, what, a thousand?" Kara said. Her eyes were tight with worry.

"They brought to the empire two thousand, two hundred and thirty-three quellers," Anoor said softly, though her voice carried. It was the first time she had been allowed to attend a Blood Forged meeting. After the guards assigned to her had been needed on the front line, she had gained a small semblance of trust from the Blood Forged for not immediately defecting again.

Sylah met Anoor's eyes, giving her an encouraging smile. Anoor didn't return it. Her own eyes were heavy with fatigue. While Sylah had been on the battlefield each day, Anoor had been working on finishing the creation.

One thousand, two hundred and thirty-three to go, Hassa signed.

Ravenwing nodded. He was still mind-linked to the group. With Jond unconscious, he was the only one who could speak through their connection; the rest could merely listen. "They will be preparing for a final assault. We need to be ready."

The night stretched out like a bow string ready to be released. Each second was spent finalising their plans on how best to utilise the remains of the sharj oil.

"The sharj oil will not be enough if Yona activates the clawmaw," Anoor murmured. She was picking at the edges of her nails, which were cracked and blood-stained from her runework.

Everyone in the room looked at her.

"What do you propose we do?" Ravenwing asked, his voice prickly and dagger-like in Sylah's mind.

"The creation I've been working on, Retribution. It's ready," Anoor said.

Sylah reached for Anoor's hand and squeezed it. "Are you sure?"

Anoor nodded slowly with only the slightest hesitation. "Yes, I think we need to use it."

Ravenwing nodded. "Well, it is now or never. So, I agree. Anoor, you release the beast on my signal during the first phase of movement."

The group looked ready to disperse, but before they did Sylah spoke up. "I have a request."

Ravenwing gestured with his arm for her to continue.

"I have surplus runeguns and not enough people schooled in bloodwerk to use them. I would like to recruit the prisoners in the old Nowerk Gaol."

The room erupted in hissing and indignant cries.

Dew held up a limb, bringing the room to silence. *I think what Sylah suggests is a good idea. Anyone willing to fight is another soldier we cannot afford to turn down. Of course, we'll need to keep them away from the main army barracks, perhaps station them in the Duster Quarter as a first line of defence.*

Sylah nodded. This was exactly what she'd been thinking. She looked to Ravenwing. As Commander General, it was his call. His lips pulled into a tight line as he spoke in her mind: "Go, but keep them in line. I cannot have a coup within the ranks."

"Do you want to come with me?" Sylah said to Anoor.

Anoor shook her head. "No, I have one last tweak I need to make to Retribution."

Sylah smiled. "I like the name."

Anoor nodded, her gaze going distant as she retreated to the place in her mind Sylah couldn't go.

Sylah pressed a kiss to her cheek before saying, "I'll see you later tonight."

She left the courtroom and made her way down to the cellar of the Keep. The walk through to the gaol was dank and dark.

When she began to smell the sea breeze, she knew she was close. The corridor opened out to a cliff face, the black of the ocean on the horizon ahead of her. For a moment she thought she saw the shadows of small ships rippling on a wave. But when she looked back, they were gone.

She stepped over rubble and entered through a wide door.

Half of the Nowerk Gaol had slipped into the sea over the years, and with rippings becoming the preferred way to punish Dusters and Ghostings, the gaol stopped being maintained.

As soon as her footsteps echoed across the chamber, there were cries for freedom.

"Let us out of here!"

"We've run out of food."

"Please, I've changed my mind!"

Sylah stood in the centre of the room and looked up at the gaol cells. There were four hundred and twenty prisoners who had either refused to join the fight against the Zalaam or had been deemed too volatile—like the wardens—to allow onto the field.

She cleared her throat. "We are in the final strikes of the battle against the Zalaam. We believe there will be one final assault against the Keep. If the Zalaam breach the walls you won't just be prisoners, you'll be dead."

There were murmurs but Sylah didn't let them rise in a crescendo before speaking again.

"I have runeguns for all of you. So, I will give you the one thing the empire never gave to me: choice. Fight for your lives or let the Zalaam kill you."

One by one Sylah unlocked the doors of the cells, asking each person the same question. Nearly all of them said yes, except one.

Wern Aldina sat immovable in her cell. "I won't do it. I cannot fight beside traitors."

"Wern, dying here is not an option," Aveed said from the group behind Sylah. The former Warden of Duty had made their choice quickly. Isolation had been good for them, it seemed.

Wern shrieked, "Warden Wern! And don't you forget it."

The cell key dug into Sylah's clenched hand. "Let's go."

Aveed moved to block Sylah. "You can't just leave her."

The atmosphere in the cell began to roil, and Sylah shifted her feet getting ready to fight if need be.

She kept her voice steady and clear as she said, "Wern made her choice, and so did you all."

At any point they could have lunged for her. They would be killed before they got out of the Keep, but Sylah knew how far vengeance could take you.

The group began to circle Aveed, closing ranks across from her. "If you attack me now, you seal your own fate. There are thousands of soldiers who want you dead on both sides of the battlefield. That's why you'll be stationed in the Duster Quarter, set apart from the barracks. For everyone's safety."

Aveed nodded and the tension left the gaol. Then the warden turned to Sylah with a look of deference she never thought she'd see.

"Lead us to the battle."

CHAPTER FIFTY-TWO

Rascal

The third day of battle

Rascal was hungry but she didn't move. She lay upon Jond's chest listening to the slow beat of his heart.

Badum. Badum. Badum.

It was soothing, but Rascal was aware that it beat slower than it had before. She was worried it would stop altogether.

His skin was cold beneath her fur and she tucked her head under his chin, trying to warm him as much as she could.

Rascal had things to do. She needed to sit in the empty medicine boxes and play with the string that was used for stitching. And she knew how much Niha enjoyed it when she weaved between his feet. But those things would have to wait.

Because Jond needed her.

She let out a small mewl.

He was her very favourite person. Her very favourite friend.

Rascal wasn't sure how long she lay on his chest. But she'd stay all night and day if it would bring him back to her.

Sometimes there were screams and loud bangs that startled her awake. But Rascal knew nothing of wars or sacrifices. All she knew was the slow heartbeat beneath her feet.

Badum. Badum. Badum.

CHAPTER FIFTY-THREE

Yona

The third day of battle

Yona looked up at the sky. The moon had faded to near transparency with the oncoming dawn, but still the Wife could feel her husband's presence with her. Her remaining troops stood at her back, watching Yona. Waiting.

"Was it always supposed to be this way?" the Wife asked the sky.

Kabut did not answer her. He rarely did, but when he did it wasn't always in words. Sometimes he would make the ground shake, like he had in the Volcane Isles, or appear as a swirling sandstorm when they activated the quellers. Every time the Zalaam went into battle, Kabut joined them in wind and spirit, a blue tornado that gave her soldiers hope.

Until the first fire.

An entire regiment of quellers were turned to molten metal before her eyes.

The only people between the Zalaam and Nar-Ruta had been a group of Ghostings. There'd been so few of them Yona hadn't even considered they'd be any trouble. The quellers' blades would have sliced through their skin like a hot knife through lard.

But then came the fire.

Later that day Yona had gone to inspect the charred ground where the godbeasts had fallen. She hadn't told her subordinates; she knew they'd be worried for her safety. But Yona had needed to see. So she'd slipped on the only blue dress she had—in the hopes that it gave her some camouflage—and crossed the desert towards the fallen quellers.

When she reached the site of the fire the godbeasts were still hot and smoking. Though the quellers were godbeasts no longer—they had been rendered down to misshapen lumps of blackened iron. And the riders who had proudly launched into battle were entombed in metal for evermore.

The air was acrid, and it burnt the back of Yona's throat.

She walked carefully around the blackened remains of the quellers, searching for any sign of how the enemy had managed to create a flame so hot.

Yona knew a lot about forges; she'd spent two years working in the smelting room in the Foundry. So when she found no signs of coal or wood, she was completely stumped. Then the wind changed and she smelt it—sharj oil.

It was the only fuel that could burn hot enough to melt metal but it was also notoriously difficult to keep alight without a controlled setting. The non-believers had used it here, but she couldn't figure out *how*.

Yona had nearly finished circling the site. Stumps of wood had been placed in sections that suggested the sharj oil had originated there.

The placement of the rubber tree stumps felt significant, but she couldn't tell why. When she inspected one, she didn't find a wick or fuse that would have sparked the oil. And there was no way the fire could have burnt as long and as big as it had without additional fuel.

Yona left without answers.

It wasn't until the report on the second fire reached her the next day that Yona began to put the pieces together.

"The Ghostings are doing bloodwerk and mixing sharj oil with their blood. It is how they have enhanced the strength of the fire," she breathed.

It sounded impossible. But as soon as she said it, she knew it must be true.

Teta looked at her with a confused expression, but Yona didn't bother explaining. Instead, she said, "Target the Ghostings, send the archers on the first rally of quellers. If there's ever another group of them on the field, kill them all before they can start the fire. It's them, don't you see?"

Teta nodded and relayed her order to the remaining troops. It had only been a few strikes later when the commune leader had suggested that she take the sentinels around the coast, to attack the Blood Forged army from behind.

Now Teta was gone, and Chah too.

And it's just me and you, husband.

Even the moon was slipping away with the oncoming dawn.

The war was not going as she had expected.

Her younger self spoke from the tomes of her memories.

"What do you think the Ending Fire will be like?" Nayeli asked her brother. They were both lying by the rocky caves of the Volcane Isles, looking out to the sea.

"We won't be alive to see it," Inansi snorted.

Nayeli threw a rock and it skimmed across the shallows. "We might, Andu seems to think it could happen this generation."

"Stop listening to Andu, you know how he rambles on."

Nayeli smiled stiffly but didn't respond. Two years in the Foundry hadn't sated her curiosity for the war that was to come. The future felt untenable and unpredictable—two things twelve-year-old Nayeli detested.

Inansi must have seen the turmoil on her face, for when he spoke, his tone was touched with wistfulness and wonder. "The Ending Fire will be spectacular. The moon won't set for a week, and Kabut's eye will shine down on the battlefield all the while. Flowers will sprout from the soil, marking where each of the Zalaam has fallen."

Nayeli huffed out a laugh at the ridiculousness of it, but Inansi wasn't done.

"The non-believers will sacrifice themselves willingly. And with each sacrifice one of our own will ascend to Kabut's realm. We will make the trip together, and our parents will be there to greet us. The four of us will hold each other tight on the threshold of paradise before entering hand in hand."

Nayeli sniffed. Until that point, she'd been unaware that she was crying.

Inansi squeezed her forearm but didn't embrace her. He knew what comfort she needed, and an embrace would have been too much.

When the tears subsided, she turned to him and said, "It sounds like a beautiful thing, brother."

It was not a beautiful thing.

But despite the blood and gore, Yona's faith did not waver. For how could it when she was so close to the end now?

Her hands gripped the metal arm of the clawmaw. The godbeast Anoor was meant to lead into battle. But the headstrong woman had escaped her clutches. Yona smiled, unable to suppress her affection for her granddaughter, even now.

Our Child of Fire was unbreakable to the end.

Losing Anoor had been difficult, and it had affected the morale of her troops.

She looked around at the remaining soldiers. Their weary eyes gazed back at her. It was time to light the final spark. Anoor should have been here, but Anoor was gone. Now it was Yona's job to raise the morale of her troops.

But Yona would see Anoor soon. In death. In paradise.

"Kabut is pleased by our efforts," she began. "Yesterday we saw the highest sacrifice of non-believers, and though that in turn resulted in heavy casualties on our side, each one of the Zalaam safely ascended to Kabut's realm. Today we prepare for our final assault."

"But what of the Child of Fire who was to lead us?" The cry came out from among the foot soldiers.

Yona's eyes flashed with irritation—her followers had never been so bold before. But she softened her expression as quickly as she was able to and painted a stiff smile onto her face.

"The Child of Fire will be sacrificed as was foretold. Though she may not lead us into battle, her blood will still be spilt." There was a murmur and Yona raised her voice to squash it. "It is Kabut's way to test us in this manner. Anoor brought us the Battle Drum, but we must strive to stop the drumbeat of her heart among the enemy lines. The non-believers thought to test our faith by taking our greatest sacrifice, but we will not let them. She will die, as will all of the non-believers."

She felt her words stir the beginnings of the soldiers' bloodlust. She had lit the final fire and now she had to tend to their flames.

"Today I will join you in battle."

The cheers weren't as robust as she'd hoped, but Yona was not done.

"The clawmaw has the ability to sway the tide of this war. So if you find your faith waning, look to the sky and you'll see me. The Wife fights at your side, and so does Kabut. For what must we do?"

The soldiers were stamping their feet now, baring their teeth as they cried: "To win we must begin again."

Yona's smile was genuine as her people shouted up at her.

"Now is the time for the final strike. We must use the enemy's isolation to their advantage."

And the clawmaw will do the rest.

Within the city there were few open spaces where the enemy could place fire runes.

"Together in death, together in life. We will live as Gods as our prophet decreed. And so it shall be done," she said with finality.

She gave the signal for her troops to mount their quellers.

Yona in turn climbed into the clawmaw. It had taken her all night to finish the placement of needles to match her measurements. The godbeast had been made for Anoor, not her. But as she settled into the rider's seat, she knew that this was what Kabut had always wanted.

Yona pressed herself backwards until the needle pushed into her spine. The ones by her hip required more force.

The pain was exquisite, and she fed it all to her God.

Her bone marrow began to bring the clawmaw to life, filling the etchings carved into its side.

A rune was painted on Yona's brow in blood, tethering her to the godbeast with a mimic rune.

The last experiment with the clawmaw had seen the godpower last for over four strikes. They had discovered that when the fresh marrow came from the person who also wore the mimic rune, they were given greater control of the creation's movements. Qwa only died when the bone marrow had drained from his body.

But death was only temporary. Yona knew that.

She willed the clawmaw forward, and when it moved, she let out a battle cry.

"To win we must begin again!"

CHAPTER FIFTY-FOUR

Anoor

The third day of battle

Anoor patted Retribution's side. The creation was complete, and she couldn't be prouder of her life's final work.

Before her guards, Rega and Jole, had been called to the front line, she had put them to work lugging in more whitestone from their reserves. Over the last few days, she had carefully chiselled and connected larger pieces of the stone together to adapt the godbeast to her purposes.

Retribution was an eru no longer. It was a clawmaw.

Gone were the short legs and the angular torso. Instead, Anoor had elongated the hind legs with extra whitestone bricks and lengthened its neck and head. Refashioning the eru into the shape of a person had been easier than she'd expected. The girth of the lizard's body had lent itself to longer limbs, and the head was wide enough to house the rider's seat.

Her seat.

Anoor had never been given the chance to work on Yona's clawmaw, and so her experience of how it had been made was limited. But now she understood that the godbeast had been created to mimic a person in shape—and the placement of the needles had been perfectly attuned to her body, feeding the clawmaw with bone marrow.

Retribution was a cheap imitation of the Zalaam's clawmaw. They'd had hundreds of years to refine the schema and here Anoor was making one by eye.

But Anoor had been a deft hand at godpower *and* bloodwerk and she'd used techniques from both to craft Retribution as quickly and as efficiently as possible.

Runeguns went off at the front line somewhere in the Duster Quarter. That's where Sylah was with her platoon of former wardens and exiled Embers.

Stay safe for me, beloved. Survive this war when I am gone.

It wouldn't be long now before Retribution would be called into battle. Then, as if summoned by her thoughts, Ravenwing spoke in her mind.

"Anoor, our scouts have spotted the wind rising in the north. The creations have been activated. Release your creation into the battlefield."

It was time. Anoor lowered herself into the chiselled seat she had carved into the neck. She lay back, her head resting against the whitestone. Until the clawmaw came to life and could lift itself she'd have to lie horizontally.

She rested her wrists on the needles she'd added to the stone, ready to press her veins into them. Though the Zalaam's clawmaw was made to be fuelled by bone marrow, the Blood Forged didn't draw power that way. Marrow was the reason the weather was changing and they wanted to ensure there was a world to live in after the war was won. Plus, she'd already seen how the wind leapt up around the Zalaam's creations, and visibility wasn't something she was willing to sacrifice. She already wasn't sure how much control she'd have over Retribution, but she planned to use a mimic rune on herself, hoping it would help.

"Here we go," she whispered to herself, and she began to press her wrists onto the needles. But a sound halted her.

"Anoor?"

Anoor knew that voice like she knew her own heart.

"Sylah?" Anoor sat up from the rider's seat.

Sylah's eyes went wide as she took in the changed creation. It seemed she had heard Ravenwing's message and come to see the eru off, leaving her platoon and her responsibilities behind.

Sylah's greatest flaw was ever her love for Anoor.

But Anoor would not be around to influence her for much longer. "This isn't an eru," Sylah said.

Anoor smiled as she shook her head. "No. I made Retribution into something more powerful."

Sylah's mouth worked silently as she circled the beast, taking it in. Then realisation hit her and she walked to Anoor's side, looking down on the rider's seat. "It's a clawmaw."

Anoor nodded.

Sylah reached for Anoor's hand and squeezed it. "But why are you riding it?" She spoke lightly, full of denial.

Anoor's voice was resigned. "It's the only way, Sylah."

Sylah shook her head sharply. Her grip on Anoor's hand tightened, pulling her away from the tip of the needles. "No, it isn't. If you do this, it'll kill you."

Sylah started crying.

And then, so did Anoor. "I have to, Sylah. Without my blood to sustain it, the beast will die in a strike, maybe less. We don't have enough sharj oil to kill all the creations."

Sylah climbed the stone structure and knelt on its chest in front of Anoor. "No."

Anoor reached forward and brushed one of Sylah's braids from her wet cheeks. When she spoke, her voice was barely above a whisper. "I was always supposed to die here. In this battle."

Sylah's eyes flashed hot and angry. "No, you cannot believe in that nonsense the Zalaam spoke of. It was all lies."

Anoor shrugged weakly. "It doesn't matter."

"It does matter, I need you to fight to live, Anoor, I need *you*—" Sylah's voice broke, and she bent forward with a ragged sob.

"Sylah, I want to fight, I want to be with you . . . but you need to understand." Anoor's voice grew stronger as she spoke. "The Zalaam *broke* me. And Retribution is the only way I can mend the little I have left of myself."

"No." It seemed the only word Sylah was capable of saying.

But then a voice spoke in their minds.

"Anoor, a larger creation has been spotted," Ravenwing said. "It appears the clawmaw is entering the plantation fields, north-west from your location."

A cold sliver of dread ran through Anoor's body. She hadn't thought Yona would be able to adjust the clawmaw in time—but she should have known. Her grandmother had been the greatest master crafter the Zalaam had ever had.

"The clawmaw," Anoor whispered. "You must see that this is the only way, Sylah. If Yona has brought the clawmaw to life, then Retribution might be the only thing to destroy it."

Sylah sat up and set her jaw. "I will do it then. Let me be the one to ride it into battle."

Anoor shook her head, ignoring her own fresh flow of tears. "This task is for me alone, Sylah."

Sylah met Anoor's eyes. She must have seen the determination in them because she didn't insist further. Instead, she asked, "Can you remove yourself from the needles? When you feel yourself fading?"

Anoor nearly winced at the hope in Sylah's voice. "I will try," Anoor said.

She reached out to cup Sylah's wet cheek. "We'll be together in the end, you and I."

Anoor leant forward and kissed Sylah gently on the brow.

"Let me go now, Sylah."

Sylah made to move, withdrawing a dagger from her side. For a moment Anoor thought Sylah was about to strike her, but then she grasped her own hair.

Sylah's braids clinked with all the pieces of her: Loot's spider brooch, the splinter from her mother's fufu spoon, the ambassador token Anoor had given her, Elder Zero's belt, Petal's cloth. All her love and loss, her pain and joy.

The dagger slipped through Sylah's braids, shearing them clean off so that they fell into her hand.

In these last few precious seconds they had together, Anoor watched as Sylah wove them together into a crown. "If a creation takes on a semblance of its former material, then let it take a part of me. The one person in this world who would protect you until the end."

Sylah pressed the crown of her woven hair onto Anoor's head. Anoor smiled and felt the weight of Sylah's love on her brow.

"I love you," she said.

"I live for you," Sylah replied.

Then Anoor pressed her wrists down onto the needles.

CHAPTER FIFTY-FIVE

Shola

The third day of battle

Ships dotted the shoreline. But as the Entwined Harbour's navy got closer, Shola realised they were hundreds of little row boats.

This cannot be the Blood Forged's fleet?

Then she saw the emblem of a spider on the soldiers' uniform and knew that the boats ahead of her were the enemy.

It had taken Shola far longer than she'd expected to reclaim the title of captain of the Entwined Harbour. Her campaigning had been long and fraught. But as soon as rule passed to her, she'd ordered her clerics to set sail for war. *The history books would not exclude the Entwined Harbour from this tale*, she'd thought.

"Captain, the Zalaam are disembarking on the beach ahead of us. They are moving west. I do not think they have seen us," one of the ocean guards said to her right.

"Eh, eh, an ambush then against the eastern front. Well, it is hard to hide the bulk of our might. They will see us soon enough. We must prepare for enemy contact as soon as we land."

"There's something else, Captain. You should see it for yourself." The cleric handed her the telescope.

She pressed the cool metal to her eye. What she had assumed was the glint of weaponry was actually the power of the fifth charter. Wolf-like creations bounded across the beach, their bladed claws kicking up sand and sea spray from the shallows.

"Three hundred of them by my count," the ocean guard reported.

Shola removed the telescope from her eye and said, "Prepare the steelweed nets. I think it's time to go fishing."

CHAPTER FIFTY-SIX

Olina

The third day of battle

Olina's furs were matted with blood. They weighed down her already tired shoulders. But she didn't remove them.

The fur had been shorn from the body of a shatter bear—the most vicious predator in the north. Its weight on her shoulders was not just a symbol of her homeland, but a representation of all she was worth. To become a helmsman in the Winterlands you had to prove your strength. For some that meant testing their will by weathering the cold, others chose to challenge a more senior helmsman to a duel. There were even some soldiers who made a show of walking across hot coals.

Each feat of strength was weighed and assessed, their rank chosen based on the outcome.

Olina wanted to rank as high as possible—she had known she was destined to be a leader since her grandmother read it in the smoke of her hearth fire. So she had navigated her narrow boat to the Silver Shores where shatter bears were terrorising the local village.

She had been fifteen when she killed the shatter bear. And its fur had hung off her back ever since.

Twenty-five years on and it still brings me strength.

She spun away as one of the Zalaam lunged for her ribcage. As she righted herself she swung her mace at the enemy's head, crushing his skull like a winter melon.

Three days of fighting and Olina's regiment were barely hanging on. She fought at the eastern edge of the battlefield, the sea to her back, the Jin-Dinil lakes to her front.

As she looked towards the swamps there, dread sank like an anvil in her stomach. Another wave of soldiers had arrived.

"Brace yourselves, more incoming!" Olina shouted to her surviving comrades. Death would come soon enough.

The Zalaam ran towards her, three hundred of them against her regiment of fifty soldiers. They did not fear death in the same way as Olina's helmsmen did. And it was that quality that made them most dangerous.

"We won't survive this," one of the soldiers to her right said.

"No, we won't, but we'll take down as many of them as we can before we go," Olina said grimly.

She sprang forward, running headfirst into the foray of oncoming enemy. But before her mace could take another life she saw something spin across the sky. She paused, which confused the Zalaam who hesitated before spotting what she'd seen.

A circular object spun through the bright blue of the sky before falling down upon the enemy.

It was a *net*.

Olina recognised the deep green of steelweed as it pinned half of the enemy to the ground. A second net joined the first and soon the Zalaam were completely trapped—not for long, but it gave her enough time to turn on her heel. What she saw made her fall to her knees.

The Entwined Harbour had arrived.

CHAPTER FIFTY-SEVEN

Sylah

The third day of battle

Sylah watched Anoor's creation disappear into the heart of the hurricane that surrounded the clawmaw on the plantation fields. Her cheeks were wet, but her heart was numb.

Though it wasn't Sylah's lifeblood that was being drained from her, it felt like it was.

"Sylah, I'm out of runebullets," Aveed said. Their words brought her back to the battlefield.

After seeing Anoor she had rejoined her regiment on the rooftops in the Duster Quarter. Runeguns and bloodwerk crossbows fired around them at the enemy below.

"I have some bullets to spare." She reached into her pocket and passed them to Aveed.

"That's not a bullet." Aveed held up a small round disc.

For a second Sylah looked at it without any recollection. Then she remembered Anoor thrusting it into her hand when the sentinels had been at their heels.

"The diffuse disc," she breathed.

Sylah snatched it out of Aveed's hand, her mind reeling. *If I time it right, I could diffuse Anoor's creation before it kills her. But not before she destroys Yona.*

Sylah turned to the former Warden of Duty. They looked up at her sudden movement. Dirt and blood crusted Aveed's face. Though there was no forgiveness for the pain Aveed had caused as warden, Sylah nevertheless had to afford them a small piece of respect for their efforts on the battlefield.

"Aveed, you'll probably never hear this again in your life—if you survive, that is. But you're in charge."

It had been a long time since Sylah had jumped across the rooftops, but her muscles remembered the landings and the launches. She even managed to avoid the septic tanks.

The exhilaration of being airborne was second to the hope that spread along her ribcage. She had found a way to save Anoor—if she wasn't too late.

When Sylah reached the end of the villas she jumped down and into the foray of the battlefield, where the Zalaam's foot soldiers were engaged with the Blood Forged.

Sylah removed her sword from its sheath, the gold of the joba tree embellishment on the blade glinting in the noonday sun. She was glad to be reunited with her sword for this final battle. Grasping the hilt was like holding a familiar hand and it gave her comfort as she charged into combat.

She began to chant as she fought:

"Stolen, sharpened, the hidden key,

We'll destroy the empire and set you free,

Churned up from the shadows to tear it apart,

A dancer's grace, a killer's instinct, an Ember's blood, a Duster's heart."

Sylah was a torrent of death and blood as she moved across the battlefield.

This was what I was made for.

She fought with the ferocity and skill of twenty soldiers, and she lost count of how many she had killed on her path to Anoor.

"Feint to the right . . . no, duck . . . see that weakness in their knee, a quick jab will do it," Azim's voice said in her mind. Coaching her, even now.

Is this what you wanted to see, Father?

She hadn't called him father in so long. But he was, he always had been. Just like Jond she couldn't stop loving him, despite his trove of flaws.

She faltered as she thought of Jond and whether he was alive or dead. A blade glanced off her forehead, showering her eyes in her own blood.

Sylah saw the assailant through the red and plunged her sword into his neck. Indigo blood covered the blade as she withdrew it.

She touched her forehead to check the wound. It was shallow, nothing to worry about.

And Sylah was off again, gliding through the front line and leaving a trail of bodies in her wake.

Her blade kissed the heart of anyone who dared look her way, until she reached the swirling wind where Yona and Anoor fought.

The battlefield was quieter here, soldiers on both sides fearful of being swept into the sandstorm.

I had thought I would never see the tidewind's like again.

But the marrow Yona was feeding into the clawmaw had summoned it once more.

Sylah took a deep breath and plunged into the hurricane's heart.

CHAPTER FIFTY-EIGHT

Retribution

The third day of battle

The creation had no thoughts except one: destroy Yona. It knew not what Yona was, only where Yona was.

The sand shifted beneath its clawed feet as it ran into the battle. The weight harboured in its heart whooped and cried as they loped across the desert.

Retribution sensed that their destination stood in the midst of the swirling wind.

As it entered the tornado of sand, it saw the beast that was Yona in front of them. Though Retribution didn't see, not really. It only held an echo of the senses that belonged to the being that fed it life. So like Yona, Retribution knew this person's name—Anoor.

Anoor sat cradled in Retribution's chest, not a part of its consciousness, but beside it. They were aware of each other, and aware of Yona, who was a beast just like Retribution, but larger and stronger.

Yona lunged towards Retribution with a swipe of its large hand. Retribution dodged, but Yona had clipped its left arm, chipping the whitestone there to dust.

It joined the blue sand churning in the wind.

Retribution lurched forward, charging with the tapered stone of its head. Stone struck metal and Yona fell backwards, the ground shaking.

Before it could rise, Retribution dragged its claws across the runes on Yona's side, paralysing its left arm. But as Yona stood, it swiped its leg under Retribution, sending the creation to the ground in a clattering heap.

Thud. Thud. Thud.

Yona's footfalls drew level with Retribution's heart.

Sounds came from Yona's chest.

"Anoor, turn your violence on the non-believers. Look at the beauty in what you have made. Let us turn our might to the Keep and tear it down as you always wished."

"A kori bird should never be caged," Anoor countered.

But Retribution knew nothing of language. All it knew was the movement that gave it life and the purpose that drove it.

And right now, that purpose was to protect.

Retribution drew its hands in a cross over its chest as Yona struck with its one arm.

Whitestone shattered but Retribution still had the means to stand. It drove Yona back until it stumbled. The metal of Retribution's feet had less friction than those made from the empire's stone.

The wind was a frenzy around them.

Yona tried to rise but Retribution sprang, landing in the centre of Yona where the metal turned to flesh, pinning the larger beast to the ground.

There was a movement on the edges of the tornado as someone new joined them on the battlefield, just in time to see the finale.

But Retribution felt its strength begin to wane as Anoor's blood supply began to ebb.

"Anoor," the newcomer cried. And Retribution felt the reverberation of Anoor's feelings in reaction to this new voice.

It was the feeling of a window being opened in a stifled room. The sweetness of a drink of water on a parched throat. The warmth and comfort of a blanket on a cold night.

It was love.

But love couldn't sustain Retribution. Only blood could do that.

So as the creation drew back to land the killing blow, it slowed to a stop.

Retribution's last thoughts were shrouded in the tenderness of a single figure.

Sylah.

CHAPTER FIFTY-NINE

Anoor

The third day of battle

Anoor was dying. Retribution had gone still, holding Yona and the clawmaw to the ground. But Yona was still alive.

Retribution had weighed down the centre of the clawmaw's body, crushing Yona's legs beneath its own.

Both were trapped in the creations of their own making, unable to move.

Her grandmother's face was tight with pain, but her eyes glittered with a manic energy as her clawmaw tried to buck off Retribution. But the damage to the clawmaw was extensive and it struggled to move.

And now Sylah was here. Beautiful, fierce Sylah, running towards Anoor through the sand and wind that cut at her skin.

Yona's clawmaw went still as Sylah approached.

Though Anoor's vision was going, she could see the glint of silver in Sylah's hand.

Clever woman, she is going to diffuse the life in the clawmaw. Using the diffuse rune on a creation was only safe once it was incapacitated, like Yona was now.

But then Sylah knelt by Anoor's side pulling out the needles from her wrist.

Did she not know Yona was still alive? Yellow and blue blood marred the battlefield, but surely she could see Yona's eyes, wide and full of malice?

"Stay with me Anoor, stay with me," Sylah was murmuring.

But it was too late. Yona had freed the clawmaw's functioning arm and its metal grip wrapped around Sylah's torso.

Anoor heard the crack of bone and a bright bloom of red before Sylah was flung to the side.

A rib, she's just cracked a rib, Sylah can survive that. Anoor clung on to the thought.

"Granddaughter." Yona's voice was a rasp. "You have served Kabut well, now sacrifice yourself willingly."

The clawmaw's hand wavered in front of Anoor's head.

"Never." Anoor tried to mouth the words, but she wasn't sure if Yona could hear them. Either way, her grandmother understood the sentiment.

The clawmaw lunged and Anoor closed her eyes and waited for death.

But it didn't come. When she opened her eyes again the clawmaw's talons were frozen a hair's breadth from Anoor's face.

"What? No!" Yona screamed.

Anoor followed the red, bloody streak in the sand until she understood what had happened. Sylah had dragged herself towards the clawmaw, pressing the diffuse disc to its side. All Anoor could see of her lover was a bloodied hand, which was still.

She's just resting, Anoor assured herself, even as the world around her grew hazier.

The wind had stopped, but it wasn't silent. Yona was thrashing in the prison she had made herself.

Anoor willed her body forward. She had to end this, end Yona. But she had no means to kill the Wife of Kabut. She had only her fists, and they weren't working. But as she managed to shift in her seat, something slipped through her shirt.

Her stylus. Perfectly pointed to pierce skin.

"How do I kill someone?" Anoor asked.

Sylah laughed and shook her head. "You don't. You call for me."

Anoor tried not to pout. "With all this strength training we're doing, I thought it would be a good idea to know how."

Sylah sauntered towards her swinging a dagger. "The final trial is 'to the blood', not 'to the death', Anoor."

"Please, just in case I need it for self-defence."

Sylah cocked her head. "Fine."

She stepped towards Anoor.

"Follow the contour of the neck." Sylah lifted Anoor's hand and placed it on her own neck, which was flushed and warm. "You feel that slight pulse?" Anoor's heart was racing. This was the most she'd ever touched Sylah.

Sylah tightened her grip on Anoor's hand. "Make a horizontal cut there, fast, and deep. It'll be a messy kill, but it'll be a fast one."

Anoor smiled as the memory gave her the last spark of strength to grip the stylus and plunge it into Yona's neck.

Yellow blood sprayed across her vision. Warm as sunshine.

And Anoor closed her eyes.

CHAPTER SIXTY

Hassa

The third day of battle

"The Entwined Harbour have joined the melee. The eastern battlefield is ours." Ravenwing's words were tinged with disbelief and Hassa too could barely believe it.

Cheers erupted as the news spread. But the joy was short-lived.

Hassa stood atop an old water tower in the Ember Quarter, the highest peak south of the bridge, except for the Keep. The vantage point meant she was one of the first to spot the wave of quellers making their way through what remained of the Dredge.

"Hassa, stand by," Ravenwing continued, having also seen the quellers from his position in the courtroom. "Prepare for the final phase. Anyone north of the Tongue needs to retreat immediately."

Blue sand, lifted by the ethereal wind the creations conjured, swirled around the spiders. Even at this distance Hassa could hear the violence they wrought.

Sha-coch, sha-coch, sha-coch. Their bladed legs slid up and down.

Hassa leant over the water tower's crumbling edge and threw a stone down, alerting the Ghosting there.

The quellers are nearly in the Duster Quarter, Hassa signed.

I'll tell the others, Captain, Sami signed back, before slipping through the streets towards the Tongue.

Hassa wasn't sure when she'd become a captain. There had been no swearing-in ceremony, or official documentation. But sometime in the last week, her retinue of Ghostings had simply started calling her it. The title chafed.

Hassa'd had many titles over the years: servant, watcher, spy. All of them had been chosen for her. She vowed this would be the last time people called her anything other than "Hassa".

Hassa was a friend, Hassa was a daughter. *Hassa was someone free,* she thought. And with the eastern battlefield won, that reality was closer than ever before.

She watched Sami move through the alleyways that led to the Tongue and found herself thinking of Ala. Her death had hit Sami hard—Hassa too—but the older man's mistake had been the reason Ala had died.

Hassa could see how the guilt ate away at him and so she increased his responsibilities. She couldn't allow the other Ghostings to take their grief out on him, so she made it clear that her trust in him had not wavered. His mistake was a collective responsibility, and any division among her taskforce would not be tolerated.

Though I hate titles, I make a good leader, she thought grimly.

She descended the water tower, following the path Sami had taken, towards the Tongue. It wouldn't be long before the quellers reached the bridge and Hassa wanted to be ready.

As she turned the final corner, she watched the horizon go dark, as the hurricane the creations raised filled the air with debris and litter. It was like watching the tidewind roll in, only more sinister as the spiders rode the wave of chaos right to the river's edge.

The Ghostings stood on the cobbled path at the southern side of the bridge. Vahi stood with them, his back hunched from lugging sharj oil from their supplies in the Keep.

Every drop of it had been used in their final assault.

It has to work. It has to.

There were a few soldiers from the Blood Forged still making it across the Tongue. Some regiments, like Sylah's squadron, had been engaging with the Zalaam's foot soldiers in the Duster Quarter and the Dredge.

Hassa looked for her friend among those fleeing across the bridge. She noticed Aveed, the former Warden of Duty, limping the last few steps into the Ember Quarter and she felt a rush of irritation that they had survived when so many others hadn't.

But from the look of the wound in their leg, their life might yet be forfeit.

Hassa didn't find Sylah among the crowds, and even as they trickled down to ten . . . then five . . . then one . . . she still hoped.

Come on, Sylah, where are you? Hassa thought.

Sami walked into her view. *We're ready, Captain, we await your signal.*

Hassa nodded and looked past Sami to cast one last hopeful look down the bridge, but instead of Sylah, something far more ominous crawled out of the hurricane—quellers. In seconds, hundreds of them had made their way onto the Tongue.

She fought the urge to run. Instead, she held her nerve. She didn't turn away from the creations as she signalled to Sami, *Set the bridge aflame.*

But then something strange happened. A flock of birds flew out of the hurricane towards them.

Not birds. *Arrows.*

The Zalaam were targeting Ghostings with inkwells.

Take cover, Hassa signed frantically. *Take cover.*

But she wasn't quick enough. Three Ghostings fell in front of her. Hassa tried to gasp but then realised she couldn't.

She looked down to see an arrow thrusting out of her chest.

"Hassa!" she heard Vahi cry, but chaos had ensued. People were running in panic.

"Ah . . ." She tried to breathe, but it was difficult. There was no pain, only pressure, but it was weight enough for her to fall to her knees.

The quellers were so close to the Ember Quarter now, only thirty handspans away.

We nearly did it, she thought.

There was a movement ahead of her and she saw that Sami had also been struck, though the arrow had only punctured his shoulder. It did however limit his signing, so instead she followed his gaze.

She had fallen five handspans from the trigger rune. All she needed to do was activate it. But she wasn't sure she had enough breath left to manage it. She either tried and failed, or she let the quellers take them.

Either way she was dead. So she might as well try.

She pulled herself to her feet and managed to stumble the last few steps to the trigger rune. Her stylus bit into her flesh and she drew the final stroke of the rune.

There could be no mistakes, not now.

As soon as she finished another rain of arrows flew towards her, but strong arms lifted her up and carried her out of range just before they landed.

Vahi set her down and began to fuss around her wound. But Hassa wasn't listening, she was watching the fire spread across the Tongue.

It was the most beautiful of performances, each flame dancing upon the iron bridge, shifting in the wind but not guttering out. Then she heard the screams—the overture. The soldiers died before the creations did. The metal turning red and burning them in their seats.

The air smelt of burnt hair and fat.

The quellers in the fire had slowed, their legs turning molten. But still new arrivals kept crossing the Tongue. For the Zalaam had no control of the quellers. The Zalaam couldn't stop what they had begun, so soon the soldiers were simply riding to their death, clambering higher and higher upon their molten brethren. But the flames reached all—including the iron of the bridge.

The Tongue was not immune to the sharj oil fire, though the protection runes placed by Hassa's Ghosting ancestors gave it a small amount of resistance. But once those had been marred by molten metal, nothing could stop the fire affecting the bridge.

There was a groan as the bridge bowed inwards, turning red and viscous in the centre. The first few quellers were slowly turning into orange-yellow liquid and they pooled through the gaps in the bridge, hissing as they struck the quicksand river below.

"Hassa, I need to remove the arrow. I need to see if it's pierced your heart," Vahi was saying urgently.

She pushed him away gently. *No, I think it is just the one lung, I have another.*

Vahi looked pained. "Hassa, you need to be healed. Let me call on a flighter."

She shook her head. *There are people in worse condition.* She tore her gaze back to the bridge and saw that it was a bridge no longer.

The entire remaining fleet of quellers had fallen into the Ruta River. Hassa got up and began to shuffle towards the river's edge. Pain sparked up her ribcage, but she didn't cry out.

Vahi started to protest but she signed, *Please, I need to see this through.*

Her father nodded and looped his hand around her arm and helped guide her towards the river. His presence was more comforting than he could know. For Hassa was deeply shaken. She wasn't entirely sure if this wasn't all a dream.

Though it hadn't gone exactly as planned, it had worked. And that in itself was a miracle worth seeing.

As they reached the edge of the ravine smoke plumed up from the riverbed. When it dissipated Hassa began to sob.

The fire had turned the quicksand into glass, entombing the creations in a crystal river.

And that was it: there were no more quellers. No more Zalaam.

The river of glass glittered blue in the sunlight, like the facets of a sapphire, but infinitely more valuable. For years to come this tomb would serve as a reminder of all they had fought for. Families from around the world would come just to look upon it. To see how beautiful death could be, and to understand how hard Ghostings would fight to survive.

Hassa laughed, a wet hiccupping sound that was full of disbelief. It was over.

Vahi wept quietly beside her. And when Sami came to join them, so did he. It was impossible not to cry at the glistening scene below them.

Sami turned to her. Someone had removed the arrow in his shoulder and bound his wound. *Captain, we did it. The war is won.*

Hassa's heart was full as she signed, *Captain no longer. Just call me Hassa.*

CHAPTER SIXTY-ONE

Jond

Jond walked through the courtyard of the Keep. A kori bird flew overhead, soaring through the soft pink of dawn.

Despite the time, the courtyard wasn't quiet. Clusters of people sat quietly talking, sharing stories of friends they'd lost.

The war was over, and they had *won*.

It was unfathomable that the Zalaam were no more. But Jond had gone to the crystal river and seen the remains of the quellers beneath the ice-like glass.

Thanks to Shola and the Entwined Harbour joining the fray in the final strikes, the eastern battlefield had been won too. Though Jond's heart soared with joy that the battle was over, they had taken significant losses.

Sylah—he stumbled as his throat constricted, and his eyes grew hot. He could barely think about her without sobbing. And so he didn't, he couldn't grieve for her. Not yet.

Not until they recovered her body.

They hadn't found Sylah or Anoor. So for now, he had to hold on to the hope that they had survived. The alternative was too painful.

Jond steadied his breath and continued on.

Rascal trotted around his ankles. The sandcat had got too big to climb in his shirt, but she seemed content to weave between his legs.

They walked past a group of mainlanders trying to explain the anatomy of a camel to some Dusters, whose mouths hung open in horror. Jond laughed but it came out as a rasp and it cut him short.

He ran a hand over his neck. The skin there was smooth, but it hid the damage underneath. Niha had done all he could to heal him with the limited strength he'd had at the time. But the blade had severed Jond's larynx rendering him unable to speak.

"I can work with the surgeons to try and break down the cartilage. The healing I did sped up some of the extraneous growth," Niha had said when Jond had awoken with no voice. "But that is where the third law comes up against its limitations. I cannot remove extra tissue without the surgeons' help."

"Will I ever get my voice back?" Jond mouthed. Niha didn't understand him the first time, so he tried again, adding a bit of breath to the words.

Rascal nudged his hand for more petting. The kitten apparently hadn't left his side since he'd been hurt.

When Niha understood he looked away. His face was grey with fatigue and Jond felt for his friend. Though the war had stopped, the job of a healer was far from over.

"I don't know. Even with the surgeons' help I might not be able to get your voice back completely." Niha's face clouded over with guilt.

Jond reached for Niha's hand and squeezed it. "Thank you for saving my life. I owe you everything."

Niha's smile was weak, but at least it was there.

Someone called Niha's name and he turned and conversed with another healer before saying to Jond, "I have to go. I'm needed with a patient."

Jond waved him off.

Niha left, moving to the southern side of the arena where the most injured patients were kept. When he'd disappeared from view, Jond swung his legs out of his pallet bed and stood on shaky legs.

There were too many people who had graver injuries than him. He wasn't about to wait around for a surgeon to cut him open again when soldiers were dying around him.

That had been three days ago.

Now as he wandered through the courtyard watching people of all blood colours converse, he felt a sharp stab of loss.

Then he saw two Ghostings on the periphery of the courtyard. They were signing slowly to a few mainlanders and Dusters. They were *teaching* them.

Jond lingered nearby watching them as they patiently explained simple words like *sky, ground, tree.*

And Jond remembered that he didn't need to speak to have a voice.

He moved away, more humbled than before.

His feet took him to a sectioned area set aside from the main courtyard. It was where the flighters were stationed.

Shola was waiting for him there. She stooped to pick up Rascal who began to purr in the captain's arms.

"You ready to go, Jond By the Way?" Shola asked.

Jond smiled at the nickname for him. It seemed so long ago that they'd met. He'd crossed oceans since then and met death more than once.

A flighter blinked into existence in the centre of the cordoned-off area. They looked tired. Jond couldn't blame them—the flighters had turned out to be an important advantage in the war. They'd been scouts before the battle began and transported the injured during the conflict. Now in the aftermath they were still working hard, helping to get people back to their ships on the shoreline.

Those who wanted to leave, that is.

"Are you sure I can't persuade you to come back to Tenio with me?" Kara had asked him last night.

Jond shook his head. He was done with courts and politics for a little while.

He wrote down his thoughts on a piece of paper before pushing it across the table to her.

Shola said there are over two hundred sign languages I can learn from the clerics of the Entwined Harbour.

Kara scoffed and stood up, her chair hitting the ground. But she didn't bend to pick it up.

"I don't like Shola," she muttered.

Jond stood and walked over to Kara, wrapping his arms around her from behind until she softened and leant against him.

He whispered in her ear as loudly as he could, "I'll come back to you, my Queen."

They stood in one of the empty rooms of the Keep where they had reunited during the celebrations in the wake of the final day of battle. The bed covers lay crumpled and well worn. For Jond had known even then that it might be the last time he could sate his appetite for a long while.

Kara sniffed. "What are you going to do out there? Read books?"

Jond smiled and kissed her jaw before saying quietly, "Yes, and heal. Grieve, and learn a new language so I don't have to whisper every time I speak. Though I don't mind so much with you."

He burrowed his face in her neck. And all thought of goodbyes fled their minds.

"Jond, are you ready?" Shola asked again, bringing him back to the present.

No, I'm not, he thought. He already missed Kara, but he nodded.

"Then I'll go first with Rascal," Shola said. Jond shot Rascal a betrayed look as she settled comfortably into Shola's arms. She closed her eyes in response.

"I'll come back for you," Windal said before flighting away with Shola.

Jond took one last look at the Dryland Republic as he waited. The joba tree stood tall against the rose-gold sky. How long had the tree been here? Centuries? Millennia? Its immovable presence had seen empires come and go.

Once again, blood had been spilt. But perhaps this time, this time the world would learn from its mistakes.

Jond could only hope.

He knew he wouldn't come back to the place that had been his home. There was too much pain embedded in the soil of its roots for him to stay.

"Jond Alnua."

He turned at the sound of the voice.

"Kara?"

She stood behind him in plain slacks and a shirt. The crown that had been entangled in her copper locks since he'd made it had gone.

"I'm coming with you," she said.

"But what about the queendom?" he mouthed slowly. Though she might not have heard all the words, she understood the meaning.

She shrugged. "The Queen died on the battlefield."

He frowned. "What?"

"Don't try and stop me, Jond, I've already circulated the news. The Queen is dead. I haven't been seen since the final battle anyway, so it's a believable rumour. Obviously, our allies know, but what can they say to stop me?"

Jond's mouth parted in disbelief, but Kara wasn't done.

"I have never wanted the throne, and though I think the Queen had her part to play in this war, she isn't needed to build Tenio back up. I see how the Dryland Republic is already giving their citizens a voice in governing and I want my people to have that too. Without an heir, the queendom ends with me."

Jond crossed the distance between them and placed a crushing kiss on her lips. When he broke away, he looked into her eyes and whispered, "Are you sure?"

Kara smiled. "This is not a sacrifice, Jond. This is what I want. This is what I've always wanted, I just wasn't sure how to achieve it. Turns out all I needed to do was die."

They laughed quietly together.

"Besides," she said, "I've been assured there are lots of botany books kept in the Entwined Harbour's libraries"

"But no soil."

"We can plant roots later, when we're ready." Kara's face grew wistful. "It could be in Tenio, it could be in Bushica. All I ask is that we have a rose garden."

"Two rose gardens," Jond added, kissing her once more.

He felt the familiar coolness of her orb on his skin, but he didn't pull away from the plushness of her lips as they flighted away.

Together, the major general of the Blood Forged army and Queen Karanomo of Tenio disappeared out of existence.

CHAPTER SIXTY-TWO

Hassa

Hassa ran her hands over the wood of the new bridge as she crossed into the Duster Quarter. She had watched Ads and the group of students of the first charter grow it a day after the battle had been won.

Terracotta tiles that they called "incubators" served as the base of the first law runework. Within a few minutes oak saplings grew from the centre of the tiles. Ads used bloodwerk runes to guide the trees to weave horizontally as they matured.

Over the course of a strike the two sides of the crystal river were stitched together once more. A wooden bridge was a precious thing, and something that had never been possible before because of the tidewind.

Two weeks on and so much of the city had already changed. As she moved into the Duster Quarter, Hassa was struck by the absence of joba trees, which had been felled to help rebuild the Dredge. Though neither of those areas were called the names they'd been given before.

The Dredge was now called the Nest, in honour of the Ghostings' home that was now crushed beneath the earth. And the Duster Quarter was called the Frontier in reverence to those who had held the front line of battle there while Hassa's operation prepared the bridge with fire runes. But there was no more housing segregation. Anyone could live wherever they wanted.

The world was changing.

It was time to rebuild the Dryland Republic into something new. But Hassa wouldn't be here to see it.

The Zwina Academy had offered her the title of councillor of the sixth charter, the newly made faction teaching bloodwerk runes. But she had turned it down.

I do not want a title, for now, I just want to learn. Will you take me on as a student? she asked the remaining councillors—Sui and Niha.

They conferred together before Niha nodded.

"You are more than welcome to join us, Hassa, but in exchange for the years of study, we do ask that you consider the title again at the end of your schooling."

Hassa nodded; that seemed reasonable. The power of her ancestors deserved to be explored and she liked the idea of being the one to do it.

I will be the first student of the sixth law, she thought.

The elders hadn't been happy. *Bloodwerk is ours to police,* Ravenwing had argued. *It should remain in the republic.*

But Hassa shook her head. *If knowledge had been shared, this war would have never happened.*

Knowledge is what gave the Zalaam power. Do you not remember that the prophet was one of the Academy's own? Reed countered.

Hassa met the blue ice of her gaze. *The wardens proved that knowledge has power. It was the greatest weapon they could have used against us.*

Dew laughed. *Always the wisest of us, Hassa.*

They had agreed in the end. Though she would have gone without their blessing.

The elders would continue to guide the Ghostings, but the government of the Dryland Republic was in a state of transformation. Jin-Laham's ideals, though so briefly carried out, had served as a successful example of how a voting-based system could work. And once Hassa had outlined how they'd done it, the elders had seen the sense in it.

An assembly of four people would make up the initial governing body. Gorn and Ravenwing had already announced their bids for nomination.

For the Dryland Republic could not just be the home of the

Ghostings. It had to be home for anyone who chose it, even the Embers who fought alongside them. After they'd been vetted, of course.

In addition to the ruling assembly, a Justice and Reconciliation Committee was being put together to process the wrongdoings of Embers and government officials. Those condemned would face restorative rehabilitation, a concept Gorn had put forward.

"They are what the empire made them to be. Some of them abused that power more than others, but education and rehabilitation need to be staples of how we move forward. Otherwise, Embers will become ostracised and the whole cycle will begin again," Gorn said.

Leadership suited the Truthsayer more than she could know. She looked to the future instead of the immediate present. Few would be able to put their lust for punishment aside to consider education and rehabilitation as a preventative tool.

As soon as the committee was put together, Vahi volunteered himself to be the first Ember to undergo trial. He'd been assessed by a group of twelve people who had unanimously exonerated him of the crimes of some of his fellow Embers.

Hassa smiled as she thought of her father. Vahi had decided to come with her to Tenio. Her father's tireless work in the Keep's forge had garnered him the respect of the Dryland Republic, but his home was with Hassa now.

She moved through the old Dredge, marvelling at the new homes that had already been erected. There were still mountains of rubble and debris around the streets, but it was starting to feel lived-in again.

Her feet took her out of the city towards the plantation fields.

It was the most she'd walked for a long time. The arrow in her chest had punctured her lung. It should have been a quick healing, but because she'd taken so long to go to a healer, some of the flesh had started to heal around the splinters of wood. She'd needed to spend a week in bed while the healers worked on getting the shards of arrow out.

Hassa paused when she reached the blackened soil where Ala had died. A ring of metal fifty handspans high circled the charred ground. The smelted quellers served as a reminder of the war that had happened here. And the loss.

Hassa climbed over the metal wall, careful not to cut herself, and dropped down into the warm sand of the Farsai Desert on the other side.

The two clawmaws lay where they had fallen. Hassa couldn't tell Yona's remains apart from that of the metal shards. The two had become one and the same, the body shattered.

Anoor's clawmaw was empty. Their soldiers hadn't found her or Sylah's bodies.

Hassa looked to the shifting dunes.

They were probably swallowed by the desert from the force of the winds.

The thought weakened the strength in Hassa's legs, and she collapsed. Her limbs pressing into the sand as a cry tore from her throat. She felt something beneath the scars of her skin, and she began to dig with her wrists.

She pulled out a braid that she recognised as one of Sylah's. She tugged it free from the sand, pulling out what was woven into it. The orb of creation shone bright in the sunlight.

Hassa held it between her wrists and brought it to her heart.

There was so much they didn't know about the fifth charter. With the Zalaam destroyed, Hassa knew that the knowledge of its runes would fade—unless she kept this orb, the last ever orb made by the Academy.

But she wouldn't. Knowledge was power, but this knowledge was death. And she'd seen enough people die to know that nothing good would come of keeping this knowledge alive.

She let it fall to the ground and dug a hole bigger than before. Then she covered up the orb.

And let the earth hide its secrets.

EPILOGUE

Sylah and Anoor clawed their way out from the sand dune, coughing. They lay on the ground for a minute, getting back their breath. The sun beat down on them from a perfectly blue sky.

There were no sounds of warfare in the distance—only a peaceful stillness. That is, until Anoor pushed herself to her elbows and laughed. "We did it, we actually did it."

The sound of Anoor's laughter made Sylah's heart soar. Sylah turned her head to gaze at her. Anoor's smile shone far brighter than the sun behind her. She ran a hand down Anoor's cheek.

"Yes, we did," she said, looking into the honeyed pools of Anoor's hazel eyes which were clear and sparkling.

Anoor's lips lifted, then she looked past Sylah to the landscape beyond where the blue of the sky merged with the blue of the desert. The sun glowed an ethereal amber, somewhere between sunset and twilight.

"Where are we?" Anoor asked.

Sylah shrugged. "Must have travelled beneath a shifting sand dune."

Anoor nodded, then she stood and crested the nearest sand dune. Sylah rested her head on the backs of her hands and watched her. Though Anoor was still in the sunlight she cast no shadow, or perhaps it just stretched away from her where Sylah's couldn't see it.

"Well, that didn't help, couldn't see anything in the distance," Anoor said upon returning, though she didn't seem concerned. Like Sylah, it was difficult to feel concerned when they'd just managed to kill the leader of the Zalaam.

Sylah pulled Anoor down beside her, vexed to be away from her warmth and her love for any short length of time. Anoor relaxed into Sylah's embrace.

A kori bird flew overhead and they both watched it glide across the cloudless sky.

Sylah smiled. "Wherever we are, at least we're together."

Anoor's face appeared above Sylah's, blocking out the blue of the horizon. Her grin was full of affection as she leant towards Sylah.

"Together," Anoor said. Her fingers intertwined in Sylah's braids, drawing her closer until their lips brushed as she spoke. "Until the end."

GLOSSARY

TERMS

Abosom The devout followers of Anyme who serve under the Warden of Truth.

Aerobatics A type of gymnastics that incorporates aerial movements.

Aerofield Ranged combat, first trial of the Aktibar for strength.

Aeroglider Wind-gliding sport, commonly practised on the hills of Jin-Gernomi.

Akoma The largest valve in the heart.

Aktibar, the A set of trials held every ten years to determine the next disciples.

Anyme The genderless deity worshipped in the empire. God of the Sky.

Ardae A religious festival celebrating the anniversary of when Anyme first climbed into the sky. It involves a blessed meal, gifts and offerings to the God.

Battle wrath A state of focus used in the martial art of Nuba.

Baqarah Submarine ship made by the Ghostings.

Blood scour Finger pin-prick checkpoints to test the colour of your blood.

Bloodink Tattoos, most commonly seen on Dusters.

Bloodwerk The ability to use your blood to manipulate objects by drawing runes. There are four foundational runes. The rest are supplementary runes which guide in direction, activation, safety and protection.

Bloodwerk rune: Ba Foundational rune: a positive pull, drags the rune towards objects.

Bloodwerk rune: Gi Foundational rune: a negative pull, drags an object towards the rune.

Bloodwerk rune: Kha Foundational rune: a positive push, presses the rune away from the object.

Bloodwerk rune: Ru Foundational rune: a negative push, presses objects away from the rune.

Book of Blood The sacred book of bloodwerk runes.

Charter The four different factions of the Zwina Academy that study:
  The first charter: the law of growth
  The second charter: the law of connection
  The third charter: the law of healing
  The fourth charter: the law of presence
  The fifth charter: the law of creation—disbanded

Choice Day The day when twenty-year-old Embers are required to choose their guild.

Clawmaw A creation made in the likeness of humans.

Clockmaster The role of time-keeping in the empire. The clockmaster projects the time every quarter strike through a chain of calls, starting with the first clockmaster based in the Keep where the only clock resides.

Crimelord The leader of a criminal organisation. Before Loot's reign there were four ruling in Nar-Ruta. Now they all report to Loot.

Dambe A form of boxing where the opponents use their strong arm as if it were a spear.

Day of Ascent The day that the winners of the Aktibar ascend the five hundred steps to join their Warden as the new disciple of their guild.

Day of Descent The day, once a decade, that the wardens of Nar-Ruta abdicate their place to their disciples by descending the five hundred steps.

Deathcraft Rune magic, called bloodwerk in the Wardens' Empire.

Disciples Second-in-command to the wardens. Leaders of the Shadow Court. They train under their warden for ten years before ascending to the title of warden themselves.

Dusters Citizens of the empire identified by their blue blood. The working-class tier of the caste system.

Duty chute The postal tubes that run under main roads. The chutes carry messages through the twelve cities of the empire.

Embers The noble and ruling class of the empire. Only Embers are allowed to rule, receive a full education and live in the Ember Quarter. Only Embers are taught to bloodwerk.

Ending Fire, the A phenomenon believed to have struck the world four hundred years ago, wiping out everything with lava, flame and flooding. Nothing survived except what was on the wardens' ships.

Eru Large lizard-like creatures that are trained as steeds. They can be ridden with saddles by the most experienced or driven with cart-drawn carriages.

Flighter Someone with the ability to harness the law of presence.

Ghostings Citizens of the empire identified by their transparent blood, their hands and tongues are severed at birth. They are the lowest class of the empire.

Godpower Magic of the fifth charter, so named by the Zalaam.

Griot Storyteller and truth-seeker.

Guild of crime A counterfeit guild, originally led by Loot, that has no true jurisdiction in the empire. It is run in opposition to the true wardens. Vow: to resist and sow chaos.

Guild of duty The guild of duty manages the smooth running of the empire and domestic services. Vow: to nourish and maintain the land.

Guild of knowledge The guild of knowledge manages the educational system within the empire. Vow: to teach and discover all.

Guild of strength The guild of strength is responsible for protecting and maintaining the peace. This includes the warden army. Vow: to protect and enforce the law.

Guild of truth The guild of truth rules the courthouse and upholds the law and religious rites. The Warden of Truth leads the Abosom. Vow: to preach and incite justice.

Gummers Members of the guild of crime, shortened from "guild members"

Handspan A unit of measurement using the tip of your thumb to the tip of your little finger.

Hollower A creation made to build tunnel infrastructure.

Imir The twelve leaders of the cities of the Wardens' Empire. An inherited position, the twelve imirs make up the Noble Court.

Inkwell A device worn by Embers that allows them to bloodwerk. The metal cuff wraps around their wrist with a slot above a vein where a stylus is inserted. The blood then runs down a channel in the stylus to the tip of the stylus, allowing them to write with their blood.

Jambiya Curved dagger.

Joba fruit A red berry the size of a small plum with an extremely hard outer shell that requires a forge to crack. The flesh is often used to create dyes. The joba tree only bears fruit every sixth mooncycle.

Joba seed The joba seed can be chewed, releasing a bitter juice that is a narcotic stimulant. Users of the joba seed often feel an initial rush of euphoria, followed by a dream-like state. It is often coupled with a depressive "comedown" and is highly addictive. Withdrawals include seizures, sickness and muscle cramps.

Joba tree Joba trees are planted in the front garden of most Ember houses. The height of the tree indicates the status and generational wealth of the occupier. The trees are white with green leaves. They are believed to be a conduit to Anyme, as the God climbed a joba tree into the sky.

Kori Small blue birds with iridescent wings.

Laambe A defensive martial art known for its open-palmed technique.

Lava fish A deep-sea fish harvested for its pearlescent scales which are used to adorn garments in glitter.

Maiden The head of a brothel.

Master crafter The leader of the Foundry on the Volcane Isles.

Milk honey A white-leafed herb used in medicine to lessen nausea.

Mooncycle A full rotation of the moon, a way to measure months.

Moonday The first day of the full moon.

Musawa A third gender.

Nameday The anniversary of the day you are born.

Night of the Stolen The night the Sandstorm stole twelve children from Ember houses.

Nightworker Someone who works in a maiden house.

Noble Court Made up of the twelve imirs, they debate and propose changes to laws and legislation, then present it to the Upper Court.

Nowerks A slur used to refer to Ghostings and Dusters who can't bloodwerk.

Nuba A regimented code of physical formations that are implemented through strict mental codes, Nuba practice is difficult to master. The user has to reach a state of complete control and focus, known as "battle wrath", where anger fuels the Nuba artist to create precise movements that become deadly when paired with a weapon.

Orb An obsidian sphere placed in an open wound in the centre of the palm. It is used to print runes in blood. This technique is taught at the Zwina Academy.

Peppashito A red, spicy pepper sauce.

Queller An offensive creation made to mimic the red queller spider.

Rack, the A wooden contraption that slowly tears the condemned into two. It is operated by a "Ripper".

Radish leaf Red leaves cultivated in the desert sand that give a rush of endorphins to those who smoke them. Expensive to procure. Slightly addictive. Smoked by Embers mostly.

Ring, the An illegal wrestling competition run by the guild of crime.

Rippers Executioners who operate the rack—always Dusters. The uniform is a blue jacket.

Runegun Bloodwerk-operated firearm.

Runelamp Bloodwerk-generated light.

Sand snail Small, white-shelled snails that live in the Farsai Desert.

Sandstorm A group of rebels founded by Loot Hisbar and Azim Iklia.

Saphridiam A blue mineral found in the sand of the Farsai Desert, derived from volcanic matter.

Sentinel A defensive creation made to mimic a wolf.

Shadow Court The court-in-waiting assigned and led by the disciple of each guild.

Shantra A game of strategy. A shantra board is made up of three different colours, patterned with diamonds. Each team has thirty-one counters, ten of each colour and one black piece. The black piece is known as the "egg". The aim of the game is to steal the egg from the opposing team, but each counter can only move onto their corresponding colour. Only red counters can collect the egg.

Sharj oil A fuel that can burn extremely hot.

Siege of the Silent The rebellion is taught in schools as the reason why the Ghostings are subjected to their penance. Four hundred years ago they rebelled against the wardens by laying siege to the Wardens' Keep for two months.

Slab The currency of the Wardens' Empire, made out of carved whitestone with former wardens printed on the underside.

Sleepglass Poison made with pepper flower and grass roots. Undetectable, it puts the victim to sleep for a short time.

Starting Drum The drum that indicates the start of a ripping.

Stolen, the The twelve children stolen from their cribs as babes and raised by the Sandstorm.

Strike A unit of time measurement; one strike is one hour.

Tannin A fabled sea monster that lives in the depths of the Marion Sea.

Tidewind A nightly phenomenon that blows in every night, whipping the sand of the Farsai Desert into a deadly frenzy.

Tio root A dark wood that is worth more than gold. Short stubby plant grown by the coast, hard to cultivate.

Trolley, the The bloodwerk-operated train that carts across the Tongue, also known as the "trotro".

Upper Court Made up of wardens, disciples and their key advisers, the Upper Court is where legislation is proposed.

Verd leaf A leaf harvested for its painkiller attributes. High in caffeine.

Wardens The four leaders of the empire of Nar-Ruta charged with representing one of the four guilds: duty, truth, knowledge and strength.

Whitestone A hardwearing substance that can withstand the tidewind, often used to build houses.

Yambrini Poison extracted from shrimp.

Zalaam, the An unknown group.

Zine Short stories featured in *The People's Gazette*.

PLACES

Arena, the Newly built amphitheatre that houses the trials for the Aktibar.

Belly, the The headquarters of the Warden of Crime.

Blooming Towers, the The central buildings in the citadel of the Zwina Academy.

Bushica A country ruled by an empire in the north-east.

Chrysalis, the Ghosting settlement in the north-east of the empire.

City of Rain A new settlement next to the Academy.

Dredge, the Previously called the Ghostings Quarter, but after the Siege of the Silent, their numbers dwindled and it was taken over by businesses of ill repute.

Drylands, the Mainlanders' name for the Wardens' Empire.

Duster Quarter A district on the north-west side of Nar-Ruta, occupied by Dusters.

Ember Quarter A district on the south side of Nar-Ruta, between the Ruta River and the Wardens' Keep, occupied by Embers.

Entwined Harbour, the A cluster of ships off the mainland.

Farsai Desert Blue sand dunes that sprawl across the centre of the empire.

Foundry, the A factory on the Volcane Isles where the Zalaam prepare for war.

Great veranda, the The open-air centre of the Wardens' Keep where functions are held. A roof automated by bloodwerk covers it during the tidewind.

Ica Sea, the East of Tenio.

Intestines, the The tunnels that run below the city of Nar-Ruta. There is a myth that one of the tunnels leads to treasure.

Jin-Crolah A city in the north; its main export is coffee beans.

Jin-Dinil A city that surrounds the central lakes of the empire.

Jin-Eynab A city in the west, known for its wine produce.

Jin-Gernomi A city in the centre-east with lots of cultivated grass hills.

Jin-Hidal A city in the centre of the island that produces the empire's coal supply.

Jin-Hubab A city in the north-west of the empire where grain is milled into flour.

Jin-Kutan A city in the south-east of the empire, one day's ride from Nar-Ruta.

Jin-Laham A city in the east that mainly exports cattle.

Jin-Noon A city in the west where the majority of cotton plantations grow.

Jin-Sahalia A city in the north known for the best eru breeding, and eru races that the imir hosts once a year.

Jin-Sukar A city in the north-east where sugar cane is farmed.

Jin-Wonta A city in the east that exports metal and mineral deposits.

Marion Sea The volatile and highly dangerous sea surrounding the Wardens' Empire.

Maroon Tavern in the Dredge where plantation workers drink.

Mistforest, the Area near the Academy.

Nar-Ruta The capital city of the Wardens' Empire, in the south-east of the island.

Nsuo A harbour town on the west of Tenio.

Ood-Lopah A village where salt flats are harvested.

Ood-Rahabe A fishing village in the north of the empire.

Ood-Zaynib A village in the north of the empire, close to the Sanctuary.

Ring, the A fighting ring operated by the guild of crime situated in the north of the Dredge.

Ruta River A quicksand river that separates the Duster Quarter from the Ember Quarter.

Sanctuary, the The farmstead where the Stolen were raised, situated outside of Ood-Zaynib.

Shard Palace, the Tenio's royal residence.

Souk, the Trading settlement near the Academy.

Souriland A country in the north-west.

Tenio The largest country on the mainland continent.

Tongue, the The black iron bridge that stands five hundred handspans above the Ruta River.

Truna Hills An area near the Zwina Academy.

Volcane Isles Area off the mainland settled by the Zalaam.

Wardens' Keep The governing centre of Nar-Ruta and home to the wardens. The cobbled courtyard is adorned with the largest joba tree in the empire. Beyond that, the five hundred steps lead to a marble platform where the wardens ascend and descend. The western side of the Keep houses the courtrooms, wardens' offices, wardens' chambers, library and the school-rooms. The eastern side houses the servant quarters, kitchens and Anoor's chambers.

Wetlands, the A country in the south ruled by a tsar.

Winterlands, the Northern most country in the world.

Zwina Academy A citadel of knowledge where people from all over the world come to study.

PEOPLE

Ads A Ghosting, unmaimed from birth. *She/Her*

Ala Ghosting servant who works for Turin.

Anoor Elsari Daughter of Uka Elsari. Disciple of the guild of strength. *She/Her*

Andu Former Yellow Commune leader situated on the Volcane Isles. *He/Him*

Aveed Elreeno Warden of Duty. *They/Them*

Azim Ikila Former leader of the Sandstorm, deceased. *He/Him*

Bisma Oharam Librarian in the Wardens' Keep. *He/Him*

Boey Elsari Blue-scaled eru owned by Anoor. *She/Her*

Chah Mastercrafter of the Foundry. *He/Him*

Child of Fire Prophesied figure of the Zalaam, believed by the catalyst of the Ending Fire.

Efie Montera Granddaughter of the imir of Jin-Gernomi. Competitor in the Aktibar for the guild of strength. *She/Her*

Elder Dew Ghosting elder. *They/Them*

Elder Petra Ghosting author of a pre-empire journal. *He/Him*

Elder Ravenwing Ghosting elder. *He/Him*

Elder Reed Ghosting elder. *She/They*

Elder Zero Ghosting elder. *He/They*

Elyzan Councillor of the first charter the law of growth. *He/Him*

Fareen Ola One of the Stolen, deceased. Had a scar running down her cheek. *She/Her*

Faro Former disciple of duty. *They/Them*

Fayl Hisbar Watcher for the guild of crime and Loot's husband. *He/Him*

General Ahmed Uka's deceased partner, father of Anoor. *He/Him*

Gorn Rieya Anoor's chief of chambers. *She/Her*

Griot Sheth Storyteller who frequents the Maroon. *He/Him*

Griot Zibenwe Storyteller, killed on the rack for writing. *He/They*

Hassa Ghosting servant and watcher for the elders. Friends with Sylah. *She/Her*

Ina A young Shariha slaver. *He/Him*

Inansi Ilrase Twin brother of Nayeli Ilrase of the Volcane Isles. *He/Him*

Inquisitor Abena Fictional main character of the zine *The Tales of Inquisitor Abena*. *She/Her*

Jond Alnua One of the Stolen who survived the massacre. Competitor in the Aktibar for the guild of strength. Member of the Sandstorm. *He/Him*

Kabut Also known as the Spider God, the deity of the Zalaam. *He/Him*

Kara Councillor of the fourth charter the law of presence. *She/Her*

Karanomo Thalis Queen of Tenio. *She/Her*

Kwame Muklis Ember servant who works in the kitchens of the Keep. *He/Him*

Lio Alyana Sylah's adoptive mother. Member of the Sandstorm. *She/Her*

Loot Hisbar Former Warden of Crime, married to Fayl. *He/Him*

Marigold Hassa's adoptive parent, Ghosting. *They/Them*

Master Inansi Leader of the Sandstorm. *He/Him*

Master Nuhan Teacher of bloodwerk. *He/Him*

Memur A Ghosting based in the Chrysalis. *She/Her*

Nayeli Ilrase Master crafter of Volcane Isles. *She/Her*

Niha Oh-Hasan A traveller enslaved by the Shariha, previously of the Academy. *He/Him*

Olina Helmsman of the Winterland's army. *She/Her*

One-ear Lazo Competitor in the wrestling contest known as the Ring. *He/Him*

Petal A Ghosting soldier and seafarer. *She/Her*

Purger, the Loot's former assassin, gummer. *She/They*

Pura Dumo Warden of Truth. *He/Him*

Qwa Former disciple of truth. *He/Him*

Rascal A sandcat. *She/Her*

Ren Apothecarist, Zuhari's partner. *She/Her*

Rohan Kwame's adoptive father. *He/Him*

Rola Duster child killed in the revolt of the hundred. *She/Her*

Shola Captain of the Entwined Harbour

Sui Councillor of the second charter the law of connection. *She/They*

Sylah Alyana One of the Stolen who survived the massacre. *She/Her*

Tanu Alkhabbir Former disciple of knowledge. *She/Her*

Teta Yellow Commune leader situated on the Volcane Isles. *She/Her*

Turin Former maiden, now Warden of Crime. *She/Her*

Uka Elsari Warden of Strength, Anoor's mother. *She/Her*

Vahi An armoursmith. Father to Hassa. *He/him*

Vona Esar Jond's guardian, deceased. Member of the Sandstorm. *She/Her*

Wern Aldina Warden of Knowledge. *She/Her*

Yanis Yahun Competitor in the Aktibar for the guild of strength. Captain in the warden army. *He/Him*

Yona Elsari Former Warden of Strength, Anoor's grandmother. *She/Her*

Zenebe Councillor of the third charter the law of healing. *He/Him*

Zuhari Member of Anoor's Shadow Court, formerly in army. *She/They*

ACKNOWLEDGEMENTS

This trilogy was a bit like making a godbeast. First I needed the faith in myself to be able to craft such a creature. From the beginning it was my family who gave me that, fostering my wild imagination. Thank you to all the El-Arifis and extended family who have supported me in every endeavour.

Then there are the limbs of the godbeast: my right hand, Juliet Mushens. An agent like no other. Thank you for always being a phone call away. And thanks must be made to the wider team at Mushens Entertainment: Liza, Kiya, Alba, Catriona, Emma—you are all wonderful. Ginger Clark, my superwoman agent in North America, my gratitude is endless.

The brains of the operation have always been my editors, particularly Tricia Narwani at Del Rey who guided me closely in this final instalment. Our girls have come so far, and that is down to you. Natasha Bardon at HarperVoyagerUK, whose spark of creativity has pushed this series so much further than I ever could have hoped. And Rachel Winterbottom, you are such a dream to work with, thank you.

To the wider teams who are the legs that keep my publishing schedule kicking. From the Del Rey team: Ayesha Shibli, Ashleigh Heaton, Tori Henson, Sabrina Shen, Scott Shannon, Alex Larned, Keith Clayton, David Moench, Jordan Pace, Ada Maduka, Ella Laytham, Nancy Delia, Alexis Capitini, Rob Guzman, Brittanie Black and Abby Oladipo.

And the Voyager UK team: Chloe Gough, Fleur Clarke, Terence Caven, Montserrat Bray, Ellie Andre, Sian Richefond, Holly Macdonald. And a massive thank you to Susanna Peden, who not only keeps me alive but is one of the best publicists I know.

My friends who I hold so dear to my chest, and so give this godbeast breath: Juniper, Rachel and Richard who have been with me every step of the way. Amy and Lizzie, you have been my guiding lights. Karin, Tasha and Sam—what did I do before I knew you?! Hannah, may we forever share voice notes in the bath. Love you all.

Then there is the heart, and that goes to you, Jim. I still remember you reading the first few chapters of *The Final Strife* and walking into the kitchen with tears in your eyes. You knew its potential back then when all I'd ever felt was doubt. Thank you for making this life worth living.

And finally there is the life blood that brings the godbeast to life. And that's you, my readers. Without you, this would all just be words on a page. We've been on a journey you and I. But for now it is time to let the runes dry and lay this godbeast to rest.